COURSE

OF

ACTION

What Reviewers Say About BOLD STROKES' Authors

❧

KIM BALDWIN

"Her…crisply written action scenes, juxtaposition of plotlines, and smart dialogue make this a story the reader will absolutely enjoy and long remember." – **Arlene Germain**, book reviewer for the *Lambda Book Report* and the *Midwest Book Review*

❧

ROSE BEECHAM

"…a mystery writer with a delightful sense of humor, as well as an eye for an interesting array of characters…" – *MegaScene*

"…her characters seem fully capable of walking away from the particulars of whodunit and engaging the reader in other aspects of their lives." – *Lambda Book Report*

"…creates believable characters in compelling situations, with enough humor to provide effective counterpoint to the work of detecting." – *Bay Area Reporter*

❧

JANE FLETCHER

"…a natural gift for rich storytelling and world-building…one of the best fantasy writers at work today." – **Jean Stewart**, author of the *Isis* series

❧

RADCLYfFE

"Powerful characters, engrossing plot, and intelligent writing…" – **Cameron Abbott,** author of *To the Edge* and *An Inexpressible State of Grace*

"…well-honed storytelling skills…solid prose and sure-handedness of the narrative…" – **Elizabeth Flynn**, *Lambda Book Report*

"…well-plotted…lovely romance…I couldn't turn the pages fast enough!" – **Ann Bannon**, author of *The Beebo Brinker Chronicles.*

"…a consummate artist in crafting classic romance fiction…her numerous best selling works exemplify the splendor and power of Sapphic passion…" – **Yvette Murray, PhD**, *Reader's Raves*

COURSE

OF

ACTION

by

GUN BROOKE

2005

CREDITS
EDITORS: JENNIFER KNIGHT AND SHELLEY THRASHER
EXECUTIVE EDITOR: STACIA SEAMAN
PRODUCTION DESIGN: STACIA SEAMAN
COVER PHOTOS: PAULA TIGHE
COVER DESIGN BY SHERI (GRAPHICARTIST2020@HOTMAIL.COM)

Acknowledgments

I want to give credit to the wonderful people who took time out of their busy lives to help me complete this project. Their input, encouragement, and support made it possible for me to keep going.

I molded Kitty McNeill after Kat, student by day and chef by night, hailing from Hunter Valley, a few hours north of Sydney, Australia. She writes fan fiction and original fiction when her busy schedule allows, posting it to her Web site http://www.wolf-fic.com. She also will publish one of her short stories in *Stolen Moments: Erotic Interludes 2* from Bold Strokes Books. Kat has an incredible sense of humor along with a refreshingly candid way of giving feedback.

Glynis is an Australian currently living in beautiful New Zealand. She posted a novel of her own, *Melting Ice*, last year and is now adding her latest, *Counting the Cost*, to her Web site, http://homepages. paradise.net.nz/glynisgriffinswriting/ This conscientious woman helps me with the hard bits that mean so much—advice about style, grammar, and spelling.

Wendy, an occupational therapist residing in Scotland, has served me several great ideas on a silver platter. Wendy writes when her muse suggests it, and her sense of humor is wickedly hilarious. Her stories can be found at http://www.gbrookefiction.com/fiction/wendys_fiction/

Jay, from Canada, and I frequently end up in discussions about what makes people tick. A lot of "what ifs" turned into plot ideas, which in turn developed into *Course of Action*. Jay's wacky sense of humor and energetic personality have many times helped me focus and keep writing.

At Bold Strokes Books:

Radclyffe, author and publisher—thank you, Rad, for believing in me.

Dr. Shelley Thrasher, editor, went over *Course of Action* with a fine-tooth comb, teaching me a lot in a friendly, professional manner. Her feedback and editing, delivered with heart and humor, enhanced this story. Shelley's skills and friendship mean so much to me.

Jennifer Knight, book doctor and editor, together with Shelley took me up a steep learning curve, teaching me invaluable lessons about building plot and characterization. Also, my thanks to Stacia Seaman, production editor, for proofreading and preparing my novel for print.

Dedication

Elon,
Without whom I would starve, literally and
metaphorically.

Malin & Henrik,
The greatest kids on the face of the earth.

My Warrior Princess,
Remember our deal; I keep you safe
and you save the world.

Lotta,
Your friendship and our sisterhood
mean everything to me.

I love you all.

PROLOGUE

That role is mine! I *am* Diana Maddox!"

Carolyn Black planted her hands on her agent's desk and stared at him like a chained panther defending a bloody meal. The meal in question was the hottest movie role on offer for an over-thirty actress since *The Hours*.

"I know you are, and so do all the fans," Grey Parker tried to reassure his best client. Carolyn had always been goal oriented and ambitious, but she seemed almost desperate over the new Supernova Productions feature. He could understand her agitation; at forty-five, she was staring down the barrels. Most actresses her age were already playing Mom in television movies of the week.

"You're my agent, and I pay you a lot of money," she hissed, abandoning his desk to pace the luxurious office. "I want this role. I have to have it."

"We don't have a script yet," Grey said in a soothing tone. "They're not casting until—"

"Oh, please. They're casting. Read the goddamned tabloids. Annelie Peterson is taking actresses to lunch. Sylvia Goodman was on E! News dropping hints." She stopped in her tracks and spun to face him, a signature move from her small-screen days as soap goddess Devon Harper. "I've earned this, Grey. I'm the one who should bring Diana Maddox to the big screen. Make it happen."

"Don't you worry about a thing, my dear." He masked an uncharacteristic lack of confidence. "Consider it done."

CHAPTER ONE

Annelie Peterson sipped her champagne and gazed down at the crowd thronging the ballroom below.

"I think we're a hit." She smiled at the boyish-looking man next to her.

Gregory Horton was the CEO of one of her companies and a trusted friend.

"Three hundred and fifty guests, a thousand dollars per plate." He rolled off the numbers with patent satisfaction. "And that's not counting the auction later. We should see half of that again with those first editions and the paintings. Of course it helps that you're the hostess—the woman everyone wants to meet."

Annelie shot her employee a mock glare. Gregory had worked for her for seven years, ever since she came to Florida, and they shared an easygoing camaraderie as well as a smooth work relationship. In his early thirties, like herself, he looked more like a surfer than a seasoned executive. His unruly blond hair attracted the attention of both men and woman, as did his green eyes and broad smile.

"We should mingle," he continued. "It'll pay to shake some people's hands before we sit down to dinner."

Annelie sighed. The mingling was the tough part. She would never get used to the kind of meaningless exchanges and air-kissing that went on at charity galas like this one. But she had spent six months planning the event for the Nebula Circle, a philanthropic trust she had established several years ago. A little mingling wouldn't kill her.

Pulling at the skirt of her ice blue Ungaro evening dress, she walked through the crowd, smiling faintly as she shook hands. She had met very few of these people personally, as she normally kept a low profile, but most of them seemed to know who she was—A. M.

Peterson, the owner of Key Line Publishing Inc., the woman whose empire was growing so fast *Fortune* magazine had labeled her the next Ted Turner. Annelie wondered if she would ever get used to people regarding her with awe—and if she did, what that would say about the person she had become.

Certainly the large mirrors lining the ballroom walls confirmed that she looked the part. The softly flowing dress fit her like a glove, and a chignon covered with a white gold web of diamonds held back her long blond hair. Annelie disliked rings and never wore any, but a breathtaking diamond necklace drew attention to her plunging neckline, and a matching bracelet encircled her right wrist. She was taller than most women and some of the men there but kept her head high, a posture she had perfected along with the rest of her carefully constructed public image.

Annelie continued to work her way through the glamorously dressed crowd. Being used to men staring at her curvaceous body, she ignored their stares yet greeted each man politely. The envious looks from some of the women disappeared when they discovered she was just as friendly toward them.

When she finally reached the other end of the hallway and scanned the crowd for Gregory, she noticed him talking to a couple and recognized the woman standing to his left. Carolyn Black wore an elegant black dress decorated with a cascade of rhinestones stretching from her left shoulder down around her waist and onto the form-fitting skirt. Her auburn hair was intricately piled on top of her head, with thin tresses caressing her neck. The actress had an obvious, quite overwhelming, charisma, which clearly held all around her captive and made Annelie catch her breath as she approached.

Gregory performed the introductions, and Annelie shook hands with Carolyn and the man she was with, Jared Garrison. As they exchanged pleasantries, she wondered if the rumors about Carolyn and Jared were true. They didn't look like lovers, but Annelie wasn't sure what gave her that impression.

"We're delighted your audio version of the Diana Maddox books has become so successful, Ms. Black," she said, thinking how young the actress seemed. Carolyn's flawless skin, lightly dusted with freckles, looked satiny smooth. Her steady blue-gray eyes, able to portray any emotion required on stage or screen, swept Annelie up and down.

"Well, thank you. And please, call me Carolyn," she said in the low, smoky voice that had convinced Annelie to hire her for the audiobooks. "Of course the role came very naturally to me. I think, in many ways, Diana and I are kindred spirits."

Annelie smiled inwardly. The actress might as well have announced her interest in the film role on a foghorn. "Your voice was perfect," she said. "I knew it would be after I saw you in *The Greenhouse* three years ago."

Carolyn's mouth stretched into a brilliant smile. "You handled the casting decision personally?"

"Of course. The Diana Maddox books are pivotal to my company."

"And you're planning to bring them to the screen now. How brave of you after the V. I. Warshawski fiasco."

A warning shot? Either Carolyn really cared about the character or she wanted it to seem that way. "Well, I haven't hired a moron to direct my film or hacks to write the screenplay," Annelie said coolly. Was it her imagination, or was this actress actually interviewing *her*—assessing her competence to extend the Diana Maddox franchise onto the screen?

Carolyn's expression was serenely self-possessed. "I'm sure, if you can attach the right cast, you'll have the distributors eating from your hand."

"Thanks." Annelie was aware her voice held an edge of sarcasm. She wasn't accustomed to having anyone imply she might lack the skills to pull off a project. Mildly irritated, she steered the conversation back to social pleasantries. "I'm so glad you could be here tonight. What are you doing in Florida, by the way? Are you filming here?"

"No, I've just closed a play in New York, and I need a break. So I'm reading a few scripts and spending some quality time with Jared."

Apparently Jared Garrison had missed the change of topic. "Do you have anyone in mind for Maddox yet?" he asked Annelie, oblivious to his date's unmistakable glare. "I hear there's a lot of interest. Even Meryl Streep and Sally Field."

Annelie had to hide a smile. She knew Jared professionally. The good-looking lawyer was a senior partner at a firm that did pro bono work for Nebula Circle clients. Her charity focused on children born with HIV and shelters for women, so they always needed volunteer legal help. She'd had no idea Jared was involved with Carolyn Black until she'd read some gossip recently. For a moment she pitied him. The actress had a reputation for chewing men up and spitting them out.

Annelie smirked faintly. "I don't see either Streep or Field as a potential Diana Maddox," she told him. "They're wonderful actresses but not the right age, to start with."

She could almost hear the wheels turning inside Carolyn's head, but the perfect face revealed nothing. Sweeping a quick assessing look around, she made an expansive gesture and projected her voice as only a Broadway star could, declaring, "Wonderful night, Annelie. I'm so glad I could come." She took Jared's arm. "Now I really mustn't keep you from your guests. Perhaps we'll chat later."

By some strange magic the crowd parted as she moved through it, people turning to gaze at her, a few even clapping. Annelie was astounded to see even the most sophisticated of her guests looking starstruck at a smile or nod from Carolyn Black. If the woman was trying to make a point, she'd succeeded. She was the consummate performer. A star.

But was she Diana Maddox? Annelie had her doubts.

❖

"You look like the cat that ate the proverbial canary," Gregory remarked as he followed Annelie off the stage after the auction.

"I'm overwhelmed," Annelie said, checking her Palm Pilot. "Someone paid $12,000 for those signed first editions of the Diana Maddox books."

Gregory grinned. "Yup, and that was none other than Diana Maddox herself, or should I say, Carolyn Black. She must want the part in the worst way."

"Gregory! Behave."

"Don't look now, but she's on her way over here. Don't make any promises you can't keep."

Annelie turned around and saw Carolyn approaching, this time without her date.

"Annelie." The throaty voice seemed to caress her name, making Annelie shiver. "I wanted to thank you for this evening. It looks like all your hard work paid off."

"I'm thrilled," Annelie said. "And everything will go directly to the children we're supporting. The hotel even donated the ballroom."

"That's wonderful."

"Your bid was extremely generous. It was very kind of you."

"You're welcome."

Carolyn wasn't going to ask about the Diana Maddox role. Annelie admired the actress's steely nerve. It wasn't often she encountered a woman with as much strength of mind as she herself possessed. She could sense that strength in Carolyn and was drawn to it. "How long will you be in Florida?" she asked.

"I'm due back in New York in two weeks."

"Are you staying in the city?"

"I'm at Jared's condo on Bal Harbour. I was hoping to swim every day since that's my favorite way to exercise. But the wind has been too strong." Carolyn smiled with faint self-deprecation. "I'm so used to swimming pools that I find the large waves intimidating."

Annelie reached into her small purse for a business card, an idea taking rapid shape in her mind. "Tell you what. I live near Jared, on Golden Beach. You're more than welcome to come use my pool. I'll leave word at the gate that you're on my guest list." A small, wry smile lifted her mouth. "Needless to say, that's a very short list."

Carolyn's eyes widened, and Annelie could hear Gregory cough in surprise behind her.

"That's very generous." Carolyn said. "I don't want to impose—"

"You're not. I promise. Any day is fine. My housekeeper will let you in. She's off on Sundays and Mondays, but I'm usually home till lunch then."

Carolyn's polite hesitance vanished. "So, would tomorrow be all right?"

Annelie smiled at the unabashed question. Being rather direct herself, she found Carolyn's manner refreshing. "Sure, why don't you come around eleven? We could have lunch afterward."

"Are you sure it isn't too much trouble?" Carolyn briefly touched Annelie's arm. "I mean, after tonight and everything?"

"Quite sure."

Gregory coughed again, but Annelie ignored him.

"I'll see you tomorrow, then." Carolyn looked delighted. "Good night."

As the actress vanished into the sea of departing guests, a soft male voice behind Annelie inquired, "What are you doing?"

"Running my business."

Gregory seemed unimpressed. "You're going to offer her the part?"

"No. I'm going to make it very attractive for her to agree to terminate the audiobook contract."

Gregory frowned. "Why? The sales have been huge."

"Once I have an actress playing Maddox on screen, we'll need to rejacket all the print books and redo sound on the audio series for the Diana character. I want the same actress doing everything. It's the only thing that makes sense, and our marketing people agree."

Gregory grimaced. "You can't seriously imagine Carolyn Black is going to take that lying down. She won't terminate. She'll sue."

"We'll see." Annelie said. "I can be very persuasive."

Gregory put his arm around her waist and gave her a quick squeeze. "Just be careful. Promise me that."

She smiled at him over her shoulder. "I promise."

❖

"Did you remember to call Beth back?" Jared pulled out into the night traffic.

Carolyn groaned. "No, I forgot. I was running late but that's no excuse. Did she say what's up?"

Beth, her eleven-years-younger sister, was a nurse, far from Carolyn's glamorous world. Married for six years, she and her husband, Joe, lived in D.C. with their four-year-old daughter, Pamela.

"No, just that she needed to talk to you about something. It didn't sound like an emergency."

Carolyn leaned back, resting her head. A familiar throbbing in her temples made her reach for her purse and pull out a nasal spray. If she disregarded the early symptoms, the throbbing would inevitably escalate into a full-blown migraine attack, incapacitating her for several days. She took her medicine, noticing Jared's concerned glance in her direction.

"Are you okay?"

"I'll be fine. Just a precaution." Carolyn gave a muted sigh. She needed to relax; she was tired after doing six performances a week for eleven months. If she wasn't careful she would end up with permanent bags under her eyes.

"Heard from your brother lately?"

"No, not in a while. He's into one of his creative spells, I think. If my sister-in-law didn't drag him to my shows, he'd never get around to watching any of my work."

"You go to every one of his exhibitions."

Carolyn chuckled at the implied criticism. "That's different. John is a genius. It's my duty to admire him, even if I think his sculptures look like deformed pieces of junk."

Jared shook his head. "You can try to sound sarcastic, but it's not working. I know you're proud of him."

Carolyn smiled. "Yes, I am."

She had been twelve years old when their mother died, hit by a car while crossing the street. John was six and baby Elisabeth just eleven months. Their father had lost his moorings when his beautiful, vibrant wife was killed, and Carolyn had soon found herself in her mother's role, taking care of her siblings.

Shawn Black had suffered a massive heart attack when Carolyn was twenty-one, and she'd dropped out of college to look after her teenaged brother and young sister. Life had been a struggle, but she had never regretted making that choice. Even now, she was proud that she'd been able to raise John and Beth without help from anyone.

Jared pulled into the parking lot beneath the large apartment building where his ocean-view condo was. After they took the elevator up to the fifth floor, Carolyn leaned against the wall and closed her eyes briefly as he unlocked the door.

"Some evening," she mused. "I don't think I've been in a room with so many people dressed fit to kill since the Golden Globes."

"Half of Palm Beach was there." Jared sounded admiring. "Annelie knows how to raise money, and she's passionate about those kids. I heard she even volunteers at the hospital when one of them is admitted."

"Remarkable," Carolyn said. "I'm amazed she invited me to use her pool while I'm here."

Jared stopped on his way to the kitchen and faced her. "I've got to admit I'm curious about two things—her motives for inviting you, and yours, for going."

"To swim, of course," Carolyn said lightly. She could see Jared wasn't buying. He knew her too well to accept the explanation at face value.

"Carolyn," he chided. "Since when did you share your precious private life, unless there's a payoff?"

"I spend hours with you, don't I?"

He laughed. "We both know it's very convenient for you to have our names linked in the media. Like I said, there's always a payoff."

Carolyn produced a mock-innocent shrug. "If it helps Annelie Peterson see I'm the only sane choice for Diana Maddox, I'll be thrilled to swim in her pool as often as it takes."

"Are you sure you really want to do this?" Jared looked uneasy.

"What do you mean?"

"It's a well-known secret that Annelie Peterson is a lesbian."

Carolyn blinked. "Are you sure?"

"As sure as I can be without actually asking her to her face."

Carolyn pictured the tall blonde in her blue dress, moving with perfect grace from one person to another in the marble hallway of the hotel, shaking hands, smiling. Her jewelry had sparkled but hadn't managed to draw attention from her ice blue eyes or her melodious alto voice. Annelie was not just attractive, she was stunningly beautiful. And gay?

"Carolyn?"

She raised an eyebrow. "If you're waiting for me to be shocked, don't hold your breath. I work in show business, for heaven's sake!"

Jared gave her a pointed stare. "Actually, I was waiting for the announcement about how you plan on using the information to your advantage."

A flash of anger burned through the effect of her medication. Feeling her left temple begin to throb again, Carolyn glared at him. "Thanks a lot. You make me sound like a callous bitch."

"You're nothing of the kind. You're a wonderful bitch."

"You horrible man," she muttered. "You make me so angry sometimes." She rubbed her temple.

"Only because I see you the way you are, and not the way you want to be seen. You're very good at playing *Carolyn Black*. It's the role of a lifetime, if you ask me."

He was an unbearable tease. Still, she felt herself relax as he put his arm around her shoulders and ushered her into the kitchen. "Let me make it up to you with a café latte," he said. "You're the only person I know who sleeps better after a healthy dose of caffeine."

Carolyn perched on a stool next to the kitchen counter, watching as he ground aromatic coffee beans. "Tell me something. What did you mean when you said you were curious about *her* motives for inviting me?" she asked.

Jared placed a cup in the espresso machine. "Does she want to get to know you before she decides whether to offer you the role? Or is there some other agenda?"

"Such as?"

"You'll have to ask her. But if I were a lesbian, I'd probably enjoy having you swim in my pool." He handed Carolyn her latte.

She sipped it with a show of nonchalance. Could Annelie Peterson be attracted to her? If so, she wouldn't be the first lesbian Carolyn had had to politely discourage. On the other hand, this could be exactly the opportunity she needed. If there was one thing show business had taught her, it was how to convert lust into an acting contract.

❖

Annelie stepped out of her blue dress and hung it carefully before taking off her lace underwear and putting on a white terry-cloth robe. She walked outside and switched on the jets in the Jacuzzi, dropped the robe on a garden chair, and climbed into the hot water. Screened from view by palm trees and high walls, her hot tub was located directly off the patio near the swimming pool. Annelie loved the sense of being in her own little world, naked outdoors. With a contented sigh, she leaned back and gazed up at the starry sky, amazed at how close it always seemed. This was one of the things she loved about Florida—in New York, you could barely make out the constellations because of the bright city lights.

Shifting in the water, she allowed the jets to reach every part of her body, teasing and caressing her flesh, rippling along the entire length of her spine like a thousand tiny kisses. Steady blue-gray eyes and auburn hair invaded her thoughts, and she closed her eyes, not surprised that Carolyn Black had lodged in her mind. The actress was more than a famous beauty; she was devastatingly sexy. Something about the way she moved, and the way she looked at Annelie, unsettled her in a way she was not used to. Face-to-face, Carolyn had made her feel like she was the only person in the room, nailing her with those amazing eyes, pulling her in and claiming all of her attention. It had taken an effort for Annelie to remain calm, at least outwardly, and just thinking about the encounter still made her heart hammer in her chest.

She wondered if Carolyn knew she was a lesbian. Annelie realized people automatically assumed she was gay just because she published an extensive range of widely successful lesbian books and never used token males as escorts to any of the functions she attended. It was not something she attempted to keep a secret, but she was not officially out either. Reserved by nature, she neither confirmed nor denied her sexual preference to anyone. It simply wasn't anybody else's business.

Annelie hadn't reached her present position in society overnight. Winning one of the largest ever multistate Powerball lotteries nine years ago had altered her life forever. After surviving the media circus with its interviews, followed by the obligatory letters and phone calls from begging strangers and acquaintances, she'd decided to drop below the radar.

Assuming her Swedish mother's maiden name, she'd moved to New York, living in Manhattan for two years while she attended Barnard College's Comparative Literature Program. During that period, she'd learned how to move among the rich and famous as if she belonged, taking lessons in deportment and public speaking. A regime of beauty treatments, massages, and regular visits to the gym changed her looks and movements.

The girl who had once been Annie Clint, bank-office clerk during the day to help pay for her literature studies in the evenings, became Annelie Peterson, businesswoman. She started a call center named Quasar Inc. at the beginning of the outsourcing boom. The business rapidly become so successful she was able to sell it at a handsome profit and look for a new business opportunity, something less crazy. Annelie never spoke about her past and had confided the truth to only three of her best friends, knowing they would never betray her. She'd learned a few difficult lessons early on, especially that people treated her differently because of her money and few had genuine motives.

As she arched her back, she tilted her head into the Jacuzzi, allowing the jets to massage her scalp. Her naked breasts rose above the surface, her nipples pebbling in the humid night air. Shivering slightly, she sank once more into the seductive warmth of the water and released a satisfied moan. She had never regretted her decision to move on. Much as she'd loved Manhattan, she had longed for a slower pace. Having visited Florida several times and fallen in love with the cosmopolitan way of life in Miami, she decided to make it her home.

She bought a medium-sized publishing company, Key Line Publishing, and promptly branched out from nonfiction and children's books to publish gay and lesbian literature as well as mainstream novels. Her strategy paid off, soon making Key Line a thorn in the sides of the industry heavyweights.

Annelie returned to her condo in New York periodically, enjoying catching up with her friends. She kept a close check on the business endeavors she was still involved with and also worked with several charity organizations. Most of her fortune remained tied up in a wide stock and bond portfolio, and under the auspices of her savvy investment manager, her net worth had almost quadrupled since her lottery win.

Annelie did not flaunt her wealth the way many of Miami's newly rich did. Her financial status made her the target of opportunists, and showing up on *Forbes*'s list of businesswomen of influence was no help. It was always a struggle to balance her need for privacy, which sometimes led to inadvertent solitude, with her need to do business effectively and provide active support to the charity organizations she had endowed.

Turning in the water, she pushed herself up over the side of the Jacuzzi, then into the swimming pool, needing to cool down. The hot water in the whirlpool was soothing, but it also made her lethargic if she wasn't careful. She swam over to the other side of the pool, completely submerged, relishing the water's silken chill against her flesh. When she reached the ladder, she climbed up and sat on the ledge, wringing out her hair as the balmy night once more surrounded her.

Droplets ran down her arms, glistening against her pale skin as they followed the rounded curve of her full breasts. They stopped at the puckered skin of her nipples, and the cooling effect of the water made her shiver. Annelie smoothed the rivulets away, running her hands over her body. The touch was oddly soothing, yet had a bittersweet tinge to it. She rarely felt lonely, but tonight she was all too aware of what was missing in her very full life. Suddenly Carolyn's eyes were there again, looking at her, her head slightly tilted as if Annelie were the most interesting, worthwhile person in the world. Not quite sure why the image of the actress was etched on her retina, she envisioned the smaller woman dressed in that elegant black evening gown, the rhinestones accentuating her figure. In person, she was everything Annelie had imagined, maybe even more.

Disregarding a sudden twinge deep inside, Annelie got to her feet and padded over to the Jacuzzi to turn off the jets. A set of patio doors opened from her bedroom, and she picked up her robe and went through these, heading for her bathroom. After a quick shower, she dried her hair and brushed her teeth before sliding into bed. For a moment, she lay completely still, enjoying the feeling of the crisp linen against her naked body; then she set her alarm for six thirty. She had a lot of work to do before Carolyn arrived to use the pool and she wanted to be clearheaded for this visit, so she could not afford to oversleep.

She hugged a pillow tight as she curled up beneath the covers, letting her mind wander to Carolyn Black once more. The actress had done a lot for Key Line, playing the role of criminal investigator Diana Maddox in their hugely successful audiobook series. It was hardly surprising that she saw herself as the logical choice for the lead in the movie.

Annelie's stomach clenched at the thought of having to disappoint her. Carolyn obviously wanted the role, and she had the necessary acting credentials. She'd won a Tony in her younger years and various film awards later in her career. But her impressive record cut little ice with Annelie's potential distributors. They'd already decided a younger star would have more box office appeal and had their sights set on Sylvia Goodman, an up-and-coming actress who'd attracted attention for her supporting roles in several major films. The fact that Diana Maddox was forty plus in the novels made no difference. In screen adaptations, everything was up for grabs.

Fastening her grip around her pillow, Annelie sighed. She was trying to keep an open mind about Goodman. The tall, fair-haired beauty had been pronounced the new Sally Field by some gushy columnists, and she certainly had the right look for Maddox when she wore a dark wig as she had in several recent supporting roles. Still, in Annelie's mind she lacked certain key sensibilities Carolyn Black possessed in abundance. Carolyn brought maturity and dimension to her roles that few younger actresses could equal. But what did that really buy these days? Audiences had been trained to accept shallow performances as long as a movie was exciting and delivered some titillating sex scenes.

Annelie wanted to make more than one Maddox film, so everything depended on how the critics and the audience received the first movie. As far as she could see, sacrificing Carolyn for Sylvia came down to simple pragmatism. Annelie didn't have the luxury of indulging her own personal preferences; too much was at stake.

❖

Carolyn reached for the phone, automatically checking the bedside clock. Her heart leapt into her throat when she saw the caller ID. What was her younger sister doing calling at two in the morning?

"Beth? Are you all right?"

"I'm fine. Really." Her voice was high-pitched. "Sorry to call you so late, but I just couldn't wait to tell you."

"It's okay." Carolyn elbowed herself upright. She could hear a male in the background, her sister's husband Joe.

"I'm pregnant!" Beth's voice cracked, and she started to cry.

"Oh, honey. That's wonderful! I'm so happy for you and Joe."

After a muted rattle, her brother-in-law started talking. "Hi, Carolyn. Beth just got a little emotional. She'll be fine, but I wish she could've waited until tomorrow to tell you."

The actress felt a pang of guilt for not remembering to return Beth's call earlier. "Is everything okay with her and the baby? When did you find out?"

"This morning. Everything seems normal this time. But she's only six weeks pregnant, so she's nervous. We both are."

"I know." Beth had suffered two miscarriages in a row, both in her eighth week. After the second, she had fallen into a deep depression. "Put her back on, would you, darling," Carolyn said, thinking quickly.

"I'm here." Beth's voice seemed a little stronger.

"Beth, honey, listen to me. Why don't you take a leave of absence until you're past the first trimester? I'll help with the bills. You and the baby are all that really matter right now. Please, kiddo?"

"Oh, Lyn. I don't think Joe would like that, but thanks anyway."

"Talk to him. Joe only wants what's best for you. He knows this isn't about his pride. Please."

"All right." Beth paused. "You're happy for me, aren't you? You don't think I'm asking for trouble, trying again?"

Carolyn's heart almost broke at the tentative voice of her little sister. Beth had needed her more than ever when their father died. She was only ten and heading for puberty. A cousin of their father had offered to raise the young girl but was not interested in their teenaged brother John. Not about to let anyone break up what remained of her family, Carolyn resisted and became her younger siblings' legal guardian.

She had carried the burden of supporting them on far too narrow shoulders. Maintaining their childhood home swallowed most of the monthly allowance from her father's life insurance, and she'd constantly hunted for part-time work until she landed the daytime soap role that had launched her career.

Like her, her brother John grew up too quickly, and she sometimes thought this was why his behavior was so often spoiled and childish now. Beth was different. Always interested in and proud of Carolyn's professional achievements, her warmhearted sister made it clear in her unaffected way that she loved Carolyn deeply regardless of her star status. The fact that her sister was now a grown woman of thirty-four didn't matter. Carolyn still felt responsible.

"I'm delighted for you, honey," she said. "Now you be careful and take good care of yourself. I promise to be better at keeping my cell-phone battery charged in case you need me, all right?"

"All right. Thank you, Lyn."

"Don't be silly. You'd do the same for me, and more."

"In case you became pregnant, you mean?" Beth teased with a glimpse of her normally wicked sense of humor.

"Smart-ass."

They continued some of their usual sisterly bantering, easing the mood.

After hanging up, Carolyn curled onto her side. Her neck and her temples hurt a bit, so she was relieved to be swimming tomorrow. It usually kept her headaches at bay. Yet again she wondered why Annelie had invited her. She had no trouble picturing the statuesque blonde. Annelie had looked down at her, masking whatever was going on behind those pale blue eyes. Carolyn sensed something was on Annelie's mind, a special reason the publisher was making her welcome this way. It had to be the movie.

This was her chance, her shot at proving they didn't need to consider anyone else for the role. Surely it was obvious to Peterson— and if not, could it be all that hard to make her see reason? The readers already knew Maddox's voice through the audiobooks; they already identified her as Maddox. She wondered about her competition. Could Supernova seriously be considering anyone else? Whoever it was, she had to convince Annelie no one else could do Diana Maddox justice. She was the one. And she would not be going home without the role.

CHAPTER TWO

Carolyn lowered the backseat window as the cab stopped at the gate and the security guard stepped out of the booth.

"Carolyn Black. Annelie Peterson is expecting me."

The guard ducked back into the booth, then motioned the cabdriver through the gate.

Looking around the exclusive residential area, Carolyn saw several different types of architecture. Most of the houses were either white or pastel and screened by large palm trees. The torpid Miami heat was already gathering, and she could hardly wait to get into the pool.

The cab stopped at the end of a cul-de-sac at a large white house set back from the road in a lush tropical garden. With its tall windows creating an exciting façade, the house seemed to wrap around its semicircular driveway. A brand-new-looking, red vintage sixties Ford Mustang sat in front of the house. She glanced to the right, spotting a vast garage with a garage apartment.

The grounds were enclosed by a high concrete wall punctuated with ornate black wrought iron. Carolyn raised an eyebrow, thinking about Jared's comments. Annelie was obviously a very private person. Was her rumored lesbianism the main reason, or was she one of those wealthy people who preferred to keep the world at arm's length? Either way, it was amazing that she'd invited Carolyn here, and little wonder Jared was speculating on her motives.

Carolyn paid the cabbie and stepped out into the Florida humidity, tossing her bag over her shoulder. Dressed in white city shorts and a light yellow tank top, she walked up to the gate and rang the bell.

"Carolyn," Annelie's voice sounded from a nearby speaker. "The gate's open."

Annelie appeared at the front door before Carolyn reached it. She looked relaxed and casual, sporting a modest ponytail, an azure blue T-shirt, and black shorts.

"Welcome. Come on in and have something to drink before you change. It's even hotter today, isn't it?"

"It sure is. What a difference from New York this time of year!"

Carolyn followed Annelie inside, looking curiously around the hallway. A blue, white, and black Persian rug adorned the oak parquet in front of the large living room's entryway, which was flanked by four-feet-tall Chinese urns full of decorative reeds.

Annelie led Carolyn into her French country-style kitchen. Opening the refrigerator, she glanced back over her shoulder. "What can I get you, Carolyn?"

"Any mineral water is fine, thanks."

Annelie pulled out two bottles of Perrier, opened them, and poured them over tall glasses full of ice. "Here you go. This'll cool you off."

Carolyn sipped the water while peering at Annelie over the rim of the glass. The younger woman looked impeccable even dressed like this, in the privacy of her own home. Her pale skin suggested she didn't sunbathe, and her lean muscles showed she was in good shape.

"You can change in my spare bedroom. Let me show you where it is. While you're in the pool, I'll go through my e-mails and then we can have lunch. How does that sound?"

"Excellent." Carolyn followed Annelie through the kitchen and out into another, smaller, hallway.

"You can reach the patio and the pool through that door. There's a guest bathroom with extra towels if you need some. I'll be out there with my laptop."

The room was a dream in blue, white, and gold. A soft carpet covered the floor, thick enough to almost hide her toes when she took off her sneakers. Carolyn changed quickly into her black swimsuit, checked her makeup, and grabbed a towel from her bag. Twisting her shoulder-length hair up with a large hair clip, she slid the glass door open and walked outside.

The large, multileveled stone patio held several tables surrounded by chairs. Closer to the pool stood six deck chairs with thick cushions. Annelie occupied one of them, a laptop sitting on a low tray table on wheels pulled across her legs. Off-white parasols provided shade.

The pool was large and rectangular, with an octagonal Jacuzzi close to the deck chairs.

"What a beautiful patio. Your home is really lovely."

"Thanks." Annelie nodded. "I enjoy decorating."

"It shows. I wish I had more time for that, but I seem to always be on location or working odd hours." Carolyn glanced at the pool. "And this looks truly divine."

Annelie made a gesture of invitation. "Enjoy!"

Carolyn flashed her a broad smile, fully aware of how it changed her face. Feeling Annelie's eyes on her, she removed her towel and tossed it on a chair, then strolled toward the deep end of pool. As she posed on the edge, she took her time before she dived in, giving her host a chance to see just how good her physique was. Women half her age had trouble keeping in the kind of shape Carolyn was in. Effortlessly, she swam half a length under water before surfacing and starting to crawl with long, powerful strokes.

❖

Annelie returned her attention to her laptop, the image of Carolyn's perfect dive and fluid swimming still in her mind's eye. She knew the actress was forty-five, but her long legs and narrow hips were firm and well exercised. Though not very curvaceous, she was incredibly feminine, and she looked amazing in the black swimsuit.

Browsing through her private e-mails, Annelie smiled to herself as she saw Kitty's name in the inbox. Her Australian friend usually wrote the most outrageous e-mails, which always made her laugh out loud.

```
From: Kitty McNeil
Subject: One week and counting!

    Hi gorgeous!
    Just wanted to let you know I finally
made flight reservations. I swear the online
booking system will be my downfall. I do
e-mails, I use word processors, but let
me loose on the Internet and I'm bound to
cause havoc. For some reason I don't seem
to be compatible with these Web sites
```

that claim to be so idiot-proof. I thought
booking a flight to Miami would be a piece
of cake. How I first ended up with a ticket
to Madrid, I'll never know! Don't worry,
babe, I straightened it out.

Sam is coming with me since we thought
we'd mix business with pleasure. We'll be
staying in Orlando cause my babe has a
soft spot for Disney World. *groan* I'm
sure I'll live, as long as I don't have
to shake hands with Pluto or Goofy. So,
bella, see you in a little less than two
weeks!

Kitty

PS. Saw the TV commercial about the
Diana Maddox audiobooks. God, the voice
of that woman!

Annelie smiled and shook her head. Kitty McNeil, one of her
authors, was also one of her best friends. She wrote feminist fantasy
and science fiction that had a large following, both gay and straight.
Like many Australians, she was refreshingly candid, and it didn't take
Annelie long to feel as if she'd known her all her life. Kitty's partner,
Sam, an artist who specialized in metal sculptures, had already sold
Annelie two of her mobiles.

Annelie looked up from her computer and watched Carolyn turn
elegantly at the far end of the pool and swim back. Wondering how many
laps her guest usually did, she admired her graceful style and fitness.
Annelie enjoyed swimming but generally stuck to the breaststroke.

After a while, Carolyn swam over to the ladder and climbed out of
the pool. Clinging to her frame, the wet swimsuit showed every muscle,
every curve of her body. She was boyishly built in some ways, yet
so incredibly feminine. Water streamed down her slender thighs, and
Annelie found it impossible to avert her eyes.

Carolyn leaned forward, arching her back as she took the clip from
her hair and allowed it to flow in disheveled auburn locks before she
toweled it in slow movements. Annelie swallowed hard when Carolyn's

raised arms made her small, pert breasts strain against the swimsuit. The outline of her nipples was obvious as they hardened against the cooling fabric.

Draping the towel over her shoulders she sauntered toward Annelie as if she had no idea of her own appeal. "Oh, that was fantastic! Thank you again for letting me borrow the pool. I just can't get enough of this particular kind of exercise."

"As I said, you're welcome to use it while you're in Florida. Mary's around most of the time, and on her days off, either I'm home or you can use a key card. Remind me to give you one later."

Carolyn's eyes widened, and Annelie watched them turn bright blue.

"This is really kind of you, Annelie. I'll certainly take you up on it. If any time is inconvenient, you'll have to promise to let me know."

"I will. Now, how about lunch? Do you like seafood?"

Carolyn ran her fingers through her hair. "Sure, and I'm starving. I'll rinse off first and get dressed."

"You can use the bathroom in the spare bedroom. The hairdryer's in the top drawer."

"I won't be long."

Annelie walked into the kitchen and slid a tray of assorted seafood out of the refrigerator, then sliced large baguettes and arranged them on a plate. Small bowls of mayonnaise and crème fraiche completed the meal. After she set one of the tables on the patio with her blue china, she placed the meal in the middle of it.

Sipping her mineral water, she had to wait only a few minutes before Carolyn joined her. Predictably, the actress's makeup was impeccable, and the two ivory combs holding back her hair drew attention to her face.

Annelie regarded the actress with outward calm, but the way Carolyn's face changed when she smiled, the way her narrow lips became lush and inviting, caused her breath to catch.

"Mmm, this looks tasty. Crab is my favorite seafood."

"Then you'll love these. There's nothing like stone crabs."

Carolyn sat down and buttered her bread sparingly. "How long have you lived here?"

"Almost six years. My first year down here, I lived in a condo near Jared's. I wanted to buy a house, but it took me a while. As soon as the real-estate agent showed me this one, I knew it was my dream come true."

"So you make quick decisions once you know they're right?"

Not sure they were still talking about the house, Annelie nodded calmly. "Yes, I do. So far my instincts haven't steered me wrong."

"That's pretty obvious. You must be thrilled with your decisions about the Diana Maddox series."

"Yes, it's all turned out wonderfully. But without the authors and the books, it wouldn't happen. It's really all about teamwork." She hesitated for a second. "I'm curious. Had you read the Maddox books before you agreed to do the audio version?"

"Only the first one, *Dying for Fame*, since it was such an instant hit. And also, the setting tied in to my own profession. After that, I intended to read the other two as they came out, but I was in constant rehearsals and never found time."

"What did you think when we approached you about the audiobooks?"

Carolyn carefully wiped her mouth. "As you know, I've done regular audiobooks before and enjoyed it, since I really love to read when I can."

Annelie leaned back in her chair. "You've probably guessed I love books too, since I'm in the publishing business. How was it, doing the audiobooks like radio plays?"

"Both challenging and fun. I enjoyed working with Helen and Harvey. I'd met them before, of course, but had never had the chance to work with them."

Annelie cocked her head. "How did you feel about doing the love scenes with Helen, even if it was only sound-wise?"

Carolyn seemed to give it some thought. "I've never played a lesbian before, so I had no idea how it would seem. But then again, this was also my first role as a criminal investigator. When Helen and I recorded the love scenes, we actually stood very close and used the same microphone. I felt very safe and comfortable with her. We're both pros."

Annelie considered this. It was a straightforward and honest reply. "So you didn't feel awkward at all?"

Carolyn gave a smile. "Perhaps I felt a little self-conscious the first time I indicated kissing her. Harvey took care of that."

Annelie raised an eyebrow. "What did he do?"

"He snuck up behind me, and when I was supposed to have ended the first, long kiss, he grabbed my waist. On tape, my gasp of surprise sounds very passionate!"

Annelie couldn't hold back a laugh. Carolyn's low purr was done tongue in cheek and utterly irresistible.

"It certainly worked for the audience. I suppose you've seen all the fan Web sites and message boards devoted to Maddox. There must be thousands."

"I confess, I'm not into computers, and I don't use the Internet. New technology just isn't my thing. It's hard to fathom how much information the fans can get hold of this way."

"We have a pretty good overview of it all. There are Diana Maddox lists, Carolyn Black lists, and several lists about the other characters."

"Honestly, I had no idea."

Annelie paused for a moment. "The Internet is a big part of our overall marketing strategy. We've also established a new company that will be organizing Diana Maddox conventions. All in all, she's quite a franchise."

Carolyn looked cautious, as if she couldn't quite see where Annelie was headed, sharing all this business information. "I'm impressed," she said. "You'll have every angle covered once you release the movies as well."

"Precisely." The perfect opening, Annelie thought, carefully composing her next sentence. "Which brings me to something I need to discuss with you." She detected an immediate flicker of excitement in Carolyn's eyes and felt bad. What she was about to say was not what the actress was expecting to hear. "We're going to have to take the current audiobooks off the market."

"What?" Carolyn blurted out in an incredulous tone of voice.

"Whoever plays Maddox in the movie will also have to feature in the audiobooks, so we'll be dubbing her voice in." She met Carolyn's stunned gaze without blinking. "We have no choice. We have to maintain homogeneity to bring readers and audience along. It would confuse them if the voice in the audiobooks is not the same as the actress's they watch on the screen. I'm sure you understand that."

A ringing sound came from the house and Annelie rose quickly. "Sorry. I left my cordless in the kitchen. Be right back."

She ran into the house, anticipating that once Carolyn was over her shock, she would rise to the bait and make her play for the role. But by the time the discussion ended, she would accept the inevitable and take the deal Annelie planned to offer her.

❖

Carolyn leaned back in her chair, stunned. Annelie had all but told her she was out of the running. Her eyes prickled and she turned her head, looking over the pool area to the well-kept gardens beyond. Tall palm trees were scattered at the perimeter, and tropical flowers bloomed abundantly in the flower beds. Annelie obviously employed a competent gardener.

Her thoughts whirled as a realization struck her. If Annelie intended to cease audiobook sales and allow the contracts to run out, where did that leave her? Thanks to a profit percentage deal, she received a steady income flow from them. She needed that money for Beth.

Rising from her chair, still holding a glass of mineral water, she walked to the edge of the lawn, her stomach churning. Annelie could do exactly as she pleased and there wasn't a damned thing Carolyn could do about it.

Except get the starring role in *Dying for Fame*.

"A penny for them?" Annelie's voice coming from behind her made Carolyn jump. "Oh, sorry, I didn't mean to startle you."

Carolyn took a long, steadying sip of the mineral water. "Let me understand this. You've chosen someone for the role already?"

"No. But my casting agent has worked it down to a short list." She had the grace to look embarrassed.

"Am I on that list?"

"Of course you are." The assurance sounded slightly hollow.

Carolyn couldn't imagine Annelie lying outright—she seemed too classy for that. Concluding that her name was right at the bottom, she said, "I get the feeling I'm not your first choice."

Annelie made a small, helpless gesture.

Carolyn lowered her gaze from the publisher's exquisite, calm face and refrained from yelling, *What's wrong with you? I'm perfect!* "Is it my age?" she asked flatly.

"No. "The denial was quick and emphatic. "You barely look thirty-five."

"Then what? Do me a favor and just tell me, okay?"

Annelie's eyes widened a fraction at the blunt request. "Okay." Her tone became very businesslike. "Your voice was always perfect for Diana. But film is a visual medium, and I'm not sure your look is quite right for her. "

Carolyn raised an eyebrow. "Clearly you wouldn't have cast Charlize Theron in *Monster*."

Annelie sighed. "Carolyn, listen. I know you want the role, and I love the work you've done for Key Line. But I can't afford to allow my own personal preferences to enter into this decision. I'm risking a lot on this movie. People depend on me for their livelihoods, so I have to listen to what industry experts are telling me or I won't get a distribution deal. You know what those guys are like."

It was the first time Carolyn had heard Annelie speak with real emotion since her presentation at the Nebula Circle fundraiser. She took a moment to consider the right way to respond. Softening her tone, she said, "At least let me read for you, and keep an open mind. Will you give me that?"

"Absolutely," Annelie said. "In fact, I'll give you more. I feel very bad about the audiobooks, and I want to make it right with you. Let's do this properly."

"What do you mean?"

"We both know I'm within my rights to stop selling the books and let our contracts with you simply expire. But neither of us gets anything from this option. I have a better idea."

"I'm listening."

"I'll pay you a hundred thousand dollars to compensate for lost earnings, and we'll terminate the contracts properly. All you have to do is say yes, and I'll handle the legal work."

Carolyn mentally repeated the offer. It sounded generous. Annelie was obviously trying to do the right thing. But her instincts told her to stall. It was a long time since she had signed the audiobook contracts. She wanted to see exactly what the fine print said before she walked away.

"I'll need to talk it over with Grey," she said.

"Of course. I'll have my attorneys fax the paperwork over to him right away. Let me know once you've had a chance to think it over." Annelie motioned toward the table. "How about some coffee?"

Carolyn shook her head. "Normally I'd love a cup, but I need to be somewhere. I'll call a cab."

"Why don't I give you lift? I have to run a few errands."

Carolyn was about to decline when she thought again. It seemed as if Annelie was trying to be a friend to her on a personal level, irrespective of their professional relationship. It would be shortsighted to shut down that possibility. The role might not be hers automatically, but it was within reach, and the more time she spent with Annelie, the better her chances.

"Thanks, that's very thoughtful of you," she said. "Now tell me the really good news—we're taking that beauty parked right outside. The Mustang?"

Annelie looked pleasantly surprised. "Yes. Do you like vintage cars?"

"Love them. I've always wanted a seventies Corvette Stingray, but since I live in New York I drive a Volvo XC90, an SUV. Safe, versatile, and a tad on the dull side. Don't tell anyone I said so, though. I'm participating in a Volvo commercial soon."

"You have my word," Annelie promised with mock sincerity.

After gathering her bag, Carolyn followed Annelie to the well-kept Mustang, where she enjoyed the feel of the smooth white leather seat. Cool air suggested the car had been modernized.

"What color would you choose if you ever bought a vintage Corvette?" Annelie asked, donning a pair of sunglasses.

Carolyn rolled her eyes at herself. "You'll think I'm nuts, but I'd like a Tweety-Bird yellow one."

"A Tweety-Bird yellow?" Annelie burst out laughing. The sound was contagious, and the actress joined in. "I'd never have guessed."

Confidently, Annelie drove through the streets of the gated community and waved at the guard. Carolyn was intrigued by the strange mix of frankness and reserve she detected in the younger woman and wondered what made her tick. She was obviously a brilliant businesswoman. Was it her wealth or her persona that opened doors for her, and was it money or power she sought? Apparently it wasn't celebrity.

"You must have a great personal stake in the Diana Maddox books since you oversee every detail yourself," Carolyn ventured.

"I guess you could say that, but also, I gave my word to Delia Carlton that I'd personally make sure her story didn't get twisted or sold out to any of the greedy Hollywood moguls. Doing the conventions, letting the fans in more without exposing Delia, is one way of accomplishing this. Keeping the movie production within the family, so to speak, is another." Annelie smiled briefly. "I'm normally not a control freak, you know. It's just that I made a promise."

Carolyn nodded. So keeping promises and honoring loyalty rated highly with Annelie. This did not surprise her since this was how everyone she'd met and worked with from Key Line operated. Still, she wondered how on the up-and-up Annelie's offer to reimburse her for the cancelled contracts was. She'd sounded so sincere when suggesting that she release Carolyn from the contract in a decent way, but something didn't ring quite true.

"How are you feeling?" Annelie asked. "You were a little pale when you came to the house, but it looks like the swim did you a world of good."

Surprised yet feeling unexpectedly cared for, Carolyn smiled. "I'm fine, thanks. The swim did what it always does for me. It's relaxing and keeps me going. I've always suffered from migraines and discovered, long before any of the newer medications, that swimming is the best way to handle them."

"I won't pretend to know what it's like, but it sounds painful. That reminds me, since you're going to use the pool a lot while you're in Florida...Do you have a car here?"

Carolyn shook her head. "No. Jared has a car, of course, but he uses it every day. I could come by cab, like today."

"No, that'd be such a nuisance for you. Here's what we'll do. Why don't you borrow the SUV while you're here? I have this car and a Jaguar, so I'm all set."

Carolyn couldn't believe the other woman's generosity. "Thanks. That's really kind, and I appreciate it. An SUV would be super, since I'm used to one."

"Great. That's settled, then." Annelie pulled over in front of Jared's condo, letting the motor run while she reached in the backseat for her purse.

The action caused her ponytail to sweep forward along Carolyn's bare arm, making her skin tingle from the soft touch. Startled, she glanced at the blond tresses, almost expecting them to be dusted with something magical.

"Here," Annelie said as she shuffled through her bag. "If no one is at the house, you can use this card." She handed over a key card similar to one from a hotel. "It automatically turns off the alarm, so pull it through the box again and it'll lock up and reset the alarm when you leave."

"You're sweet to trust a stranger, Annelie. I'm honored, of course, and it'll be so good for me, but still…"

"You're not really a stranger." Annelie shrugged. "I've known *of* you for years, and you're working for me too, in a way. I'll give you the keys to the Navigator tomorrow and tell the guards to expect you."

"Thanks again. I'm really grateful," Carolyn said as she stepped out of the car.

Annelie hesitated as if meaning to say something more, but shifted into Drive and waved. "Talk to you later. Have a nice afternoon, Carolyn."

"You too."

Walking toward the apartment building, Carolyn looked down at the key card, feeling almost disoriented. Nothing had gone as she'd planned, and she now had to regroup mentally. It hadn't crossed her mind that Annelie would virtually rule her out before the casting process began in earnest. She was infuriated that the decision could be influenced by men who thought any actress over thirty-five should be playing Grandma. What did they know about the audience for a powerful female character like Diana Maddox?

She had to figure out how to show Annelie Peterson exactly what it took to captivate that audience, how to make herself indispensable as Diana Maddox. *I know Sylvia Goodman is a good actress, beautiful… younger.* Carolyn gave a mental shrug, pressing her lips together. *She may be good, but she's not me. She's not Maddox.*

CHAPTER THREE

Annelie waved to the security guard at the desk in the foyer of a carefully renovated art-deco building by the boardwalk.

"How are things today, Earl?" she asked, as she passed him on her way to Key Line Publishing.

"Just fine, Ms. Peterson. The wife and I have bought tickets to the Diana Maddox convention."

"I'll see you there, then." Annelie returned his smile. "I hope the two of you have a good time."

"I'm sure we will. My wife adores the books."

"Tell her to keep an eye on our Web page. We're planning a few surprises."

With another wave, Annelie walked through the glass doors leading into the building and down the hall to her beachfront corner office. She greeted her administrative assistant with a smile, then paused to enjoy the view and watch the waves wash onto the sand. Noticing a large envelope sitting on top of her inbox on her desk, she reached for it and instantly recognized the distinctive logotype of a famous photographer, Corazon Perez.

Curious, Annelie opened it and pulled out a set of publicity photos. Suddenly breathless, she had to will her hands not to drop them. Carolyn Black gazed at her from the glossy pictures, her persona radiating off them with a subtle force. A note from Grey Parker was attached to the top photo, again stating Carolyn's interest in the Maddox role.

Annelie had glimpsed Carolyn several times since the actress had begun to use her pool. They rarely conversed, but she had been very aware of the actress's presence.

Reluctantly looking at the first picture, Annelie saw Carolyn dressed in a black, sleeveless turtleneck, resembling a panther. With her hair pulled back from her face in a tight twist that accentuated her features, she exuded both arrogance and danger as she leaned back in an armchair. Carolyn looked almost haunted, which made Annelie wonder what Corazon Perez had said or done to bring out this expression.

The second picture was completely different. With her auburn hair clouding around her shoulder, Carolyn wore a long white caftan made from a thin, lacy fabric. One of its wide sleeves had fallen back a little, revealing her arm up to the elbow. Her makeup was discreet, emphasizing her intense eyes. She smiled faintly, as if privy to a special secret.

The third picture made Annelie gasp inaudibly and sink into her desk chair. Corazon must have used a fan to blow the hair off Carolyn's shoulders, making it flow behind her. At first it looked like she was naked, but when Annelie examined the picture, she saw Carolyn wore a transparent, light tan shirt that fit like a second skin. Small silver threads were woven into the fragile fabric, making Carolyn's skin seem to sparkle. In this picture, the actress focused on something behind the photographer, a dreamy expression in her eyes.

The glamorous pictures bothered Annelie. She rose from her chair and paced over to the window. As she placed a hand on the cool glass and watched the beach fill up with people, she was flooded by inexplicable emotions. She frowned, simply not used to feeling so vulnerable.

Annelie hadn't allowed herself to become involved with anyone the last few years. The last time she let anyone close, the relationship had ended in heartache. So far it had never seemed worth the effort to figure out if someone loved her for her money or for herself. *I promised myself not to let it rule my actions. I guess I have.*

She recalled Carla, the one who had hurt her the most. The mere thought of the dark-haired girl she'd met at the university made her heart recoil. Though hardened by the sudden transition from being ignored to being fawned over, Annelie had still lowered her guard and let the other woman approach her.

Attending some of the same classes at Barnard, they became close and Annelie began to nourish hope for a future with the exciting brunette. She never admitted to anyone how it broke her heart when she heard by chance of Carla's plan to seduce the "ice queen." When Annelie learned Carla had known about her financial status all along, she had in her wounded state assumed the other woman was a gold digger as well.

Pulling out of the relationship and changing her curriculum, Annelie stayed within the close circle of her study group, never exchanging more than polite words in passing with Carla.

She glanced at the remaining photos of Carolyn Black, but then opened a drawer in her desk and pushed the pictures inside before closing it. Feeling childish about her uncharacteristic behavior, she closed her eyes briefly.

"Annelie? I'm going nuts! Will you take a look at this?" Jem Sanderson burst through the open door to her office. A shock of short brown hair streaked with a few gray strands framed a strongly chiseled face with azure blue eyes and a firm mouth. Waving a thick stack of documents in her right hand, the chief editor of Key Line was obviously agitated. "This is only since yesterday."

"Good morning to you too, Jem," Annelie said, grateful for the interruption. "What's this?"

"E-mails! I'm suddenly getting at least two to three hundred e-mails every day insisting we use Carolyn Black as Diana Maddox and Helen St. Cyr as her love interest. They're clogging my inbox! I can't work like this."

"Calm down. Let me see." Annelie reached for the documents and began browsing through them. "Oh, my." She read a sample aloud. "I, and every one of my friends who have read the books and listened to the audiobooks, am hoping Carolyn Black will play Diana Maddox in the upcoming movies. After hearing Ms. Black read Maddox's part in the audiobooks, there simply can be no other."

"Amazing, huh?" Jem stated. "How fans can be this devoted and loyal."

Annelie shook her head. "Mind-boggling."

"When will you be seeing Black next?"

"Probably tomorrow. This is a busy week for me, so it'll be the only day I can work from home." Annelie had no plans to mention the audiobook contract termination to her staff, or anyone else, until after the upcoming convention, so she smoothly changed the topic, "Speaking of which, you're not bailing on the luncheon at my house Friday, are you?"

"Of course not! It'll be fun. Did Kitty manage to change her ticket? I'm really looking forward to meeting her and Sam after all this time."

Annelie laughed quietly. "Yes, after nearly strangling me for changing the dates. She'd bought tickets to fly in just after the weekend, and then when I e-mailed her, asking her to come earlier, she had a fit. Only the fact she managed to save several hundred dollars saved my neck."

"Will she be here for the convention too?"

"Yes, she and Sam decided to extend their vacation since they haven't really taken one for the past two years."

Jem nodded, looking pleased. "Good. Maybe we can spend some time with them after the convention."

Annelie agreed.

"I guess I'll go work on a standard reply to the Maddox fans. There's no way I can correspond with them individually." Jem waved, jumped off the chair, and left.

Alone with her thoughts, Annelie sat down at her computer and opened her desk drawer. Glancing down at the envelope with the photos she'd left on top, she sighed inaudibly. Carolyn looked absolutely wonderful in the pictures, almost as irresistible as in real life. Impatient with the direction her thoughts were taking, Annelie pivoted in her chair and gazed at the ocean again.

It was obvious the actress had a large following. Numerous Web sites were dedicated to her long before the audiobooks—now there were hundreds more. Annelie reached under her hair, rubbing at the tension in her neck.

Audiences were only faithful to a degree. If the actress they chose for the Maddox role did her job right, Carolyn Black would soon be forgotten by this part of her fan base, especially if the audiobooks were discontinued in their present form.

She's the one I always saw as Diana Maddox. Annelie made the acknowledgment uneasily. For her, Carolyn was perfect as the headstrong, daring criminal investigator. However, she had to set her personal bias aside and listen to the show business expertise. So far, the marketing experts had suggested three different names of actresses they deemed more suitable than Carolyn—younger, edgier, and less glamorous, definitely less glamorous.

Perhaps that's it. Her personal appearance is too glossy, and even too strong? They don't think she can play the role convincingly. Annelie doubted herself, her own assessment, since she reacted the way she did to Carolyn. *Perhaps the investors and marketing experts fear she's too much herself. The very part I find so intriguing.*

Diana Maddox was the kind of character who seemed to jump off the page. From the moment she'd read the first chapter of *Dying for Fame*, Annelie had been convinced that Maddox could attract just as large a fan base as other fictional female heroes. Getting to know the lesbian investigator was perhaps even more absorbing than author Delia Carlton's compelling plot lines. Though Annelie knew they were sitting on a winner, she could never have anticipated the books would stay on the best-seller charts for several years or that sales would skyrocket worldwide.

Fans of Diana Maddox, and of Delia Carlton, had flooded the publishing company with letters and e-mails, wanting to know more. Delia was not comfortable with the attention, so after brainstorming with Gregory and Jem, Annelie decided to give Diana Maddox a voice, if not yet a face, and purchased the rights to turn the novels into audiobooks. And instead of hiring a talented unemployed actor or actresses for the recording, as she usually did, she assigned a cast, a different actor for each character in the book, plus a narrator.

For Maddox, Annelie had thought of Carolyn Black instantly. The actress's voice held a rare quality that made people stop and listen. It could vary from a dark growl to a seductive purr, and because they would need a wide range of tones for the series, she was the obvious choice for the lead.

Carolyn and the other actors signed contracts to read three novels. Annelie had expected only the devoted fans to buy the audiobooks, but when sales of the CDs and tapes not only tied with the hardbacks and paperbacks but surpassed them, Key Line wrote publishing history. Now they were set to expand their market exponentially, and she didn't have much time left before they began filming. Even Delia Carlton was asking if the lead actress had been cast yet.

Annelie would have to make her decision soon.

Not even glancing at the glossy pictures of Carolyn, she clicked on her first e-mail. She had work to do.

❖

Carolyn had lost count of her laps and the time. Muscles quivering, she climbed out of the pool and reached for a large towel draped over a deck chair.

"I can make you some coffee and a bagel with cream cheese, if you like, Ms. Black," Annelie's housekeeper said behind her. The petite, wiry woman had greeted her at the door when she arrived, informing her that Annelie would be at the office all day.

"Thank you, Mary. I'd like that. You spoil me, you know."

"Ah, think nothing of it. I was going to have a cup anyway."

"Then why don't you join me here on the patio?"

Mary looked shocked and appalled. "Now, how would that look? I have work to do."

Amused over her apparent faux pas, Carolyn walked into the guest room to change. When she returned to the patio, she found coffee, orange juice, a bagel, and assorted fruits.

Carolyn reached for the coffee cup and, inhaling the aroma of her favorite type of coffee, Royal Copenhagen, she sipped it carefully. Black and strong, it seemed to go straight to her veins, rejuvenating her after her strenuous workout, and she secretly commended herself for bringing two packages as a gift for Annelie.

A beeping sound came from her bag. Pulling out her phone, she grimaced when she noticed two missed calls from Beth and one from Grey Parker. Immediately worried, she dialed her sister first, but the phone went dead the moment Beth answered. When it wouldn't power up, she realized she'd probably forgotten to charge it again.

Carolyn grabbed her wallet and rushed into the house, looking for the housekeeper. "Excuse me, Mary? Is it okay if I use the phone? My cell died on me, and I have a calling card."

"Of course." Mary led her into Annelie's study. "Here you go. You can use the one on the desk."

Thanking her, Carolyn sat down in the black leather chair behind Annelie's large cherrywood desk.

While she waited for her call to go through, Carolyn studied the room curiously. The walls were a pleasant forest green and the carpet off-white. The bookshelves, also made of cherry, held numerous reference books and long rows of binders. Two wine red chairs on the other side of the desk were obviously for visitors. Soft classical music from an invisible source permeated the entire house, including the office.

"Hello!"

"Beth, I'm sorry. My phone died again."

"For goodness' sake, Lyn. You're the most technically challenged person I know." Her sister sounded much more her feisty self, which was reassuring.

"Was there something you wanted?"

"Yes, I know you'll be pleased. I've taken a leave of absence, and my boss says whenever I want to come back, my job's waiting for me."

"That's wonderful." Carolyn smiled and leaned back in the chair. The scent of leather mixed with perfume soothed her senses. "So Joe's willing to let me help?"

"To be honest, he was more willing to accept than I was." Beth paused. "I was worried about his pride. You know what I mean."

"I know." In Carolyn's experience, Joe didn't have an ego. He focused on what mattered. "Listen, I won't have any problem helping you guys out during the pregnancy. If you need help around the house, just hire somebody. The sky's the limit."

Beth's voice was warm. "You're so thoughtful, sweetie. Thank you. Tell me, does anyone else ever get to see this side of you?"

Carolyn smiled. Sisters were allowed to see through one another. She had to keep the rest of the world at arm's length or they would eat her alive. "No. I have to maintain my image as a witch on wheels to keep them on their toes."

A small sigh. "Are you coming back this weekend?"

"That's the plan. I'll call you when I know which flight I'll be on. Take care of yourself and hug Joe and Pamela."

"I will. You take care too."

About to call Grey, Carolyn glimpsed a small picture in a silver frame at the far end of the desk. It was one of the promotion shots from *The Passing of Time*, taken during the second season. A much-younger Carolyn Black gazed at her with confidence that was only skin-deep at the time.

Her success as Devon Harper had opened many doors for her in show business, especially when the show's ratings climbed and she was credited for attracting a wider audience. She'd played Devon Harper for more than two years, at the same time seeking minor big-screen roles.

Carolyn took a deep breath and stared down at the photograph once more. Why did Annelie Peterson keep a picture of her in her study?

The only other picture she could see was a group photo on one wall. It looked like a class reunion—Annelie with a bunch of other women.

A twitch at the corner of her mouth developed into a smile. Tapping the picture frame with a well-manicured nail, Carolyn thought about it some more. Annelie, it seemed, could be a fan of hers from way back. If she played her cards right, this could prove rather useful.

Her mind racing, she set the picture back on the desk and dialed her agent.

❖

Jem stuck her head in the door of Annelie's office. "Can I talk to you?"

"Come on in." Annelie gave her chief editor a quick smile. "What is it?"

"A couple of things. First, we're going to have to find at least two more authors in the fantasy genre or we'll have an unbalanced catalogue. I'm sure I saw a promising manuscript and now I can't find it!"

Jem was famous for losing things. Keys, cell phones, wallets… Annelie couldn't keep track of how many times the whole office had been in uproar—all pitching in to help the energetic editor find her missing belongings.

"What was the title? Who was the author?"

"I think it was something with *Dragon Dreams*."

"Ah, sorry. It's at home. I wanted to read it over the weekend, but I didn't get around to it. I'll try and finish it tomorrow morning."

"You're going to read an unsolicited manuscript while Carolyn Black is visiting?" Jem asked, clearly aghast.

Annelie blinked. "How did you know about Carolyn coming over?"

"Your housekeeper dropped a hint big enough to sink the *Titanic*." Jem grinned. "Smart move. You can ask her about the convention and sound her out about the film role."

"That's not what this is about, Jem. I offered Carolyn the use of my pool while she's in Florida, and she was truly grateful. That's it—no agendas."

"I can't believe you've had her spending hours swanning around your house in a swimsuit and didn't say a word! What's she like in person?"

"She's very nice and very charismatic, every bit as fascinating as she seems on stage and TV. Even more so, in my humble opinion."

"Is someone I know starstruck?" Jem teased.

"You know me better than that." Annelie tried to hide her faint embarrassment with a cough. "She bought first editions of the Diana Maddox books for $12,000 during the auction. I thought that was pretty amazing. She was there with her boyfriend."

"Who's her boyfriend?"

"Jared Garrison. He's from the law firm we use for the Nebula Circle's clients."

"Oh, him. He's a nice guy."

"That he is. Great taste in women too, obviously."

This drew a small gasp. "Annelie, what are you saying?"

Stunned at what had jumped out of her mouth, Annelie lapsed into momentary silence. She did find Carolyn Black very attractive, but she never mixed business with pleasure, and certainly not with involved straight women.

"Well, she's gorgeous and has *it*, don't you agree?" She stalled, knowing Jem wouldn't be fooled for a second.

"Uh-huh."

"Anyhow, I'll bring the manuscript tomorrow and we can discuss it." Assuming her most businesslike tone, she said, "So, are we going to take a look through that convention merchandise?"

"Yes, but there's something else." Jem's eyes narrowed slightly. "Those e-mails flooding in—our Web guru says they originate in Grey Parker's office."

"Really?" She should have guessed.

"I wonder if your screen idol knows." Jem needled her gently.

Annelie shot her a look. "My first guess would be she doesn't. I get the impression Carolyn can barely cope with cell phones, let alone computers."

"I'm sure she's smart enough to find people who can. Seems like her agent follows the trends."

Annelie knew her chief editor was right. "Well, Grey Parker can do what he likes to stir up the fans. But it's not going to buy his client a thing."

"I hear you." Jem snapped her fingers. "By the way, I'm going to the Blue Beach Café for dinner with my sister and her husband tonight. Want to join us? We have reservations at eight o'clock."

Annelie was not looking forward to yet another evening home alone, especially knowing where her thoughts kept taking her at the moment. "Sounds like a good idea. I'll meet you there."

❖

The Blue Beach Café, located where the most popular beach in Key Biscayne began, was a long, single-floor building with a waterfront deck.

Carolyn and Grey Parker strolled out on the long porch, the soft, scented evening wrapping around them. Still not over the shock of learning that her agent had flown down to Florida yesterday, she had agreed to join him for dinner. Following the waiter to a table by the railing, the actress wrapped her shawl tighter, feeling a chill. She smiled briefly and politely thanked the waiter who pulled out a chair for her.

"I'll have a scotch, please," she ordered, surprising herself. She was a little cold, and perhaps the alcohol would ignite a much-needed fire inside.

"A beer, thank you." Grey leaned back in his chair, glancing around the large deck. "Apparently it's hard to get a table here. At least that's what they said at the hotel."

"Yes, I believe so. It's popular." Carolyn focused on the menu until the waiter returned with their drinks and some iced water. Sipping the alcohol, she realized she enjoyed the warmth it spread through her system way too much.

"You look uneasy." Grey frowned.

"I'm fine, it's just...I'm...well, I admit I do feel a bit stymied by the last turn of events. I don't know what to do about the contracts, Grey. Ms. Peterson is trying to be decent about it, so I can cut my losses without actually losing too much."

"Not so fast, my dear. I went over the contracts before I left New York, and my advice is for you to hang on to them. We're not throwing in the towel just yet. It's going to take a bit of engineering, though."

"I was so certain...My mistake," Carolyn huffed, fumbling in her purse. "Mind if I smoke?"

"No, go ahead." He nudged an ashtray closer to her.

Carolyn lit up and inhaled deeply. She had cut back a lot over the last few years but always craved a cigarette when she felt like this— rattled, on edge. *Damn it, what's wrong with me? It's not like me to feel so...defeated this early in the race.* She had been having trouble sleeping. Worrying about Beth, seeing the Maddox role just beyond her grasp were making the veins at her temples throb painfully. *Why can't Annelie see I'm the perfect choice?* She knew the answer. Over the years, she had made a few enemies in the business for refusing to play their game. One of the more illustrious movie reviewers once accused her of being "too much." *Perhaps I am too much. Too much me. Too much Carolyn Black.*

"Maybe it's better to just bow out," she murmured. "Peterson's advisers seem determined to cast Sylvia Goodman. From what I understand, Annelie's a rookie executive producer. She's bound to listen to them."

"We can still sway them. Listen to me, Carolyn. I have some news for you. A sister company to Supernova Productions is planning an event in Orlando, on Saturday two weeks from now."

"What kind of event?" She squinted at him through the smoke.

Realizing she sounded angry, Carolyn tried to calm down. It wasn't Grey's fault she was feeling stung that the role seemed to be sliding out of her grip.

"They're holding a Diana Maddox convention, and fans from all over the world will attend. Some of your colleagues from the audiobooks will be there. This tells me they've been cast for their respective roles in the movie." He paused, eyeing her carefully. "Exactly how far are you prepared to go to land this role?"

"I don't know what you mean. I feel I've earned the right to play Maddox. The audience connects me to this character."

"Audience attention is fickle, and you know it. You have to cause some disturbance in Supernova's plans. Stir the pot, in a manner of speaking." Grey's eyes sparkled; the agent was obviously excited at the prospect of causing trouble.

"What do you suggest?"

Grey leaned closer over the table, speaking in a mock-secretive voice. "I suggest we crash their party."

❖

Jem spotted her first.

"Damn, isn't that Carolyn Black sitting over there?"

Annelie's first reaction was to immediately turn around; instead she made herself casually pivot on her chair, looking over at the smoking section.

"Yes, it is. The man she's with is Grey Parker, her agent." Her voice was calm. "If the Blue Beach Café weren't so popular, I'd say this was quite the coincidence."

"It *is* a coincidence," Jem insisted. "Here, come sit next to me so you can see her."

Not quite sure why she complied, Annelie rose and changed seats. The first thing she noticed was Carolyn's erratic smoking. The actress's hands jerked when she put the cigarette between her lips or tapped restless fingertips against the tablecloth.

Jem noticed too. "She seems on edge."

"Yes."

Annelie watched Carolyn snub out her cigarette and toss down the last of her drink. She looked furious, every taut movement a testament to her control. Of course Carolyn would not permit her public to see her having some kind of tantrum. The actress stared into her glass, only to follow the smoke's journey toward the ceiling, and gazed out over the ocean. When she turned back to Grey, her face was serene.

A waiter brought the actress a new drink, and the sight of Carolyn holding onto the glass with both hands made Annelie frown, then look quickly away. So far, it seemed Carolyn hadn't noticed Annelie and her party. She briefly wondered what the New York–based agent was doing in Florida. Not wanting Grey Parker on her case this evening, she decided not to acknowledge the two unless Carolyn spotted her.

"I don't get it," Jem said. "Why aren't we asking her to guest speak at the convention? She'd be such a draw."

"Because if we do, the entire planet will assume she's going to be playing Diana Maddox in the movie."

Clearly Jem thought this was ideal. "I don't see the problem. I mean, I know you have to go through the motions of casting, but—"

"The problem is distribution," Annelie said. "I'm negotiating with prospective distributors as we speak, and, frankly, no one is talking about Carolyn Black. Those guys are hot for Sylvia Goodman."

Jem looked startled. "But she's too young. And that voice—Marilyn Monroe on helium."

Annelie laughed at the description. Jem was right. Sylvia's squeaky breathlessness was totally wrong for Maddox. But although Annelie was financing the movie, she was not a distributor. If she didn't get decent distribution, it would make no difference how good her film was. It would wither at the box office or, worse, end up going straight to video.

"I know she's not ideal, but I have to consider her," Annelie said. "I can't afford to cast an actress they won't get behind."

"I see the problem." Jem's dismay was palpable. "What are you going to tell Carolyn about the convention?"

"Nothing at all. She's a busy woman. With any luck, she won't even realize it's happening until it's over."

When Jem's sister and her husband joined them at the table, Annelie was thankful for a change in topic. But despite their friendly banter, she found it hard to focus on the conversation.

As the evening continued, more people entered the restaurant, now and again obscuring Annelie's view of Carolyn, who sat smoking an endless number of cigarettes after finishing her meal. Still her eyes constantly sought the actress out, staring hungrily, feasting from a distance, which was utterly unsatisfying. But it was all Annelie could ever do.

❖

Driving up to Annelie's house the next day, Carolyn felt resolved and oddly detached. She parked and, pulling her bag toward her, stepped out of the Navigator.

To her surprise Annelie, dressed casually in white slacks and a light yellow top, appeared in the doorway and waved at her.

"Hello! You're early today, Carolyn."

The bright sunlight reflected in Annelie's long hair, which hung down around her shoulders today. Her smile was friendly and open.

"Yes—" Carolyn broke off before she let the other woman know she hadn't slept a wink the night before. Adjusting her features to not betray her cold determination, she returned the smile.

Annelie gestured toward the hallway. "Before you swim, I need to run something by you if you don't mind. Join me in my study?"

"By all means." Carolyn pushed her sunglasses on top of her head.

Fastening her gaze on Annelie, she donned a bright expression. "As you said, I'm early."

In the study, her eyes immediately fell upon several large glossy photos stacked on the desk. She was still amazed at how well they had turned out. Corazon was talented, making her look young and vibrant in every shot. Not that it had made any difference to Annelie, who quickly picked up the glossies and put them aside.

"I see my promotion pictures arrived," Carolyn remarked pointedly.

"Yes, Grey Parker sent them. They're wonderful. Corazon Perez is a very good photographer. I admire her work tremendously."

Still looking at the picture of herself in the ethereal outfit with the silver threads, Carolyn saw, out of the corner of her eye, Annelie move to the other end of the desk and stealthily lay the picture of the nineteen-years-younger Carolyn facedown.

Amazed, her heart pounding at the unexpected movement, Carolyn continued, "I needed new pictures taken since I've received so much mail from Maddox fans wanting to put a face to the voice." Instinctively, she pretended she hadn't noticed Annelie's subtle maneuver and filed this information away for future reference. Looking up at the other woman, she gave a broad smile, knowing from experience how it could entice people. She touched Annelie's shoulder, squeezing it gently. "Anything for the fans, right?"

"Of course." Annelie sounded collected, but her shoulder felt tense beneath Carolyn's touch.

Letting her hand drop, she removed her sunglasses from the top of her head and put them into her bag. "Are you going in to work today?"

"Yes, in a little while. I thought we could go over the contracts first."

"Oh, yes, the contracts. Well, Grey advised me to hang on to them. He takes care of these matters for me, and I trust his opinion." Carolyn shrugged. "We talked things over last night, and if need be, I'd be happy to screen-test, to prove I'm the right one for the Maddox role."

Folding her arms, Annelie seemed taken aback. "I still intend to withdraw the audiobooks as they stand from the market," she pointed out. "This will mean a significant loss of royalties to you. I think Mr. Parker's advice is not in your best interest, financially."

"Perhaps. Grey, of course, agrees with me that I'm right for the role and stand a very good chance compared to the other actresses on your list. A screen test ought to prove that beyond a shadow of a doubt." Carolyn let the steel in her voice become more apparent. "Regardless how you look at it, I'm more experienced and the one closest to Maddox's age. I also *know* the character in a way they don't."

Leaning with her hip against the desk, Annelie hardened her eyes. "A screen test is of course always useful for a comparison, and I know it's a stretch for someone of your fame to have to do one. Why put yourself though this when I've already explained to you how the marketing experts reason?"

"As I recall, you also promised I could read and you would watch with an open mind," Carolyn said, not acknowledging Annelie's attempt to put her off. "So how about sometime this week?"

The other woman seemed to force back a deep sigh. Shrugging, the politeness only marginal in her voice, she said, "I'm sorry, but my schedule is full. I can't fit you in that quickly, and also I have to have the director present, as well as the casting director."

"Next week, then? Surely that will give everyone ample time to coordinate." Carolyn adopted a cheerful tone of voice. "I'm available any time, except the weekend."

"I'll see what I can do and get back to you through your agent." Her eyes narrowing, Annelie took the promotion pictures and put them back into the envelope with rigid movements. "Now I have to get ready for work."

Remaining completely charming despite the barely concealed irritation in Annelie's voice, Carolyn hoisted her bag over her shoulder, giving the other woman a wide smile. "Well, I better go take my swim. Have a great day, Annelie."

Looking at her with an unreadable expression in her eyes, Annelie nodded regally. "You too, Carolyn."

CHAPTER FOUR

Unmistakably, it was Kitty McNeil at the gate. Her Australian accent carried through the intercom system.

"Hey, gorgeous. We're here and we're starving!"

Annelie buzzed the gate open and hurried to meet Kitty and Sam. As always she was amazed at the couple's appearance. Kitty was dressed in dark jeans, a sleeveless denim shirt, and a baseball hat jammed on her short blond hair. Sam, the taller of the two, wore black jeans and a T-shirt with an enigmatic print decorating the front. A Celtic tattoo stretched from her shoulder down along her abdomen, which Annelie had admired in a private *showing*. Sam moved effortlessly between classic elegance and street-smart toughness.

"Kitty, Sam, welcome. I can't believe you're finally here. I thought I'd exhausted our friendship by dragging you to the opera when I stayed in Sydney."

"It was close," Kitty muttered good-naturedly, pulling Annelie into a warm embrace. "You look great but you're so thin. Are you working too hard, darl'?"

"It's hard not to with so much happening—launching the first Maddox convention and starting to cast the movie. It's been hectic." She embraced Sam and gestured for them to follow her. "I'll show you your room, and then we'll have dinner."

After washing up, her guests joined her in the dining room. Decorated in a modern Nordic style with pinewood furniture, soft blue walls, and an off-white carpet, the room inspired a sense of serenity. The table could seat ten people easily, but Annelie rarely used it for formal entertaining. Mostly she enjoyed gathering her small group of close friends to enjoy Mary's cooking.

"I like the colors in here," Sam said. "I'm glad you didn't put up curtains. Looking out on the pool and the patio gives it a real outdoors feel."

"Thank you. I was hoping to buy one of your galvanized steel mobiles to hang right there." Annelie pointed at a rafter on the patio.

"So, now I'm so curious, I'm tempted to bounce," Kitty exclaimed after the first couple of bites. "I want to hear all about Carolyn Black. How many times have you met her?"

"Almost every day. She comes here to swim."

"Hey, you! Remember who you're talking to." Kitty smirked. "Don't try and fob me off with a nonanswer like that one."

Annelie gazed calmly at her Aussie guest. "She needs to swim every day for her health. I can't tell you any more than that."

"Will she play Maddox in the movies?" Sam asked.

"I don't know yet. Casting will begin soon, and I have the final say on the four major characters. It'll be an interesting experience, that's for sure."

"You've done this before, haven't you?" Kitty questioned. "I mean, you've backed several plays in New York and here in Florida?"

"Yes, but I've never been involved with the casting. I trusted the directors to get it right. But the company has much more at stake this time."

"I guess if the films bomb that'll be the end of Diana Maddox," Kitty observed.

"Precisely. Which is why Delia Carlton wanted me to be very hands-on with every aspect of the project before she would sell the movie rights."

"So when do we hear if Carolyn Black's getting the role?"

"Not yet," Annelie said mildly.

"Okay, I won't hassle you," Kitty conceded, making Sam raise an incredulous eyebrow. "So, what's on the agenda for the next couple of days?"

"We have the authors' luncheon here at the house tomorrow. Jem's coming, so you two will finally get to meet."

"It's about bloody time! She's only edited six of my novels."

"Is Carolyn coming over to swim tomorrow?" Sam asked hopefully.

Annelie seriously doubted it after their last chilly conversation. "I'm not sure of her plans," she said in a noncommittal tone.

Kitty sighed. "If I were you I'd be crawling on my hands and knees to get her in the movie."

Annelie maintained a placid smile. "I'll keep that in mind."

❖

Carolyn woke with her head throbbing. She'd hardly slept, her mind working overtime on her plans for the coming week. Annelie still hadn't given Grey a time for the reading, but no other actresses had read either, so that was always something. She had decided to swim today, for the first time since their unhappy discussion, just to keep Annelie under pressure. The convention was only eight days away, and she was determined to deliver a superb reading that would set the benchmark when Annelie had to consider other actresses.

After showering, she scrutinized her eyes in the mirror and carefully applied Vitamin K cream to the slight bagging and dark circles she noticed. The sea-kelp masque she had used in the shower had eliminated most traces, and she dealt with the last faint shadows with a concealer pencil. Once she had finished dusting a little powder over her usual discreet foundation, she checked herself again, then put the makeup into her bag so she could reapply it after swimming. The last thing she needed today was to look anything less than camera-ready.

Although the guards knew her now, they always stopped the car anyway. Carolyn was uncertain whether this was because the Golden Beach residents insisted on strictest security measures or because they just wanted to ogle her. As always, she was charming to them. Stars who ignored the little people soon found themselves wondering how unpleasant stories got around and secrets were exposed.

As she parked the car and walked up the stone path, she was surprised by an unexpected flutter in her midsection. The thought of facing Annelie again was nerve-wracking, and she steeled herself for the possibility that she would not be made especially welcome. Not that it would matter. She'd all but decided she was going to tell Annelie she no longer wished to take advantage of the pool.

She was about to let herself in when the door opened and Annelie stood there smiling at her. "You're early." she said. "Perfect timing."

"Excuse me?"

Annelie startled Carolyn by extending both hands to take hers. "I have some people here I want you to meet. Don't worry. It's very casual and—"

"You're having guests?" The sound of several female voices laughing made her flinch. "Look, I don't want to intrude."

"I have a few friends over for lunch, and I'd love for you to join us. Please say yes."

The straightforward invitation seemed genuine. Carolyn gazed at Annelie, trying to gauge her expression. She saw nothing but honesty.

"They'd kill me if they knew you were here and they didn't get to meet you. Please?" Annelie continued her pitch. "You'll make me look good."

This unexpected playfulness was irresistible. "All right," Carolyn said. "I'd be glad to stay and meet your friends. Who are they?"

"Most of them are authors." Annelie led her indoors. "Also Jem, my chief editor, is here. She's one of my best friends, and so is Kitty McNeil."

"Kitty McNeil? Jared loves her work. He's really into science fiction and fantasy. I read one of her novels when I visited him last spring and found it intriguing."

"Really?" Annelie sounded surprised. "She'll be thrilled when you tell her."

Walking toward the living room, Carolyn realized she was nervous about meeting Annelie's friends. Inhaling deeply, she slipped into her professional skin. This was nothing but another audience and, to quote Jared, her best role was playing herself.

The women were sitting comfortably around the coffee table. The actress was sure she heard an exhaled, "Oh, my God," from someone.

As Annelie made the introductions, Carolyn reached across the coffee table and shook hands with everyone. She had to smile when she noticed how stunned they seemed by her presence.

"This is unbelievable," Sam exclaimed. "I knew there was a chance we'd get to meet you, but I didn't think it would be today."

"It's very nice of Annelie to include me," Carolyn said.

Sam grinned. "Yeah, nice for us."

❖

They moved to the adjoining room, where chairs ringed the oval table. A white linen tablecloth set with white china and decorations of light blue and peach made the table look festive. Sitting down after complimenting Mary, and keeping an eye on things, Annelie made sure Carolyn ended up next to her.

"What brings you to Florida, Carolyn?" Deena, a Canadian romance novelist, asked as she unfolded her napkin.

"I'm visiting a friend and also attended the Nebula Circle's fundraiser. I hear the evening made a lot of money for the children."

"It did," Annelie agreed, "thanks to generous people like you."

"I just bought a few books," Carolyn said. "I saw somebody buy a painting for a tidy sum."

"True." Annelie nodded. "We had some nice things for sale."

The women spent the following half hour mixing their appreciation of Mary's food with conversation. Sarah, a diminutive woman from Texas, entertained them with an outrageous story about her mother's latest adventure.

"I can't believe it!" Carolyn gasped for air between bouts of laughter. "They called 911 because of a beeping hearing aid?"

"It's a true story," Sarah vowed. "My mother and her sister honestly thought the mysterious sound came from a crashing satellite from space."

Annelie laughed until her stomach hurt. Suddenly she felt Carolyn put a hand on her knee for support as the actress doubled over, laughing deep in her throat—a thoroughly sexy sound.

"Right!" Sarah sighed. "And this is why my partner says she's genetically concerned!"

Annelie looked at Carolyn, amazed at how relaxed the other woman seemed. She had joined in the fun, listened intently to Sarah's story, and the sound of her laughter had made Annelie shiver.

Throwing her head back and laughing again, Carolyn wiped tears from her eyes with a peach napkin. She winked at her hostess and began, "That reminds me of an incident while I was filming in Spey Valley, in Scotland…"

The women around the table listened intently to Carolyn's story of strange noises in the night turning out to be rampaging sheep. Animated, her eyes sparkling, the actress had them all in her hand, and she obviously knew it. *Her hands. I always loved her hands.* Well-kept and expressive, they moved with the tale, emphasizing Carolyn's horror when the sound outside the cottage had come closer. She demonstrated vividly her trepidation when she approached the window, reaching out to open an imaginary window above the table, only to recoil quickly, pressing the right side of her back against Annelie's shoulder.

"I heard something go 'bah.' Very loud." Carolyn's voice was a mere whisper. "I stopped in midair and leaned forward again, actually sticking my head out the window." She leaned forward again, eyes wide. "Something wet, and cold, and in dire need of a breath mint, appeared half an inch before me!"

Pulling back, Carolyn again pressed against Annelie, to demonstrate her dismay. "At least a dozen sheep had escaped their confinement and were crowding my garden."

Unable to keep from laughing along with everybody else at the look on Carolyn's face, Annelie realized the other woman had once again placed her hand on her knee. As if Carolyn had just noticed this as well, she casually withdrew, resuming her relaxed posture on her chair.

The conversation kept flowing easily among the women, and Carolyn seemed to appreciate the friendly banter. She was the center of attention but also utterly charming as she questioned the others. Each of the women present was obviously flattered that Carolyn Black showed an individual interest in her. When, occasionally, she turned directly to Annelie, her eyes held nothing of the resolute defiance from the other day. Instead, they seemed more blue than gray, indecipherable. *How much of this is an act, Carolyn? All of it? Some? It could be so easy to merely assume you're being honest. That this is really who you are.*

A few moments after Mary cleared the lunch plates away, Annelie rose and said, "I'll just go see if Mary needs a hand with dessert."

"I can help as well," Carolyn offered, getting to her feet.

This raised a few objections from the other guests, who seemed to be enjoying her company. Lightly, Carolyn said, "Talk among yourselves, but make sure it's about me. Okay?"

Annelie was astonished to hear Carolyn make this small joke at her own expense. Peals of laughter followed them down the hallway to the kitchen.

Mary was loading the dishwasher. "I've whipped the cream but that's all," she said. "You can decorate them if you want."

"We're having chocolate mousse with whipped cream and raspberries," Annelie explained, opening the refrigerator. She located the cream and spooned some of it into a piping bag. Then she started drawing small circles of cream on the mousse.

"Looks delicious, but then again, so was the entire lunch," Carolyn said. "Are the berries going on top of this?"

Annelie shot her an amused look. "Yes. If you'd like, you can stack some raspberries just inside the circle of cream—about five of them on each." Glancing at Carolyn, she smiled again, watching her stick the tip of her tongue out while focusing on her task.

"I normally don't cook," Carolyn confessed.

Annelie laughed. "I have news for you. This isn't cooking. This is decorating."

"Ah, semantics." Carolyn wrinkled her nose at her hostess. "This is harder than putting butter and marmalade on toast, which is where I normally draw the line."

Annelie shook her head. "You've got to be kidding. Marmalade on toast? That's about the least nutritional thing you can possibly eat."

"Nope, not kidding. And I happen to love apricot marmalade."

After decorating the last bowls of mousse, Annelie moved to her left. Carolyn moved to the right at the same time, reaching for the last of the berries. Standing close enough for their arms to touch, she arranged five berries on the last two bowls and ate one of the two leftover fruit.

Lifting the other, she held it close to Annelie's lips. "Want the last one?" The suggestive gesture was contradicted by what looked like innocence in her eyes.

Ignoring her instinctive reservations, Annelie lowered her head and took the berry. Her lips briefly touched Carolyn's fingertips, and as she crushed the fruit with her tongue, she watched those remarkable eyes widen.

Annelie did not avert her gaze, and for a long moment the two women stood transfixed, Carolyn's attention riveted to Annelie's mouth. Moving slowly, as if unaware of what she was doing, the actress placed a slender, caressing hand over Annelie's elbow and stepped well within her personal space, leaning in as if to kiss her.

Annelie could sense heat radiating off Carolyn's body, permeating the air around her. She could hear the blood rushing in her ears and feel its telltale presence in her cheeks. Not until Carolyn was just a breath away from her lips did she attempt to pull herself together. Mustering enough strength, she managed to withdraw a step.

"Annelie?" Carolyn's voice was almost inaudible, her eyes dark and wide.

Swallowing hard, Annelie found her voice. "I'm sorry. I can't."

Their eyes locked; neither woman was able to pull back completely. Annelie tried to gauge Carolyn's expression. She didn't seem hurt, but instead surprised and bewildered—stunned at her own initiative. Annelie couldn't imagine why Carolyn had tried to kiss her. Surely she knew Annelie was gay; it was virtually an open secret. Touched by something completely vulnerable in her expression, Annelie raised a tentative hand, wanting to temper the rejection. But before she could speak, rapid steps announced Mary's presence and Carolyn sprang back a step.

"I see you've done a great job. Do you want me to bring it in?" the housekeeper asked.

Annelie immediately snapped out of her daze. "No, no, that's okay. I'll take them. Why don't you bring the coffee, Mary?"

She did not know whether to give Carolyn a reassuring smile or not, so she lifted the tray and walked out of the kitchen, hearing the actress follow her.

As they entered the dining room and were swept up in laughter and conversation again, Annelie stole a glance at Carolyn. For some reason, she was sorry to see the vulnerable woman from the kitchen had disappeared. In her stead Carolyn Black, the ambitious actress, once more took possession of the room.

❖

Mary set coffee cups on a side table while Annelie handed out the chocolate mousse. Jem took the chair next to Carolyn's, and Annelie resumed her seat on her other side. Carolyn caught her breath at the brush of that lithe body so close to hers. Her heart was still thundering, as if trying to escape her rib cage. The incident in Annelie's kitchen had caught her off guard.

What had gotten into her? Only her ability to slip into her star persona had saved her from running away and embarrassing herself further. Standing there with two leftover raspberries in her hands, she'd acted on impulse. Annelie had stood there, her hair like a golden cloud around her narrow shoulders, looking at her with darkening ice blue eyes. *I could have sworn she responded to me at first.* Carolyn wondered what the publisher was thinking now.

Having been approached by several lesbians over the year, most of them working in her line of business, she had more or less standardized a way of politely letting them know she wasn't interested. She used the same technique with most men; she was nowhere near the man-eater some gossip columnist had pegged her to be. Sure, she used her sex appeal when it suited her, but compared to some of her colleagues, she was practically a nun. *Is that what I instinctively did?* Glancing around the table, she barely kept from biting her lower lip as it began to tremble. She didn't think anyone noticed.

Carolyn felt Annelie's presence next to her like heat radiating against her skin. She had never felt even the remotest attraction toward a woman. *How could I possibly find the catty, competitive women I know even the slightest alluring? It's not like we're buddies, exactly.* Annelie was not a friend, nor was she a colleague or rival. *She holds my future.* The thought made Carolyn swallow hard and almost forget to smile toward Kitty, who was discussing something with Annelie. *Focus. Don't let them see you lost your footing.* Carolyn sighed. *Why did I do it? Why the hell did I lower my defenses like that?*

"Oh, chocolate mousse," the woman across from her exclaimed, interrupting Carolyn's thoughts. "I've loved this since I was a child."

"So does my niece," Carolyn added, trying to find her bearings by willing her thoughts in a different direction. "Pamela loves chocolate, just like I do."

"How old is she?" Gillian asked.

"She's four, going on forty."

"I know the feeling. My best friend's daughter is just like that!"

"Pamela is quite inventive and, being an only child so far, she's used to getting her own way. Once, when she was barely two and I was taking care of her for the weekend, she wanted to go out and play in the sandbox in the park. I told her no, it was raining and we'd have to wait until the sun came out."

"I guess this didn't go down well."

"It did, at first. She could see the rain from her window and seemed to take no for an answer." Carolyn sipped her coffee, pleased to see everyone hanging on her words. Somehow it helped her find her bearings again. "Anyhow, I was doing some ironing for my sister... now, don't look so shocked, Kitty. I *can* iron."

Ignoring the comment after giving Annelie a half grin, Carolyn continued. "You know how suddenly you realize the house is way too quiet—which normally means the kid, or the pet, in question is up to something. I went looking for Pamela and—speaking of pets—I found her in their cat's litter box, scooping kitty litter into her little plastic bucket."

"Ew." Jem frowned. "And God knows what else."

"Exactly," Carolyn said. "And, of course, she used her most angelic smile when she looked up at me and said 'sandbox, Auntie Lyn,' looking absolutely adorable."

The women laughed, shaking their heads as they commented on children and pets they had run into.

"'Auntie Lyn'?" Annelie murmured next to Carolyn. "It sounds very cute."

Carolyn raised an eyebrow at her hostess. "Don't even go there."

Annelie only laughed. "We'll see."

❖

Annelie waved goodbye to her guests who were returning to their hotel. The cabdriver holding open the door for them watched in bewilderment as the four laughing women seemed to literally take over his vehicle.

"See you soon!" Annelie raised her voice for them to hear, and they waved back.

Annelie turned to Jem, who remained by her side, waiting until the cab drove off before walking to her own car.

"Aren't they great? I think the luncheon was quite the hit."

"It was and, of course, having Carolyn Black as a surprise guest of honor didn't hurt."

Annelie smiled. "No. I thought Sam was going to faint when Carolyn hugged her."

"True, but Carolyn only had eyes for you."

Annelie had started walking toward the living room where Kitty and Sam were waiting, but now stopped in her tracks. "What do you mean?"

"It was very subtle but also very obvious, at least to me. I think the rest of them were so enthralled with her presence, they weren't paying attention. But she couldn't take her eyes off you."

Looking at her good friend, Annelie didn't know what to say. "Was it that obvious?"

"Maybe only to me. When you came back from the kitchen, you looked flustered, and she put on quite a show with the story about her niece. Did something happen?"

"We decorated the chocolate mousse," Annelie managed, trying to sound casual. "That's all."

Jem's eyes softened. "I don't think that's all, honey, but I won't pry, 'cause it's none of my business. I'm just looking out for you. Carolyn wants that part, and who knows what she's prepared to do to get it."

Annelie winced at the candid words. "I know," she whispered. "And yet, she has her vulnerable moments, Jem. When she's just Carolyn and not acting…I've seen it."

"Just don't buy into it too much, kiddo. Be careful and think of what's at stake here." Jem put her arm around Annelie's waist and hugged her quickly. "I don't want you to get hurt—or used."

"I won't."

"All right, fair enough."

They walked back into the living room where Kitty and Sam looked decidedly sleepy.

"The jet lag has set in, I see," Jem remarked. "I think it's time for me to head home, but I look forward to seeing you in the office Monday before you leave for Orlando, Kitty. I still have three chapters of your latest novel to edit, and I'll try to finish them this weekend."

"Excellent." Kitty yawned. "I'm honored you'd work through the weekend for my sake."

"Not a problem. I'd go with you if I had the time. I may try to visit Disney World after the convention, unless everything goes crazy around the office afterward."

"I think we can leave it for Gregory to handle," Annelie suggested. "You should take a few days off then. I know how you love Epcot."

Jem grinned sheepishly. It was a standing joke around the office how much the strong-willed, classy editor adored "the House of Mouse."

Sam rose from her slumped position on the couch, stretching and making a face because of her sore muscles.

"I don't know about you, but I'm off to bed. I'm exhausted." She gave Annelie a quick hug. "Today was wonderful and Carolyn Black was great."

"I second that," Kitty said, and followed her partner's example. "She was very nice and a lot of fun to talk to. She honestly seems to like us."

Annelie nodded. "I think she had a great time too—she told me so before she left."

"Sam smiled. "I can't wait to tell my mother—she's also a great Black fan—I've actually shaken her hand, talked to her for an entire afternoon, and even had a hug from her."

After the two women said goodbye to Jem and left the room, Annelie turned to Jem and shrugged. "Glad they didn't pick up on any special glances. I don't want any rumors. If—and I say if—I give this role to Carolyn, it's by merit only, no other reason."

Jem raised an eyebrow. "I hope you'll be able to tell the difference. Be sure any decision you make is made for the right reason."

Annelie knew the other woman was right. "I will."

"You look tired too. The luncheon turned into an all-day event. Are you going to get some rest?"

"It's too early for me yet. I have some correspondence to take care of, and then I'll unwind with a glass of apple juice on the patio. It looks like it's going to be a lovely evening."

"I should go home and get started on those last three chapters. I didn't want to raise false hopes, but it looks like Kitty may have her biggest hit so far. I had to force myself to read slowly and make notes, when really I wanted to plow through the pages and devour the book."

"That good, huh?"

"That good."

The two women hugged again, and Jem left.

Annelie strolled into her study and opened her e-mail, looking for messages marked "urgent." She wanted them out of the way before the weekend, since she had several things planned with Kitty and Sam. An hour and a half later she turned off the computer, went to the kitchen, and poured a glass of juice, then wandered out to the fully screened-in part of the patio. Sitting down in a deck chair, she inhaled the humid, scented evening air. It was still early, and she had no desire to go to bed yet.

Carolyn had taken her by surprise in the kitchen. The narrow lips, becoming so full when she smiled, had parted as Carolyn had touched her arm. It had taken all of Annelie's willpower not to respond to the beautiful woman.

Annelie thought about Jem's warnings. She agreed with the other woman's assessment of Carolyn Black in many ways. Still, Jem hadn't seen Carolyn when the diva persona left and made room for the real woman.

She sipped her juice. Maybe that was it. They'd joked around in the kitchen, decorating the chocolate mousse and acting like two friends— not the producer and the actress. Carolyn had offered the raspberry with a truly innocent look in her eyes, and only when Annelie's lips had grazed her fingertips had the situation altered.

To watch Carolyn slip back into her part as herself, the diva with an image to uphold, had been like witnessing a miracle. From looking flustered and embarrassed in the kitchen, the actress had swept into the living room as if she had entered a Broadway stage in front of adoring fans and simply owned the situation. She had told her anecdote, her voice steady and humorous, and her audience had swallowed it hook, line, and sinker.

Still, there had been several moments when their eyes had locked. The fact that the two of them had been sitting almost touching hadn't helped.

Annelie had, as a starstruck teenager, followed Carolyn's career, first as Devon Harper on TV and later as a stage and screen actress. She had never kept a scrapbook, and the small allowance her mother could afford to give her did not provide her enough cash to go and see her movies, except on special occasions. Something about the elegant face with the compelling eyes and the throaty, purring voice spoke to Annelie on so many levels. She suspected it always would.

Annelie drank the last of her juice and rose. Whatever Carolyn's motive was for trying to kiss her, it wouldn't happen again, she was pretty sure. The actress had seemed devastated when Annelie pulled back. Remembering how tired and subdued she looked just before she left, Annelie wondered if she should have offered to pick Carolyn up at the airport when she got back from D.C. on Sunday. Considering it for a moment, she decided that making such an offer might imply she was willing to compromise her principles. Carolyn was bent on getting that reading, and Annelie didn't want to do it before the convention. That would be asking for trouble.

She walked into the quiet house and put the empty glass into the dishwasher and continued to the bedroom. Running the shower, she frowned. What could have happened if she'd let Carolyn kiss her? As far as she knew, all of Carolyn Black's previous relationships had been with men, suggesting she didn't harbor any authentic interest in Annelie. More than likely, Jem was right to caution her. Carolyn was not above manipulating anyone who stood in her way. She had a solid reputation for being an arrogant star.

Undressing and stepping into the shower, Annelie closed her eyes, enjoying the pulsating water massaging her stiff shoulders. Despite what Jem said, a strange feeling had existed between her and Carolyn in the kitchen, something almost tangible. She had glimpsed the real Carolyn just for a moment, and she wanted to see her again.

The water streamed down her body like caressing hands. Chastising herself for indulging in futile fantasies, Annelie reached for the soap and a sponge, then scrubbed her skin until it glowed.

An annoying voice inside her head kept asking if she was trying to wash away the feeling of Carolyn's touch, however brief.

She simply did not know.

CHAPTER FIVE

Carolyn was relieved that only a handful of people were on the return flight to Miami. She had both seats in first class to herself, and even if the flight attendants' glances revealed they recognized her, they were professional enough to leave her alone. They probably saw enough celebrities to last them a lifetime.

Pulling her legs up under her, Carolyn moved restlessly in the seat. She had not slept well during the stay with her sister. Little Pamela had been nothing short of ecstatic to see her and demanded most of her attention. Beth, in turn, looked pale and nauseated most of the weekend, and all Carolyn could do was provide supportive comments about her tenuous pregnancy.

Late that Saturday, after Carolyn gave up falling asleep in their guest room, she ran into Joe in the kitchen. Her migraine had escalated since the flight on Friday evening and was now close to unbearable.

"Are you okay, Lyn?" Joe looked concerned.

"Just need some juice for my pills. I'll be okay."

"Headaches again?"

"Yes."

After a brief silence her brother-in-law walked up to her and put a reassuring arm around her shoulder. "You're so protective toward Beth, but you'd tell me if something was really wrong, wouldn't you?"

Fighting back tears, Carolyn leaned into the brotherly touch, tempted to actually cry on his shoulder. "Of course I would. It's nothing I can't handle." *Nothing I haven't handled before in so many different ways.*

"I've never seen you this pale and tired," Joe insisted, his voice kind. "I know this weekend isn't turning out to be much of a rest. It's just that Pamela adores you, and Beth…well, I guess Beth will always be your kid sister if you don't cut her loose a bit."

Carolyn gave him a sharp look. "What's that supposed to mean?"

"Beth's thirty-four, but I guess to you she'll always be the baby you mothered from the time you were twelve."

Carolyn had swallowed an acerbic retort, knowing he was right. Beth and John had depended on her for motherly affection for so long. Their struggles had strengthened their ties, and when John moved out of the house at twenty-one to go to art school, Carolyn had missed him terribly.

Carolyn stared wordlessly at her brother-in-law. Wondering, not for the first time, if Beth knew what a treasure he was, she raised her hand and patted his upper arm.

"I know, Joey, I know. One day, I'll get around to it."

Her half-joking tone of voice had worked. Joe grinned. "Just let me know if there's ever anything I can take care of for you. Promise."

Carolyn shifted in her seat again, affected by the pressurized air. Her temples throbbed, pulsated in painful waves, and not even the nasal spray seemed to work. She had not been able to go swimming anywhere in D.C., but perhaps she could swing by Jared's, pick up her gym bag, and head for Annelie's house.

The thought of Jared, of being under her friend's knowing gaze, made her recoil and suck in her lower lip, biting down on it hard. He always seemed to see right through her. Jared was her friend and he knew her well, too well, and sometimes he took it upon himself to point out her weaknesses.

Carolyn sighed. She had a feeling he thought much about her needed fixing. Jared's clear-sightedness could be unnerving as well. A small voice inside insisted that a true friend accepts you, and likes you, for who you are. *But how could he know who I am? Maybe I'm the one to blame. I never let him in completely.*

When they met five years earlier, she had been relieved when all Jared seemed to want from her was friendship. Only then did she begin to relax around him, feeling for the first time in years the budding signs of camaraderie.

Jared had not been too impressed that her college boyfriend, and later her first and only husband, had "chickened out," as he called it, because of her circumstances. "Beth and John were only kids," he'd said. "Where were they supposed to go, if they couldn't be with you?"

Carolyn smirked at the memory. She had long forgiven Derek, her first serious boyfriend, for not wanting to be a father figure at age twenty-two. Still, the very young, grief-stricken woman she was at the time felt desperately abandoned and rejected.

Her marriage to Frank Thorpe three years later lasted just that, three years. After a stormy engagement while filming together during her first feature-film role, they got married. *I sure landed on my ass pretty fast after the honeymoon was over. He could never make up his mind. Either I was not at all what he wanted, or I was too much.* Turning her head toward the dark sky outside the window, Carolyn felt her tears reach her eyelashes, but she refused to let them fall any farther. *I spent three years being lonely.* Eventually his ultimatum that she had to choose between him and her siblings terminated the marriage. *He knew how I'd choose.*

After that her relationships were short, burned white-hot, but ended before any of the flames reduced her life to ashes again, leaving her feeling unfulfilled and unsatisfied. Carolyn had rebounded from one of these—two heated months with a Broadway producer—into a platonic friendship with Jared, and over the years they'd found a comfortable tone between them, which worked as long as he didn't try to change her too much. Right now she felt his Argus eyes on her, judging her motives and challenging them. It bothered her more than usual, probably since she was at a loss herself over some of her most recent actions.

"Ladies and gentlemen, we're now approaching Miami International Airport and will be landing in ten minutes…"

The plane bounced twice before rushing down the runway. Nausea rose within her, making Carolyn swallow hard repeatedly. What she wouldn't give to be in the tranquil neighborhood where Annelie lived, stretching out on a deck chair after a long swim.

❖

Annelie floorboarded it and smiled as the Mustang gave a muted roar. Driving down the busy street toward the on-ramp, she settled against the backrest after switching on a Debussy piano prelude. The soft, romantic music filled the car and toned down the engine. Having spent four hours at the office, she was on her way home to meet her friend Charlotta. They went back many years, at least twenty, Annelie calculated. Growing up in the same neighborhood in Chicago, they had attended the same school before Charlotta had moved to a different district north of the city.

Annelie frowned while thinking of the hard time her childhood friend had gone through. Charlotta had become ill two years ago and lost her job while recuperating. Then her ex-husband had gained custody of their three children, claiming she was an unfit mother and couldn't support them. Charlotta had been too weak to fight, too ill to stand her ground, and Annelie blamed herself for not staying in touch.

She had learned of Charlotta's situation only four months ago and had convinced her to move to Florida temporarily to regain her health. She had helped her by paying for a rehab clinic and later cosigning a lease for a small, but nice, apartment on the city's outskirts. Having reached rock bottom, the other woman was beyond false pride. She had gratefully accepted Annelie's help, desperate to regain custody of her children.

Annelie knew Charlotta loved her new place and had already begun preparing two small rooms for the children. She was coming over to pick up the last of her things from Annelie's home that morning, having stayed there several weeks earlier. She would be thrilled with the contract Annelie had in her briefcase formalizing Charlotta's new position as an assistant at the Nebula Circle. The job would at least end her financial problems.

Adjusting to the quicker pace on the highway, Annelie thought about the recent meeting with Gregory and Jem at Key Line. Gregory had updated them on all the signed contracts for the upcoming convention and also reported on how well prepared the merchandising was. Apart from the usual photos of the stars, audiobooks, and more third-edition copies of all the Maddox books, he'd also ordered mugs, posters, key rings, and terry-cloth towels, all displaying Key Line's logo and the Maddox book titles. Then Annelie had disclosed the final evening's big surprise—three first-edition copies signed by Delia Carlton, first prize in a raffle for Nebula Circle.

"We'll take a chartered Lear jet to Orlando International," Gregory had continued, "and I've arranged for shuttles. We all have suites on the eleventh floor, as Annelie requested. Most of them consist of adjoining suites, so we'll be a close-knit group. I made an additional reservation for Ms. McNeil and Ms. Jordan, so they can join us there, as well as Charlotta Hazelwood."

"Did you find out how many guests have booked rooms?" Annelie asked.

"There are no vacancies. They decided to bring in the adjoining hotel located on the other side of the large mall. The two hotels have booked six floors and are still receiving inquiries."

"How many tickets have we sold?"

Gregory pulled up the numbers on his handheld computer. "All of the all-events passes went as soon as they were released. About 75 percent of the day-only passes have gone. We have a thousand unclassified tickets allowing the visitor to attend certain events, and about half of those are gone."

Annelie did some mental calculations. "So, we've sold about two thousand tickets?"

"Exactly." Gregory beamed. "We're well past breaking even."

"Amazing," Annelie said. "Well, it'll be interesting to see what the photos, books, audiobooks, and other merchandise bring in."

After the meeting, alone with Jem, Annelie had given a soft sigh and leaned back into her chair, reaching for a glass of mineral water.

"Some days I feel the responsibility weighing on me," she admitted when she saw Jem raise her eyebrows. "I haven't undertaken this much work in quite a while."

"And now the pace is full speed ahead," Jem offered.

"Yes. Also, I'm nervous about not making the right decision about the movies. I promised Delia and she trusts me. If I choose the wrong person to play Diana Maddox, the whole project could be ruined." Annelie made a face at her self-doubt. "Sorry, I don't mean to sound so gloomy."

"It's okay, kiddo. It's good to vent, don't you know that? I wouldn't want to be the one making that decision. Who would want to make an enemy of Carolyn Black for life?" She laughed at her own joke.

Annelie didn't find it so funny.

"Did she come over during the weekend?" Jem reached for a bag of lime-flavored chips.

Annelie shook her head. "No, she's been in D.C. Some family issues."

"Ah. Well, I've been thinking. I know the suits want Ms. Breathless…" She broke off when Annelie groaned. "Oh, excuse me, Ms. *Goodman*, to play Maddox, but I'm not convinced. I think

Carolyn Black can play any damn role they throw at her. She's a true chameleon."

Annelie knew Jem had a point. Carolyn's career was proof of that.

"I've never doubted her ability as an actress, but that doesn't mean she's right as Maddox." *What if she's right...and I make the wrong decision, for the wrong reason?* Annelie tried to examine her feelings, but merely doing what the experts advised her seemed the most logical way out. Or simply the easiest? No, there was nothing easy about disappointing Carolyn.

Jem eyed her closely. "Don't you think you owe her the benefit of the doubt?"

Wincing at the truth behind her friend's words, Annelie sighed. "Her contribution to the audiobooks...well, she's the major reason they're doing so well." Voicing this undeniable fact made her reasons for procrastinating regarding Carolyn's reading seem petty. *I'm being unfair. She's earned it.* "Still, I'm against giving Carolyn the role by default, just because of that." *Or because I was once a starstruck teenager who would've given my right arm to see her perform.*

"I guess you do need to know a lot more about her before you make your decision. When's her screen test?"

Was Jem reading her mind? Annelie sipped her water. "I haven't scheduled it yet, but I ought to call Parker. Perhaps later today."

"All right." Jem closed the bag of chips and gave a sly grin. "If you ask me, I think she'll blow everyone away as Maddox. But that's just me."

Now as she drove through the gates, Annelie wondered how she would be able to deal with Carolyn after what took place in the kitchen during the luncheon. She could still vividly picture how the actress had leaned into her, the soft hand on her arm, as the fine lips came closer.

Once she'd parked in her driveway, Annelie grabbed her briefcase and jumped out. Pushing the thoughts of the beautiful woman out of her mind, she fought to focus on the last-minute things to do before Charlotta arrived.

❖

The cul-de-sac was filled with cars, blocking the driveway to

Annelie's house. Muttering under her breath, Carolyn drove back to a small parking lot at the beginning of the street and managed to find the last available spot. She opened the door, and the humidity engulfed her as she grabbed her bag from the passenger seat.

Carolyn pulled the card through the reader and listened to the familiar sound of the gate clicking open. Deciding to go straight to the pool, she took the garden path around the house. As she rounded the corner, Carolyn glanced toward the large windows and stopped abruptly. Annelie was home and stood in a tight embrace, her arms around a petite woman with fiery red hair in a pageboy. The stranger had buried her face against Annelie's shoulder. Oddly disturbed by the sight, Carolyn stalked to the patio and removed her shorts.

She was already wearing her swimsuit under her clothes, and she dived into the deep end of the pool without ceremony, swimming half a length underwater.

As the cool water closed above her, she felt protected. She remained below for as long as she could before she surfaced unwillingly, inhaled deeply, and dived again. Carolyn kept this routine up until she was so out of breath she had to stop and grasp the edge. Pulling herself up with the last of her strength, she sat in the sun gasping for air. Her head pounded, and she cursed inwardly at her treacherous body.

When her dizziness from lack of oxygen had dissipated, she leaned toward her bag and pulled out her cigarettes. Lighting one, she sucked the smoke deep into her lungs, coughing as it stung her throat. Tears burned behind her eyelids as scattered emotions whirled through her mind. She tried to calm down but failed miserably. What the hell was the matter with her?

"Carolyn? I walked my friend to the door and didn't see the Lincoln. Where did you park?"

The alto voice cut through her tumultuous thoughts and made it possible for her to focus. Glancing up, Carolyn squinted toward the sun. "I parked down the street at the visitors' parking lot. Your driveway's blocked."

"Yes, I saw that. Charlotta's cab had problems getting here too." Annelie sat down next to Carolyn, water soaking the hem of her khaki shorts as she dipped her feet in the pool. "Welcome back. How was your flight?"

"Okay. I had a couple of seats to myself." Hating herself for sounding so short, Carolyn put the cigarette to her lips, inhaling deeply again.

"You look pale," Annelie observed. "Is something wrong?"

"I'll be fine. I guess I'm just tired after spending the weekend with my niece."

Apparently not buying into the explanation, Annelie reached out as Carolyn raised the cigarette to her mouth again and stopped her midway.

"You're trembling," she insisted in a soft voice. "You've got dark circles under your eyes, and you look exhausted. Please let me try to help."

Annelie's voice wrapped around Carolyn like a soothing blanket, yet she still instinctively withdrew, determined to protect herself from becoming too vulnerable.

"The woman earlier…Is she why you didn't let me kiss you?" she blurted out, shocked at her own defensive tone of voice.

"Who…" Annelie frowned. "Oh, you mean Charlotta?"

"Whoever. I saw the two of you."

Obviously she was losing her mind, alienating the woman who held her immediate future in her hands. Carolyn wished she could take the words back, but now her head pulsated with every beat of her heart.

"Charlotta is one of my oldest friends. I hug my friends, as I'm sure you do too. She came over to sign some papers and to fetch her things. We grew up together, and she's been very ill. Unlike you, I'm not in a relationship, Carolyn. I just don't date straight, married, or curious women. It makes life complicated and brings too much heartache." Annelie's voice was kind but firm.

Carolyn opened her mouth to speak, but her voice failed her twice before she spoke the truth. "Jared and I are not a couple. I don't *do* happy couples, Annelie." She fought back the stupid tears and looked down at her cigarette, humiliated by the bitterness in her tone.

It had not been her intention to reveal anything of herself to this woman, certainly not to appear weak. *The actress of a certain age admits her personal life is not exactly fulfilling…what a cliché.*

To compound her embarrassment, Annelie took the cigarette from her and pressed it down into the closest flowerpot. "Have you eaten anything since you came back?"

"No. I came straight here. I needed to swim."

"I see." Annelie rose to her feet before extending a hand toward Carolyn and pulling her up. "Well, before you do, it might be a good idea to eat something. Mary has the day off, but my omelets aren't too bad." She led Carolyn through the door into the guest room. "Why don't you take a shower? Make it a hot one. You're still shivering. If you like, you can use the robe hanging behind the door, and then join me in the kitchen. Okay?"

"All right," Carolyn whispered, feeling strangely relieved someone else had taken command for once.

"Good. I'll start lunch."

❖

Annelie arranged some lettuce, tomatoes, and cucumbers next to the omelets and filled two glasses with ice water. Deciding it was too hot on the patio, she placed everything on the small kitchen table.

"It smells good," a throaty voice from the doorway said.

Annelie glanced up and saw Carolyn hesitating on the threshold, dressed in a gray terry-cloth robe. Her slightly tousled hair was almost dry and framed her pale face.

"You okay?"

"Yes, thanks. I used one of the guest toothbrushes."

"That's what they're for."

The two women sat down to eat, and Annelie waited until Carolyn had managed half of her serving before continuing their conversation. "Want to talk about it?" Her voice was noncommittal.

"What do you mean?"

"I see you're not feeling well, and it looks like you're not at all as rested as you should've been after going away for the weekend."

"It wasn't that kind of *going away*. I had to fly up to D.C. to check on some family matters, and I…" Shoulders slumping, Carolyn laced her fingers into her hair. "I'm worried about my sister. She acted fine around me during the weekend, and yet…There's something. I don't know. Perhaps I'm reading too much into it."

"You care a lot about her."

"She's fragile right now. I know she's a grown woman, but she's the baby of the family." Carolyn lifted a shoulder in a shrug. "You could say she and her husband Joe are my only family."

Annelie thought there was more behind the light words than Carolyn let on. "Families are important," she murmured, the words leaving a hollow feeling in her heart.

Carolyn leaned forward, her eyes clouding over with a darker shade of gray. The hurt in those eyes made Annelie's heart skip a beat. There was a raw, naked pain in Carolyn's voice that sounded genuine as she spoke. "Yes, families can be everything. I just wish *Jared's* family didn't have to be my concern right now. I've got too much on my mind at the time."

"What do you mean?"

"Jared's parents, sister, and brother-in-law are flying down from Boston. They're going to be staying with him for a few days."

"Sounds a bit crowded." Annelie fought to sound casual.

"It's not that. The condo is big enough. His sister never gives up on wanting to pair us off. His mother, on the other hand, never gives up hoping we never do." Carolyn sighed, rubbing the back of her neck. "Right now it's more than I can deal with. I think I'll have to return to New York for a while."

She has to leave? Unwilling, and perhaps unable, to examine the quick stir of panic, Annelie thought quickly. From a professional standpoint, it would be easier to deal with the casting situation with Carolyn out of town. *But I don't want her to go.* Recoiling from her muddled motives, Annelie knew what to do. Sensing she would have to make the offer sound matter-of-fact and logical, she waited until Carolyn had finished her omelet.

"You know what? I have an idea." She smiled innocently, extending a hand across the table. "Come with me."

"But I'm not dressed," the actress objected as Annelie took her by the hand again. "Where are we going?"

"I want to show you something. Don't worry, it's not far."

Not letting go of the small hand, Annelie again led Carolyn through the kitchen door, into the garage. Carolyn quirked an inquisitive eyebrow at her. Annelie smiled broadly at her and opened the garage door. Outside she took a left turn and climbed a narrow staircase. Pulling out a key card, she pulled it through the reader next to the white door at the top of the stairs.

"There you go, please step inside," she invited her surprised guest.

Carolyn hesitated for a moment, giving Annelie a cautious smile. "Should I be concerned?"

"Don't be silly. Go on."

They entered the small garage apartment, and Annelie watched Carolyn walk from the tastefully decorated living room into the small kitchenette and then examine the bathroom and two small bedrooms.

"Do you like it?" Annelie asked.

"Yes, it's wonderful. What a lovely little apartment."

"Can you see yourself spending a couple of nights here?"

There was a stunned silence. Annelie knew she had to convince Carolyn this was a good idea. "Look at it this way," she continued. "I know you have some family issues going on—and I'm not prying—and you're about to be swamped by opinionated relations of a friend. Here you can relax, just hang out, and take your swim. The place is fully equipped. You can make calls…and there's a computer installed in the niche over there—" Annelie's voice broke off, and she had to laugh at the disgust on Carolyn's face. "Okay, so you don't have to use the computer—just the phone, then."

"You wouldn't mind me staying so close to you?"

Annelie opened her mouth to answer but closed it again. Was there something more behind Carolyn's question? "It's just for a few nights, so I'm sure we wouldn't crowd each other. You'd be my guest."

Carolyn turned around, looking the elegant apartment over again. "I'd be a fool not to accept," she replied, her voice soft. "Thank you, Annelie. I appreciate your offer."

"You're welcome. You can just pick up a few of your things at Jared's. I'm sure he'll understand."

"I don't keep many personal belongings at his condo." Carolyn walked toward the bedroom overlooking the patio. "I think I'll sleep in here, away from the driveway."

"Good point. Let me know if there's anything else I can do to help."

Carolyn pivoted and walked up to Annelie. Looking up, her eyes calmer than before, she said, "You've done so much already. Today's been…different. I'm not used to anyone taking care of me like this."

Annelie was stunned to hear this. Somehow she had pictured someone as renowned as Carolyn being fawned over everywhere she went. Furtively, she studied the other woman as she moved around the living room, looking at the delicate figurines on a shelf. Instead of pushing her shoulders up and hunching over as before, Carolyn now seemed more relaxed.

"Then I'm glad I can offer a refuge of sorts." Annelie flipped her ponytail back over her shoulder. "Take your time looking around. I'll be in my study working if there's anything you need."

To Annelie's surprise, Carolyn raised her hand and quickly brushed two fingers along her benefactor's cheek. "You're truly a kind person."

Trying to swallow past the sudden lump in her throat and feeling her skin tingle, Annelie only nodded. She gave Carolyn a quick smile and then disappeared down the stairs.

❖

After watching Annelie leave, Carolyn slowly turned around, taking in her surroundings. The living room was tastefully decorated in the same earthy tones as the main house—browns, blues, and yellows. The leather couches faced a large window, to the left of which stood an open fireplace.

The bedroom, decorated in different shades of white, featured a queen-size bed and a fully stocked linen cabinet. As she glanced out the window, Carolyn saw her bag still sitting by the pool. Feeling energized, she walked through the apartment and down the stairs to retrieve it.

She had brought a change of clothes and would only need to pick up a few things from the condo for her brief stay. Returning to the apartment with the bag, she walked into the bathroom. As she checked her reflection in the mirror, Carolyn saw her hair fall in tousled waves around her shoulders.

In the drawers next to the sink, she found a hairdryer, which she plugged in and used with her hairbrush to form her trademark shiny, straight hair. Her makeup kit held everything she needed to emphasize her eyes, and Carolyn expertly hid the dark circles beneath them.

She hung up the bathrobe and wandered into the kitchenette. Though the cabinets held most items needed in a kitchen, she would need to stop at the grocery store before stopping at Jared's. She thought of buying something she would be able to share with Annelie. Carolyn didn't cook, but she knew where to get excellent takeout.

She grabbed the car keys and left the apartment, making sure the door was locked before she left. When she reached the bottom of the stairs, she met Annelie.

"You look much better. My magic omelet, no doubt."

"No doubt. I'm off to do some shopping and pick up my things."

"Good. Can I help you with anything?"

Resisting the urge to say yes, Carolyn shook her head. "No, thank you, Annelie. It's really nice of you to have me over. I appreciate it. So let me buy us some takeout tonight, as a sign of my appreciation."

Annelie seemed to mull her offer over for a moment and then smiled broadly, transforming her features completely. Carolyn was suddenly aware how seldom Annelie smiled like this. "I'd love that."

"What kind of food would you like?"

"I get to pick?" The younger woman pursed her lips, drawing Carolyn's attention to their fullness. "I don't mean to sound predictable, but what about Chinese?"

Carolyn laughed. "I don't think anyone can accuse you of being predictable. I love Asian food, so Chinese it is. I should be back around seven or eight. See you then?"

"I'll be here."

❖

To Carolyn's surprise and dismay, Jared had not yet left for the airport to pick up his family and now questioned her motives for accepting Annelie's offer.

"Why would you want to stay there when you have access to everything right here?" he demanded. "Or are there additional perks to staying at her place?"

Carolyn stared at him, not sure what he was referring to.

"Don't give me that well-rehearsed look of innocence. I'm not buying it," Jared growled. "You're up to something, no doubt something that'll get you ahead in the game."

Refusing to take the bait, she fought to remain calm. "What on earth are you talking about?"

"I'm talking about you staying at Annelie Peterson's home! I don't know how you did it, but you must have pulled some pretty amazing stunts to get under the skin of someone like her."

Carolyn's temper flared. "What's wrong with you? What the hell are you implying?"

"You're up to your usual tricks and schemes. Annelie obviously thinks you need rescuing. What's the next step? Climbing into her bed?"

Feeling herself go pale, Carolyn stepped back, staring at Jared. "You bastard," she managed, her mind whirling back to last Friday and the near kiss in Annelie's kitchen. She thought of Jared's urge to tell her about Annelie's lesbianism. Inhaling deeply, she saw what she hadn't seen before.

"You're jealous! That's what this is all about. For years you've been my only friend, apart from Beth and Joe. And I just don't get it! I thought you'd be pleased not to have to sit through your mother's and sister's endless arguments about my place in your life. Annelie is someone who might become a friend one day. How can you ask me to back away from that? This isn't like you, Jared." Hurt constricted Carolyn's throat, making her cough.

"But it is *so* like you! You've never hesitated to use whatever means to suit your needs. Me included."

"True. I go after what I want. I never hide who I am. But I can tell you this, once and for all. I don't intend to sleep with Annelie, nor is that why she made this offer."

She pulled away from me and made it pretty clear why. Taken aback by the sudden thought, Carolyn frowned at the unexpected twitch in her chest.

Jared paced back and forth, staring at the large roller suitcase at her feet. "So you're not even going to stay and say hello to my parents? They love you."

"Your father likes me. Your mother barely tolerates me because she's afraid I may turn our friendship into something else—even outright seduce you. Your sister is an avid fan who'd like nothing better than to brag to her friends about being closely related to a celebrity." Flinging her hands in the air, Carolyn took a deep breath, trying to calm down. "I don't want us to part this way. We're supposed to be friends—and you're not being my friend right now."

Stopping in front of her, Jared looked tired and suddenly shamefaced. "I know. Listen, I'm sorry. I just want you to be clear over your own motives."

"Are you clear about yours?"

"Point taken."

Her pulse as well as her breathing calming, Carolyn held out her hand. "Jared, please, this isn't about not needing you as my friend. This is about finding some peace of mind, being able to call Beth and not be interrupted, and planning what to do next from a professional standpoint. I still haven't given up hope of playing Maddox. I guess I won't throw in the towel until they actually sign someone else." Clenching her hands, she forced back tears. "To tell the truth, I don't have anything lined up right now except a Volvo commercial, and…I'm terrified." She offered a halfhearted smile.

"Don't be. You're too talented and sought after to go without work. In the meantime, no doubt, you'll be performing your favorite character—yourself." Only the fact that he winked at her and wriggled his eyebrows removed some of the sting in his words.

"Bastard," she accused softly.

"Bitch," he retaliated, pulling her into his arms.

"Friends?" Carolyn's voice broke, and she buried her face against his shoulder.

"Friends."

They remained still for a moment, and then she disentangled herself to grab the handle of her rolling bag. "Say hi to everyone for me?"

"Of course." Jared smiled. "Drive carefully."

Swiftly kissing his cheek before stepping out into the corridor, Carolyn nodded. "Don't I always?"

At the elevator, Carolyn glanced back toward Jared's door. He had already gone back inside.

❖

Carolyn put down the novel after finishing the last chapter, her mind reeling from the twists and turns the author had taken her on. Delia Carlton's tale was a spellbinder, her characters' interactions full of deep emotions. She had read the book quickly, but she found herself wishing it would never end. Though Carolyn had not read the second and third Maddox books before doing the audio versions, it seemed like a good idea to familiarize herself with all of the stories since she was now planning to invite herself to the convention.

The last few days in Annelie's small garage apartment had been peaceful. Carolyn, emotionally exhausted, had slept the entire afternoon once she returned from Jared's condo and had been catching up on rest ever since. She would be sorry to leave.

Stretching, she decided it was time for her swim. She changed into her swimsuit, pondering if she should go out for a late lunch after her exercise—perhaps a quick trip to the nearby coffee shop. Tossing a short bathrobe over her shoulders, she strolled through the garden to the swimming pool, dropped the robe on a deck chair, and dived into the deep end.

Enjoying the cool, satiny feeling against her body, she swam one lap after another until the tension in the back of her neck and shoulders had disappeared. Then she turned over on her back and floated as she caught her breath. The sun was hot and unforgiving, and she realized she needed to be careful to not burn herself.

"That looks relaxing," a familiar voice said, startling Carolyn and making her cough as she sank half-below the surface.

"Annelie!" she gasped. "God, woman, you surprised me. I didn't know you were home. Where's the Mustang?"

"The staff down at the clubhouse picked it up. They clean it inside and out every two weeks." Annelie was wearing dark blue shorts and a white tank top, with her hair in the usual low ponytail. She extended a hand as Carolyn swam toward the ladder. "You're getting a little pink around the shoulders. Better watch out."

"I know. I burn easily even if I've managed to get a little tan. I need to be more careful. The swim just felt so good." Carolyn walked over to the deck chair and pulled her bathrobe on, tying the belt around her waist. "I'm getting hungry. Join me for a late lunch? Maybe do takeout, like last time?"

Annelie cocked her head. "Hm, we've done Chinese so why not—oh, you know something? I'd love a family-size pizza with everything on it, and perhaps chicken wings on the side!"

Unable to resist the eager look in the other woman's eyes, Carolyn laughed and nodded. "Why not? I haven't had pizza in a long time. I'll just go take a quick shower. We could have it out here."

"I'll call the Pizza Parlor," Annelie offered. "They have the most divine supersize pizzas. Hurry back, because they're quick."

Carolyn promised and walked back toward the garage. At the corner of the house, she turned around with a grin and wrinkled her nose. "Just hold the anchovies, okay?"

CHAPTER SIX

The hotel was buzzing with activity. Marble floors, white and golden walls, and blue furniture gave a luxurious impression. Located not far from Disney World, it was full of Maddox fans of all ages and from all walks of life instead of the usual families and senior citizens this weekend.

Jem walked in front of the group of Key Line women who had just stepped out of the airport shuttle. Several bellboys handled their luggage.

"I'm glad Gregory decided to come a day early," Jem said, turning to face Annelie. "This is a madhouse! Do you see him anywhere?"

Annelie rose on her toes, trying to find Gregory's tall, lanky form in the crowd of people. Relieved to see him standing by the desk, she waved him over. "Greg, great to see you. What's going on here? I thought if we came a day early we could avoid all this."

Gregory ushered them to the side of the check-in counter. Pulling Annelie aside, he lowered his voice. "I've taken care of most of the details. However, we have a bit of a problem."

"Shoot."

"We had to do some rearranging. The hotel doesn't have any vacancies, as you know, and we wanted to keep all the stars and your personal guests on the same floor."

"So, give me the bottom line."

"Carolyn Black arrived here last night."

"Carolyn?" Annelie felt blood receding from her cheeks. The actress had already left yesterday when Annelie came home from work. She had assumed Carolyn was back at Jared's place.

"It gets worse. They put her in the Presidential Suite."

"What are you talking about? We reserved that months ago."

"They seem to be under the impression that she's your personal guest."

Annelie stifled a gasp. The nerve of the woman was monumental. Was this her way of paying Annelie back for not giving her the reading last week? *Very nice, after I made her welcome in my home!* "Well, tell them she's not."

Gregory lifted an eyebrow. "See all these people? They know she's here. And not just that, they think she's your last-minute celebrity speaker. Do you really want to have her thrown out of your room in front of a legion of fans?"

Annelie muttered a rare expletive. Carolyn had backed them into a corner with expert ease. "What do you mean they think she's a speaker?"

Gregory opened a copy of the *Orlando Sentinel* he had tucked under one arm. On the front page of the entertainment section was a photo of Carolyn looking like a goddess. The article next to it was headlined *Carolyn Black to Speak at Maddox Convention.*

Annelie couldn't believe her eyes. "When did you know about this?"

Gregory looked embarrassed. "There was a lot of chatter on the message boards, but I didn't think anything of it. You know how the rumors have been."

"Yes, rumors circulated by Grey Parker," Annelie hissed. "This must have been his idea. A huge publicity stunt."

"It's working." Gregory swept a glance around the lobby. "And now that the story has hit the papers, it'll be everywhere by registration time. This explains the last-minute surge in ticket sales."

"We'll have to give her the stage," Annelie concluded. *Unbelievable.*

"And you won't have a room unless you want to share with one of the staff," Gregory pointed out. "But most of theirs are full."

Annelie's mind ran riot. "I'm going to kill Grey Parker."

"That won't get you comfortable accommodations." In a tentative tone, he said, "The Presidential Suite has four bedrooms."

"You want me to ask Carolyn Black if I can camp in the suite she stole from me? You must be joking."

"You can take my room," he offered. "I can get something at a Motel 6 down the road."

Annelie took a deep, steadying breath. "That won't be necessary. I'll sort this out with her."

She willed herself to calm down and think rationally. Perhaps she could turn this disaster to her advantage. No one could deny the presence of Carolyn Black would attract media. It would generate a lot of extra exposure for Diana Maddox, even if it did mean Carolyn's name was associated more emphatically with the character.

"There's one more thing," Gregory said, looking like a man eating his last meal before execution.

"Yes." Annelie eyed him with unease. Could this get any worse?

"Sylvia Goodman is here too."

"Here? Do you mean in town, or here at the hotel?" Annelie groaned inwardly.

"She's at the hotel and she has convention tickets. I think she was hoping to steal the show."

Annelie smiled. In a mess like this what else could one do? "Well, she was just outplayed. We all were."

❖

Taking a deep breath to calm down, Annelie knocked on the door to the Presidential Suite. After a moment's silence she heard rapid steps from inside. As Carolyn opened the door, the actress's smile was in place.

"Annelie! So you've arrived. Please come in." Gesturing for Annelie to enter, Carolyn looked every bit the gracious hostess.

In the suite I booked. Annelie was fuming. "I see you've made yourself comfortable," she murmured between gritted teeth. "How did you persuade them to let you into the Presidential Suite?" She walked inside, placing her briefcase on the floor to stake her own claim.

"I merely assumed it was a mistake on your part to not invite me to the convention." Carolyn's eyes grew wide in mock disbelief. "When I told them who I was, and that I was your personal guest, they scrambled to accommodate me."

"I bet. Nothing like a little name-dropping, right?"

Looking around, Annelie was impressed with the accommodations. The Presidential Suite was luxurious. Complimentary fruit, chocolate, and champagne were displayed in the living room, and everything they could possibly need was either there or just a phone call away. She looked through the open doors leading into large bedrooms, each with a king-size bed.

"I'm sorry for any misunderstanding, but you're not my personal guest, so you'll just have to get another room."

"And we both know there are no vacancies at the hotel. I have nowhere to go."

Setting the stakes, are we, Carolyn? "There are other hotels nearby."

"They're full too. Not even a motel room in sight, I'm afraid." Carolyn probably knew better than to sound triumphant. Instead she had the good taste to pretend to be regretful.

Annelie moved past the other woman, their shoulders brushing, and walked over to the panoramic window. She could smell Carolyn's musk-and-sandalwood perfume, so familiar by now. Refusing to let her body react, she stood by the window for a moment, faking an interest in the view over Orlando while she gathered herself.

Eventually she pivoted, pressing her lips to a fine line. "The reservation is in my name." She was surprised at the ice in her voice. "I could have you thrown out."

"You wouldn't do that." Carolyn's smoky, velvety voice wrapped around Annelie. "You wouldn't humiliate me like that."

Damn you. "You placed all your bets on my benevolence. I resent being taken advantage of." The constriction in Annelie's throat made it hard to speak. "This is a clever plan. No doubt Parker masterminded it."

"He did what you should've done. He informed me of the convention, and we agreed I should be here. The fans want me here."

"The fans are here to meet some of the stars and try to find out who'll play Maddox. Not necessarily you."

"That's bull." Carolyn's face darkened. "You weren't here when I arrived yesterday. The way the fans received me in the lobby says it all. They see me as Maddox. No one else, and certainly not a silicone-enhanced starlet."

Wanting to groan out loud at the manipulative woman in front of her, Annelie clenched her fists. "You're forcing my hand and I don't like it."

"I have to! You're making a mistake if you think anyone else can portray Maddox the way I can. You're blinded by the talk of money, investments, marketing…You have to listen to your heart, and then you'll know what the right course of action is."

Carolyn's voice lost its animated tone. Her eyes turned bluer than Annelie had ever seen them as the actress seemed to speak from the heart. "You know the stories about Maddox better than most. You discovered Delia Carlton and published her books. Don't let any Hollywood moguls run over you. Trust your instincts." Carolyn paused, raising a hand as if to touch Annelie, but lowered it again. "Then, if you still can see someone like Goodman in the role…I guess there's nothing I can do about that."

She's reading my mind. Annelie studied the expression on Carolyn's beautiful face for a few more seconds. Was she acting? Was that impassioned plea just part of her diva routine?

"You've left us with little choice but to put you onstage tomorrow," she said stiffly. "People in the hotel think you're the main event."

"Yes. They do. And you hate me for it." Sorrow was hidden in the other woman's stubborn voice.

Wincing, Annelie shook her head. "I don't hate you." *How could I?* Annelie pulled herself together, keeping her voice matter of fact. "We have to share the suite. Which one is free?"

"Excuse me? Oh, you mean which bedroom? I'm in the one to the far right."

Annelie chose a room to the left, placing her briefcase on the bed inside. She dialed the front desk and asked for someone to bring her luggage up. As she glanced over her shoulder, she studied Carolyn through the open door. The actress looked a little weary, she thought, as she walked back out into the living room. Standing just behind Carolyn, she watched as street lights began to light up, drawing dotted lines in the distance. Suddenly Carolyn's conniving actions seemed temporarily unimportant.

"What's wrong?" Annelie kept her voice low, as if speaking softly would make the question less intrusive.

"I'm fine…I…" The other woman seemed at a loss for words. "An angel walking over my grave, that's all. Suddenly I'm nervous as hell."

There was a brief silence after the rare admission.

"You're betting the role of a lifetime, as well as your immediate future, on one card. Seeing all these fans downstairs, rooting for you, made you think this would work out."

Carolyn pivoted quickly, almost losing her balance. Annelie automatically reached out and steadied her, putting both hands on the actress's shoulders. Her palms tingled instantly, making her shudder.

"You're right." Carolyn sounded surprised. "That's exactly it. How did you know? And why are you being nice when you're so mad at me?"

Annelie lowered her hands, letting them slide down Carolyn's bare arms before clasping them behind her back. *Why did I do that? Like a caress, for heaven's sake!*

"I'm trying very hard to distinguish between our professional relationship and..." She swallowed hard, not wanting to show just how conflicted she was. "...and a potential friendship. You're skating on thin ice. I don't like being manipulated, especially by someone I've begun to actually..."

Annelie stopped short of admitting just how much she'd started to like Carolyn. Right now, she thought she could detect the vulnerable private person behind the diva persona, but...*How can I be sure? She could be acting her little calculating heart out right now. Still, there's that haunted expression in her eyes. Can a person fake that?*

"As I said before, we have to put you onstage since we can't disappoint the fans," Annelie continued, smiling faintly. Feeling tired, she was suddenly desperate to lighten the mood. She was still upset, and she knew it shone through as she lifted a hand in a dismissive gesture. "There'll be a question-and-answer session tonight."

"I'll be there. What will be expected of me? I mean, by the fans."

Refraining from a curt reply to hide the tremor in her voice, Annelie pulled herself together. "Just go out there and be the star. Let's be honest, Carolyn—you do that so well."

❖

It was quite the entrance. Carefully orchestrated and with finesse, Sylvia Goodman sashayed into the hotel restaurant, her long blond hair in perfect ruffled waves. Glancing around the room, she let her publicist speak to the head waiter.

"Never mind. I see her!" Sylvia suddenly exclaimed, homing in on Annelie sitting alone at a table in the corner. "Ms. Peterson! How delightful to meet you."

A tad on the theatrical side. "Ms. Goodman, it's great to finally meet you too." Annelie extended a hand and was not surprised that Sylvia's grip was loose and quick. "What a surprise to find you here at the Maddox convention. I understand you've bought tickets to all events."

"I sure have." The breathless voice, normally high pitched, was toned down to a level Annelie guessed was supposed to be sultry.

No doubt the voice coach had been listening to Carolyn on the audiobooks. The result was as if the young actress did some sort of strange impersonation. *Surely she doesn't think it sounds sexy?* Realizing she was not being fair, Annelie tried to gauge the eager starlet from an objective standpoint.

Sylvia Goodman's body had clearly been sculpted by Hollywood's, or perhaps Fifth Avenue's, best plastic surgeons. Her breasts were not too big, but just right for her slender frame. Her bottom was high and firm, with no excess weight in sight. The tight-fitting jacket and skirt, over a blouse with a plunging neckline, left very little to Annelie's imagination. Creamy white skin glimmered, and she wore Obsession, a perfume that would soon give Annelie a headache.

"Please sit down. I've ordered already." *Because you're twenty minutes late.*

Sylvia ordered a salad and water, only pushing the food around when it arrived. Instead the actress focused all her attention on Annelie. Speaking about Diana Maddox's character, she sounded knowledgeable, obviously well read on the subject.

"I believe the actress who'll portray Maddox needs to do extensive research as a criminal investigator. I've got a friend in Seattle who dates a police officer. He put me in contact with their investigation unit, and I spent two days with them. All the guys there were so attentive and helpful."

Somehow Annelie found it hard to concentrate. Wondering briefly how much Sylvia could have picked up being admired by male cops, she tried to picture her as Maddox. With the right makeup, the younger woman could perhaps look the part, but the voice was all wrong. Too bright, too breathless, and not at all like the dark, velvet huskiness Annelie associated with the tough character in Delia's books. *She sounds nothing like Carolyn. She may be younger, perhaps even more beautiful, in a smooth, wrinkle-free kind of way. But she's not right.* Leaning back in her chair, Annelie let Sylvia continue with her interpretation of the role.

"I think Maddox should be sexier than she was in the audiobooks. No critique on your judgment when choosing actors, but Maddox is a tough woman in a man's world. She needs to play on her femininity more."

Was Sylvia suggesting Maddox should flaunt herself among her male colleagues? *Oh, God.* One of the things that had attracted Annelie to Delia's novels was the self-assurance of Maddox, her what-you-see-is-what-you-get attitude, which fell apart when her attraction to Erica Becker became apparent. She was not a tease, and Maddox surely didn't flaunt herself to anybody.

"When is a good time for me to read for the role?" Sylvia came right out and asked.

Taken aback by the actress's straightforward display of confidence, Annelie thought quickly. Even if she couldn't see this woman as Maddox, she might be wrong. Perhaps Sylvia Goodman possessed the skill to create a Maddox completely different from Carolyn's take, but just as good. And every suit involved in the project wanted her.

"Why not Tuesday? Can you be in Miami then?"

"Sure. For this role, I can be anywhere." A broad smile showed even, white caps, rendering Sylvia's a camera-perfect smile.

"Hello, Annelie."

The unexpected sound of Maddox's—no, *Carolyn's* voice, of course—made Annelie sit up ramrod straight.

"Carolyn. Hello." Momentarily stumped, she looked from one actress to the other. "Sylvia, this is Carolyn Black. Carolyn, meet Sylvia Goodman, a colleague of yours."

Carolyn's demeanor didn't change. Looking at the younger woman, she smiled politely and extended a hand. "Welcome to Orlando and the Maddox convention. How nice of you to drop in, Ms. Goodman."

Sylvia's eyes widened. "Thank you, Ms. Black. Please, call me Sylvia. I'm too young to be uptight about titles."

"Then call me Carolyn, Sylvia."

Annelie could have sworn there were icicles hanging from Carolyn's words.

"I'm a huge fan," Sylvia gushed, pointing at a chair. "Won't you join us?"

"I'm sorry, I don't have time. I have errands to run before I participate in tonight's major event."

"Yes, I heard you were speaking. What a great way to say goodbye to the audience." Sylvia's smile became razor sharp. "Your career has been so inspirational and a wonderful motivator for me. It's great that you can still find challenging parts at this late stage in your professional life."

Holding her breath, Annelie darted a look at Carolyn, stunned to watch her eyes turn slate gray. "Yes, it's a welcome development when the moguls in Hollywood and Broadway realize that an actress with talent, no matter her age, is worth much more than a young starlet who slept her way to her position."

Wanting to hide her face in her palms and groan out loud, Annelie refrained from both, watching the two women stare at each other. On the surface they maintained their composure, but the undercurrent was wild and unbending. Wondering if the rest of the lunch guests were going to witness an honest-to-God catfight for free, Annelie sighed with relief when Carolyn suddenly laughed and shook her head.

"Well, I'm off to find as stunning a dress as I can possibly scare up at the last minute." She placed a soft hand on Annelie's shoulder, its warmth permeating the thin shirt and making Annelie jump. "I'll see you later in the suite, then."

"Yes, see you later."

Flustered, Annelie saw Sylvia's jaw drop. Wanting to throttle Carolyn, but at the same time forced to admire how her roommate had handled the situation, she speared another shrimp from her salad. "You were saying about the screen test, Sylvia?" Frowning at the menacing look in the actress's eyes as they followed the disappearing competitor for the role, Annelie tried again. "Sylvia? The screen test?"

Turning her attention back to Annelie, Sylvia altered her expression completely. All smiles and charm, she gushed in her breathless voice, "That's right. I know I can convince you…"

Annelie's mind drowned out Sylvia's words with Carolyn's voice. Low and with a definite purr, along with the soft touch, it made it impossible for her to think of anything else.

❖

"Ladies and gentlemen, I'd like to introduce the woman who made all this happen. Delia Carlton wrote the books"—Gregory was interrupted by the roar echoing through the large auditorium when the audience acknowledged the mention of the author's name—"but had this lady not seen the genius, the potential, in Ms. Carlton's manuscript, who knows? So put your hands together as the owner of Key Line Publishing joins us to introduce the next guest. Here she is—Annelie Peterson!"

Annelie felt a rush of awkwardness as she walked onto the stage. The large audience rose in their seats, and she was met by thundering applause, whistles, and cheers. The noise went on for half a minute before she raised her hands to calm the crowd.

"Thank you, thank you very much. Please take a seat. Thank you." She paused as people sat down. "Wow, that's some welcome—and I haven't really done anything apart from printing the books." Loud cheers erupted again, and Annelie smiled, shaking her head. "Thank you again. Now, I have two treats for you. First, I have a message for you from someone who has chosen not to be a public figure."

Annelie glanced to the left, searching for Carolyn among the faces in the wing. She could not spot her but knew she was out there, probably pacing back and forth, focusing hard and looking pale, like she had been doing only a minute ago. *She came here on her own volition, forcing her participation on all of us. Why should I worry whether she's pale and nervous?* Pulling out a piece of paper, Annelie read a short message from the author of the Maddox books, making the audience go wild again.

"We are taping parts of this convention, and I'll be sure to send a copy to Delia. Am I wrong in assuming you're having a great time?" The audience applauded and cheered again as Annelie pulled the microphone from its stand. "Have all of you listened to the Maddox audiobooks?" The crowd went wild as the majority yelled yes. "Then you know who the star of these books is. You've already met the lovely Helen St. Cyr, and now it's time to introduce…"

Annelie glanced to her left, seeing Gregory give a thumbs-up.

"…the lady who gave Diana Maddox her first voice. Please welcome Carolyn Black!"

The response from the audience was deafening as Carolyn stepped onstage. Walking toward Annelie, the actress surprised her by wrapping her in an embrace and kissing her on both cheeks before taking over the microphone. *What was that about?* Annelie raised a hand as if to touch her cheek but quickly turned it into a wave while walking hastily out of sight of the audience. *Was that for show? Or for me?*

"Thank you, everyone." The trademark throaty voice rose over the whistles and cheers. "I'm so glad to be here among you. Thank you!"

Annelie was relieved to be back in the wings again. Standing as close as possible without being seen, she watched Carolyn in action as the applause slowly dissipated. The audience seemed ecstatic, cheering loudly as Carolyn posed. Red highlights sparkled in her auburn hair, and her pale complexion, emphasized by skillfully applied makeup, made her look beautiful and fragile at the same time.

Photo flashes hammered the actress as she stood center stage. Waving at the audience, she raised the microphone to her lips again. "Can we make a deal, my friends? How about I walk slowly along the stage and give you the opportunity to take pictures; then you won't have to do it while we talk. The flashes blind me, and I want to be able to see you lovely people."

Annelie watched Carolyn slowly parade along the stage, smiling at the people who rushed forward with their cameras. After a few minutes, the actress held up her hands, and the audience obediently retook their seats. Amazed at Carolyn's control over the crowd, Annelie decided to just sit back and see how the performance would unfold.

"We all love Diana Maddox, don't we?" Carolyn began. "Let me tell you how I came to portray her in the audiobooks. Would you like to hear that story?"

A loud yes resounded throughout the auditorium.

"I had read the first Maddox book. You know it takes place in New York, at the School of Performing Arts. Of course that setting captivated me. Key Line Publishing approached me about a year later to do a theater version, really, of the books. I was intrigued. You younger people may not know this, but in the old days, first on the radio, and later on television, actors gave live performances—entire plays. Key Line's concept was similar. They had already signed Helen, Harvey, and a few other actors, and, for some unfathomable reason, they saw me as a good candidate for Maddox."

The audience cheered, making Carolyn smile and give an exaggerated shrug. "I was of course eager to get such a high-profile part—I mean, who could resist playing a savvy, headstrong criminal investigator?" Laughter broke out, and some people applauded. "I see you agree with me," Carolyn continued.

"So I accepted, and it was the most fun I've had in years. Harvey is, of course, a delight to work with—when he's not driving the rest of us crazy with his pranks. It was an honor to work with Helen St. Cyr, whom I admire so much. The kids in the story were handpicked, just like the rest of us. All in all, doing the audiobooks was one of the best things I've ever done."

Carolyn waited until the applause had died down. "Now, I see a long line of people in the aisle who need to know things. Please, fire away."

Annelie smiled cynically as she watched Carolyn make the large auditorium feel like an intimate little club, with the entire audience listening intently to every word she uttered. Her voice wrapped around them, captivating them completely. *What a snake charmer she is*, Annelie thought. *If they only knew the real Carolyn Black.*

"Oh, hello, Ms. Black. It's so wonderful—"

"Hello, darling, and forgive me for interrupting you." Carolyn beamed. "I just want to say, right off the bat, we're all on a first-name basis here. I'm Carolyn. What's your name and where are you from?"

"I'm Ally, from Los Angeles, and I'm thrilled—"

"Hello, Ally. You've traveled a long way to be here. What's your question?"

"I've just adored you ever since you played in *The Passing of Time*. You were so beautiful. I couldn't wait to see you every day. But I'm dying to know if you regret being in that show, when you're so famous and all now?"

Carolyn walked to the edge of the stage, glancing down at the doting older woman. "Of course not. I wouldn't be where I am today if I hadn't played Devon Harper. Working on a soap is tough, and it's a good way to learn your trade. The fans like yourself who liked me as Devon have been kind enough to remain loyal through the years. Does that answer your question, Ally?"

"Yes, thank you so much. And I've got to tell you, I just love your voice. I've got all three of the audiobooks and—"

"Thank you. That's so sweet of you."

A tall man stepped up to the microphone in the aisle, nervously cleared his throat, and introduced himself as Mike from Minneapolis. Annelie, watching his Adam's apple bob, estimated him to be about thirty and rather full of himself.

"First of all, I am one of your biggest fans. I have seen every one of your movies and, also, I have seen you onstage in Boston."

"Really? That's wonderful, Mike."

"I would be curious to know if you are going to play Maddox in the movies as well. Personally, I have a huge problem picturing anyone else as Maddox."

Carolyn gave a broad smile. "From your mouth to—well, we'll see what happens. The decision is not mine to make, Mike."

Annelie smirked, knowing full well that Carolyn realized she was listening.

The endless line of people wanting to talk to Carolyn questioned her about both her personal and private life. Annelie watched Carolyn bewitch everyone, even the ones who tried to overstep the boundaries of the strictly personal. Obviously in her true element, the actress managed to extricate herself slickly from questions she didn't want to answer, without ever appearing evasive.

Finally, a teenager dressed in an elaborate black leather jumpsuit adorned with zippers, chains, and rivets stepped up to the microphone.

"How's it going, Carolyn? I'm Cassandra, from New York. See what you think about this question."

Carolyn walked closer and gazed down at the youngster. "Go ahead, darling. Just let me say your outfit is stunning."

The girl gave a surprised smile. "Thanks, Carolyn. If you were peanut butter, which kind would you be? Crunchy or smooth?"

Annelie quickly covered her mouth to keep from chuckling out loud and wondered what went through Carolyn's head. As if she had read Annelie's mind, the actress glanced in her direction. "Funny you should ask," Carolyn answered, her voice a low purr. "There's no contest. I'd be…smooth." The way she said it, her head tilted to the side, one hand on her hip, seemed to shake Cassandra's bravado.

When the girl recovered, she grinned like a Cheshire cat. "I need to ask one more question—for my friend Paula over there. She's too shy to—"

"Come on, Paula. I won't bite, and I'm dying to meet you." Carolyn put her hand up to block the light from the rig above her. The audience laughed as an obviously mortified teenager dressed similarly to Cassandra slouched up to the microphone, giving her friend a murderous glare.

"Don't be shy—we're all friends here," Carolyn smiled. "Fire away!"

"Hi…eh…well…driving here we were talking…uh…and we wondered…uh…if you and Helen St. Cyr really…you know…kissed. You know. In the audiobooks."

Complete silence fell. Annelie wondered how many people had wanted to ask that particular question but hadn't had the nerve. Falling into old habits, she slid her thumb into her mouth, about to bite her nail when Jem swatted her.

Carolyn gave a charming smile. "No, Helen and I didn't really kiss. We did just like they did in the old days. We mimicked it by making the appropriate sounds."

"If you're gonna…uh…play Diana Maddox in the movies, you know…er…you're gonna have to kiss, you know, whoever plays…eh… Erica Becker, though," Paula reasoned, making the audience cheer.

Carolyn didn't miss a beat. "Should I get the role, I'm sure I'll enjoy making it as authentic as I can…in every way."

Annelie released a small gasp. Of all the calculated comments Carolyn had made during her presentation, this one was aimed squarely at her. Was Carolyn simply letting her know she could be completely comfortable as a straight actress, playing a lesbian? Or was she saying something much more personal? Annelie could not imagine Carolyn hinting at a casting-couch opportunity, yet the woman had made it very clear she would do her damnedest to get the role. Uneasily, Annelie forced her concentration back to the proceedings.

The next question fell to a stylish woman in an austere business suit, wearing her dark hair in a bun. She introduced herself as Penelope from Atlanta.

"Welcome to Orlando and the convention, Penelope. How do you like it so far?"

"It's superb, better than I ever could have dreamed. My question for you ties rather neatly into the previous one."

"Go ahead." Carolyn tilted her head, as if listening intently.

Annelie watched the actress, increasingly amazed that she had been onstage, answering questions and entertaining the crowd with anecdotes, for over an hour without any sign of fatigue. In fact, she seemed energized by the whole experience. The woman was a real professional, she admitted grudgingly.

"Carolyn, did you know that a huge number of us in the lesbian community love and admire you, not just as an actress but as a person? And how do you feel about that?"

"Honestly, I just became aware of my popularity among different groups when my agent told me how many Web sites are dedicated to Diana Maddox, and also to me personally. I was stunned, and very flattered, since I assume a lot of time and energy goes into maintaining a Web site.

"How I feel about it? Honored to be the object of anyone's admiration and appreciation, no matter who they are."

Annelie smirked. The politically correct answer was smart, much smarter probably than Sylvia Goodman could have ever come up with. If the distributors could only see Carolyn in action they might open their hard-shell minds.

"May I become personal and say that I think you're wonderful, and your voice is such an incredible turn-on," Penelope said.

Carolyn gave her photo-ready smile and then laughed. "Thank you for the compliment."

The following questions were less personal, and soon Gregory concluded the session, promising that the stars would shortly sign autographs.

Carolyn waved to the audience and looked both touched and delighted when the standing ovations seemed never to end. Finally she walked offstage and into the wings where Annelie waited.

"Congratulations," she greeted her. "That was an amazing performance, Carolyn." *You were so in your true element. You thrive on their admiration and you loved every second of it.*

"I'm glad you think so." The actress beamed. "I had a great time out there."

I bet you did. You continued to cement your status as the perfect candidate for Maddox.

"I could tell. I found the question-and-answer session very informative."

"I bet you did." Carolyn's eyes twinkled as she tilted her head.

"You know, your voice turns *me* on," she echoed the words of the woman in the audience.

Annelie gave a faint smile, determined not to let Carolyn get the last word in this friendly banter. "And your legs do it for me," she returned the favor, watching Carolyn's eyes widen.

Walking toward Jem, who was gesturing for them to hurry up, Annelie had a feeling the comments might come back to haunt them.

"People are lining up for the autographs," Jem said, shaking her head. "I hope you're prepared for it, Carolyn. The line is a mile long already."

Carolyn cast a look of seasoned resignation at Annelie. "Don't worry," she told Jem. "It's nothing I haven't handled a hundred times before."

❖

Carolyn looked around the dinner table, pleased they were all seated in a private area of the restaurant on the top floor. Most of all she was pleased that Sylvia Goodman, who had invited herself to the gathering, sat at the far end of the table. Carolyn was sitting between Annelie and Jem, and everyone was buzzing about what a success the convention had been. Helen St. Cyr was giving her impression of the audience and the response she had received while signing autographs.

"They were mostly women," the Canadian actress mused, "and they were so sweet to me. Some of them had brought presents, and I think I have at least fifteen little teddy bears and fifty cards. There even was a woman who had knitted me a blue sweater."

Carolyn smiled, knowing she had received just as many gifts and feeling amazed at the audience's generosity. "I think all the continents were represented. Three women even came from South Africa. Diana Maddox must appeal to all types of people, because I signed autographs for both men and women of all ages."

Helen concurred. "Honestly, I haven't experienced anything like this in my life." She shook her head. "What do you think, Carolyn? Is your ego as massaged as mine?"

"You bet." Carolyn nodded. "Any more of this, and I'll be impossible to deal with."

"And that differs from now…how?" Helen grinned.

"All a matter of degree, my dear." Laughter erupted around the table when Carolyn put on her best diva look before wrinkling her nose at her colleague. Sitting among these people, she felt more at ease than she had in a long time. Her performance was a success, and she had experienced such a rush when the audience yielded to her. It had been magical, the way they absorbed every word and constantly wanted to know more.

Carolyn reached for her glass, enjoying the soft, fruity taste of Le Volte 1999. Gregory had made numerous toasts during the evening, and she felt warm and relaxed after sipping her wine each time.

As if reading her mind Jem suddenly stood up, raising her glass. "We've toasted everyone but the person who's responsible for this tremendous success. I say we raise our glasses in a toast to Annelie! This whole endeavor would have been impossible without you."

"To Annelie," they all echoed and sipped their drinks.

"Or should I say *Annie*?" Carolyn smiled slowly at the blonde next to her.

"Hmm, I prefer Annelie, thank you, *Lyn*."

Carolyn laughed. "Touché."

The laughter and companionship around the table continued for another hour before Harvey and his wife rose to say good night. Suddenly, Annelie grabbed a digital camera and sprang from her chair.

"Please let me get some group shots as a memory of the first Maddox convention," she said. "I want one of the audiobook cast first, and then one of all of you…"

Soon, Carolyn was laughing out loud as Annelie arranged and rearranged different constellations of people, totally confusing everybody. Harvey didn't help by doing rabbit ears behind whoever stood next to him. When she glanced to her left, Carolyn's grin became even broader as she spotted Sylvia Goodman struggling to look as if she were amused by everybody's antics. Carolyn could tell Sylvia was equal parts fuming and exasperated.

When Annelie was finally ready to sit down, Kitty pointed out the publisher had not been in any of the pictures. The absolute dismay on Annelie's face made Carolyn laugh again, and Annelie gave her a mock glare, which turned into a broad smile.

After the impromptu photo session, Harvey and his wife retired, followed by Kitty and Sam. Annelie excused herself and went back to the Presidential Suite, explaining that she had to go over the numbers once more and send a few e-mails. One by one, the rest of them parted and went to their rooms.

CHAPTER SEVEN

Carolyn walked into her bedroom and undressed, still on an emotional high after the performance. It would be a while before she could settle, and she contemplated taking a swim in the hotel's outdoor pool. Of course, the idea was completely impractical unless she wanted to be surrounded by eager fans while she attempted her laps.

Resigned to the next-best thing, she strolled into the luxurious bathroom and ran the water in the shower until it was as hot as she could tolerate. She could feel the adrenaline slowly leaving her body as she stood beneath the spray. She was always jittery after a performance, especially a premiere. And tonight's had been one of the most important she had ever given.

If Annelie Peterson needed any proof that Carolyn was a hot ticket, she had it now. The publisher had been oddly silent when Carolyn returned to the room. No doubt she was trying to play it cool. Carolyn's coup must have been an embarrassment on some level. Carolyn took some satisfaction knowing Annelie had to act as if it was all her idea or look foolish.

Smirking a little, Carolyn dried herself off with a thick towel and pulled on the complimentary bathrobe. After drying her hair and brushing her teeth, she stared at her bed without enthusiasm. It seemed pointless even to try to go to sleep; her body was still tingling and her mind reeling. With a sigh, Carolyn headed for the living room.

Annelie was just putting her computer away and looked up in polite welcome. "Planning to stay up?"

"Thought I'd watch some TV. It usually puts me to sleep."

Annelie checked her watch. "Would you like some company for a little while?"

Carolyn studied Annelie, noticing how different she looked in casual clothes. Dressed in gray slacks and a white, long-sleeved T-shirt, she wore no makeup, her hair framing her face and waving around her shoulders. "You're beautiful," she blurted.

Annelie's eyes darkened. "Thank you." Her tone was cautious. "So are you."

"You think so?"

"Of course, and everyone in the audience agrees with me."

Carolyn sat down on the couch, noticing how it virtually embraced her. Pulling a pillow closer, she invited, "Join me?"

Annelie stood frozen for a moment and then sat down next to her. "What is it you want?"

Carolyn let her eyes roam Annelie's face, traveling from her full lips, as the other woman repeated the question, to the huge blue eyes that examined her with a guarded expression. Unable to resist, Carolyn raised a hand and cupped Annelie's chin. "I'm not sure," she tried to explain. "I just know I find you so beautiful, inside and out. I've never met anyone like you."

Softly sliding her fingertip along the amor arch of Annelie's upper lip, she discovered a faint tremor. Annelie was not indifferent to her.

❖

Annelie felt the soft touch against her lips, and it started a fire inside her she was unprepared for. Carolyn was sitting too close, looking breathtakingly beautiful with her damp hair loose around her shoulders. The robe revealed slightly freckled skin just below her neck, and the left sleeve fell back along her arm as she cupped Annelie's chin. *Just like in the photo.*

"So you don't know what you want, and yet you touch me this way," Annelie breathed, fighting to stay in control. This was quickly leading toward disaster. "You're playing with fire, Carolyn."

"Am I? How?" the actress whispered.

Unable to reply, Annelie turned her head and pressed her lips against Carolyn's palm. A soft intake of breath escaped the other woman as Annelie placed her own hand over Carolyn's, urging the soft palm closer to her lips before placing a trail of kisses on the sensitive skin inside the actress's arm.

Carolyn leaned in closer, hooking her arm around Annelie's neck. "Annie," she whispered. "I'm trembling."

Feelings rampaged. Alarm bells echoed madly inside her head. Everything she knew and had learned told Annelie to stop.

Carolyn was looking at her with stormy gray eyes, her lips slightly parted. "I'm all wrong, I know," she continued in a low, throaty voice. "Still..." She leaned in farther, closing the distance between their lips until she was little more than a breath away.

Annelie knew she ought to pull back, but she simply couldn't resist. Closing her eyes, she wrapped an arm around Carolyn's waist. "You want me to kiss you?" she said huskily, her voice barely audible.

Not waiting for a reply, she leaned down and pressed her lips against Carolyn's. Afterwards she knew she might have been able to kiss her and then pull back, if only Carolyn had not moaned softly and whimpered Annelie's name into her mouth.

"Annie..."

Parting her lips, Carolyn wordlessly invited Annelie to explore further.

Annelie resisted for a fraction of a second before plunging her tongue into the warm darkness, finding its counterpart and caressing it over and over. Carolyn whimpered again, returning the kiss feverishly. Her soft, yielding body trembled in Annelie's arms, and Annelie felt like she was drowning in the sweetness. Her hands roamed Carolyn's back, tugging at the robe as if they had a mind of their own.

Soon the actress's shoulders were naked and accessible to her mouth. Annelie wasted little time, letting her lips and tongue explore the warm skin. Carolyn cupped Annelie's head and held her as if afraid to let her go.

Annelie finally sat up, gazing at the disheveled woman beneath her on the couch. Somehow the robe had opened fully, and she could not stop looking.

"Bedroom?" Carolyn managed, her voice husky and filled with desire. "Bedroom, please, Annie?"

Unable to stop the madness, Annelie pulled Carolyn to her feet. "Come." She guided the other woman to her room.

At the foot of the bed, Annelie pushed the robe off Carolyn completely. Standing there naked, she looked young, vulnerable, and almost frightened. Annelie took her into her arms and kissed her again, suddenly wanting nothing other than to reassure her. "Carolyn, open your mouth…let me in…" she whispered against the wine-colored lips beneath hers.

❖

Carolyn's head was spinning. Trustingly she opened her mouth, allowing Annelie to deepen the kiss. She felt the bed at the back of her legs and gave in to the urge to lie down and just let everything happen.

Annelie helped her get comfortable and then stood gazing down at her reclining form for a moment. Suddenly aware of the age difference, of the unmistakable signs of her forty-five years, Carolyn blushed.

"You're exquisite," Annelie murmured.

"Please undress," Carolyn said, her voice trembling.

With hesitant hands, Annelie unbuttoned her slacks and let them fall to the floor. She pulled the T-shirt over her head and stood dressed in a whisper-thin satin tank top and skimpy panties that left very little to the imagination. Keeping her underwear on, she joined Carolyn on the bed.

"Don't be scared," she said, placing small kisses on Carolyn's forehead, along her nose, down to her lips.

"I'm not. Just feeling clumsy and, I guess…a little shy."

"We can stop."

Carolyn's heart almost quit beating. She was more turned on than she had been in a very long time, if ever. Now her heart was racing, and the moisture pooling between her legs was going to make it embarrassingly clear to Annelie just how much she wanted her.

"No, please…Annelie…" Carolyn reached out and was rewarded when Annelie parted her legs, settling between them.

"Hold on to me," she suggested. "There, that's it." Leaning down, Annelie unceremoniously took a rigid nipple in her mouth, sucking it in between her teeth. She flicked her tongue over it repeatedly, making Carolyn moan aloud and arch her back. "So this is what you like, what you want," she murmured around the pebbled surface before letting it go.

"Yes…" Carolyn's voice betrayed her when Annelie pushed herself closer between her legs.

"Oh, Carolyn, you're so ready for me…so ready to be touched," Annelie whispered, sneaking a hand between her thighs. "Like this?"

She pushed her fingers along swollen, drenched folds. "Oh, yes, just like this." Rubbing Carolyn's aching clitoris, she began to rock against her.

Feeling tender fingers enter her, Carolyn knew it would not take long before she was completely lost to sensation. She pulled her knees up and circled Annelie's hips. Wrapping her arms around that beautiful neck, she cried out softly as their lips met in a profound kiss.

"Oh…oh, God, Annie…oh…"

❖

The sound of that famous voice giving in to passion, the feeling of Carolyn surrendering in her arms, made Annelie hold her breath as heat surged through her. The way Carolyn clung to her, calling her *Annie* in a longing tone of voice, almost broke her heart.

"Now, now…" Carolyn whimpered, and her inner muscles began to contract, pulling Annelie's fingers deeper inside.

"I've got you. I've got you, Carolyn," Annelie whispered as one long shudder after another gripped the woman she held. Rocking against the convulsing woman, Annelie felt the fire between her own legs erupt and spread to her stomach and down her thighs. "Carolyn…" She hid her face in the other woman's hair, knowing her own orgasm was close. "Carolyn!"

Still holding on tight to Annelie, the actress whispered huskily in her ear. "Oh, you're amazing. You take my breath away. Never before…" Carolyn's voice faded. "Don't let go."

Annelie shivered and rolled over on her side, pulling Carolyn with her. Sensing the deep need and pent-up desire in the other woman, she knew it was going to be a long, passionate night.

❖

Dawn was breaking, but the woman standing on the large balcony dressed in only a robe did not care about the spectacular sunrise. Tears streamed down her cheeks, and her shoulders shook as she cried soundlessly.

Annelie had made love to Carolyn all night, taking her from one height to another, making her sob from a pleasure so intense it seemed to border on pain. Annelie had never fully undressed, nor had she allowed Carolyn to touch her intimately. It was impossible for her to let her guard down.

Carolyn had hugged her close and kissed her deeply—wonderful, passionate kisses that left Annelie feeling robbed of all the oxygen she needed to think clearly. She would have given anything to be able to just let go—to allow herself to give in to Carolyn and let the other woman reciprocate every erotic caress.

"Annelie? You okay, darl?" a familiar voice to her left said, making Annelie jump.

"Kitty! Oh, God, you startled me." Annelie blinked away her tears as she walked over to the balcony adjoining hers. "What are you doing up so early?"

"Still on Aussie time, I guess. What's your excuse?"

"I…eh, I'm thinking of what to do next, really." She fiddled with the belt to her bathrobe.

"Something's happened, hasn't it?" Her friend sounded concerned.

"Yes, Kitty, something happened," Annelie whispered. "I've done the most stupid thing. I'm such an idiot."

"Tell me about it," the other woman said in a gentle voice. "It can't be that bad."

Swallowing hard, Annelie wiped her wet cheeks. "It's worse, actually."

"You're beginning to scare me, babe. Tell me what's up."

Annelie had to clear her throat again. Looking at her friend with eyes burning from tears still unshed, she couldn't be anything but honest. "I made love to Carolyn."

Kitty paled. "Oh, shit."

Annelie gave a bittersweet laugh at the other woman's choice of words, so in character. "Yes, I agree."

"What are you going to do?"

"What I have to. Will you help me?"

Kitty extended a hand, barely able to reach Annelie over the distance between the balconies. "Of course. You just tell me what you need, babe."

❖

Carolyn slowly opened her eyes, squinting at the bright sunlight flooding the room. Rolling onto her back, she felt aching muscles she didn't even know existed. She reached over, letting her hand slide across the other side of the bed. The fact that it was empty rattled her, and, sitting up, she realized two things—she was naked, and she was still in Annelie's room.

Looking around for Annelie, she was about to call out her name when she saw an envelope lying on the bedside table. Puzzled, she noticed her name written on the front, and her heart fluttered as she reached for it.

Carolyn's fingers trembled when she opened the envelope. The card within contained only a few handwritten words.

Congratulations, Carolyn.
The role is yours.
Annelie

CHAPTER EIGHT

Carolyn picked up the robe from the floor and walked back toward her own room, noticing Annelie's computer bag was missing. Thinking her suitemate had gone to a meeting with Gregory or Jem, Carolyn went to her bathroom and ran the shower until the room filled with steam.

Her body ached from the previous night, and memories of endless passionate kisses and soft hands roaming her body made Carolyn shiver inside as she stood there nude, pacified for a moment by the sound of the rushing water.

Feeling unsettled, she replayed the night she'd spent in Annelie's arms, being thoroughly taken, pushed over the edge repeatedly. She stepped into the shower, welcoming the hot, streaming water. She regretted washing Annelie's fragrance from her body, which surprised her. She had never before wished to savor a lover's scent upon her skin.

She had never experienced such abandoned pleasure, and realizing that this earth-shattering lovemaking had occurred with someone of her own gender made her head spin.

Annelie, beautiful and vibrant behind her cool exterior, had shown Carolyn a side of herself the actress had never known. Not until this stunning woman entered her life, her mind...*My heart? God. Does this mean I'm a lesbian? What if I am? What will that mean? What will people think?*

Carolyn thought of the emptiness she felt when she woke up alone, and she rubbed her eyes, trying to force the feeling from her mind. Annelie had taken her thoroughly, several times, and Carolyn blushed when she remembered how she had whimpered and begged for release. When Carolyn had reached for Annelie's full breasts, which were barely covered by the thin fabric of the tank top, Annelie had pulled her hands away, distracting Carolyn by kissing every inch of her. Annelie had pressed her heated sex against Carolyn's throbbing center several times, but always with fabric between them, never skin to skin.

Carolyn had felt Annelie come at least twice, though never from her direct touch. The realization left her feeling unsettled, a dark tone reverberating through her whole being, leaving a desolate feeling in her stomach. *Maybe she thought I was totally inept as a lesbian lover. Go figure. Perhaps I'm not only a lesbian but totally incompetent, to boot.* Her throat clenched and she fought against the sting of her self-deprecating thoughts.

Her mind reeled at the short message Annelie had left her. Wanting the role for so long, then finding out she had landed it, seemed unreal, but she knew euphoria was not far away. Still, she was disappointed that Annelie was not there to share the excitement. *How could she leave this morning without telling me in person?*

She turned off the shower and wrapped herself in a large towel. Wiping off the foggy mirror with a washcloth, she examined her reflection. Her eyes were huge and stormy gray, as expected, with a definite fire burning in them. Jittery, with an overwhelming feeling of excitement for getting the role, Carolyn wanted to shout it out from the balcony. *I'll be playing Diana Maddox in the film, damn it!*

A knock on the door startled her and made her reach for her robe. "Just a minute."

Tying the belt around her waist, she disregarded her dripping hair and rushed through the suite. When she peeked through the peephole, she saw Kitty.

Her caller's eyes widened when Carolyn opened the door. "Oh, did I interrupt your shower? I'm sorry."

"No, no, I was done. Please come in."

Once inside, Kitty turned to look at her. "I thought I'd come by and ask if you'd like to have breakfast with us before you leave for the airport."

"Sure, I'd love to. I'll be ready soon." Carolyn hesitated briefly. "Do you have any idea where Annelie is?"

Kitty's expression was unreadable. "Annelie's gone, Carolyn. She had to leave unexpectedly."

It took all Carolyn's acting skill and self-discipline not to show

Kitty how her stomach lurched. "She left? Oh. I didn't hear her pack. I must have been out like a light after yesterday."

Carolyn thought she glimpsed a look of sympathy in the other woman's eyes. "Yes, she left very early. Apparently she managed to get a last-minute ticket. I talked to her briefly out on the balcony, and she told me she had to leave."

Making herself stop fiddling with the bathrobe belt, Carolyn gestured toward her hair and then the room in general. "Just give me a minute to dry my hair and pack, and I'll be down for breakfast. Can't miss my caffeine."

"I know what you mean." Kitty nodded. "We'll be waiting for you in a private section of the breakfast room." She looked at Carolyn intently. "Are you all right, Carolyn? You look a little pale."

Not about to make a fool of herself in front of Annelie's friend, Carolyn gave a broad smile, slipping into her comfortable role as the diva. "I'm probably a little hungover, but it was worth it. We had a lot of fun, didn't we? I'll be fine as soon as I get my hands on some coffee."

"It was a blast." Kitty looked as if she was about to say something else, but apparently changed her mind. "See you downstairs in a little bit, then?"

After closing the door, Carolyn stroked one hand along her face, letting it linger over her mouth. She shivered when cold water dripped from her hair inside her collar. Wavering between feeling overjoyed and desolate, she decided she better pull herself together before she faced the others. It wouldn't do to let anyone see her like this.

❖

Annelie looked down at the dense quilt of clouds preventing her from seeing anything of the New York area as the plane descended at LaGuardia. She had lowered the backrest fully and stretched out in her first-class seat, pretending to browse through some documents, but her thoughts had whirled aimlessly—all about leaving Carolyn. Carolyn, looking like a sleeping angel, lying completely relaxed, her hair spreading like a dark red shadow across the pillow. She hadn't even stirred while Annelie packed. Annelie had watched her for a few precious minutes before grabbing her bags and leaving the bedroom, closing the door softly behind her.

She automatically checked her seat belt during the turbulent landing, but her mind was still on the previous night. Blue-gray eyes looking up at her with a wondrous expression as passion rode the petite body beneath hers. For those moments, she'd allowed herself to drown in Carolyn's eyes, reveling in her responsiveness. However, she feared last night could never lead to anything more. She was all too aware of Carolyn's reputation for always having a plan or an ulterior motive.

She was jerked from her reverie by the plane's erratic course along the runway. It taxied toward the terminal, and soon she was walking on the moving sidewalks, too impatient to stand still and be carried along. After she claimed her bags, she continued toward the exit when suddenly a reporter followed by a camera crew stopped her. Bringing her sunglasses down from her hair to cover her eyes, Annelie answered her questions regarding the Maddox movies in a short, polite manner while she kept walking, wanting nothing else than to find refuge in her large two-floor apartment. Telling the TV reporter goodbye, she hailed a cab and gave the driver her home address in Manhattan.

As she leaned her head back against the neck rest, she drew a deep breath. She still had Carolyn's musky scent in her hair.

❖

Carolyn briefly closed her eyes as the cab drove up to Annelie's house. She had dropped her bags off at Jared's, to her relief finding the condo empty. Wanting to talk to Annelie face-to-face, she had taken a cab to Golden Beach immediately, hoping to find her at home.

She pulled the large hair clip from her hair, letting it flow freely around her shoulders. *Why am I so down when I should be walking on air? I must have been crazy last night. Waking up alone hurt like hell, and I simply can't understand why she left—especially after all that...passion.*

The note—despite its positive message—didn't convey anything about Annelie's state of mind. Carolyn thought back to the empathetic look on Kitty's face when the Australian came to fetch her. *She knew, damn it. Annelie told her what happened.* Mortified at the sudden realization, she flinched as the cabdriver tried to get her attention by raising his voice.

"You okay, ma'am?"

"Fine, thanks. Here you go. Keep the change." She stepped out into the scorching sun.

Had anyone asked her before yesterday what could ruin such a day, Carolyn would have replied, "Nothing on God's green earth." Now, her happiness about getting the coveted role was overshadowed by the fact that Annelie hadn't waited to tell her in person. *How dare she?* The note left her feeling more alone than ever, with a queasy sensation erupting in her stomach. She didn't usually read more into things than what seemed reasonable, but now she felt vulnerable, an easy target. *And I hate it.*

When she reached the gate leading up to the paved garden path, Carolyn pressed the buzzer, since she had returned the key card to Mary when she left three days earlier. The speaker came to life with Mary's voice, and the gate swung open seconds later.

"Welcome back, Ms. Black," Mary greeted her at the door. "What can I do for you? Did you forget something above the garage?" The wiry woman studied her closely.

"Hello, Mary, I didn't realize you worked on Sundays."

"Usually I don't, but I'll have a week or two off and wanted to make sure everything was in order before I left."

Carolyn frowned. "Annelie isn't home, by any chance?"

The housekeeper raised her eyebrows. "She had to leave directly from Orlando to fly to New York. I thought you were aware of this, since you were there with her. She originally planned to go tomorrow or Tuesday."

"Something came up, I assume." Carolyn tried to sound casual, her mind reeling. *What the hell...To New York?* Had Annelie run away? "I'm going back to New York myself, and I'd like to get in touch with her. Do you have her address?"

Mary nodded her head. "Of course. Come on. I've started a light lunch."

Feeling reprieved from her increasing depression, Carolyn followed Mary into the kitchen and sat down at a small table. "There you go, Ms. Black. I'll go find a business card and then join you."

As Carolyn contemplated the large salad and Melba toast in front of her, she suddenly felt nauseous. Mary's assumption only emphasized the reality of the situation. Annelie had opted for New York without so much as a goodbye, rather than return to Miami with Carolyn.

Her jaw tensing, she held on tight to the fork, staring down at the salad. *Was facing me in the morning so incredibly embarrassing, she'd rather act this rudely? So out of character?* Carolyn could only surmise that her first fear was correct. *For whatever reason Annelie was forced to go to New York, the way she did it...*

Mary returned with the card, interrupting Carolyn's train of thought. Accepting the card, Carolyn raised an eyebrow. "Annelie Peterson, Peterson & Associates. This is a law firm?" she asked. "Her own firm?"

"Yes." Mary said. "She employs several young lawyers, and they only do pro bono work."

They ate in silence while Carolyn digested this new information. Stunned, she was more than impressed with Annelie's multiple ventures. *Perhaps there was a perfectly logical reason for Annelie to return so hastily to New York.* The thought was comforting, but a persistent voice within her cautioned Carolyn not to assume this was true.

Refusing to go down the path of self-pity and anger again, Carolyn gazed down at the business card next to her plate. The idea of Annelie owning a law firm and turning out to be even more dedicated to putting her wealth to good use was not a surprise. It was the extent of Annelie's involvement, which was impressive, far beyond anyone Carolyn knew, that was astonishing. Carolyn knew people richer than Annelie who clung to their wallets like life rafts in a storm.

Something Mary had said earlier surfaced. If Annelie had originally meant to leave Monday or Tuesday, she *must* have run from Carolyn. *Was she overwhelmed with regret for breaking her own rules?* Knowing full well her own part in what had happened in Orlando, Carolyn wanted to bury her head in her hands and moan aloud. *And that damn note...I'll go confront her. She's not going to get away with this. We'll just see what she has to say for herself. Nobody treats me like a whore and gets away with it!*

After finishing what she could of her salad and thanking Mary, Carolyn called a cab and headed back to Jared's condo. She didn't offer much of an explanation for her hit-and-run stay, immediately reserving a flight for early the next morning. She would be in New York just after lunch Monday.

Dodging Jared's inquisitive looks, she locked herself in the guest bathroom, letting her clothes fall to the floor. She looked at her body in the mirror, seeing the clearly visible traces of Annelie's passionate caresses. Carolyn let her hands trace the reddened skin on her left breast, wincing when the nipple proved to be more sensitive than usual. She could still feel Annelie's full lips closing over the puckered skin, drawing it into the warm, moist cavity of her mouth…

Snap out of it. Carolyn turned on the shower and stepped into the cool stream of water. Scrubbing her sensitized skin, she tried to wash the memory of Annelie out of her mind.

Of course she was doomed to fail.

❖

"Morning, Grey. How are you today?"

"Carolyn! I've been trying to reach you!" The agent sounded excited.

"Sorry, I forgot to switch on my cell phone earlier. The only good thing about that is at least the battery's still fully charged."

"Well, I'm delighted you called. I have contracts waiting here for you, several of them."

Carolyn stopped walking, causing a man to stumble into her from behind. Miami International Airport was buzzing with activity, and all the corridors were crowded.

"What on earth are you talking about?"

"A courier was waiting for me when I arrived this morning. He refused to let anyone but me sign for the documents—and I can't blame him. You have four different contracts waiting for your signature, Carolyn! The three Maddox movies and a special contract for more Maddox conventions. We're talking about roughly fifteen million dollars."

Carolyn was stunned and had to clear her throat twice before her voice would carry again.

"Oh, my God," she said huskily. "Good thing I'm on my way to New York, then. I'm at the Miami airport."

"That's what I like to hear. Get yourself right to my office when you land, my dear."

Inwardly shaking her head at her agent's enthusiasm, Carolyn couldn't blame him for being excited. This would be a nice feather in his hat, as well as a profitable 10 percent fee.

"I'll call you when I get there, okay?"

"Looking forward to it."

Carolyn disconnected and dialed her sister as she resumed walking toward her gate. "Beth, honey, it's me. How are you doing?"

"Lyn, I'm so glad you called. I have some news for you," her sister replied. "I've hired someone to help me around the house, part-time. Her name's Frances and she seems great."

Exhaling deeply with relief that the news wasn't bad, Carolyn smiled. "I'm delighted. Now, have her address ready for me when I call you next time, and I'll arrange to send her a check every week."

"But, Lyn…"

"No *buts*, darling, just humor me. Let me do this for you."

There was a sigh of mock exasperation. "All right, then. So, how was the convention? I haven't heard from you since you got back."

"The convention went very well, sweetie. Actually, I just wanted to let you know I'm on my way home for a bit. I have some things to take care of with Grey."

"Sounds exciting. Anything you can tell me?"

"No, not yet," Carolyn smiled and began to walk toward the gate as they called her flight. "I promise you'll be the first to know, though, when I can." The energetic tone in her sister's voice was reassuring.

"You better." Beth laughed.

"Hey, I have to go. It's time to board. Say hi to Joe and Pamela for me, okay?"

Beth promised and Carolyn disconnected, making sure she switched the phone off. Passing the smiling flight attendant, she returned to her thoughts of Annelie, wondering how the other woman would react to seeing her so soon. Impatient with herself for letting her nerves get to her, she found her seat, stowed her only bag in the overhead compartment, and sat down.

A short time into the flight, the screen embedded in the backrest in front of her lit up, and Carolyn was able to choose from a variety of TV shows. Browsing through the channels, she found E! News. She smirked as she watched with some amusement how several of her colleagues had made fools of themselves at a Hollywood mogul's housewarming party. Carolyn sipped her mineral water and almost choked on it when a familiar face filled the small screen. The narrator continued by presenting the next interview.

"E! News had the pleasure of bumping into the elusive publisher of the best-selling Diana Maddox books, Annelie Peterson, at LaGuardia Airport on Sunday morning. Several sources have confirmed Ms. Peterson is in the process of casting the movies based on the famous books. Here's what the blond beauty had to say on the matter."

After a shot of the covers of the three Maddox books, Annelie's face came into view again. "Ms. Peterson, can you tell us who's going to play Diana Maddox?" a reporter asked as Annelie, wearing large black sunglasses, hurried toward the exit.

"We're going to start the casting process tomorrow," Annelie replied. "I'll get back to you when I know more."

"So no hot tip about who the lucky actress is going to be?" the reporter insisted.

"No, we're considering several interesting names. As I said, I'll have to get back to you when I know more."

"Is Carolyn Black among the interesting names you're referring to?"

"Carolyn Black did a wonderful job portraying Diana Maddox in the audiobooks and was instrumental in making them even bigger best-sellers than the hardbacks and paperbacks. She's definitely of interest to us, but so are several other actresses."

"Can you give us a few more names?"

"No, that'll have to be a surprise. Supernova Productions will hold a press conference as soon as we have made a decision."

Annelie acknowledged the members of the press with a regal nod. Giving an equally royal wave, she disappeared into a cab and drove off.

Carolyn sat staring at the small screen, her blurring eyes making it impossible to see the face of the famous singer who'd been arrested during a cocaine bust in downtown L.A.

Unsure why the sight of the other woman would twist her stomach into a knot, she clenched her fists, her hands suddenly cold. Seeing Annelie in her professional role only added to the emotional distance she felt from the woman she had been intimate with so recently.

As she blinked back tears of confusion, Carolyn followed Annelie's example by putting on her large sunglasses and reclined her seat so she could lean back in it. Biting her lower lip, she was even more determined to obtain answers to her growing set of questions.

❖

Annelie walked into her office, smiling at the receptionist sitting at the front desk.

"Good morning. How are you?"

"Ms. Peterson! Just fine. I didn't know you were expected in today, ma'am. I thought…" The new employee looked slightly panic-stricken as she browsed though her day planner.

"Don't worry about it. I flew in a day early."

The nervous young woman looked relieved. "Should I page Ms. Dillon, ma'am?"

Annelie's personal assistant, Margo Dillon, was also her personnel manager. The energetic woman hired everyone from the law clerks to the janitors at the firm. Annelie now headed for the main desk in Margo's office where the personnel manager usually sat, queen of her domain.

"Margo, do you have a minute?" she asked blithely, walking up to her and making her jump.

"Annelie! Jesus, Mary, and Joseph. Are you trying to give me a coronary? You're here already?" Margo exclaimed in her familiar Irish accent. Rising, she freed herself from her headset. "Good to see you, girlie!" She rounded the desk and wrapped Annelie in a bear hug.

Margo was the only one who could get away with calling Annelie "girlie." A close friend of Annelie's mother, Margo had lived next door to them in Chicago and, after Annelie's mother died, stepped in and took the lanky seventeen-year-old under her wing. She became a different kind of female role model. Feisty, with a colorful vocabulary, the energetic, caring woman had been just what Annelie needed.

"It's wonderful to see you too, Margo." Annelie beamed at her friend, placing her briefcase on the closest desk before returning the hug. "I came earlier, which means I can participate in the meeting with the lawyers from city hall."

"Yeah, that petition is going to take some fine-tuning," Margo sighed.

After hearing the latest on the pending case, Annelie grabbed her briefcase and walked toward her office. Pushing the door open, she looked involuntarily at the two posters above the couch. One was of the first off-Broadway play she had sponsored, *Dream Catcher*. The critics had been impressed with the new playwright, and the audience had kept the show going for a year.

Annelie's eyes narrowed when her glance fell on the other one, a collector's item. *Little Women* had played on Broadway eighteen years ago with a young Carolyn Black as Jo. Annelie had bought the poster at a charity auction five years ago. As much as she longed to do so, she refused to think about the woman she had so recently left behind in Orlando. Doing so would only bring her pain and confusion.

Her cherrywood desk was empty, but Annelie knew it would become cluttered with documents after the meeting. She welcomed the busy day ahead of her; hopefully it would take her mind off her disastrous weekend.

CHAPTER NINE

Carolyn stepped out of the cab in front of the large office building. When the security guard looked inquisitively at her as she signed her name and identified herself, Carolyn knew he probably recognized her but was reluctant to ask. She gave him her automatic diva smile before heading toward the elevators.

The mirror in the elevator didn't reveal how nervous she felt. *Am I doing the right thing, barging in here like a wounded wildebeest? Will she toss me out and tell me to tear up my contracts? Or will she act like an ice goddess and freeze me out? I'm afraid I'm going to throw up, but this is the only way I know to get in touch with her. She's so damned private I'd never find her home address. Oh, to hell with it. Here goes nothing. I'll just have to play my charm to the hilt.*

Large glass doors with Peterson & Associates, Attorneys at Law painted on them in gold letters led into a formal reception area. A dark-haired woman wearing ultramodern black glasses looked up as Carolyn approached the desk and gave her a welcoming smile.

"Good afternoon, ma'am. How may I help you?"

"I'd like to speak to Annelie Peterson. Is she in today?"

The receptionist nodded. "Do you have an appointment, Ms....?"

"Black. Carolyn Black. No, I don't, but if you ask Annelie, I'm sure she'll see me. It won't take long."

"I'm sorry, Ms. Black. Ms. Peterson is in a meeting and can't be disturbed. If you can wait just a second, I'll page Ms. Dillon, Ms. Peterson's assistant."

Carolyn bit back an impatient reply and waited while the receptionist made a quick phone call.

"Ms. Dillon will be right with you, Ms. Black," the receptionist said. "Here she is already."

A slender middle-aged woman, dressed in a cobalt blue suit and high-heel pumps, approached. "Ms. Black, welcome," she greeted Carolyn, extending a hand. "What a pleasant surprise. We had no idea you were in town. I'm Margo Dillon."

Slightly taken aback by the other woman's energy, Carolyn shook her hand. "Hello, Ms. Dillon."

"Oh, call me Margo, please."

"Nice to meet you, Margo. I know I don't have an appointment, but…"

"Don't worry about it. I'm sure I can pry Annelie out of the conference room for a minute or two. Could you please come with me? And would you like something to drink?"

Having gone directly from the airport to her apartment to change, Carolyn hadn't bothered to eat. "I'd love some coffee. Black, please."

"Like the name, should be easy to remember." Margo chuckled. "Here's Annelie's office. Make yourself comfortable and I'll bring you some coffee and, hopefully, the woman herself."

Rushing off, the energetic woman left quite a void. Carolyn stepped into the corner office and looked around the room curiously. Ivory walls and peach and forest green furniture gave the room a feminine elegance. Dark peach drapes framed the large panoramic window overlooking Manhattan.

Several diplomas hung on the wall behind the desk, and a painting, which on closer examination proved to be an original, hung across the room. Carolyn had never heard of the painter, but the name Carl Larson sounded Scandinavian. This portrait of a woman holding a child, called "Idyllic Studio," soothed her. Turning around to sit down, Carolyn discovered two large posters. One was of a play she had actually seen a few years back, and the other…was of her. Or of her as Jo March, many years ago.

Not sure what to believe, Carolyn sat down on the couch only to rise again, feeling jittery. She scrutinized the empty desk, wondering if Annelie had already started working today.

Quick steps approached and Margo returned with a tray. The Spode china and Georgian silverware didn't surprise Carolyn. "Thank you," she managed. "Is she going to be long, do you think?"

"No, just give her a few minutes. Enjoy the coffee."

Margo smiled and left after pouring the black, steaming-hot beverage. Carolyn sat down again and sipped her coffee, comforted by the familiar, rejuvenating taste. Anticipating how the caffeine would enter her bloodstream, travel to her brain, and energize it, she finally began to calm down.

"Carolyn," a soft voice said from the doorway. Looking up, she had to force herself to carefully place the delicate coffee cup back on its saucer since her fingers had begun to tremble. "This is a surprise."

Annelie was dressed in a black pantsuit over a crisp white blouse. Silver-white pearls gleamed around her neck and in her earlobes, reflecting the light in an expensive, understated way. A larger pearl was attached to the jacket's left lapel. She wore a white gold watch on her left wrist, but no other jewelry on her hands.

This was another side of Annelie. Having become accustomed to seeing her only in casual clothes, Carolyn was awed as she looked at the professional vision before her. As she stood with her arms folded over her chest, her hair swept up in a tight twist without a strand out of place, Annelie looked untouchable.

"I need to talk to you, Annelie," Carolyn said, amazed at how calm she sounded. "I'm sorry to barge in here like this, but I didn't know how else to get in touch with you. I couldn't talk to you about this over the phone."

Annelie stepped inside and closed the door behind her. "You're right," she admitted. "We have to talk but not here, like this."

"I just flew in today. I went home to change and then came straight here. I...I just don't know what to think."

A slight frown marring her forehead, Annelie remained standing just inside the door. "I'd have thought you'd be paying a visit to your agent first, or hasn't he contacted you?"

"Grey? I talked to him when I was waiting for my flight in Miami. He told me about the contracts."

"I'm surprised you didn't go by and sign them right away."

Not sure if Annelie was being sarcastic, Carolyn recoiled. "I wanted to talk to you first. I'm amazed you're offering me the role. I've wanted it ever since the rumors about the movies started spreading. Now I'm all confused and—" She flung her hands into the air. "Damn it, Annie, I don't know what to think! You leave me behind with no explanation other than a note that makes me feel like...for heaven's sake—" She broke off again. "You're giving interviews talking about people auditioning for the role. What the hell's going on?"

Hearing her voice almost break, Carolyn forced herself to stop before she embarrassed herself further.

"I had important meetings here in New York," Annelie explained. "I can't talk now. I have to go back in there." She gestured vaguely behind her. "As for the media asking me questions at the airport yesterday—that was merely for the sake of appearances. Surely you realize that? We can't go public with who will star in the movies before the contracts are signed—and if you'd actually read the contracts before you came here, you would've seen we added a confidentiality clause. You won't be able to tell anyone you got the role until a certain date, when Supernova hosts a press conference with the director and the actors."

Carolyn noted that Annelie avoided the issue about leaving her alone in Orlando.

"I understand you're busy, but this is important too. When I called Grey from the cab on my way to my apartment, he almost bit my head off for not going directly to his office. It's just that I'm not so sure I *should* sign the contracts."

Annelie's eyes narrowed. "What are you talking about? What's the problem? They're standard contracts for this kind of project. You're the perfect choice for the role, and you've made it very clear you want it more than anything."

Carolyn lowered her eyes, a pang of guilt and other undefined emotions exploding in the pit of her stomach. "Not more than *anything*," she murmured.

"What do you mean?"

"Saturday night," Carolyn murmured huskily, "something more than the physical part of it happened. If signing the contracts drives a wedge between us…If it means I'll miss the opportunity to…"

Suddenly Annelie seemed to relax. Lowering her arms she walked over to Carolyn and gently touched her left shoulder. "Listen to me. I promise we'll talk, but not here. I won't be done until late this afternoon. Why don't we have dinner at my apartment? We can talk uninterrupted in a more private setting and," she gestured at herself with a faint smile, "in comfortable clothes."

Carolyn swallowed hard, forcing her breathing to become even. "Sounds good to me."

"And, Carolyn, do me a favor? Go by your agent and sign the

contracts. You're the one we want for the Maddox role. Nothing that's taken place between the two of us has anything to do with that, nor will it, in the future."

"All right." Carolyn's voice was noncommittal.

"Here, let me give you my home address." Annelie walked over to her desk and pulled out a small notepad and a pen. "I'll let the doorman know you're coming. How about sevenish?"

"See you tonight, then." Carolyn watched as Annelie turned to walk toward the door. She was elegance personified—the black suit tailored to fit her curvaceous body, the high heels adding to her length.

Annelie surprised Carolyn by stopping in front of her and raising a hand to cup her cheek. "Yes, see you then." After she disappeared out the door, Carolyn could hear her talking to someone outside. "On my way."

Carolyn reached for her coffee again, taking a large gulp of the still-warm liquid. Her eyes reverted to the *Little Women* poster on the wall, narrowing as she tried to figure out its potential importance. Something had made Annelie put this up in her office, and she was dying to know what it was. Adding it to the picture Annelie had of her in her house in Florida, Carolyn was indeed mystified.

"Everything all right, Ms. Black?" Margo poked her head through the half-open door. "Anything else I can do for you?"

Carolyn shook her head and put the coffee cup down. "No, thank you, Margo. I'm fine. I'll be going now, so thank you for being so obliging."

"Not a problem." She escorted Carolyn back to the reception area. "If you need a cab, this young lady will be glad to call the company we use."

"That would be great."

Margo motioned for the receptionist to make the call, smiled, and said goodbye to Carolyn before returning into the inner regions of the office.

"The cab will be here shortly."

"Thanks. I'll head downstairs, then."

Riding the elevator, Carolyn glanced at her reflection, noticing she had more color in her cheeks than when she'd arrived. Meeting Annelie for the first time after their night together had gone reasonably well.

Squaring her shoulders, Carolyn took a deep breath and willed herself not to return to her previous confused frame of mind. Right now she would take Annelie's advice and go by Grey's office. She had contracts to sign.

❖

Annelie pondered what to wear. Riffling through the rack of clothes in the walk-in closet, she let her fingertip bounce off the hangers and finally settled for dark blue stretch jeans and a white T-shirt.

She'd called for Italian takeout, though not pizza this time. Glancing at her watch, Annelie tried to ignore the butterflies cavorting in her stomach.

The doorbell startled her, making her drop her hairbrush. Chastising herself for being so jumpy, she picked it up and placed it on the dresser before walking to the front door and opening it.

Dressed in a long black coat, Carolyn looked completely calm as she leaned against the wall, one leg bent over the other, her arms crossed over her chest.

"Hi, Annelie," Carolyn said, a slow smile making goose bumps appear on the other woman's arms. "Colorful fellow downstairs. Chatty."

"Yes. He's quite a character, but somewhat overwhelming."

"I could tell. I think he likes me. I thought he was about to propose before I could escape to the elevator." Carolyn paused, raising an eyebrow. "May I come in?"

Blushing faintly, Annelie stepped aside. "Forgive me. Of course you can. I might as well level with you—I'm nervous."

Something vulnerable flickered across Carolyn's features before she smiled and patted Annelie's arm. "Don't worry, so am I."

"Want to look around the apartment?" Annelie asked, knowing she was stalling. "It's going to be another ten or fifteen minutes before our food gets here."

"I'd love to see your home. Lead the way."

Annelie took Carolyn's coat, noticing the other woman had changed into khaki chinos and a chocolate brown turtleneck. She started the grand tour by showing Carolyn the large living room with the open fireplace, then moving through the kitchen and the long hallway with oak parquet floors. The guest bedroom was decorated similarly to the one in Florida, but the rest of the apartment was more of a mix between East Coast style and Scandinavian influence. Walking toward the recreation room, Annelie looked at Carolyn as she opened the door, not about to miss the other woman's reaction to what was hiding behind it.

"Oh, my God. A pool!" Carolyn's jaw actually dropped.

"Thought you'd like it," Annelie grinned. "Actually, it's more than just a pool. It's called an Endless Pool. Let me show you."

She pressed a button next to the eighteen-by-eight-foot pool, causing the water to move.

"You swim against the current," Annelie explained.

Carolyn looked impressed. "You know about me and swimming…" She smiled.

"You're welcome to try it anytime." The words left Annelie's lips before she realized what she meant to say. The invitation hung between them, and Carolyn had opened her mouth to reply when the doorbell interrupted them.

"The food's here. We can finish the tour later." While switching off the controls to the pool, Annelie wondered if she sounded as relieved as she felt.

After she took the bags from the delivery woman, Annelie carried them out into the kitchen with Carolyn in tow.

"Did you mean it?" Carolyn's voice was low.

Not about to pretend she didn't understand what Carolyn meant, Annelie busied herself with the bags of food. "Of course I did. You can use the pool if you like." She took heated plates out of the oven and arranged their meals on them.

"You said anytime."

Pausing, Annelie shot Carolyn a glance. Carolyn looked serious, and she had an unreadable expression in her eyes.

"I meant that too."

Carolyn moved closer, standing next to Annelie at the counter. Frowning, she pressed her lips together before she spoke. "Why did you run? I mean, I can think of several reasons, and I have, ever since yesterday morning when I woke up alone."

Reaching for the bottle of Bettinelli chardonnay breathing on the counter, Annelie carried it over to the table she had set for two when she came home. Picking up the two plates, she motioned with her chin toward the table. "Please have a seat."

Carolyn complied, not taking her eyes off the other woman.

"I guess I did run. I panicked," Annelie admitted. "You must have seen by now how I live my life. Inviting you to stay at the garage apartment was out of character for me, but I wanted to help. Usually, I'm not this open with someone I hardly know."

"You've treated me very well," Carolyn allowed. "I know about your reputation for keeping a low profile."

"And I told you about my rule never to get involved with curious, married, or straight women."

"You saw me as all of the above, I assume. Until last Saturday." Carolyn speared a mushroom.

"Some of them, I still do." When she saw Carolyn flinch, Annelie regretted her harsh tone of voice. "And I was very angry with you for showing up uninvited and forcing my hand. You left us with no other choice but to allow you to hijack the convention."

"I'm not apologizing for fighting dirty when it comes to the Maddox role...but about what happened later...it certainly wasn't anything I had planned to do."

"And you still fit the description of women I stay away from." Annelie's voice sank.

"I'm aware of my ineptness in making love to another woman," Carolyn murmured. "However, you know by now Jared and I are just friends, and I've never questioned my sexual preference. I always assumed I was heterosexual. Until you."

Feeling bad for the hurt she detected within Carolyn, Annelie sighed. "*Ineptness* doesn't factor into it. I don't think you're that type of curious either. But you have a reputation for going after what you want—no holds barred."

"Yes, you're right. I have done that. I did that by showing up in Orlando. But ending up in bed with you was not part of my plan!"

Annelie stopped with the fork halfway to her mouth. "But we did."

"Yes. We did." Carolyn's voice became huskier. "We did. And now I don't know what to do."

"What do you mean?"

Carolyn hesitated and then shrugged. "I simply don't know how to proceed. I'm puzzled. I guess I should have second thoughts about what happened and disregard it, but I can't."

Cocking her head, Annelie reached for her wineglass. "That's a very honest reply."

"Coming from someone like me, you mean?" Carolyn made a face. "Will you give me an equally candid answer? Do you regret making love to me?"

Annelie was about to say yes, even knowing it wasn't true. Rolling the wine around in the glass, she stared down at the minivortex forming. "No, Carolyn, how could I?" she whispered. "You were beautiful… wonderful, in my arms."

"I've never experienced anything like it in my entire life," Carolyn confessed. "Nobody's ever made me feel that way. Nobody."

Something in Carolyn's voice gave Annelie courage to meet her gaze. To her surprise, the other woman's eyes shimmered a bright blue. "I couldn't resist you," Annelie admitted hoarsely. "I wanted to. I knew you might be in my arms for all the wrong reasons."

"What reasons are those?"

"You have a reputation for being an opportunist, Carolyn. The last few weeks, I've felt your interest and just didn't know what to make of it."

"*My* interest?" Carolyn raised her voice. "Your interest in me is just as plain!"

Annelie carefully put her utensils down and leaned back in the chair. "What are you talking about?"

"I'm talking about the picture of me, a very young me, on your desk at the house in Florida. I'm talking about the old theater poster of me when I did *Little Women* that I saw in your office today. It's a little too obvious to be a coincidence."

Annelie felt herself pale. She rubbed her forehead, looking into Carolyn's angry eyes. "Touché."

"You've obviously followed my career." Carolyn sounded calmer. "Want to tell me about it?"

"You'll laugh."

"Maybe, but who cares. It's just the two of us." Carolyn sipped her wine. "Fire away."

"When I was twelve, my mother was holding two jobs to support us. During the summer break, I began watching *The Passing of Time*. I fell in love with you as Devon. The network aired reruns every weekend and I didn't miss a single episode. I would watch every Sunday morning, five episodes in a row. Whenever you were in a scene, I'd move closer to the TV, watching your every move, every facial expression. When you quit the show, I was devastated and stopped watching it. I kept track of your career from a distance, watched your TV movies and feature films, as well as all the other appearances you made, like talk shows and so on."

"I'm flattered, Annelie. I really am. What's there to laugh about?"

"I was trying to get to know you through the media, even though I realized that image couldn't capture all of you. You're as private as I am, if not more so. There's very little known about your family, other than the basic stuff, which I respect completely. When I said you have a reputation for being an opportunist, I meant it literally—a *reputation*. I'm aware of how wrong it can be but, then again, it's all I had to go by."

Carolyn frowned. "I went by my agent's and signed the contracts. I don't want you to misunderstand. I'd rather tear them up if signing them somehow means losing your friendship…"

"No, Carolyn, I'm not sure why you think I'd ask you to make such a sacrifice. Don't even consider it."

"Because you left the note the way you did. It suggested you thought I'd seduced you to get the role, and this was your way of saying *I'm on to you*. The night was so wonderful. Nothing we did or felt gave me reason to think otherwise—but the note did. You say you want nothing but honesty from me, and the truth is, the note was like finding money on the nightstand. It hurt like hell."

"I'm sorry, Carolyn. I should have stayed. I'm normally not such a coward." Annelie pressed her lips together. "The note was a bad idea and certainly not meant to hurt you." Noticing Carolyn had barely touched her meal, she gave up on the idea of eating. "Why don't we put the food away and sit on the couch and talk?"

Carolyn nodded. "Yes, please. It's delicious and deserves more attention."

They put their meals in the refrigerator and then walked into the living room. Annelie motioned toward the big leather couch by the fireplace. "Want a blanket?"

"Yes. I'm cold for some reason." Carolyn nodded.

Annelie took a wool blanket from the armchair next to the couch and spread it across both of their laps as she sat down next to Carolyn.

"Better? Good. Now listen to me. You're perfect for the role. The convention proved it. Everyone in the audience identified you as Diana Maddox. You're a most professional, conscientious actress, and your reputation in that respect is impeccable. Of course, some of your female colleagues have made catty personal remarks about you, and a few men have made acid comments, probably because you've turned them down. I can't think of anyone else doing a better job with Maddox than you."

Carolyn looked stunned. "And personally? You idolized me for years, and now that you've known me for more than a month, are you disappointed?"

Thinking to herself, *In for a penny, in for a pound*, Annelie inhaled deeply and slowly exhaled. "You're more than I ever thought."

❖

Carolyn studied the telltale pink cheeks of her hostess. Annelie looked embarrassed but also strangely relieved after her confession.

"In true Hollywood manner, I have no problem calling perfect strangers *darling*, *sweetheart*, and *honey*." Carolyn smiled ruefully. "And now, when it counts, all I can think of is I called you *Annie* last Saturday."

"Yes, you did."

"Did you mind?"

"No, not at all, coming from you. You must've realized how... turned on I was by everything you said."

"That was another new thing for me," Carolyn admitted. "I've never been that vocal in bed before."

"Your voice is amazing. Now—your turn." Annelie leaned her head against the backrest, her legs pulled up underneath her.

Carolyn knew she had to stay truthful or she would lose any of the ground she had gained.

"I've always considered myself heterosexual, though I've had plenty of chances to experiment. I simply wasn't interested in the women who came on to me, so I didn't need to reflect on my sexual preference until I met you. In the kitchen, when we were fixing dessert, I didn't mean to try and kiss you. I just had this overwhelming urge and—"

"And I pulled back."

"I thought I'd offended you. When you explained, I was prepared to accept and respect your standpoint." Carolyn smiled ruefully. "After the convention, which frankly was quite the ego trip, I was on such an emotional high. I was feeling giddy, excited, and simply unable to wind down. When we were on the couch together and you looked so beautiful...oh, God, Annelie..." Reaching out for support, Carolyn took the other woman's hand in hers. "I was hot and cold at the same time, and more so, I knew I had to hold you. I had no ulterior motives, no thoughts of the next day. I can be a calculating bitch, but I had no plans to seduce you, I swear."

Annelie studied her for a moment, as if trying to make up her mind. "I want to believe you. What I couldn't believe, though, was how your voice, the look on your face, made me feel. I was about to pull back, to leave you alone to watch TV, when I saw the passion in your eyes."

"You did pull back, in a way. You never let me touch you, Annie." The words were hard to say. Carolyn cleared her throat. "I was naked but you never fully undressed."

"Self-preservation. I was trying to protect myself somehow." Annelie paused. "I thought, if she touches me, like I used to fantasize, I'll break. It wasn't because I didn't want you to. I was afraid."

"I wanted to touch you, the same way you caressed me, so much. I wanted to know how it felt to make love to you. Not just any woman. You."

Annelie's eyes welled up with tears. Blinking them away, she squeezed Carolyn's hand hard before she let go. "Me?"

Carolyn rose on her knees on the couch. Framing Annelie's face with her hands, she didn't take her eyes off her lover. "You. I'll go out on the proverbial limb now and tell you the truth. I have to."

Annelie swallowed and pressed her lips together into a thin line. "Will I like it?" she whispered huskily.

"I don't know. You might feel awkward or look at me with pity. Or you might give me a chance, despite your principles." Carolyn let one of her hands stroke Annelie's hair down to her ponytail. Freeing it from the large hair clip, she watched as the blond abundance cascaded down around Annelie's shoulders. "I'm falling for you, Annie. I really am."

Annelie gave a muted gasp.

"It's true," Carolyn repeated.

Annelie suddenly rose, making Carolyn's hands fall into her lap. She paced back and forth in front of the couch a couple of times, making

Carolyn hold her breath, fearing she'd overstepped the final boundary and made her presence in Annelie's life impossible.

"Please, Annie." Her voice was merely a whisper.

Annelie stopped pacing and knelt in front of her guest. "I have to be blunt, Carolyn. This whole situation scares the living daylights out of me. I'm independent and treasure my freedom. I keep to myself for a lot of reasons. Now…having you here…I'm afraid! You have a reputation for doing just about anything to get what you want—even if it means sleeping your way to it. How can I possibly know this isn't just part of your plan?"

Knowing there could be no excuses if she was going to stand a chance with Annelie, Carolyn reached out and pulled the visibly distraught woman up next to her on the couch. "Some of those rumors are true, and I deserve to be criticized for some of the things I've done, especially in my younger days. But listen to me. This is important.

"I have never cheated on anyone. I have never had a one-night stand with anyone to get ahead. I've schemed and also lied, fought tooth and nail for roles, but I've never willingly or deliberately lied about personal feelings.

"Grey constantly tells me I'm too frank for this business—he could be right." Forcing herself to stay calm, Carolyn sighed. "I care about you. I don't want to lose what I've found with you. That's why I'd rather tear up the contracts than risk—"

"No, don't even say that." Annelie's eyes probed hers. "If I'm to take a chance on you…on this…it will be my decision, based on how I feel—not on how much you're prepared to prove or give up."

Carolyn held her breath when Annelie leaned forward, sliding her hand underneath Carolyn's hair, caressing the soft skin on her neck.

"Carolyn, tell me. Will you spend the night? Will you sleep next to me and, I mean, just sleep? Things are moving too fast, and I'm afraid of doing the wrong thing. I don't want you to go, but I don't want us to rush headlong into it—making love. Not yet. Last Saturday we ended up in something way too soon. We couldn't resist each other, and we risked destroying a budding friendship and a great working relationship. Now, as I said, I don't want you to go. Please stay?"

Taken aback, Carolyn nodded. "I don't want to go either. I'd love to stay all night. We'll take it slow. We can take it at any pace you like or feel comfortable with, just as long as you know I'm sincere."

Annelie looked intently at Carolyn. "There's still so much to settle, to learn, about each other. Is it enough for you if I say I believe in your good intentions?"

Carolyn realized this was the most she could hope for at this point. "Yes."

Suddenly Annelie blushed faintly, looking down at her hands before raising her gaze again.

"You can have the guest room, if you prefer. I didn't mean to assume…"

"Shh. I want to sleep next to you. I don't want the guest room."

❖

Annelie watched Carolyn approach the king-size bed. After they had finished their reheated meal, they had listened to soft music, both of them lost in thought, until bedtime. Annelie's mind had wandered to how Carolyn had sounded, asking Annelie to trust her motives, without sounding pleading or begging. The whisky voice rose and fell, its timbre setting off the strangest sensations inside her. It was the voice she had admired for so long and yet completely different. Mulling it over, Annelie had finally realized the new qualities, the urgent tone, in the famous voice had been the sincerity so clearly present. *And here she comes, dressed in one of my T-shirts. Oh, God, she looks so innocent, shy almost…and so sexy.*

Carolyn climbed into bed, the fragrance of Annelie's citrus shower gel clinging to her. As she looked at Annelie hesitantly, she raised an eyebrow. "So, where do you want me?"

Annelie gave a faint smile. "Right here. Any way you want."

Poking at the big pile of pillows, Carolyn pushed a large one encased in a satin pillowcase close to Annelie's right shoulder. Then she settled down next to Annelie without touching her.

"Comfy yet?"

"Getting there." Carolyn moved around a bit.

"May I assist you, ma'am?" Annelie joked, trying to take some of the tension away.

"I'm all right, I just…I usually fall asleep on my right side."

Annelie's chest filled with tenderness when she realized Carolyn was feeling shyer than she let on. "Then lie down on your right side.

There, that's it." She moved until she could almost feel Carolyn's back. "Lift your head." She pushed her arm under the pillow. "Now lie down again."

She adjusted her position, spooning behind Carolyn, her right arm under her neck, her left hand stretched down along Carolyn's thigh, touching the naked skin just below the hem of her T-shirt, though feeling no sexual sparks.

"Comfy?" Annelie repeated.

"Oh, yes," Carolyn sighed. "Very."

Placing a tender kiss on the auburn hair, Annelie closed her eyes. Nothing could have prepared her for this day. She was playing it by ear now, completely against her normal method of operation.

Carolyn stirred slightly. "Good night, Annie. Sleep tight."

"You too."

CHAPTER TEN

Jazz music seemed to come out of nowhere. Carolyn stirred, unsure of where she was until she managed to open her eyes and see blond hair cascading across the pillow next to her. Lifting her gaze further, she looked at Annelie's relaxed face, realizing she was still asleep.

"Annelie." Carolyn gently rubbed the naked shoulder next to her. "Annie, your alarm clock says it's time to get up."

Slowly ice blue eyes opened, and the head next to her turned. "Carolyn?"

"Yeah, time to wake up."

Obviously still half-asleep, Annelie rolled toward Carolyn and wrapped a slender arm around her waist. "Good morning."

"Good morning." Carolyn's heart raced as she inhaled Annelie's sweet scent. Unable to resist, she buried her face against her neck, amazed at the softness. "Did you sleep well?"

"Very well. And you?" Annelie whispered, stroking her hands up and down Carolyn's back.

"Dead to the world. I don't even remember dreaming."

Annelie rose on one elbow and looked down at Carolyn. "You look rested," she murmured. "You look wonderful."

"You're beautiful any time of day, but I don't think I've ever seen you look this way." Carolyn traced Annelie's face with soft fingertips. "No makeup, no jewelry…just you."

Annelie smiled faintly and placed a gentle kiss on Carolyn's forehead. "Time to get up, I'm afraid. I have meetings all day."

Carolyn glanced at the alarm clock again. "Seven o'clock…I guess I should go home and change before I meet Grey. He wants to go over some business details with me."

Annelie stood up and stretched. Looking at Carolyn, she hesitated. "Want to have lunch today? There's a nice restaurant a block from the office."

Carolyn smiled broadly and rose from the bed. "I'd love to. What time?"

Walking up to Carolyn, Annelie wrapped her arms around her. "How about one o'clock?" She kissed the top of Carolyn's head. "You want to hear something silly? I was about to suggest dinner tonight… but suddenly I didn't think I could wait that long."

"That's not silly," Carolyn objected. "So, do you want to have dinner tonight?"

"Yes. We need to talk more, don't you agree?"

"I do. And I want to look at you. I can't seem to get enough of that."

Placing her fingertips under Carolyn's chin, Annelie tipped her head back. She leaned down, kissing her with more tenderness than passion. "We promised to go slow," she murmured. "Is this slow enough, Carolyn?"

Wrapping her arms around Annelie's slender waist, Carolyn rubbed her cheek against her silky tank top after returning the soft kiss. She was still stunned at how Annelie filled her with equal parts of passion, joy, and fear. "Yes, this is slow enough for me."

❖

"So you're meeting Carolyn Black for lunch?" Margo asked while she poured them another cup of tea. She glanced at Annelie. "Is that why you're blushing, girlie?"

Annelie dropped the Sweet'n Low dispenser dangerously close to the cup. "What?" She fiddled with the sweeteners before managing to add one to her tea.

"Aw, come on, Annelie. I've known you all your life. You practically bounce in here, cheeks flushed, eyes aglow…I'm not blind."

"And certainly not subtle in your approach," Annelie smirked. "All right. I'm silly enough to be giddy about having lunch with Carolyn."

Margo studied her, making Annelie smile sheepishly. "Want to talk about it?" She raised an eyebrow.

Annelie had worked hard all morning and already finished a productive meeting with her associates. On a small break with Margo in her office, she leaned back against the couch and kicked off her pumps.

"She's all wrong for me," Annelie confessed, "but I can't stop thinking about her. I simply want to be around her as much as I can."

"Are you in love?"

Annelie's heart stopped, only to race a second later, pumping color to her cheeks. "I guess I am."

"I thought Carolyn Black was straight."

"So did I. And she. Now we're both confused." Tracing the rim of her cup with a finger, Annelie sighed before continuing. "She says she's falling for me. We talked all of yesterday evening, and she was very blunt, making no excuses. Still, I'm afraid. I just don't know if I can trust her. Her reputation isn't exactly encouraging."

"It's a reputation, not a universal truth. Whatever she did in the past—we know nothing about her motivation, and she certainly didn't do any of it toward you."

"I know."

"We can all change. Things can happen in our lives that change everything. You of all people should know that, Annelie." Margo's voice was soft. "You won all that money, and it was the start of your new life."

Annelie knew the other woman was right. Margo had been with her every step of the way, even long before she began creating a new life for herself. "I've known Carolyn for about a month and have become good at spotting when she's in her professional skin and when she's just herself. Last Saturday after the convention, as well as last night, she was herself. She let down her guard with me in a way that took courage."

"You must be important to her."

Annelie sipped her tea. "I believe I am. She stayed the night, and the way she fit in my arms..." She could feel herself blush and was unable to stop a smile. "And before you ask, no, nothing happened."

"Oh, girlie, you've got it bad." Margo returned the smile, cupping Annelie's chin. "I swear, if I thought for a second Carolyn had a hidden agenda, I wouldn't say this. I've seen people circle you like predators, out for your money, influence, or your endorsement for whatever product they're hustling. I don't believe she's one of them. Seeing her come here, practically straight from the airport, gave me the impression very little else but you mattered to her."

Annelie's eyes widened at Margo's candid words. The Irishwoman was not easily fooled, and to hear her speak this openly about Carolyn meant a lot.

"Anyway, I have no idea where this is going," Annelie confessed, "but I know I'm not about to let her slip away from me. I've dreamed about getting to know her for years. Now that I'm starting to, she's everything I thought and more."

"Then go to lunch with her, talk to her, and learn who she really is."

"I will." Annelie glanced at her watch. "I've got a few more things to do, and then I'm out of here for an hour or so."

Margo drank the last of her tea and winked as she set the cup down. "Have fun."

❖

Grey Parker rushed through the reception area, greeting Carolyn as soon as she stepped inside the door.

"There you are!" He beamed before turning to his assistant. "Camilla. Bring us some coffee and those chocolate biscotti, please."

Guiding Carolyn into his office, the balding agent grinned at her. "So, sweetheart, I'm taking the best care of you possible. I had Camilla work out the details yesterday. She printed your schedule for the three films and the conventions. You'll be busy the next three years, darling, but not to worry. It's a comfortable pace. You start preparing to shoot *Dying for Fame* in about two weeks." He pulled out a chair for Carolyn.

"Have you gotten the script yet? Any news of who's going to play Erica Becker and Gordon Fisher?"

"I've got it all under control. Chatted up Greg Horton, of course. You'll all get your scripts Friday at the big press conference at the Pierre." He handed Carolyn a document. "Here's the schedule for that, by the way. Starts at two o'clock on the dot, and the media will get a chance to talk to you, Harvey Davidson, and Helen St. Cyr."

"I was hoping for Helen and Harvey." Carolyn smiled broadly. "Will we do individual interviews or a joint session?"

"Just a joint session at this point. Horton's saving the individual interviews for the premiere. You know—Leno, Letterman, Conan, the works. You're going to be very busy, my dear. I also renegotiated the contracts for the three commercials you were supposed to do for the Volvo Corporation. Have to earn my keep, you know."

Carolyn had to laugh at her agent's obvious delight. She remembered how she, as a young actress, had practically stalked him until he agreed to see her. Their cooperation had been fruitful during the years, and now she considered him a friend.

"Good. I'm still trying to wrap my brain around the fact I'm going to play Maddox, let alone all the stuff that comes with it," Carolyn confessed. "I can't even begin to fathom the idea that this is just the beginning."

"You'll be identified as Maddox worldwide, sweetheart. The books have already been translated into ten languages. The Internet will probably overflow with rumors the next few days."

Carolyn smiled, shaking her head. "From what I experienced with the Maddox fans at the convention, there's no doubt about that." She reached for her bag. "Well, I'm on my way to have lunch, so I'll get out of your hair. Do you have the contracts I signed handy, by the way? I can take them with me."

Grey raised his eyebrows. "I told Camilla to send them by courier down to Supernova."

"I'm lunching with Annelie Peterson, so thought I'd give them directly to her."

Fortunately the courier hadn't arrived yet, so Camilla handed Carolyn the thick envelope containing Supernova's copies.

As Grey walked her to the door, he gave Carolyn's shoulders a friendly squeeze. "My best to the lovely Ms. Peterson, my dear."

"Of course."

Walking out the door and crossing the hallway to reach the elevators, Carolyn was already thinking about Annelie. It was only hours since they'd parted after a quick cup of coffee, and yet she couldn't wait to see her.

❖

Annelie spotted Carolyn taking a sip of mineral water and smiled as she glided toward her famous friend.

"Hi, you."

"Hi." Annelie sat down next to Carolyn. "How's your day going?"

"Fine, thanks. Before I forget, I've got something for you." Carolyn reached into her bag. "Here are your copies."

"The contracts?" Annelie put them in her briefcase.

"Signed, sealed, and delivered," Carolyn quipped. "When I went by Grey's office, I realized how many plans I have to change to do these movies. It's a good thing I'd put off committing to any major projects after my last season."

"I'm glad you were available. I did check your schedule before I offered you the role, though. Just to be sure you wouldn't delay the project."

"I've never broken a contract in my life, but this could have been a first."

Annelie wrinkled her nose at the cheeky gleam in Carolyn's eyes. Knowing Carolyn's reputation for complete professionalism, she doubted it.

"Speaking of contracts," Carolyn continued, "I'm so glad to be working with some of the audiobook cast, especially Harvey and Helen." She paused. "Did they know during the convention?"

"Actually, they signed a few weeks ago, but they have a confidentiality clause too. Choosing Diana Maddox was the last piece of the puzzle. Your performance at the convention ended any doubts on that score."

"Thank you. So, how was your morning?"

"Very productive. We're trying to start new homeless shelters in several cities. It's just typical that several of my pet projects come to a critical point simultaneously." Annelie smiled and cocked her head. "And before you ask, yes, you're one of them."

Not sure how Carolyn would take the joke, she was delighted when the other woman tossed her head back and laughed. Several heads in the restaurant turned, and Annelie suddenly felt proud to be the one there with Carolyn. Of all the people who adored Carolyn Black, Annelie was the one who'd spent the night with her and was the center of her attention.

"So I'm a pet project." Carolyn grinned. "Well, I take that as a true compliment."

"Good. Now, have you ordered?"

"No, I waited for you. I peeked at the menu, though. The pasta looks tempting, but I don't know…Should I start watching my weight again?"

"Absolutely not. You're perfect, and if you're thinking of the role, remember your character is a real woman, not a supermodel."

Carolyn raised an eyebrow and pursed her lips. "So you mean I shouldn't try to look like something I'm not?"

Appalled before realizing Carolyn was yanking her chain, Annelie groaned. "Funny. You know what I mean. Be yourself. A little more you, a little less Carolyn Black."

As soon as she'd said the words, Annelie understood something about her final casting decision. It was not Carolyn's glamorous public persona that made her ideal for Maddox; it was her private self, the woman Annelie was coming to know. The fact that Carolyn could thrill the film's target audience would certainly help convince distributors to get on board with her, but the role itself needed the real person.

To her surprise, Annelie felt a soft caress along her stocking-clad leg under the table. Staring at Carolyn, she didn't see any indication the other woman was guilty of the furtive touch. "What are you up to?" she murmured, opening the menu.

"Me? Nothing. Except being myself, of course."

The foot kept up the caress, well hidden by the long white tablecloth. When it reached her knee, Annelie quickly grabbed it and tickled underneath. Watching Carolyn bite her lower lip, probably to keep from giggling, she let go after a stern look. "Behave."

"I would've, if you hadn't winked at me when you said it," Carolyn replied sweetly, but relented. "Okay, for now."

Amazed at Carolyn's unexpected playful side, Annelie tried to focus on the menu. Glancing up, she caught Carolyn looking at her with a warm expression.

"Are you going to the next convention?" Carolyn asked after they ordered pasta. "I went over the next month of commitments with Grey, and Los Angeles is coming up in less than four weeks."

"Yes, I'll be there. I haven't been to California in quite a while, so it'll be fun."

"I think so too. I usually stay there several months a year when I'm filming, but I haven't been at all this year."

Annelie gazed at her. "Do I take it you'd like me to be there?"

"Of course I would. I can't think of anyone I'd rather be with."

Feeling warmed inside by Carolyn's remark, Annelie fought to keep the exchange casual. "I'll arrange for all of us to travel from LaGuardia. This time, the crew from Florida won't go. Jem told me they're up to their necks with work. She sounded exhausted." Annelie shook her head.

"Jem's a good friend of yours from way back, isn't she?"

Annelie nodded. "I've known her since I was nineteen. When I moved to New York, she followed suit, and we shared an apartment the first months. And, no, Jem and I were never lovers." She smiled at Carolyn's sheepish look.

"I wasn't going to ask."

"But you wondered."

"Yes."

Annelie appreciated the honest reply and, slipping out of her shoes, gently tapped one of Carolyn's feet, making her jump. "It's okay to be interested."

As they ate in silence for a few minutes, Annelie wondered how much Carolyn knew of her past, how much Jared might have told her.

"What about you? Who's your oldest friend?" Annelie broke the silence.

Carolyn looked surprised. She opened her mouth as if to answer, but hesitated. "I guess my sister Beth is my best friend."

"I always wanted a brother or a sister." Annelie's voice was wistful. "I grew up in a neighborhood with lots of children, though. There was always someone to play with."

Carolyn only nodded and smiled. "I was a very serious child. I didn't have much time to play."

Though this last statement sparked Annelie's interest, she realized this wasn't the time or place to pursue it. She and Carolyn would have plenty of time to get to know each other.

"About dinner tonight..." Annelie began, her eyes narrowing at Carolyn's expectant look.

"Yes?"

Carolyn seemed as anxious about the future of their relationship as she was. "Is it okay if we just stay at the apartment? I'd planned for us to eat out, but on second thought, perhaps we need our privacy to talk."

Carolyn seemed to relax. "I like the idea of having you to myself." Blushing faintly, she paused before continuing. "Do you want me to… stay the night?"

"I'd love for you to stay, just like last night."

"All right." Carolyn leaned back against the leather backrest. "When do you want me?"

Annelie wanted to groan out loud at the other woman's ability to talk in double entendres. Not convinced Carolyn was unaware of it, she pushed her empty plate aside and leaned in closer across the table.

"Any time after seven o'clock."

❖

Carolyn leaned down and let her fingertip lightly bounce along Annelie's CD collection. Jazz, classical, musicals, pop, and rock—Annelie had an eclectic taste in music. She selected Ella Fitzgerald, one of her favorite singers, letting the legendary voice calm her nerves.

"Good choice," Annelie said as she entered the living room carrying two large coffee mugs. "Want to sit out on the balcony?"

"Sure, it's a nice evening."

Annelie placed the coffee on a small table in front of a cane furniture suite and then walked over to a console by the door. After she pressed a few buttons, Ella's voice drowned out the distant noise of the traffic. Carolyn sat down on the soft cushions.

"Not too loud? Good." Annelie sat next to Carolyn. "It's been a while since I've been out here. I try to stay in Florida as much as I can, but I make sure the apartment is ready at a moment's notice."

"The view's wonderful." Carolyn reached for a mug and sipped the strong coffee. "Mmm, I needed this."

Annelie tilted her head to one side. "So, is it beginning to sink in yet—you playing Maddox?"

"Yes, and I meant to ask you, is it okay if I tell Beth and Joe? They won't tell anyone."

"That's fine. I trust your judgment. Does your sister know you were interested in the role?"

"I'm not sure, really. Our conversations have mostly been about her recently. So giving her something else to think about is probably a good thing."

Annelie angled her body toward Carolyn, pulling one leg up underneath her. "What does your sister do for a living?"

"Beth's a registered nurse."

"A nurse? She must possess a special kind of strength."

Carolyn stopped with the mug halfway to her mouth. "Yes," she said, "I think you're right. I guess I'm rather protective where she's concerned, since I raised her."

"I can understand that. What's her husband like?"

"Joe's a great guy and adores Beth and Pamela. He's not overly impressed with my fame, either, which makes it possible to talk to him like a human being. Actually, he treats me more like a sister than John does."

"John's an artist, isn't he?"

"Yes. I haven't seen him in a while. His choice more than mine. When he's in one of his creative phases, he treats me like a leper. You know, I'm so commercial I might contaminate his process." Carolyn smirked. "Personally, I think he's going through either a midlife crisis or a seriously delayed puberty."

Annelie smiled but didn't avert her eyes. "That's hard to take, isn't it?"

Carolyn shrugged. "Jokes aside, it feels like a rejection. I've always been proud of him and for some reason…" Her voice trailed off. "I'm not so sure he feels the same way."

Annelie reached out and took Carolyn's hand. "You have every reason to be proud of your success."

"Thanks, and I am. I've worked hard. Sometimes John seems to think I worked *too* hard at mothering him and Beth over the years. He was really angry after our father died."

"That was a long time ago."

"Yes, but he's still stubborn as a mule. It was easier with Beth. She just remembers losing one parent, not two."

Annelie pulled Carolyn's head onto her shoulder and encircled her with an arm. Resting her chin on Carolyn's head, she said in a low voice, "I know what it's like to lose a parent. My mother died when I was seventeen. In my case, my only parent."

"What about your father?"

"He left us when I was a little girl. I have no idea where he is. Sometimes I wonder, but I try not to dwell on it."

"That's so sad, Annelie. I'm sorry." Carolyn relaxed against her, inhaling the faint smell of lemon and enjoying the soft warmth of Annelie's skin above the neckline of her T-shirt.

"Have you thought about what we discussed last night?" Annelie asked. "About us?"

Annelie's faint tone of caution worried Carolyn. "Yes, but I wanted to tell you this first. I slept better last night than I have in a long time. Sure, I woke up a few times and didn't know where I was. But when I felt your arms around me, I went right back to sleep."

Full lips pressed against her hair, making Carolyn sigh and wrap one arm around Annelie's waist.

"I thought about you all day at work," Annelie murmured. "Margo picked up on it. She knows me so well. I told her about you. No details, of course, but she knows I'm interested. You don't have to worry. She'd never tell anyone."

"Does she know it's mutual?"

Annelie paused briefly. "Yes."

Carolyn tipped her head back, wanting to see Annelie's face. "What did she say?"

"That I should give you a chance. Give *us* a chance, really. She told me to form my own opinion about you."

"Smart lady. I like her."

"Margo isn't easily swayed. I could tell she was impressed by you. And I was too. It took a lot of courage to come find me yesterday."

Carolyn felt her cheeks grow warm. "I had to."

Raising a hand, Annelie traced her lover's lower lip. Suddenly finding it hard to catch her breath, Carolyn opened her mouth and inhaled deeply.

"So…" Carolyn's voice trailed off as she tried to focus. "What did you think…when you thought about me today?" She was afraid of the answer.

Annelie's hair tumbled down over her right shoulder as she turned her head to one side. As her fingers traced the arch of Carolyn's left eyebrow, she murmured, "Hearing your voice first thing in the morning. Waking up in the night, snuggled up behind you, how easily I could—" Annelie broke off.

"Could what?" Carolyn coaxed after a minute of silence.

"Could get used to you being there."

Tenderness overflowing at Annelie's apprehensive tone, Carolyn raised both hands to cup her face. "Oh, Annie," she whispered. "I don't know what to say to reassure you. I just know how right this feels, how much I want to hold on to you."

"What if you decide this isn't for you after all? What if you stumble on a man who can give you everything? What if another role comes along and you…It would hurt me so much, Carolyn. I don't think I could take it."

She knew Annelie's fear was talking, so Carolyn placed her fingertips over her lips. "Shh." Shifting on the couch, she pulled Annelie closer. "Life doesn't offer many guarantees. But I can't imagine ever feeling this way about anyone else, male or female. I've never felt this way before."

The tiny light that appeared in Annelie's eyes encouraged Carolyn to continue.

"There will always be roles I want, and I'll probably be prepared to walk through fire to get them. But I promise I won't do anything without talking with you.

"Doing the Maddox films, I'll have the luxury of being financially independent, so I can wait and pick the roles I really want. You know…I dream of going onstage again, doing a play, maybe in a small format."

"So, no big productions after Maddox?"

"Oh, I never say *never*—perhaps, if the script and the circumstances are right. I simply can't imagine doing anything that doesn't involve you." Carolyn felt tears sting behind her eyelids. "I'm beginning to understand I don't have to run anymore."

"What do you mean, run?"

"I've run to or from things so many times. I admit it's a rare feeling, and I'm a little afraid, but it feels so good to be where I want to be."

"And where is that?" Annelie asked gently.

Carolyn tipped her head back, looking into the ice blue eyes. "Here, in your arms, in your life." Unable to resist, she took Annelie's hand and raised it to her lips, placing a soft kiss on the fingertips.

Annelie's eyes darkened, her lips parting as she inhaled deeply. "Carolyn," she murmured and slid her fingers along Carolyn's cheek, moving up into her hair.

Closing her eyes, Carolyn felt satin-smooth lips brush her forehead, dip down to kiss her eyelids, then follow her nose, only to bypass her lips. Annelie nuzzled her cheeks, kissing her way down Carolyn's neck and making her sigh when pleasure rippled down her spine.

"Oh, God...don't tease," Carolyn breathed. "Kiss me." She opened her eyes enough to see the desire in Annelie's before her lover claimed her mouth.

Carolyn's eyes fluttered shut again when she parted her lips, allowing Annelie access. Tongues met, played, and tasted the softness, their passion overwhelming. Carolyn drew Annelie closer and felt strong hands move over her back and pull her silk blouse loose from her slacks. With slow caresses Annelie stroked up and down underneath her clothes. Wanting to experience the same, Carolyn slid her arms down along Annelie's back.

As she suddenly remembered how Annelie had avoided her touch in Orlando, Carolyn stopped and held her breath. Feeling utterly clumsy, she withdrew, ending the kiss.

Annelie didn't let go completely, but gave Carolyn some space. "You okay?"

"Yes."

Annelie scrutinized her. "Really? I can see there's something."

Carolyn swallowed hard and tried to smile, failing miserably. "I'm sorry, I...I want to touch you, but I was afraid you'd pull back, like before." Her heart pounded in her chest, as she waited to see how Annelie would react. To her surprise, Annelie rose from the couch, still holding her hands.

"Come with me. It's getting chilly out here. No, no, leave the coffee—it can wait till tomorrow."

Silently, Annelie circled Carolyn's shoulders with her arm and guided her toward the bedroom. The room was lit by two small bedside lamps, which cast a soft glow on the walls. Stopping at the foot of the bed, Annelie turned toward Carolyn and held her gently at half an arm's length.

"I wasn't about to pull back, not this time. We agreed to take things slow, as slow as it takes to still feel comfortable, but you can still touch me any way you want."

Her mouth suddenly dry, Carolyn tried to moisten her lips with the tip of her tongue. "I feel clumsy."

"You're not." Annelie pulled Carolyn's arms around her waist. "Here. Hold me." She buried both her hands in Carolyn's hair.

Carolyn rubbed her cheek against Annelie's shoulder, again inhaling the faint scent of her citrus soap. Her hands slipped under the T-shirt, and she spread her fingers wide, trying to feel as much of Annelie's smooth skin as possible. Stroking up and down along her back, she reveled in how exquisite Annelie felt. Carolyn moved her hands up farther, finding the clasp to Annelie's bra. Her fingers lingered there, carefully examining it.

"You can unhook it, if you want," Annelie whispered, gently pulling Carolyn's head back, kissing her lips.

Carolyn gave a muted gasp but managed to undo the white lace bra. With no obstacle in the way, she slid her hands up and down the satiny skin. "You feel wonderful," she murmured. "Simply wonderful."

Annelie let go of Carolyn for a moment and pulled her own T-shirt over her head, taking her bra along with it.

All Carolyn could do was look. Annelie's full breasts were pale compared to the rest of her slightly tanned body, with plump, pink nipples, now pebbled and, she hoped, eager to be touched. Carolyn lifted her gaze, looking up at Annelie, who stood there half naked, with her hair tousled, trusting her.

"Annie..." She raised her hands, cupping Annelie's shoulders, pulling her closer and kissing her right collarbone. "I'm not sure this qualifies as taking it slow, but I'm certainly not uncomfortable." Turning her head sideways, she nuzzled the curve of the soft breast.

"Me either." Annelie's voice was husky. "Mmm."

With reverence, Carolyn lowered her hands and cautiously cupped the full breasts, tingling as she touched Annelie in this intimate way. The hard nipples pushed against her palms, making her want to explore precisely how rigid they could become. Her own breasts ached to be touched, but she focused on Annelie, absorbed with the feel of her body.

As she moved her hands in slow circles, the puckered skin tightened even more. "Am I doing this right?" Carolyn was breathless and a trembling smile formed on her lips. "Do you like it like this?" Her fingers tweaked the nipples in a way she herself liked.

Annelie swayed and held on tighter to Carolyn's shoulders. "Yes, yes...please, I need to...sit down."

"Here, let's get undressed first," Carolyn suggested, suddenly feeling self-confident. She unbuttoned her own blouse and pulled it off and was reaching for the clasp of her bra between her breasts when Annelie's hands stopped her.

"Let me." Annelie unhooked Carolyn's black satin bra, her eyes locked on the skin she was revealing. She reached down and undid Carolyn's slacks, pushing them down slender hips.

Standing before Annelie, Carolyn felt her heart overflow with emotions. Fast-growing tenderness rose within her, along with the arousal stirring deep inside. She trembled, unable to take her eyes off the enticing curves before her.

Annelie undressed until she too was wearing only sheer white panties. "Are we going too fast?" she whispered.

"I think we are," Carolyn allowed, her voice throatier than usual. "I just don't know how to slow down or stop. I can't even remember why I should..."

She pulled Annelie into a firm embrace, their bodies meshing together as she claimed the other woman's mouth, parting her lips to kiss her feverishly. When she felt Annelie's tongue enter her mouth, caressing hers over and over, she nudged her toward the bed, and they both tumbled onto it, inadvertently breaking the kiss. Reaching for Annelie once more, she held her close while she let her lips trace her lover's jawline, down her long neck toward her breasts.

Closing her mouth over Annelie's taut nipple for the first time and hearing her name whimpered in response was something Carolyn knew she would never forget. The taste and texture of the pebbled skin, combined with the trembling hands laced in her hair, made her forget any insecurities. She hooked one leg across Annelie's legs, holding her tight, while she cupped her lover's breasts, alternating between them.

"Carolyn, please...oh..." Annelie gasped. "You're driving me crazy. Please come here." She pulled Carolyn up against her, hugging her and placing kisses on her forehead. "Shh...now we're moving too fast."

"Don't you want me?" Carolyn murmured huskily, her heart hammering in her chest.

"I want you more than I can say," Annelie vowed. "I could ravage you all night and it still wouldn't be enough, but I don't want to rush things." She leaned over Carolyn and kissed her lips gently. "I want us to do this slow, and right."

"But it feels so right." Carolyn blushed but kept her promise to level with Annelie on everything. "I'm on fire. I want you so much."

A faint smile appeared on Annelie's lips. "And I want you. Your touch, your body…everything about you." She reached down and cupped Carolyn's left breast, gently flicking her thumb over the nipple, which was as hard as her own. "I could go into detail about what I want to do with you and for how long…" She slowly licked her lips.

"Annelie," Carolyn growled, her voice a low purr. "So, what do we do when we feel this way, then? Leave the room?"

Annelie kissed the tip of Carolyn's nose. "No, silly. Let's just play it by ear. We'll know when the time's right. Tonight, I wanted you to see how much I want you."

Carolyn tugged at a blanket lying at their feet. "And you did," she whispered. "You let me touch you. You liked how it felt."

"No, you're wrong," Annelie objected, pulling Carolyn closer under the blanket. "I *loved* how it felt."

❖

The limo driver navigated through the heavy Manhattan traffic on the way to the Pierre, a famous hotel next to Central Park. The press conference would take place in the Wedgwood Room.

Annelie glanced at Carolyn, noticing a frown on the otherwise smooth forehead as she stared out the tinted window.

"You were exhausted when you got back yesterday. I never had a chance to ask what your sister and brother-in-law said when they heard about the role."

Carolyn turned her attention from the traffic and gave Annelie a quick smile. "Beth was delighted, of course—partly because I'll be working in New York once we start to shoot. I tried to tell her I won't be able to go to D.C. very often during filming, but I'm not sure she heard me."

"How's she doing? She okay?"

Carolyn raised a hand and rubbed the back of her head. "I think she's doing fairly well. However, she seemed a bit…I don't know, too animated. She couldn't sit still while we were talking. She kept getting up to fetch things or to go to the bathroom. Joe seemed concerned."

"Did he say anything to you?" Annelie had felt Carolyn's stress level rising ever since she'd returned from the capital the previous night.

"We talked when he walked me to the cab. Sounds like all her test results are fine. She doesn't show any of the signs she did when she lost the other two babies. Still, I couldn't help feeling something was wrong."

Annelie took Carolyn's hand. "She's scared. Perhaps her fear's affecting her more than she realizes. She's at a crucial period, isn't she?"

"Yes, she's eleven weeks now. I know time will work in her favor, and I tried to tell her so."

"I'm glad you could be the bearer of good news. They must've been thrilled you're going to play Maddox."

"Me too. The news did distract Beth for a bit."

They rode silently in the limousine the rest of the way, Annelie careful not to let go of Carolyn's hand until the vehicle stopped at the back entrance of the Pierre.

"We've arranged to come in through the back door, since we don't want to spoil the surprise. If everything goes according to plan, Harvey and Helen should be there already." Annelie squeezed Carolyn's knee reassuringly just before the driver opened the door and offered them a hand.

"Welcome." Gregory met them at the hotel's rear entrance. "Nice to see you again, Ms. Black. Annelie, everyone's here and we're ready to begin."

"I know you wanted me to speak, but I'm glad we decided for you to make the introductions," Annelie said.

"Only if you listen in the wings and keep an eye on us." He grinned.

"That's my specialty. So, how's the media turnout?"

"The place is packed. All the major networks and entertainment channels are here, as well as newspapers and magazines, even several e-zines."

Annelie discussed some last-minute details with Gregory while they walked through the hotel toward the Wedgwood Room. She glanced at Carolyn gliding beside them, concerned as she saw the other woman press her lips together. She hoped this was merely a sign of how Carolyn focused before an appearance.

Harvey, his wife, and Helen greeted them in the green room. To Annelie's relief, Helen's presence seemed to distract Carolyn, who lit up as soon as she saw the other actress.

Gregory winked at them, rubbing his hands together. "Wish me luck, folks. This is it."

As he disappeared through the doorway, Annelie could hear cameras go off before the door closed behind him. Someone spoke Annelie's name, making her turn around.

"Annelie, good to see you again." Regina Carmichael extended a hand. A striking woman in her mid-fifties, she had been Annelie's first choice as director of the Maddox films. The charismatic woman was known for adapting several other best-sellers for the big screen. Regina kept a strict regime on her sets and enjoyed an impeccable reputation for sticking to budget without compromising on quality.

"Regina, you look wonderful. Carolyn, this is Regina Carmichael. Regina, Carolyn Black."

"Regina, how are you? It's good to see you again."

"I'm fine, and you look ravishing. I told you, black's your color."

Carolyn gave a husky laugh. "Oh, please, not again."

"A private joke?" Annelie looked from one woman to the other. "Now I'm curious."

"I directed Carolyn in a movie made for TV about five years ago. Our designer insisted on dressing Carolyn in psychedelic colors, so we had constant battles with wardrobe. We tried to tell her—where this lady is concerned, less is more, and preferably black."

Annelie had to laugh at Carolyn's visible distaste. "Psychedelic colors? Oh, goodness, that must've been a sight."

"It sure was. I confiscated the negatives." Carolyn smirked.

"Ms. Carmichael, you're on."

Regina squared her shoulders. "See you in there."

Annelie watched as Carolyn began to dig frantically in her purse. "Did you forget something?"

"Damn it, I need a smoke before I go out there." She sighed impatiently when her search seemed fruitless. "Shit."

Annelie cupped the other woman's elbow and guided her toward a private niche. "Carolyn, you can't smoke in here, and you don't have time to do it anywhere else."

Dark gray eyes looked back at Annelie. Frowning, Carolyn slapped her palm against the wall. "God, I don't know why I'm so damn nervous. I hate when my nerves do this to me. I should know how to deal with the jitters better."

"I know a way to beat them." Carolyn's eyes narrowed, and Annelie knew she was taking a big chance.

"You do?"

Glancing over her shoulder to make sure they were out of sight, Annelie pulled Carolyn into her arms.

"You'll do just fine out there, and I have something for you far better than any cigarette."

"Really?" Carolyn breathed, wrapping her arms around Annelie's waist.

"Yes."

Tipping Carolyn's head back with a gentle fingertip under her chin, Annelie brushed her lips softly.

"Annie…" A soft gasp.

Taking advantage of the half-open mouth, Annelie deepened the distracting kiss, which turned into a passionate embrace. Only the fact they were close to Helen and Harvey kept Annelie from losing herself in the woman in her arms. Slowly letting go, she looked down at the dazed expression in Carolyn's eyes. "There, you see, all relaxed."

Relieved to see the familiar slow smile appear, Annelie dared breathe again. "So, purely for medicinal purposes?" When Carolyn wrinkled her nose, she added, "I aim to please."

Carolyn laughed and reached into her purse. "Lipstick for me and handkerchief for you. You were wearing colorless gloss, right? Here, let me help you." She carefully wiped Annelie's lips before reapplying wine-shaded lipstick to her own.

As Carolyn turned to go back into the green room, Annelie stopped her. "I have a suggestion," she said in a low voice. "When we're done here, we have a week before the whole circus begins. Why don't we go back down to Florida in the meantime? I have things to take care of down there and—"

"And I need to start studying the script. Sounds like a plan. Can we leave tonight?"

"If possible, or tomorrow morning."

"Deal."

They walked back into the room where Helen was sitting on a couch, talking with Harvey and his wife. Annelie looked at Carolyn as she made her way over to the other three, now every inch the self-assured professional.

The door opened to the Wedgwood Room, and they could hear Gregory announce, "I present to you two amazing actresses and an equally splendid actor, who will portray the key characters in Delia Carlton's famous novels."

The actors walked over to the door.

"First, in the lead role, as Diana Maddox—Carolyn Black!"

Carolyn took one step through the door before turning her head over her shoulder and shooting Annelie a broad smile. Winking, she mouthed, "Showtime."

CHAPTER ELEVEN

A nnelie smiled as she regarded the sleeping form to her left. Carolyn had rushed from the hotel to her apartment, picked up a few necessities, taken a cab to Annelie's place, and ridden with Annelie to LaGuardia. Though excited about the press conference, she had eventually fallen asleep on the flight to Miami.

"Can I get you anything?" a flight attendant inquired.

"No, thanks, I'm fine," Annelie said, glancing up. "Oh, wait. May I have a blanket for my friend?"

When the flight attendant returned with a blue blanket, Annelie tucked it around Carolyn, careful not to wake her. Leaning back in her seat, she smiled at the thought of a week in warm weather, alone, more or less, with Carolyn. She longed to hold the other woman in her arms, undisturbed, just being close. Imagining Carolyn's body fitting so well with her own, when they snuggled during the night, made Annelie's heart beat faster.

There was something frail about her delicate hands, and yet they could be so strong when pushing Annelie onto her back, roaming her body. Carolyn's eyes, changeable, commanding, yet vulnerable, were one of her biggest assets, adding to her mystery. Annelie had seen them shoot daggers, well up with tears, darken with passion, and light up with mischief and laughter.

At first, she thought it was yet another actor's trick, a learned trait the other woman could switch on and off like a faucet. She still considered Carolyn artful but had consciously decided to trust that her lover wouldn't put on an act around her, at least not when it mattered.

Carolyn stirred next to her, reaching out a hand from underneath the blanket. "Annie?"

GUN BROOKE

"I'm here, Carolyn." Annelie took the hand in hers. "Go back to sleep. We won't be in Miami for another hour."

"Thought you'd gone," the husky voice whispered. "Perhaps a dream."

"Shh. I'm not going anywhere without you."

Annelie kept Carolyn's hand, stroking across it with her thumb. This touch seemed to soothe the exhausted woman, who snuggled closer and let her head fall on Annelie's shoulder. "You promise?"

"I promise."

The soft scent of Carolyn's musky perfume enveloped Annelie, making her stealthily kiss the auburn hair. Tenderness almost choking her, she rubbed her cheek against the top of Carolyn's head, not caring about the flight attendant's curious looks.

❖

"Home, sweet home," Carolyn exclaimed when the cab drove away.

"Glad you think of it that way," Annelie remarked, pulling her bag up the driveway. "It's a nice change from the busy streets of New York. It's amazing how quickly you get caught up in the pace up there."

Carolyn smiled at Annelie as she wrinkled her nose. "I know. We were there less than a week, and still it's such a relief to be back here. Perhaps the fact we're going to stay in New York while shooting the movie factors in?"

"Sounds plausible."

They walked up the driveway and Carolyn stopped at the stairs leading up to the garage apartment, suddenly feeling hesitant and ridiculously shy. "Well, I—"

"Do you—"

They both laughed and indicated the other should continue.

"You first," Carolyn insisted.

Annelie shrugged. "I was going to ask if you'd rather stay at the house with me. I mean, you can use the garage apartment as much as you like…but I'd miss you if…" Her voice trailed off as she gestured between the house and the apartment, a faint blush on her cheeks.

"Same here, but I didn't know how to put it," Carolyn confessed. "I didn't want you to think I was taking things for granted."

"I know you're not. I want you with me as much as possible while we have some free time."

"You're right. So, should I unpack in the guest room in the house for now?"

"No, I'd rather you unpack in my closet and stay with me in my bedroom."

Carolyn inhaled deeply. "But what about Mary?"

"Mary's loyal and won't raise an eyebrow. She's as straightforward as can be and protective of me, which extends to friends and people I love."

Carolyn wanted to ask Annelie what category she fit in but knew the driveway in front of the house, fully visible to the neighbors, wasn't the right place.

"Lead the way," she murmured, feeling her cheeks burn.

Annelie gave her a curious look before they walked inside.

The cool house was a welcome change from the humid evening outside. Annelie walked up to the small marble table in the hallway and picked up a note. "Mary's shopped for us and fixed something to eat."

"Great, but I'm not hungry yet."

The women walked to Annelie's bedroom, Carolyn stopping on the threshold to take it all in. The warm, golden sand walls, chocolate brown curtains, and elevated queen-size bed reflected their owner's personality, Carolyn thought. Feeling how exhausted she was, she couldn't wait to lie down on the golden brown and off-white checkered bedspread and rest her head on the large pillows. The Polarfleece blankets folded neatly at the foot of the bed looked soft and were just what she needed to wrap around herself.

Annelie turned off the ceiling light and switched on the small lamps in the window and on the nightstands.

"Better," she said. "I don't like ceiling lights."

"Cozier," Carolyn agreed. She pulled her bag into the room and looked around for the closet door.

"I'm so tired. I think I'll unpack tomorrow. It's late."

"Good idea. Why don't I run the shower—" Annelie stopped as Carolyn pursed her lips. "What?"

"You have a tub?"

"Come here." Annelie smiled as she nudged Carolyn toward another door, next to the closet. "Voilá."

Of course Annelie's bathroom was a study in understated elegance and functionality. It featured a large shower stall and an oval Jacuzzi.

"Oh, wonderful." Carolyn sighed at the sight of the large tub. "I've never seen a Jacuzzi with that many jets."

Annelie leaned down, turning the faucet to fill it up. "It'll only be a minute."

"Great." Carolyn turned and walked into the bedroom again, rummaging around her bag for her short bathrobe. She tossed it on the bed and had begun to undress when gentle hands wrapped around her waist from behind.

"I can see who my biggest rivals are going to be," Annelie breathed against her neck. "Anything with water...pools, tubs, showers, oceans, lakes..."

Pivoting, Carolyn gave a smile as she raised one eyebrow. "Oh, you don't have any rivals, Annelie—none whatsoever. In fact..." She hesitated and her heart picked up speed. "In fact, I'd like you to join me, if you want."

Annelie's eyes darkened, and her lips parted. "You sure? We're supposed to take things slow, remember? I don't want you to feel obligated to—"

Carolyn interrupted Annelie by kissing her quickly on the mouth. "You must be joking. Obligated? Obligated to have the most beautiful woman in the world in the tub with me?" She wiggled her eyebrows, making Annelie laugh.

"All right, I'd love to take a bath with you."

The women undressed, each careful not to ogle the other too blatantly, but Carolyn was very aware of the tall, voluptuous body next to her. They returned to the bathroom, Annelie holding Carolyn's hand as she stepped into the tub and slowly sank into the hot water, moaning at its effect on her sore muscles.

"Oh, God, I was stiffer than I realized. This is heaven."

"Just wait till we start the jets," Annelie said as she joined her. "You want me behind you?"

"Yes, please. It seems to work well when we sleep, so why not?"

Carolyn jumped when Annelie started the jets. The water flowed and bubbled around her, massaging every inch of her body. Leaning back against her lover, she savored the feeling of soft skin. Annelie stretched out her legs on both sides of Carolyn, wiggling to get comfortable. Carolyn moved, twisting to the left so she could wrap an arm around

Annelie's hips and rest her head between her breasts. She closed her eyes, sighing in relief.

"Comfy?" Annelie asked, raising her voice to drown out the jets.

"Sinfully so."

"Good. Me too."

They lay in silence for a while, every now and then softly stroking each other wherever their hands made contact with hot skin. Eventually Carolyn raised her head and looked drowsily at Annelie.

"Think it's time to rinse off and go to bed. I'm too tired to eat. I'll do Mary's food justice tomorrow, I promise."

Annelie reached out and turned off the jets. "Let me help you. You look positively drunk."

"I'm very sober—but drained."

"I know. Come here."

Annelie helped Carolyn to her feet and into the shower stall. Slightly cooler water rinsed them off, helping Carolyn find her bearings. Annelie wrapped her in a large towel from a heated bar next to the tub and then took one for herself. "You okay?"

"I'm fine. I'll just grab my toothbrush out of my bag and—"

"Here, use one of my new ones." Annelie pulled out a drawer. "You're too exhausted to do anything but stumble into bed."

"That's what old age brings you," Carolyn joked.

"Oh, don't worry. I'm going to stumble right behind you."

Folding back the covers, Carolyn climbed in between the cool Egyptian cotton sheets, too worn out to bother with a nightgown. Annelie switched off the bathroom light and left on only a small lamp on the dresser before joining Carolyn. Unlike Carolyn, she wore a long white T-shirt.

"Mmm," Carolyn murmured and rolled into Annelie's arms. "We smell very nice. Is it vanilla?"

"Uh-huh."

Soft lips brushed her forehead. Drowsily looking up at her lover, Carolyn smiled. "Whatever it is, I like it." She raised a heavy arm and pulled Annelie down, kissing her. "And…I like you." Another kiss. "A lot." Her voice was a mere whisper. "Oh, God, an awful lot…"

"You're slurring. Come here." Annelie took the naked woman in her arms. "Temptress." Snuggling close, she arranged them with Carolyn's back toward her, one arm under her neck and the other along her hip. "We have the whole weekend to relax before I have to go to work."

"Good."

Carolyn felt herself drift off, her backside covered by Annelie, feeling utterly safe.

"Annelie?"

"Yes."

"Sleep tight."

Annelie brushed a kiss along Carolyn's shoulder. "You too."

❖

"I can't believe I'm this late!" Annelie rushed through the kitchen, grabbing a shoulder bag and a briefcase before turning to Carolyn, who sat enjoying her first coffee of the day. "I never oversleep."

"Must be me, then." Carolyn grinned. "Calm down. They won't start without you."

Annelie made a face. "I hate to keep people waiting." She shot the amused woman a questioning look. "What'll you be up to today?"

"I'm going to start reading the script, swim, and also...I might meet Jared for lunch. He left a message on my answering machine. I've still got some clothes and other things at his condo—my address book, for one."

Carolyn noticed a subtle change in Annelie's demeanor. Squaring her shoulders and slightly setting her jaw, she gave an automatic smile. "Of course." Her voice was polite.

Uncertain what to say, Carolyn rose from the chair and tried to change the subject. "Are you sure it's okay if I move my things in here instead of the garage apartment?"

Annelie avoided her glance for a moment. Finally looking straight at Carolyn with expressionless eyes, she spoke in a low tone of voice. "Naturally. Feel free to use any space you see fit."

Knowing something was wrong, Carolyn walked up to Annelie and pulled her into an embrace. "Thank you." She tipped her head back and was surprised when Annelie's lips descended on hers, making her open her mouth and allow Annelie's tongue to examine her completely. Her head spinning, Carolyn clung to the woman now pressing her against the counter as she plundered her mouth. Caught up in the passion, Carolyn returned the kiss as fire rose inside her. She gasped for air as they pulled back, and she could see a myriad of emotions in Annelie's eyes.

"How am I supposed to let you go to work when you kiss me like that?" Carolyn said huskily. "Goodness, Annelie…"

"I'll be home around three, an hour later at the most."

Carolyn swallowed hard. "I'll be here. I can't wait."

A faint smile flickered over Annelie's beautiful features. "Me neither."

As Annelie walked through the house and out the door, Carolyn grabbed her mug of coffee and took a deep sip to calm her aching body.

What the hell just happened? She sensed she had involuntarily caused Annelie pain, and it stung her deeply. The mention of seeing Jared, no matter how trivial the reason and even though he had never been her lover, obviously tapped into Annelie's fear that Carolyn would leave her for a man. *Me and my big mouth. I should have realized…* Imagining the reverse situation, that Annelie was meeting an ex-lover at this fragile point in their budding relationship, made her stomach twitch. Later, once they were more established and secure in their roles together, it would be another matter.

"Damn," Carolyn whispered and picked up the cordless phone. She left a message on Jared's answering service asking him to ship her things to her New York address. No way would she risk seeing him; in fact, she was relieved not having to do so.

Carolyn sat down on the living-room couch, eager to start on the script. After only a few pages, she realized Delia Carlton must have been pivotal in adapting the novel. The language flowed, and the scenes were poignant, exciting, and occasionally even heartbreaking. Several scenes between Maddox and Erica Becker would challenge her and Helen. Carolyn read several of her lines aloud, absorbed in her work.

She wondered how Regina would tackle the romantic scenes, especially the controversial and quite explicit scene where Maddox and Becker made love in Maddox's office late one night. It would obviously entail partial nudity, which she had no problem with as long as it moved the story along. Reading through the scene again, Carolyn blushed, suddenly imagining Annelie as Becker.

Sleeping close to Annelie every night, Carolyn had shared passionate caresses with her, yet both women still restrained themselves. Carolyn had learned a few things that drove Annelie insane with pleasure. To her surprise, the serene and composed woman loved for Carolyn to lavish her with rough but loving attention. Carolyn had once used her teeth on Annelie's nipples during a particularly heated moment, chewing and tugging at the sensitive tips. Suddenly afraid she had gone too far, she apologized for being too eager, but Annelie arched beneath her, moaning and begging for more. That was the closest they had come to making love since Orlando. Carolyn had eventually pulled back, forcing herself not to spread Annelie's legs and plunge into the softness between them.

Checking her watch, Carolyn realized it was already time for her swim. She still felt a little unsettled after the emotional scene this morning, a warning tension around her temples. Hopefully, swimming would relieve it.

Dressed in her black swimsuit, she dived into the pool and began her laps, relieved how the strenuous exercise soothed her muscles. Carolyn lost track of time, and only when her legs felt like lead did she swim over to the ladder and climb up, her muscles trembling with an exhilarating fatigue.

A movement in the corner of her eyes made her jump. Mary was not due until tomorrow. Then she saw Annelie enter her study, not even looking toward the patio or the pool area.

Carolyn wrapped a towel around her shoulders as she padded through the living-room door and toward the study. When she entered, Annelie was browsing through a folder, her back toward Carolyn. A quick glance toward the wall clock let Carolyn know it was one thirty.

She wrapped her arms around Annelie from behind and planted a kiss on her neck just below the ponytail. "Welcome home. You're early."

Annelie gave a muted gasp and pivoted in Carolyn's arms.

"Whoa, Carolyn, you scared the living daylights out of me! I didn't think you'd be home."

"I never went out. Truth be told, I was relieved to just leave a message for Jared to ship my things. I've been reading the script and, as you can tell...swimming."

A small light, a glimpse of hope, glimmered in Annelie's eyes, making Carolyn's heart gallop. "I was stupid," Annelie whispered. "And jealous. I'm sorry."

"Don't be. I reversed roles, and the mere thought made me turn green. We're not ready for male companions and the Lisa-Betty-Jennys of our past yet."

Annelie leaned back against the desk and raised an eyebrow. "The Lisa-Betty-Jennys? What are you talking about?"

"I don't know the names of any of your exes—and I don't want to, yet."

"Lisa-Betty-Jenny. Sounds like you think I've had a complete harem," Annelie muttered, but the happy spark was back in her eyes.

"Of course you have. You're the most beautiful woman in the world—who could ever resist you?"

Annelie tossed her head back and broke out in uncharacteristically resounding laughter. "God, you kill me, Carolyn," she snorted. "Your sense of humor. Wicked and wacko."

"Wicked and wacko, huh?" Carolyn shook her head. "Sounds like a sordid C-movie to me."

"If I ever produce such a movie, I know who to typecast."

"Watch it, Peterson. You're skating on thin ice."

"Oh, yeah?" Annelie disregarded the fact that Carolyn was soaking wet under the towel and pulled her in for a kiss. "How's this for melting the ice?" She dipped her head and captured the smiling mouth beneath hers.

Feeling both relieved and euphoric because they were back on track, Carolyn returned the kiss, losing herself in Annelie's familiar taste. "You melt me...you turn me on like no one has ever done," she moaned. "You are so wonderful."

"And you're shivering. You can't stand here, half naked and wet, with the air-conditioning going."

"I should take a shower, I guess."

Annelie raised a hand and tucked a dripping lock of hair behind Carolyn's ear. "I can scrub your back, if you like."

Carolyn sighed in contentment. "Please, feel free to scrub any body part you like."

"I'll remind you that you said that."

❖

Annelie checked the rearview mirror of the powerful car she was driving. The tan leather seat smelled of lemon leather polish. The 1969

Tweety-Bird yellow Chevrolet Corvette Stingray was in mint condition, and she had given the dealer a handsome tip for making this happen.

She had called him from New York. Remembering the longing tone in the actress's voice when she talked about such a car, Annelie had decided to surprise her with one.

The dealer had connections all over the U.S. and Canada and found the exact brand and year within two days. His mechanics installed air-conditioning, a Bose sound system, and airbags in the hardtop.

Checking the rearview mirror again, Annelie spotted Jem driving her Mustang two cars behind. Her friend had raised not one, but two, inquisitive eyebrows when Annelie revealed her surprise.

"A car?" Jem asked as she sat down in Annelie's office. "That's pretty special. I mean, it doesn't have the same connotation as giving her a diamond necklace, but..." She hesitated. "You really like her, don't you?"

Annelie leaned back in her chair, folding her hands in her lap. "Yes, I do. I know you're suspicious of her, but she's different when you manage to find the real Carolyn behind the diva."

"I saw some of that at the luncheon and then in Orlando," Jem said. "Still, her rep isn't exactly encouraging. Don't lose your head...or your heart."

Annelie tilted her head, regarding her protective friend fondly. "I think it's too late for the latter."

Jem's eyes widened. "Oh, kiddo, are you sure? You're not just... well, starstruck?"

"I'm falling head over heels, and I'm terrified. I can't help it."

"And what about her?"

"She says she's falling in love with me." Annelie could hear her voice soften and knew Jem picked up on the change. "She's bewildered, especially regarding the physical aspect. Guess she never realized she could be attracted to a woman. I'm trying to give her space and time."

"But?"

"She seems not to want it—or need it."

Jem's lips stretched into a broad grin. "So, she can't keep her hands off you?"

Blushing, Annelie shook her head. "It's mutual. You know I don't kiss and tell, but you're my best friend and...well, I haven't felt this way, ever. I'm not sure where we're heading. I want to make her happy, and giving her this car is an attempt to show her how I feel. Also, I'm dying to see the look on her face. For some reason she's as crazy about this kind of car as I am about the Mustang."

"Hey, I'm not arguing. If anything comes between me and my Beemer, I won't answer for the consequences."

After she and Jem pulled into the driveway, Annelie jumped out of the Corvette and shouted, "Wait here. I'll go in and find her. She's probably in the pool."

"All right."

Jem stepped out of the Mustang and leaned against it while Annelie walked toward the door. As she strolled through the quiet house, she saw several signs of Carolyn's presence. Her purse on the hallway table, the script on the coffee table, and in the kitchen, several bags of Royal Copenhagen stacked next to the coffeemaker.

Annelie could hear Mary humming in the laundry room as she walked out to the patio. She found Carolyn resting in a deck chair in the shade, half a glass of orange juice next to her on the ground. Annelie knelt beside the chair and kissed Carolyn's lips softly. "Hello, there."

She had to admire the other woman's composure. Carolyn merely opened her eyes and gazed at Annelie from under heavy eyelids, a lazy smile on her lips. "You're home early."

"Yes, and I have a surprise for you." Annelie tugged at Carolyn's hand. "Come on, it's out front."

"A surprise?" Carolyn raised an eyebrow. "Will I like it? Maybe I should've told you. Surprises make me nervous."

"You'll love it." Annelie tried to sound reassuring, hoping she was right. She wanted Carolyn to accept the gift in the spirit it was given. Holding her lover's hand, she led her through the house and opened the front door.

Carolyn stopped dead and stared at the Corvette. Glancing between the vehicle and Annelie, she looked like a spectator at a tennis match. "Annie?"

"It's for you. I want you to have it, for landing the role…and also I know you'd never indulge yourself."

"What do you mean, for me? Oh! Oh!" Carolyn padded on bare feet down the garden path and over to the driveway.

She waved absentmindedly at Jem, who looked astonished at the sight of the usually elegant star circling around the Corvette in only a swimsuit and damp hair. Moving her feet quickly, actually skipping from one foot to another, she looked like an eager child, even though Annelie knew the hot cement was the real cause.

Annelie sauntered down to join the other two, not taking her eyes off the dumbfounded woman, who was now opening the door and climbing into the car. Carolyn slid her hands over the wheel and up over the dashboard, a reverent look on her face as she touched the tan leather.

"Annelie, how on earth could you remember? I told you about this when I was here to swim the first time."

Annelie bent down, resting her forearms on the door. "I remember everything you tell me."

Carolyn sat still for a moment and then smiled tremulously. "You do, huh?" Her voice was a mere whisper. After a few seconds her expression changed, and a hopeful gleam appeared in her eyes. "Can we go for a drive?"

Jem had walked up to Annelie's side. "I think you should. But there's just one problem, Carolyn."

"What?"

"You don't have anything on but a swimsuit."

Annelie started laughing at the surprised look on Carolyn's face as she looked down at herself.

"Not a problem," Carolyn insisted. "Two seconds!" She jumped out of the car, almost knocking the other women over in the process, and ran up the garden path and into the house. Before either of them had time to utter a word, she rushed back out again, ran down the path, and hugged Annelie fiercely. "Oh, I forgot…thank you, thank you, thank you!" Letting go, she disappeared again.

"I think she likes it," Jem offered. "I make this assessment despite her restrained and ladylike reaction."

Sending an elbow into Jem's side for being a smart-ass, Annelie shook her head. "I hoped she'd be happy, but I had no idea she'd be this excited. Think my idea was a brilliant move?"

"Yup, that, or she'll expect childhood dreams to be fulfilled at the drop of a hat from now on." Jem elegantly avoided elbow number two. "She damn near choked you—I think you must've picked the perfect present."

"Funny. As a matter of fact, I wouldn't mind fulfilling a few more dreams—if she reacts this way."

As they began to stroll toward the house, Jem glanced at Annelie musingly. "And all jokes aside, I really hadn't expected Carolyn to be this...well, I guess, not blasé. Goes to show you should never assume."

"True."

To their surprise, Carolyn met them just inside the door in khaki shorts and a green tank top with the text "A verbal contract isn't worth the paper it's written on." Her hair was pulled back into a simple ponytail, still damp.

Jem nodded approvingly. "Cool outfit, but you might need shoes."

"Damn!"

Carolyn slapped her forehead and disappeared again, while Jem reached into her purse for her cell phone. "You two go ahead. I can let myself out when the cab gets here. If we keep her waiting, she'll explode."

"I think you're right. Here she is now."

"Oh, Annie, I can't wait to drive that beauty," she enthused. "Where should we go?"

"You decide. It's your car."

Hooking her arm around Annelie's, Carolyn smiled brightly. "I'm going to have to pinch myself to really believe that."

"No pinching—can't have bruises on Diana Maddox." Jem grinned as she approached them. "The cab'll be here in a few minutes, so you girls have fun."

Carolyn grabbed Annelie by the hand, pulling her toward the door. "Thanks, Jem! Bye!"

Running down the path toward the car, Carolyn suddenly stopped, releasing her hands and pressing them over her mouth.

"Carolyn?"

"It's beautiful."

"And yours. I had all sorts of reasons for buying it for you—but mostly, I just wanted to make you happy."

Not caring if anyone saw them, Carolyn turned around and hugged Annelie close. "And you did. You have no idea how much."

After they climbed into the vehicle, its new owner made the powerful V8 thunder. Carefully, she backed out into the cul-de-sac and turned around.

"You buckled up?" Carolyn asked, winking at her lover.

"Of course."

"Tweety and I are going to take you for a spin, baby!"

Tweety? Baby? Annelie groaned out loud.

Carolyn grinned broadly, slid the car into gear, and roared down the road.

❖

Annelie turned off her computer and switched off the light in her study. Going through the e-mails marked "urgent" had taken longer than she expected.

"Carolyn?" Annelie poked her head into the living room but got no reply. After a quick glance into the kitchen and the bedroom, she smiled knowingly and opened the front door.

Carolyn was sitting on the top step of the four that led down to the driveway. Her eyes were fastened on the yellow car she had driven for two hours that afternoon.

"Carolyn?" Annelie repeated, walking down the path and sitting down next to her. "Hard to tear yourself away from your new love?" she joked.

Carolyn turned her head and smiled. "Yes. I still can't believe you went to all that trouble. I wonder if you have any idea how incredible this is?"

"I think I have some idea, but why don't you tell me?"

Scooting close, Carolyn sighed. "You know, when Daddy died I gave up several dreams. I lost some things, and some people, because I didn't want to let Beth and John down or have them miss out on anything. Don't get me wrong—I've never resented that—or them. It was my choice to make the sacrifices I did, and I'd make them again.

"But you giving me the Corvette—it means a lot. I dreamed of so many things growing up, especially this car. But I denied myself such dreams. You've given me back part of my youth. Thank you."

Annelie swallowed hard, fighting back tears. She'd detected that the car was somehow important to Carolyn, but had no idea what it symbolized. Carolyn's gratitude untied a knot deep inside that she had not even realized was there. Warmth spread through her veins as she regarded the soft expression on Carolyn's face.

"I'm glad you like it. I'm even happier I followed through on a spur-of-the-moment idea. As I said, I have several reasons for this gift, but most of all I wanted to make you happy. Honestly, when I drove the car home to you, I was afraid you'd think I was nuts."

"No, never. Nobody has ever done anything like this for me. Nobody. You've introduced me to more firsts than anyone else."

"I hope that's a good thing."

"It is."

After a brief silence, Carolyn reached out and stroked Annelie's arm. "It's getting late. Want to go to bed?"

"Yes."

They rose and went up to the house, switching off the lights and undressing in silence. Carolyn had put on one of Annelie's T-shirts, and Annelie kept her matching La Perla camisole and panties on as they climbed into bed.

Reaching out for Carolyn, Annelie nuzzled her hair, placing a trail of kisses across her smooth forehead and down her temple and cheek, only to find Carolyn's mouth half open, ready to be devoured. She slipped her tongue inside and caressed its counterpart, which met hers eagerly. The kiss went on until they both were out of breath and began to tug at what little clothes they wore.

"Please, let me…" Annelie whispered, pulling Carolyn's shirt up. "I want to touch you."

Wordlessly, Carolyn pulled it up the rest of the way and over her head, then tossed it into the shadows. "Then touch me." Her voice, a low purr, made Annelie tremble.

Moving closer, half on top of her, Annelie felt Carolyn's nude body. She let her hands move along the irresistible curve of her lover's slender hips, up toward her chest. Annelie greedily filled her hand with Carolyn's small breasts. The dark nipples pebbled into hard peaks, and Carolyn inhaled sharply when Annelie's fingers tugged gently at them, molding them into even harder points.

"Annie…" Carolyn arched into the touch. "More…"

Not about to object, her own heart pounding hard in her chest, Annelie lowered her head and took one nipple between her lips. She sucked it deep into her mouth, letting her tongue work it relentlessly before grazing it with her teeth. Carolyn whimpered and moved her legs restlessly, as if trying to get closer.

"Shh…" Annelie said around the wet, rigid nipple. "There's no rush, Carolyn. Just relax and enjoy it." She moved to the other nipple, rewarding it with the same attention. The incredible sound of the famous voice moaning her name over and over caused Annelie's own body to respond. Moisture pooled between her thighs, and she knew she wouldn't pull back tonight.

She temporarily let go of the reddened nipple and moved atop Carolyn, careful not to place too much weight on her. Carolyn readily parted her legs, making room for her.

"I want you," Annelie whispered into the delicate ear beneath her lips. "If you want to stop, you have to tell me now."

"No, no, don't stop. I'm on fire...burning for you." Carolyn's voice was barely audible. "I want you so much. But..."

Annelie waited a moment, but when Carolyn didn't continue, she supported herself on one elbow, tipped Carolyn's head back, and looked into her eyes. "Yes? Tell me."

"I want you...but please, can I take your clothes off?"

Annelie tried to moisten her suddenly dry lips. "Of course." Sitting up, she pulled Carolyn with her. Annelie raised her arms, allowing Carolyn to pull the camisole over her head. Lying down in one fluid motion, she raised her hips, indicating with her hands for Carolyn to pull her panties off.

❖

Carolyn watched as Annelie stretched out next to her, her hips elevated to make it possible for Carolyn to remove her last garment. With trembling fingers, Carolyn pulled at the hem of the panties, totally sheer except for a modest triangle of embroidered roses. She slowly slid them off the long legs that seemed to go on forever and tossed them on the floor, registering the fact they were damp from Annelie's arousal.

She looked at the soft shadows forming valleys and hills all over Annelie's sensuous body. She had naturally pale skin, which tanned slightly in the Florida sun. Blond curls at the apex of her thighs made her catch her breath.

"You're so beautiful. It makes me nervous to touch you. I'm afraid I'll do something wrong...even hurt you."

"You could never hurt me." Annelie's voice was low, trusting.

"You can do anything you want. Touch me anywhere. Nothing is forbidden or wrong."

"You sure?" Carolyn bit her lower lip, wanting nothing but to explore her lover's mysteries.

"Very sure. I want your touch."

"Promise to tell me if I—"

"Carolyn...I promise."

Reassured enough to move on top of her lover, Carolyn sighed in relief when she finally felt all of Annelie's body against her own. They fit so well together, despite their difference in height.

Carolyn placed kisses in a blazing-hot trail along Annelie's neck, tasting the warm, damp skin. Tight nipples filled her mouth, creating a need to suck them hard, bite them, but she relented, merely licking them until Annelie arched her back, begging her to do more. Carolyn obliged, wanting to please. She let her teeth rasp over the sensitive skin, eliciting moans from Annelie at each touch.

When both nipples were pink and raw from her lavish attention, Carolyn moved down and kissed the taut stomach, circling the belly button before blowing into it and making Annelie shudder. "Ticklish, huh?" Carolyn murmured. "Good to know."

She moved farther down, hesitant to touch the damp curls. Annelie trustingly parted her legs farther. "Carolyn, please touch me. Any way you want."

Lying along Annelie's right side, Carolyn placed her palm against the warmth of her moist sex. Amazed at the familiar silky feeling, she moved her fingers while looking into Annelie's eyes, searching for signs she was doing this right. Darkening eyes narrowed and full lips grew even fuller when she slid her fingers between the drenched folds to find the swollen clitoris.

Gently, slowly, Carolyn circled it, spreading the wetness around the protruding ridge of nerves as she did when touching herself. Annelie whimpered almost inaudibly at the careful touch. Reveling in the feel of her, Carolyn slid her free arm under Annelie's neck, pulling her closer as she kissed the damp hair at her temple. "There. Like that?"

"Mmm...yes...and more."

Pleased she was on the right track, Carolyn tried to disregard her own aching body, aware of how utterly aroused she was. When Annelie pulled her legs up, involuntarily moving toward her hand, she hummed in response. "Yes, that's right. Open up to me…" She moved her fingers down to find her lover's entrance. Circling it, she felt Annelie turn toward her and hide her face in her neck.

Taking this movement as a sign of approval, Carolyn slid two fingertips inside, delighted to feel Annelie's muscles contract as if to draw her in. Though she had no idea where she found the courage, she plunged her fingers inside, careful not to let her blunt nails scratch the sensitive tissues.

"Ah!" Annelie arched her back and placed her feet on the bed again, her hips undulating against the tentative hand. "Carolyn!"

Resting on her elbow, making sure she held Annelie close with her left arm, Carolyn thrust her soaked fingers in and out, a variety of feelings rushing through her as she realized Annelie was about to come.

When Carolyn felt a small, fluttering sensation around her fingers, she pressed her thumb against her lover's engorged clitoris, rubbing it fiercely until Annelie gave a muted cry against her neck. Muscles clenched around her, over and over, and the slender body in her arms trembled long after Carolyn had gently extracted her fingers.

Slowly, Annelie caught her breath, still clinging to Carolyn, who was rocking her. Feeling protective, proud, and almost giddy, she placed a series of kisses on the damp forehead beneath her. "You okay, sweetie?" she asked, her voice husky.

"Mmm…more than okay. More like wonderful." Annelie sighed, moving to look at Carolyn. "You sent me through the ceiling."

Still in awe at the experience of being able to drive this amazing woman over the abyss, Carolyn willingly spread her legs to accommodate Annelie as she settled between them. "Oh."

"Your turn," Annelie murmured. "Your turn to go flying." She slid an arm under Carolyn's leg, raising it as she allowed her sex to rub against Carolyn's.

Carolyn felt her moisture blend with Annelie's, and the aching need between her legs reignited, making her hips move. Annelie lowered her head and sucked a stiff nipple into her mouth, a hot sensation traveling along the sensitized nerve ends as she used her tongue relentlessly.

Carolyn buried her fingers in Annelie's hair, holding her close while murmuring her name. Soon she realized her lover was moving down slowly, placing open-mouth kisses along Carolyn's stomach.

When she reached the damp curls between Carolyn's trembling legs, she spread them more, caressing the inside of her thighs. Moaning aloud in anticipation, Carolyn felt Annelie part her folds, and then a hot tongue was there, finding every inflamed nerve ending, not relenting until the fire consumed her.

"Annie...oh, God..." Arching, Carolyn pressed against the greedy, loving mouth, wanting to experience it all. After a brief pause, which almost drove her insane, slow fingers entered her, pushing inside with gentle force as the agile tongue resumed its activities.

Unable to hold back, and unsure if she was even supposed to, Carolyn let the waves wash over her, flood her system when she was tossed over the edge. Arrows of pleasure shot from between her legs, through her legs and stomach. Tugging at Annelie, she pulled her up on top of her, clinging to her lover as she kissed her deeply. Tasting herself on Annelie's lips, she lost the last of her fear of inadequacy, in bed or otherwise—at least during this shared moment of safety, security, and intimacy.

"Oh, sweetie," Carolyn sighed as Annelie settled next to her, pulling up the sheets to cover them. "Annie..." She snuggled close, slowly catching her breath.

Annelie stroked Carolyn's hair and smiled faintly, gazing deeply into Carolyn's eyes.

"I'm not sure if what you're looking for can be found in a person's eyes," Carolyn said.

"So, what am I looking for?" Annelie frowned.

"You're looking for how I feel, aren't you?"

Annelie looked caught. "I guess I am."

"Let's do it this way. Let's use words." Carolyn cupped Annelie's chin. "I've already told you I'm falling in love with you. It's true, Annie. I love you."

Tears welled up in Annelie's eyes. "Carolyn..." She coughed, blushing profusely.

Carolyn winked at her. "Now, don't choke. I'm not dangerous or anything."

"Yes, you are," Annelie said, sounding serious. "You're very dangerous to my peace of mind, my heart, and my concentration. Then again, I wouldn't have it any other way." She paused and drew a trembling breath. "I love you too."

Carolyn leaned in for a kiss. "I'm glad. I think I knew, but I love hearing it." She snuggled close again, getting comfortable against the pillows. "This feels so good."

Mimicking Carolyn's movements, Annelie spooned behind her, nuzzling her hair. "I agree. I don't think this bed has ever felt better." She slid her hand down the curve of a hip. "I hope you're not too tired."

"Still a little breathless, but not really tired. Why?"

Annelie's low alto voice reverberated against Carolyn's skin. "I want you again."

❖

In a drafty trailer far from Annelie's home, a thin, balding man raised a bottle of beer to his lips and sipped it while he kept his eyes glued to the old TV set. The beautiful blonde on the screen had changed from a scrawny, gangly child into a stunning woman. His lips parted in a smirk to reveal nicotine-stained teeth, and he gave a husky chuckle.

"How about that. Little Annie grew up."

CHAPTER TWELVE

Carolyn's hair fluttered in the wind from the open window as she drove toward a newly opened shopping mall. Handling the yellow vehicle as if it were an extension of herself, Carolyn looked more content and relaxed than Annelie had ever seen her.

After a quick breakfast of Carolyn's Royal Copenhagen coffee and toasted bagels with cream cheese, Annelie had announced she would take the day off and just be available via her cell phone.

"What about going shopping?" Carolyn had asked, glancing at Annelie over the rim of her mug. "I need to pick up a few things, and we could take the Corvette." Carolyn wiggled her eyebrows at her own suggestion, making Annelie laugh aloud before she agreed.

Annelie was amazed by the calm and soothing ambiance between them, a restful camaraderie that she hadn't expected. Leaning back in the passenger seat, she enjoyed the ride to the mall.

When Carolyn pulled into a large parking lot and carefully parked away from any other vehicles, Annelie smiled at her knowingly, the smile turning into a worried frown when she heard Carolyn groan after she got out of the car.

"What's wrong?"

Carolyn sighed, smiling sheepishly. "I used muscles last night I didn't know I had. All night, I might add."

"Oh, my. Well, that'll teach us not to be so enthusiastic," Annelie joked.

"Don't say that. Practice makes perfect."

Hooking her arm under Carolyn's, Annelie leaned down to whisper in her ear. "Well, in that case, I'm all for perfection."

Once inside the mall, they headed for a store that carried clothes by several famous designers. An efficient shopper, Carolyn bought several pairs of chinos and short-sleeved shirts, as well as a new denim jacket and sneakers, which Annelie suggested.

"Are you planning something special, since you want me in shoes like these?" Carolyn asked, winking as she pulled out her credit card.

"As a matter of fact, I do." Annelie hadn't realized until that very second she had a plan brewing. "I have a brilliant idea."

They walked out of the store and headed toward the center of the mall where several smaller vendors had kiosks. "You can't hold back on me like this. You have to tell me." Carolyn raised an eyebrow.

"You're cute when you're demanding," Annelie teased. "All right, all right. Tomorrow's Friday, and I've given everyone the day off because they worked overtime to put the Orlando convention together. How would you like to drive up to Orlando and spend the weekend at Disney World?"

Annelie kept walking and finally realized Carolyn was no longer beside her. Stopping, she turned around and saw her standing a few steps behind, looking cemented to the floor. "Carolyn?"

"Disney World? As in rides, exhibits, and…Mickey Mouse?"

"Exactly. Fireworks…parades…restaurants…"

Carolyn's eyes began to twinkle, and then she tossed her head back, laughing huskily. "Oh, you never cease to amaze me, Annelie," she said. "I'd never have guessed you were thinking about Disney World…but why not! I'd love to go. Once we get back to New York, we won't have much time to run and play."

"I'll call Jem and have her make the arrangements."

They walked in silence for a moment, looking in the windows of the shops they passed. Carolyn glanced at Annelie with a thoughtful expression. "I just thought of something. You'll be stuck in New York for the time being too and won't be able to spend time with your friends down here…Annie, why don't we ask some of them to join us at Disney World? I mean, unless they already have plans."

Annelie's heart overflowed. Part of her wanted Carolyn to herself, but another part wanted to introduce her into her circle of friends, to make them understand she belonged. "Are you sure? It could be fun, of course."

"I wouldn't have suggested it otherwise. Just so I still have you to myself all night, naturally." Carolyn gave a broad grin.

"That goes without saying. We can fit several more in the Lincoln, plus luggage. How about Jem and Charlotta, and…I think Kitty and Sam are still in Orlando."

"Great. Sounds like we could have a lot of fun."

Annelie turned to Carolyn, looking down at her smiling eyes. "So it's settled, then."

"I can't wait."

❖

They continued their shopping, and at one point Annelie asked Carolyn to wait while she disappeared into what Carolyn called a gizmo store. Turning around to scan the windows of the store opposite it, Carolyn had a sudden idea.

She glanced over her shoulder to make sure Annelie was occupied with the salesperson, then hurried across the marble floor toward the store. Less than ten minutes later she placed a neatly wrapped item in her large bag, smiling inwardly as she walked back to the other store just in time to greet Annelie.

"Did you find whatever you wanted in there?" Carolyn raised an eyebrow.

"Yes, I did. Sorry, it took longer than I thought."

"Not a problem, but now I'm hungry. Should we grab something in here or…?"

"Why don't we drive down to the beach and see what we can scare up?"

"Sounds like a plan. Let's go."

They gathered their bags and headed toward the parking lot. As Carolyn drove the car out of the parking lot and headed toward the highway, Annelie opened her purse and pulled out her cell phone, pressing the speed dial.

"Jem, Annelie here. Yes. Shopping, actually. Good. Now, Carolyn and I have a great idea. How would you like to join us and go to Disney World over the weekend? Friday to Sunday. You do? Great! I want to take Charlotta, if possible. As far as I know, Kitty and Sam are still in Orlando. I don't think they'd mind switching to our hotel. Can you take care of the bookings? Brilliant. Thanks. I'll call Kitty and Charlotta later. Okay, talk to you soon. Ciao."

"I take it Jem's game?" Carolyn asked.

"Yes, she didn't have any plans for the weekend. She'll take care of everything."

"Super. I look forward to it." Carolyn smiled, not taking her eyes off the traffic ahead of them. A soft touch on her thigh made her give an inaudible gasp.

"Why don't we take the scenic route, along the beach drive?" Annelie suggested, making little circles on Carolyn's leg.

"Oh, goodness, Annie, I'll do whatever you want, but you better not touch my leg like that while I'm driving."

"I thought you were completely absorbed in driving this car. How can one little caress have such an impact?"

"Depends on who's giving the *little caress*. Cut it out." Carolyn smiled, not taking her eyes off the traffic. "That, or I'll be forced to pull over and have my way with you."

Delighted, Carolyn heard Annelie moan quietly before withdrawing her hand. "Okay, so drive, then."

Caroyn laughed as she drove toward the beach, turning south on the smaller road following the coast. They passed the tourist-filled areas, and when the traffic thinned, Annelie pointed to the left. "What about that place?"

"Barnacle Bill's Crab Shack?" Carolyn read. "You've been there?"

"No, but it looks genuinely quaint enough to be worth a try."

Feeling her stomach growl, Carolyn agreed. She turned into the gravel parking lot, looking for a remote spot for her beloved car. Under a group of palm trees, she switched off the ignition and stretched before she opened the door.

"Still sore?" Annelie frowned. "We might have to get you to a massage parlor before you start working next week. We can't have Diana Maddox limping or flinching every time she moves."

"Very funny. No, I'm not sore—just…a little tender."

They stepped up on the large veranda that circled the house, noticing the rustic tables and chairs. The door was flung open, startling both of them, and a tall, skinny man boasting a red ponytail and mustache stepped outside.

"You like seafood?" he asked abruptly, glaring at them.

"Yes," Annelie replied, raising an eyebrow.

A broad smile spread across his freckled face. "Then you've come to the right place! Step inside where it's nice and cool, and I'll pour you a glass of our homemade iced tea."

Carolyn sighed inwardly. "You have coffee?"

"Sure do! We don't have any of the fancy latte stuff, but we have fresh-ground beans, and the brew is strong enough to knock your socks off."

"Sounds wonderful." Carolyn sighed in relief at the prospect of not having to drink tea, since she detested the stuff. "Are you Barnacle Bill, perhaps?"

"Nope, I'm Pete. His son."

Annelie smiled faintly. "There really is a Bill, then?"

"Yup, he's in the kitchen."

Carolyn had to stifle a giggle or risk offending the colorful man showing them inside.

Large ceiling fans kept the air cool around tables with red-and-white checkered tablecloths. The walls were covered with postcards, odd signs, and maritime art, together with fishnets. Pete showed them to a corner booth, motioning for them to sit down before handing them worn leather-covered menus. "I'll bring you your drinks. One iced tea and one coffee?"

"Yes, please," Annelie said.

Carolyn opened the menu, and she widened her eyes at the many choices of different seafood. "I think we might have stumbled on something extraordinary," she said. "If it tastes as good as it sounds on the menu, we have a winner."

"I agree. I think I'll have the medium seafood platter."

"Me too."

They placed their order when Pete returned with their drinks, Carolyn hard-pressed not to giggle when he nodded in agreement at their choice.

Remembering the small package in her pocket, she pulled it out discreetly, holding it in her hand before raising her glance to Annelie.

"I have something for you," she began, "and I hope you'll like it."

"You do? What?"

Mutely, Carolyn pushed the gift across the table, not taking her eyes off Annelie as she took the small package. Shooting Carolyn a curious glance, she slowly removed the black-and-gold paper. When

Annelie looked at the brand name on the small wooden box, her eyebrows rose.

"When did you have time…?"

"When you were in the gizmo shop."

"Ah." Annelie carefully opened the box and lifted the cotton to reveal the item underneath. "Oh, Carolyn, it's beautiful," she breathed. Tears suddenly welled up in her eyes, startling Carolyn.

"Annie, don't cry." She reached across the table. "Here, let me put it on for you." She lifted from the box a white gold bracelet, a simple chain with three charms attached to it—a heart, a cross, and an anchor. Carolyn had fallen for its old-fashioned look and immediately thought of Annelie. "There. It looks wonderful on your wrist, but of course you can take it back if you—"

"Never," Annelie said huskily. "I love it. Nobody has ever given me anything so romantic."

Carolyn couldn't hold back a broad smile. "I'm glad you like it."

Annelie looked up, her face composed once again. "I do." She held on to Carolyn's hand. "I can't believe I'm here with you. I'm afraid I'll wake up and find it's a dream."

Carolyn stroked her thumb across the back of Annelie's hand. "In that case, we're having the same dream," she said. "I never thought I'd ever feel this way about anybody—and there's no place I'd rather be."

Approaching steps announced Pete's presence, but Annelie kept Carolyn's hand in hers. Whistling off-key, Pete placed their food in front of them, giving no indication he had noticed their joined hands.

"Eat and be merry," he said and walked away to greet a new group of guests.

Carolyn winked at Annelie as she tackled a jumbo shrimp. "Be merry…sounds good to me."

"Speaking of that, I picked up something for you, but I'll give it to you in the car."

Carolyn licked her lips suggestively. "Something you can't give me in public. Now I'm curious."

"I can see what you're thinking, but don't let that imagination run away with you," Annelie warned, raising her fork in mock admonishment.

"What are you talking about? What imagination?" Carolyn did her best to look innocent.

"You know what I mean." Annelie grinned. "Eat your lunch and stop trying to make me blush."

Carolyn gave a resounding husky laugh, making several people turn their heads. "All right, Annie. I'll behave and let you reveal your gift in private later."

Annelie looked down at her bracelet, the expression in her eyes softening. "It's beautiful."

Carolyn found it impossible not to smile as she gazed at the beauty before her. She leaned in closer. "It's pretty," she agreed in a low voice. "But *you're* beautiful."

❖

Annelie had to laugh at the expression on Carolyn's face when she gave her the hands-free device for her cell phone.

"What's this?" Carolyn frowned. "You know me and tech stuff. We're not compatible."

"Yes, I know. This is to make your life easier. You plug it in here, in the cigarette lighter, like this. Then you attach your cell phone to the cord…like this…and now you can talk without using your hands. And also, it charges your phone. Smart, huh?"

"Very smart…wait, how do you mean, without using my hands?"

"All you have to do is press one button if the phone rings, and then you can just talk out loud. It's like a speakerphone. It'll make your driving safer. You can focus on the traffic around you instead of the cell phone."

"Amazing." Carolyn grinned. "And here I thought you'd bought something naughty."

Annelie rolled her eyes and laughed. Feeling a slight blush creep up her cheeks at involuntary images flashing before her eyes, she had to ask. "Naughty? Such as?"

It was Carolyn's turn to blush. "Oh, I don't know. Like massage oil, or…well, some tech toy, or something. I mean, after all, you were in one of those stores. They have all sorts of things."

"Oh, Carolyn." Annelie smiled. "If I wanted to buy something like that, I'd be a little more subtle about it. You're just teasing me."

"A little. This was a very thoughtful gift. Thanks, Annie." Carolyn leaned in and kissed Annelie's cheek.

"You're very welcome. As for the other suggestions, I'll give it some thought. I'm all for massage oils and, well, I suppose a toy can be fun." Annelie winked at Carolyn, who promptly started the car and pulled out of the parking lot.

❖

The sun was low on the horizon, barely above the waterfront, as Annelie stepped out of the Lincoln in the parking lot outside her office.

"About time." Jem greeted her and Carolyn with a yawn. "Here I set four different alarm clocks to not be late, and you have the nerve to show up…" She checked her watch. "Six minutes late."

"Ah, quit whining, Jem." Annelie grinned. "So we're ready to go, then?"

She glanced around and saw Charlotta walking toward them, pulling a small bag on wheels. Waving to the diminutive redhead, Annelie turned to Carolyn.

"Looks like we can take off right away."

"Mmm," the husky voice behind her agreed. "Want to drive? You sound incredibly perky."

The soft purr took the sting out of the words, and Annelie just smiled. "Sure. You had a hard time waking up this morning."

Jem raised an eyebrow at the information, but refrained from commenting. "I wouldn't mind driving," she suggested.

"That's okay. I'll take the car through the morning traffic," Annelie offered diplomatically. Jem was a good driver but possessed a fiery temper, which made being a passenger quite an experience. On more than one occasion, Annelie had tried to point out that the driver in the offending car couldn't hear her colorful remarks.

Looking slightly disgruntled, Jem opened the trunk to the Lincoln and stowed her bag inside. Charlotta followed suit and then climbed in the backseat next to Jem.

"Everybody set?" Annelie asked, glancing over her shoulder.

The morning traffic wasn't too congested yet, so they drove quickly through the city and headed north.

Annelie sat lost in thought as the other women chatted behind her. *Such an ordinary thing to do, going away for the weekend with friends. Still, so much rides on this. Will they accept Carolyn when they realize I love her? Will she be comfortable around them, knowing they know? This'll be her first, granted, very small, experience of being out.* She glanced down at her right wrist and watched the bracelet sparkle, the small charms glimmering as the rising sun shone through the windows.

"I haven't been to the House of Mouse in at least five years," Jem said from the backseat. "It's really one of my favorite places, but I guess I've just been too busy lately."

Annelie smiled inwardly at her chief editor's words. Not many people knew of Jem's more playful side, and she could see by Carolyn's raised eyebrows that she was surprised.

"I went to Disneyland with my brother and sister years ago." Carolyn turned her head toward Jem. "They loved it, of course, but I mostly remember how hard it was to keep up with them. It'll be great not having to chase children around."

"I especially love Epcot," Jem said. "It's my favorite part of Disney World."

"I've never been to Disney World," Charlotta confessed. "I'm a terrible wimp when it comes to roller coasters. I hope you won't think I'm a complete bore."

"No, don't worry," Carolyn replied. "I'm not so daring myself. I prefer the slower rides."

The conversation flowed easily as they drove toward Orlando. Annelie enjoyed the facetious comments and laughter, occasionally glancing over at Carolyn, who sat half-turned toward the backseat, taking part in the friendly banter. Annelie smiled, her heart aglow, as she watched Carolyn enjoy herself and take an active interest in what her other friends had to say. The weekend promised to be wonderful.

❖

The one-bedroom executive suite held everything they could possibly need. Carolyn walked over to the window and pulled the curtain aside to admire the view of the lake and the Dolphin Hotel on the other side.

"Cute." She grinned, turning to Annelie. "I have to say, the swans on the roof of our hotel are slightly more elegant than the chubby-looking dolphins on that one."

Annelie walked over and put her arm around her lover's shoulders. "I agree. It's quite a view. Look. There are the Friendship boats that'll take us to the different parks."

Annelie pulled her closer. "I enjoyed the drive up here. You seemed to connect with Jem and Charlotta."

Carolyn grinned. "I hope so. They seem to like me."

"Don't sound so surprised. Of course they like you. You're wonderful." She brushed her lips against Carolyn's.

"I don't take it for granted. I know I'm respected in the business. Actually, I think I frighten a lot of people. It comes with the territory, and I can be abrasive and a little too candid at times."

"Well, you have a kindred spirit in Jem. She calls a spade a shovel, if you understand what I mean. You don't have to pretend with her, and I don't think you did. You all seemed to have a good time chatting."

"We did." Carolyn nodded, hugging Annelie. "Now, come here and kiss me properly."

Annelie readily dipped her head, capturing Carolyn's lips in a kiss initially more loving than erotic. When it deepened, Carolyn felt her knees buckle as she slid her hands up underneath Annelie's T-shirt and moved them over the smooth skin. Instinctively she pushed the thin fabric up to reveal the white lace bra.

"Oh, Carolyn…please…" The husky whisper from Annelie made her hands tremble.

"I know, I know, we have to get out of here and go play." Carolyn nibbled at Annelie's full lower lip. "You're just too tempting, my love. You're so…" Her voice broke off when Annelie pulled back, her eyes wide. "What? What's wrong?"

"Nothing." Annelie swallowed. "You…you called me *my love*."

Realizing how effortlessly the words had passed her lips, Carolyn blushed. "I did. I know I have a habit of using terms of endearment pretty freely, but I never call anyone *love*."

Annelie's eyes sparkled. "I liked it."

"Me too."

Hearing a knock at the door, Annelie gave Carolyn another quick kiss before she answered it. The sight of the other women, both dressed in shorts and T-shirts, Charlotta boasting a bright yellow baseball cap, made Carolyn smile.

"You ready?" Jem asked, sounding impatient. "I'm starving. Kitty and Sam are checking in later this afternoon and meeting us tonight for dinner."

"Sounds great. We're ready." Annelie and Carolyn grabbed their daypacks. "Let's go play."

Jem looked closely at Annelie as she made sure the door was closed and locked. "You look a bit flushed. You okay?"

"Of course," Annelie assured her. "I've never felt better."

❖

Kimonos, the Japanese restaurant at the Swan Hotel, had subdued lighting and a cozy atmosphere. Annelie sat close to Carolyn on the couch, resting her arm behind her shoulders. Across the table, Kitty and Sam had joined them and were now focusing on Jem, who sat at the short end of the table busily filling out the form that replaced a regular menu. She had commandeered the form and endured a lot of outrageous comments as she scribbled on it.

When the waitress arrived with their drinks, Jem handed her the form with an apologetic smile. "Sorry about this. I hope you can read all the changes we made. These people can't make up their minds."

The other women raised their voices in protest, claiming it was Jem who had made a mess of the menu. Smiling indulgently, the waitress assured them everything was fine.

When Charlotta started lancing innocent California rolls with fervor rather than using her chopsticks correctly, Carolyn said, "Charlotta, they're already dead. Hold the chopsticks like this, and move them like so."

"I've tried," Charlotta muttered. "They work better this way." She stabbed another roll. "See?"

Laughter erupted around the table at her violent efforts.

"Excuse me, aren't you Carolyn Black?" a female voice interrupted.

Annelie glanced up at two women standing next to her, their eyes fastened on Carolyn.

"Yes, I am." Her voice was low and noncommittal.

"We just love you, Ms. Black. Please may we have your autograph?"

Carolyn squared her shoulders, her eyes a dull gray as she lowered her chopsticks. "Normally, I'd love to, but I don't sign autographs while dining out with friends and family. Please respect my rule. Catch me later in the foyer and I'll be glad to."

"We don't mean to interrupt," the other woman persisted, to Annelie's dismay. "But now that we already have, couldn't you make an exception? Just sign *To Dolly* here, on my receipt." She pushed a small piece of paper forward, holding out a pen.

Carolyn's voice was polite, but cold enough to make Annelie shiver. "Please, not now. Thank you."

The two women hesitated for a moment, but relented and left with sullen looks on their faces. Muttering between them, they stomped toward the door. Carolyn took a deep breath and then smiled toward Charlotta. "Now, where were we? Here, let me help you."

In awe, the others watched as Carolyn gently placed Charlotta's fingers in the correct position around the chopsticks, and the smile on the redhead's face broadened when she managed to grip a piece of salmon on her plate and bring it over to the soy sauce, dip it, and then pop it into her mouth. "I did it!"

Jem leaned closer to Annelie, lowering her voice. "Damn, did you see that? She just blows me away."

Annelie had yet to recover from Carolyn's reaction to the rude fans. Glancing around the table, she saw Kitty and Sam look at Carolyn with a new respect.

"Do you get that a lot?" Sam asked.

Carolyn shrugged. "Yes, unfortunately. It's a definite downside to fame. I try to always remember the fans and sign autographs whenever asked to. But I do have a rule. I want to eat in peace. Later, I'll sign any paper or photo they bring, but not now."

"I thought you handled it very well. You were more restrained than I could ever be," Jem said. "I'm impressed with how you slipped into the Carolyn-Black-the-diva role. You slipped out of it even faster."

Carolyn rolled her eyes. "The diva, huh? I guess it's second nature to me by now."

"I've never quite realized how fame can be," Charlotta remarked. "To be a household name and never enjoy complete anonymity like the rest of us."

Annelie felt a hand touch hers. Looking down, she interlaced her fingers with Carolyn's. Her first instinct when the two women approached her lover had been to protect her, but she had quickly realized Carolyn was much better equipped, and used to handling such situations. Squeezing the hand in hers, Annelie wanted to convey her empathy. The thumb rubbing the back of her hand suggested Carolyn understood.

❖

"Let me undress you."

Annelie's eyes widened at the soft growl behind Carolyn's words. Her arms remained at her side as her lover began to unbutton her white cotton shirt. Slowly, but without hesitation, Carolyn unveiled bare skin covered only with a bra.

"You're exquisite." Carolyn looked at the trail of wine red lipstick marks she'd left on Annelie's pale collarbones. "Beautiful."

She nudged the shirt off Annelie's passive arms and watched it fall to the floor. Kneeling to pick it up, she changed her mind and unbuttoned the beige chinos instead. As she slid them down over voluptuous hips, she tugged at the panties underneath and removed them as well. Utterly exposed, Annelie closed her eyes, visibly trembling as she moved her feet and stepped out of her clothes.

Carolyn rose with the clothes in her hands, folding them with teasing slowness and placing them on the chair by the desk. She turned her attention back to Annelie, reached around her for the clasp, and removed her bra. Tossing it on the chair, she slowly rubbed Annelie's back, down over her bottom.

"Oh, so good..." she murmured. "And so mine..."

"Yes." Annelie's voice sounded weak.

"Come here, love." Carolyn guided her toward the bed. "Lie down and relax. I'll be back in a second."

Annelie obeyed, glad to be off her feet since her knees felt weak. She watched her lover walk into the bathroom, only to return a few minutes later, just as naked, carrying something in her hand.

"I have something for you," Carolyn murmured. "I think you're going to like it. You're so sensitive, so responsive. Yes. I definitely think you're going to like this, Annie."

Annelie looked at the item in Carolyn's hand—a white bottle of unknown origin. "What's that?"

"I used to burn badly in the sun, and this saved me. It still keeps my shoulders from burning to a crisp. Being out all afternoon in that tank top…you've burned your shoulders a bit."

"What's in it?"

"Herbs. Aloe vera mostly, but also another herb, very invigorating and…stimulating, you could say. It stings for a minute, but then it feels great. Trust me."

Carolyn opened the bottle and squeezed some of its contents into the palm of one hand, then rubbed it against the other. Moving onto the bed on her knees, she cupped Annelie's red shoulders and began to massage the cream into them.

At first it did sting, painfully so. Annelie was about to object when the pain turned into a tingling, soothing sensation. She moaned in pleasure as Carolyn spread the cream down her arms.

"There, I told you. Doesn't that feel good?"

Annelie could only nod. It felt better than good.

Carolyn took more cream into her hands, now massaging down Annelie's front, between her breasts toward her stomach.

"I'm not burned there," Annelie murmured, not really objecting.

"I know, but this'll feel good anyway."

She felt limp as Carolyn's soft hands rubbed the tingling cream into her stomach, down her hips, and along her legs. Unable to resist, she parted her legs to help Carolyn reach around them.

"Roll over. Let me do your back."

Annelie complied, moaning aloud when Carolyn's strong hands massaged more cream on her back. The sensation was everywhere, tingling, sparkling against her skin, enhancing the touch of the loving caresses.

"Roll over again." Carolyn's voice was throatier than usual, vibrating with desire.

Annelie turned onto her back, watching in anticipation how Carolyn took more cream and lowered her hands. She arched her back, striving to prolong the touch as Carolyn's hands cupped her breasts. The cream heated and chilled her nipples at the same time, making them impossibly hard. Loud whimpers broke from her throat as the intensity of the pleasure rose.

"Now, like this…" Carolyn put the bottle aside and moved on top of Annelie, placing kisses over her forehead and cheeks before hovering over her lips. "You drive me crazy, you know. Absolutely insane…" Finally a kiss, the one Annelie had been waiting for, hot and intense. She parted her legs, allowing Carolyn to settle between them. "You…only you…"

Annelie couldn't take it anymore. Needing release more than she ever had, she rolled them over on the king-size bed, lowering her head to Carolyn's breasts. She captured a nipple between her teeth, tugging at it only to soothe it with her tongue a moment later. Reaching down, she found the damp folds between Carolyn's legs and unceremoniously entered her when she felt the copious moisture there.

"Ah!" Carolyn clung to her, apparently quite willing to have them switch roles. "Yes…oh, yes…"

Rubbing her own swollen sex against Carolyn's thigh, Annelie pressed her fingers deeper, a thumb on the aching clitoris above, while lavishing open-mouth kisses from one breast to another.

"Oh, Carolyn…I need you so much…I love you." Her voice broke. "You make me want you so much."

"I'm yours. Yours to have. Yours to do anything you want to. Yours." Carolyn arched, wrapping one of her legs around Annelie. "Take me…"

The last words sent Annelie over the edge. Pressing herself hard against her lover, she flicked her thumb over Carolyn's drenched ridge of nerves. She was desperate for Carolyn to follow her into the depths of endless pleasure. Convulsing from her orgasm, she kept caressing the woman in her arms, determined to give her what she herself was feeling.

"That's it…" Carolyn murmured. "Yes, yes…"

Just as Annelie's tremors began to slow, Carolyn went rigid beneath her, caught in her own landslide, calling out Annelie's name. Carolyn's strong muscles clenched Annelie's fingers, fluttering for precious moments until Carolyn began to settle down.

Annelie tried to catch her breath as she raised her head to look down at Carolyn. Flushed and tousled, she had never looked more beautiful. Slowly, Annelie removed her fingers, cupping Carolyn's overindulged sex. Then she lay down beside her lover.

"Carolyn…" Annelie pushed errant strands of hair out of her lover's eyes. "Wow."

Those unforgettable eyes looked dimly up at her, and a slow, bright smile spread across Carolyn's lips. "Wow, indeed. Very good choice of words."

Pulling at the covers, they created a nest in the middle of the bed since the air-conditioning would soon chill them. Turning her back against Annelie, Carolyn snuggled close, as was her habit.

"I love you, Annie." Her voice was a soft whisper.

Annelie, not yet accustomed to Carolyn's open-hearted declarations, felt her heart beat erratically. "I love you too. So much." Hearing her own voice about to break, she blushed and hid her face in Carolyn's hair.

"I know. I feel it." The husky voice held a multitude of emotions. "Sleep tight."

Annelie placed her hand on Carolyn's hip and closed her eyes. Tired beyond words, she enjoyed the soft throbbing inside her body, knowing sleep was only minutes away.

❖

Carolyn and Annelie had pulled up six chairs around one of the small, round tables in the breakfast area and sat waiting for Charlotta and Jem to join them. Sipping her coffee, Carolyn thought about the preceding night. To her own surprise, she had woken Annelie twice during the night, initiating more of the irresistible lovemaking. She ought to feel just a little embarrassed about not being able to resist her, she thought, but she couldn't. Annelie was so responsive and the sexual energy between them incredibly overpowering; it enthralled them both. Carolyn stretched her right leg discreetly, feeling an unfamiliar, but pleasant, soreness in her muscles.

Charlotta looked rested and ready to face the day when she approached the table, a café latte in her hand. Jem, however, looked bleary-eyed.

"You all right, Jem?" Annelie asked as the two women sat down.

"I'm fine," Jem muttered. "I just didn't get much sleep last night."

"Sorry to hear that."

"Our neighbors were so noisy. I couldn't tell if the sound came from below or above."

"I slept like a baby," Charlotta said. "Didn't hear a thing."

"You must be deaf," Jem huffed. "Somebody was going at it like there's no tomorrow. Honestly, this is a family resort, for heaven's sake!"

Carolyn had to bite her lip not to laugh aloud. Glancing at Annelie, she watched her blush a deep crimson.

"Annelie, I told you you were too vocal," she whispered, leaning closer.

"What?" Charlotta exclaimed, sitting on the other side of Annelie. "Come to think of it, I heard some commotion too. That was you?"

"You're a dead woman, Carolyn," Annelie muttered between clenched teeth.

Carolyn looked at Jem and Charlotta, who suddenly dove to the floor, apparently retying already neat shoestrings while their shoulders shook unmistakably. When she sat back up, Charlotta covered her mouth with one hand, her eyes twinkling.

"Oh, God," Annelie sighed, shaking her head as she joined in the laughter. She nailed Carolyn with her eyes. "I'm going to get you for this," she vowed, unable to erase a broad grin from her face. "Sooner or later."

"Promises, promises," Carolyn replied with a carefree wave of her hand.

Annelie grinned. "You're damn right."

❖

"Oh, we have to go on this ride," Jem enthused. "It's brand-new! Everybody's talking about it."

After a full day of fun in the warm weather, the six women had enjoyed most of the Epcot rides and now approached the newest attraction.

Annelie looked at the brochure in her hands. "Mission: Space. It sounds fun. You go in four at a time, take on roles as navigator, pilot, commander, and engineer, and land a space shuttle on Mars. It's quite a wild ride."

"I'm not sure…" Charlotta looked hesitant, as did Sam. "Wild?"

"Don't worry. You're on the ground, in a seat, spinning in a centrifugal chamber, creating g-forces. Says here you should avoid it if you're prone to motion sickness, though."

"I'm usually not so bold, but I want to try it," Carolyn said and rose. "Who else?"

Eventually they all decided to go. After waiting in line and watching an instructional video with actor Gary Sinise, they were ushered into rows of four, which meant Sam and Charlotta had to wait.

Entering their pod, Kitty climbed in first, followed by Carolyn, Jem, and Annelie.

"Oh, cool," Kitty said. "I'm the engineer. That's a first."

"I'm the commander." Carolyn grinned.

Jem was happy to be in the pilot's seat, and Annelie rolled her eyes at being the navigator. A bar locked them safely into their seats, and the wall opposite them suddenly moved closer to provide each of them buttons and a joystick.

After Gary Sinise instructed them how to operate the controls, they awaited takeoff. Annelie kept her eyes on the small screen that showed the view from the space shuttle's window. The engines ignited with a thundering vibration, and a surprisingly strong g-force pressed her into her seat.

"Whooohooo!" Jem yelled next to her. "You feel that?"

"Focus on the mission and steer this thing," Carolyn replied. "You have maneuvers coming up, pilot!"

"Yes, ma'am," Jem replied merrily.

Each had different assignments during the mission to Mars, but, despite trying their best, they still came close to crashing on the landing strip at the Mars colony. Carolyn kept barking out orders, making the other three want to double over with laughter.

They skidded along the runway, breaking through the barriers. Annelie listened to Gary Sinise's somber voice as their space shuttle teetered on the edge of the abyss, swaying back and forth. "Don't move a muscle."

"I'm not!" Kitty squealed from the engineer's station. "Oh, God!"

"Welcome to Mars!"

The lights went on, and the safety bars released their vise grip. The four women stepped outside on wobbly legs, all smiles.

"Wasn't that fun?" Jem grinned. "I think I did an awesome job of piloting, if I do say so myself."

"An awesome job?" Kitty raised her eyebrows. "We practically crashed!"

"It's indicative of how she drives a car," Annelie teased, as Jem shot her a mock glare.

"I can't believe how much fun that was," Carolyn added. "It all felt so natural to me, being starship captain. Who knew?"

Annelie exchanged glances with Jem and Kitty before bursting out in a fit of laughter.

Carolyn looked at her companions with mild surprise. "What? What did I say?"

Deciding it was time for ice cream, they sat down on a bench in the shade, and Annelie suddenly felt a hand on her knee. She wondered if Carolyn was aware of the public display of affection as she placed her own on top of Carolyn's and rubbed her thumb over her knuckles. Hearing a soft intake of breath, she noticed Carolyn's slightly startled eyes.

"Good ice cream?" Annelie asked innocently.

"Wonderful," Carolyn said huskily. "I love chocolate."

"Oh, goodness, look at Charlotta and Sam," Jem snorted, breaking the mood.

The two women were stumbling toward them, both looking queasy and pale.

Carolyn rose. "Charlotta, come take my seat. Here, let me help you." She held the ill-looking woman around the shoulders. "Take a couple of deep breaths. Annelie, open my backpack. I have an unopened bottle of water left."

"Charlotta, you okay?" Annelie said, as she handed the water to her friend.

"Uh, yeah, I think so. They did warn people about motion sickness. Ew."

Sam had recovered more quickly and kept fanning herself with a brochure. "I think it's time for dinner," she suggested. "Charlotta will feel better with some food in her."

"Good idea," Jem agreed. "Any suggestions?"

"What about the Scandinavian part of Epcot?" Annelie said. "My Swedish heritage needs meatballs."

"Sounds good to me," Carolyn agreed.

The sun had set by the time they found the right restaurant and ordered their food. Charlotta started looking better after eating an appetizer.

"Your color's improved, at least," Carolyn noted as the waiter served their main course, meatballs.

"I'm fine now, thanks. Can you believe how wild that ride was?"

"I thought I was going to go deaf from Carolyn barking orders." Jem rolled her eyes. "Is she always this bossy, Annelie?"

Annelie looked at her lover, noticing Carolyn's wink. "She's normally very bossy, except when it comes to doing one thing." She saw Carolyn's eyes widen as the other women whistled and laughed. Annelie leaned closer to Carolyn. "Told you I'd get even."

"I can't believe you said that."

"What do you mean? I was talking about our professional relationship, as actress and executive producer."

"Aha. Right." Carolyn gave a slow smile.

Annelie focused on the way her friends teased Carolyn about her ability to slip into character at the drop of a hat, as Charlotta put it. Seeing everyone so at ease around her warmed Annelie's heart.

Sam's voice broke her reverie.

"Annelie, can you call the odd little guy over here? I want some Norwegian dessert."

❖

Having pulled out the box he had forgotten about until he watched the television show, the thin man tugged at the rubber band circling a small stack of letters. The box had been sitting in the cabinet for ages, and now it could come in very handy. Opening the first letter, he laughed with a hissing sound.

"'Annie asks for you all the time,'" he read aloud. "Great."

CHAPTER THIRTEEN

No, not like that. I look like I've been in a hurricane," Carolyn said, trying hard to remain patient. She hated having her hair and makeup done but was determined not to convey her aversion to the makeup artist working on her.

"It's a contemporary style," the hair stylist explained. "Diana Maddox—"

"Is a hardworking criminal investigator with little or no time in the morning to create this!" Carolyn gestured toward the mirror. "You're wasting your time. I know Regina Carmichael. She's not going to run with this look." Truth be told, she simply could not imagine going through the rather painful process of creating the wild hairdo every morning before filming.

"Let's take a picture of it anyway." The stylist gestured toward the photographer. "Just in case."

Muttering under her breath, Carolyn stepped up on the dais and allowed the studio photographer to do his job. "I liked the first version you created," she said. "The simple French twist was in character."

The other woman looked like she was about to object when Carolyn's cell phone interrupted them.

"Black."

"Oh, dear, you sound miffed," Beth greeted her at the other end. "What's up?"

"Nothing, sweetie. I'm at work, doing my fittings."

"Welcome back to New York."

Wanting to slap her forehead for forgetting to call her sister the previous evening, Carolyn took a deep breath and moved out of earshot. "I'm sorry I didn't call right away, kiddo. When we got in last night I fell into bed, unconscious."

"Did you have fun?"

"We had a great time, especially at Disney World, going on all the rides and eating well."

"Great. Listen, Lyn…" Beth's voice wavered. "I'm not sure, but I picked up on something on TV and had the feeling I should tell you."

"What is it?" A sudden, inexplicable pang made Carolyn square her shoulders.

"It's about your new boss. I saw something on E! News first and then a short segment on NBC."

Chills dashing down her spine, Carolyn pressed the cell phone closer to her ear. "Go on."

"Apparently Annelie Peterson's father has come forward, accusing her of letting him live in poverty, on welfare. He's claiming her charity work is nothing but a hypocritical act, since she doesn't even care about her own flesh and blood."

"What?!"

"I didn't like the sound of it. It came across like she was this heartless rich bitch with a poor, sick, old dad."

Carolyn's heart raced as cold fury exploded in the depths of her stomach. This was the type of story that signaled a media hunt. With so much press about the Maddox film and interest in the woman behind the project, the media would beat up any hint of scandal into a salacious exposé. Knowing time was all-important, she scrambled to figure out the best plan.

"Thank you for letting me know so quickly, honey. This will cause problems for Annelie, so I need to get right on it. Can I get in touch with you later tonight?"

"Sure. I'll be here."

Carolyn hung up and walked over to the makeup area where she kept her purse. Combing her hair, rolling her eyes as she destroyed the ridiculous hairdo, she held up her hand dismissively when the beautician approached her. "Sorry, we'll have to continue tomorrow. Something came up that can't wait."

"But…"

"Tomorrow." Rummaging around in her purse, Carolyn found Margo's business card. She looked up and saw the stylist still standing there. Sighing inwardly, she fought not to take her irritation out on her. "Can you call for my car? I'll see you in the morning at eight." Carolyn grabbed her coat and was already dialing Margo as she left the room.

"Margo, this is Carolyn Black."

"Carolyn, how are you? Annelie's not here. She's working from her apartment today." The Irish accent smoothed out the other woman's energetic way of speaking.

"I know. I'm on my way back there. It's you I need to talk to. Something's come up."

"Go on." Margo's voice was guarded.

"I had a call from my sister in D.C. who saw something disturbing on the news today about Annelie. It's not good." Carolyn relayed what Beth had said.

There was a pause, making Carolyn think she'd been cut off.

"Margo, are you still—"

"The bastard!" Margo exploded. "We'll take care of him. Why the hell did that lowlife have to crawl out from under his rock?"

"That's a no-brainer. Money."

"Yeah." Margo cleared her throat. "You realize this is going to hit her hard, don't you? When the media's witch hunt is on, all bets are off."

"I agree." Carolyn walked over to the car pulling up at the curb, got into the backseat, and gave Annelie's address. "I can't imagine how she'll take it. Privacy is so important to her."

"Tell her I'll be there as soon as I know more. And Carolyn, thanks for calling."

Forcing herself to relax against the headrest and rubbing her forehead, Carolyn hoped Annelie wouldn't be watching TV while she worked. Knowing Annelie preferred listening to soft jazz or classical music, she doubted it. Fifteen minutes later, the car pulled up to the condo.

Outside the door to the apartment, Carolyn had to stop and draw a cleansing breath. She was furious, angrier than she had been in a long time, and at a ghost of a man who was only out to get his hands on some of his daughter's money.

As Carolyn unlocked the door and stepped inside, she heard the bittersweet voice of Billie Holiday.

"Annelie?" Carolyn dropped her purse on the small dresser in the hallway and strode toward Annelie's study. Stopping in the doorway, she felt her heart melt when she spotted her lover completely focused on her computer. Her hair was in a ponytail, and she wore powder blue sweats. "Annie?"

Flinching, Annelie looked up, a soft smile spreading on her lips at the sight of her lover. "Carolyn, what are you doing home already? I thought fittings would take all day." A frown appeared on her forehead. "You look so serious. Is something wrong? Oh, God, is Beth all right?"

Carolyn walked over to the desk and sat down on the edge, leaning down for a quick kiss. "Beth's doing fine. She called me earlier and… she had some news that I wanted to share with you in person."

"What news? It can't be good. I can tell from your face. Come on. You're scaring me."

"Now, listen to me, love." Carolyn cupped Annelie's chin. "Seems your father has decided to float to the surface and make an appearance."

There was a stunned silence as Annelie went pale.

"Probably saw you on TV and put two and two together," she continued. "I've called Margo. She's dealing with it as we speak."

"My father?"

"Yes."

"Who…I mean, where…wh…" Annelie's voice gave out. When the words still didn't come, she reached for a remote sitting on her desk and pressed a button. Doors slid open in the bookshelf to reveal a plasma-screen television. Pressing another button, she clicked to the entertainment channel. After a commercial, a news segment featuring an elegant blond woman appeared.

"We're talking to Miranda Lewis, who has the latest on the Annelie Peterson story. As you know, Annelie Peterson is the publisher and executive producer responsible for bringing the famous character Diana Maddox to us in printed form as well as award-winning audiobooks. There has always been some mystique around the elusive beauty, who is one of the wealthiest women in the country. Share the scoop with us, Miranda."

Carolyn moved to stand behind Annelie, placing both hands on her shoulders.

"Well, Cathy, it turns out the stunning Ms. Peterson, also known for her generosity and philanthropic endeavors, has been hiding a secret that seems out of character. We know her, among other things, as the president of the Nebula Circle, a company devoted to building shelters for the homeless and raising money for needy children. Here's what's hard to understand. It turns out Annelie Peterson's father has lived in poverty most of his life, and he claims she hasn't raised one finger to help him."

"He's never...I didn't know," Annelie whispered. "I..."

Carolyn caressed the top of her right shoulder through her sweatshirt.

"He's disabled, unable to work for a living, and getting by on welfare. His name is Stuart Clint, and I met him a few hours ago in the Laguna Trailer and Camping Park." The scene shifted to a run-down trailer park, zooming in on a skinny, gray-haired man with piercing blue eyes. Dressed in a faded red T-shirt and torn jeans, he certainly looked the part.

"Tell us, Mr. Clint, why you've chosen to step forward right now?"

"I've missed having my daughter in my life for a mighty long time. I didn't want to mess things up for her, by showing up, you know, looking the way I do. I wouldn't fit in. She's a, well, I guess you could call her a jet-setter. I'm at the other end of the rope—real down on my luck, you could say. Lately, I've been sick, and there's no insurance and all. When I seen her on TV with her fancy friends, I figured maybe she might help her old dad out. So I been trying to get in touch, but she never answered my letters. Couldn't even pick up the phone."

"What? There have never been any letters, let alone calls!" Annelie rose from the chair. "He's lying, Carolyn."

"You don't have to convince me. I know he is." Carolyn reached for her.

"She was a real sweet child. Beautiful, with that golden hair and all. Can't believe the change in her since she come by money. Imagine, she's running these charities but leaves her own flesh and blood to suffer like this. Just isn't right. I've been quiet long enough. Hypocrisy, that's what we're talking about."

"He's lying!" Annelie grabbed the remote and switched off the TV. "I have to call Margo." Her hands trembled so much, the phone slipped through her fingers and landed on the floor, knocking the battery from its compartment. "Damn."

"Annelie, listen." Carolyn held her gently by the shoulders. "Margo's on her way here, as soon as she's informed Greg Horton."

At first, Carolyn thought Annelie was going to break free from her touch, but then she relented, turning into the embrace. Her slender form was shivering.

"I can't believe this is happening," she whispered. "I can't believe he'd do this after all this time. He left *us*! One day when I came home from school—I was in the first grade—he was gone."

"Come into the living room, love." Carolyn kissed Annelie's cheek and realized her lover was crying. "Let's go sit on the couch." She guided her through the apartment, one arm around her waist. Sitting down, she held Annelie, who clung to her. "There. I've got you."

They sat in silence for a moment, while Annelie regained her composure. When she finally pulled back, the expression in her eyes made Carolyn's heart ache.

"There's no way he can know anything personal about me," Annelie murmured, settling back against the pillows on the couch. "I certainly wasn't a beautiful child, as he says. Still, he has an eerie sense of what would hurt me the most." She clenched her teeth, blinking back new tears.

"I've worked so hard to get to where I am. I never wanted to be in the public eye. When I won the lottery, I was suddenly famous in the Chicago area and all over Illinois. People who normally wouldn't give me the time of day suddenly wanted to be my best friends. Women who gave me the cold shoulder all through high school now talked to me like we'd been pals since childhood.

"In fact, when I was a geeky preteen, they despised me. After I blossomed one summer and boys began acting nuts around me, they hated me. It also turned out my so-called geeky friends started seeing me as a kind of traitor. But when I became rich, all of them were suddenly my long-lost friends."

She shrugged, drying her tears on the sleeve of her sweatshirt. "So I left. I only stayed in touch with Margo, Charlotta, and Jem. I took my mother's maiden name…I *paid* someone to teach me how to walk, talk, eat…everything, so I could fit into circles of high society and big business. I just wanted to put the money to good use, to be left alone, and to, maybe…just maybe, find someone to love."

Carolyn reached out for Annelie's restless hands, pulling one of them up to her lips. Not taking her eyes off her lover, she kissed the palm and rubbed it against her cheek. "You *did* find someone to love, who loves you right back. I know your privacy is important, and I can imagine how this must hurt. The fact that it's your father doing this…is terrible.

"But listen to me, love. I know how this works. The press smells a scoop, and they aren't stupid. They see a story here. You're a beautiful, rich woman whom they know very little about. I mean, you've covered your tracks pretty well. A family drama unfolds in public, and they jump on it. The thing is, in a day or two, they'll lose interest. It's the nature of the media."

"But this reflects on more than just me, Carolyn," Annelie said, her eyes glistening. "He's questioning my credibility in my charity work. Never mind what he can do to me personally. This could seriously damage our projects."

Carolyn knew Annelie was right. "I understand that. But you need to see beyond your pain. Start thinking about damage control. Then you'll feel empowered, not victimized. Margo will help, and so will all of us."

Annelie's eyes narrowed. "You've been in a similar situation, haven't you?"

Carolyn shrugged. "Several times. I'm a celebrity, so the press treats me like public property. They invade my private life on a whim. It's the same for anyone like us, Annelie."

Annelie gestured toward herself, her hand shaking. "I feel…naked. I hate not being in control, not calling the shots. Guess that makes me a control freak." She gave a joyless smile.

"For not wanting your private life on display on TV? Hardly. Listen, early on I made a deal with myself where to draw the line. I never let them close to my house or the kids, but I just ignored so-called personal scandals. I taught John and Beth to ignore anything the media said about me. You know…as long as the three of us know what's true."

"I'm not used to this kind of scrutiny. I should have known to expect it," Annelie said.

"Well, you don't have to handle it alone. When I first met you, you seemed very reserved, aloof, even intimidating. But I was determined to get to know you. In the beginning it was to get the Maddox role, of course."

Annelie's eyes widened. "And later?"

"It soon became about something else. In Orlando at the

convention, it escalated to something I never could have imagined. You're a contradiction, Annie. So private and withdrawn, yet with a strong network of friends and colleagues. You attract very nice people who'd do anything for you, because they know you'd be there for them in a heartbeat."

Annelie blushed faintly. "They're quickly becoming your friends too."

"They let me in and try to get to know me only for your sake. I have to make them my friends, which hopefully I can, with time. Anyway, for such a reclusive individual, you have an extensive private life."

Annelie sat in silence for a moment, considering Carolyn's remarks. "You're saying I'm not as private or standoffish as I think?"

Cupping Annelie's chin, Carolyn leaned in for a quick kiss. "Not anymore. You were, for several valid reasons, but as you succeeded in business and made your way through law school, your confidence grew. And you learned who your real friends were. Don't you see? Just taking a chance on me, going against pretty much all of your principles, points to one thing. You've changed."

Scooting closer to Carolyn, Annelie wrapped her arms around her. "How is it you can see things so clearly? How?"

"I don't know. I love you. I love observing you when you don't know it, watching your expression change, hearing your voice when you talk to someone else. You're the most beautiful woman I've ever seen. Your body moves with such litheness and grace and—well, you're of course very hot." Carolyn felt, rather than heard, Annelie give a short laugh. "I can't take my eyes off of you. Let alone my hands."

"You know, that's what Jem told me after the luncheon. You were looking at me the entire time. Even then?"

"Even then."

Carolyn let her body slide back, ending up against the armrest of the couch, taking Annelie with her. "Why don't we just relax until Margo gets here? She's a smart lady, and she loves you."

"Okay." Annelie moved to the side and wrapped an arm and a leg around Carolyn, as if she needed as much contact as possible. "I'm so glad you're here. When do you need to go back to the studio?"

"Not till tomorrow."

Annelie sighed and relaxed more into her lover. "Good."

Carolyn closed her eyes. Annelie's soft lemony scent surrounded her, reminding her of Florida, and had the circumstances been different, nothing could have prevented her from making love to her.

❖

Annelie inhaled Carolyn's musky scent, remembering how she first became aware of the soft perfume when Carolyn tried to kiss her at the luncheon weeks ago. It seemed longer than that; so many things had happened since then. Her heart was still hammering painfully, as if trying to break free from her rib cage. Every breath was hard, and she hated how the hurt of what her father had done seemed to permeate her body.

Carolyn had soothed her, helped her get the initial panic under control. Annelie was glad her lover had been the one to break the news to her. Falling apart was horrible, but doing it in front of Carolyn wasn't so bad. Realizing the implications of this thought, Annelie turned her head and kissed the soft cheek next to her on the cushion.

"What's that for?" Carolyn sounded drowsy.

"Because you're here."

Smiling with her eyes still closed, Carolyn turned her head and pressed her lips against Annelie's. "Yes, I am, and I'm not going anywhere."

The sound of Carolyn's throaty voice was reassuring. It wrapped around Annelie's heart like armor, and for a moment, she instinctively knew as long as Carolyn was there to love her, nothing could really pierce it.

The doorbell made her jump and sit up so quickly she almost shoved Carolyn onto the floor. "That must be Margo."

"How long was I asleep?" Carolyn asked, clutching at Annelie so she wouldn't fall off the couch. "Hey, easy there, she'll wait for you."

Annelie helped Carolyn regain her balance. "You slept an hour or so. I thought you were awake earlier. You talked to me."

"I did? What did I say?"

Turning her head over her shoulder as she walked toward the hallway, Annelie smiled softly. "Mushy stuff. Should've known you weren't quite lucid."

"Oh, funny," Carolyn muttered, winking at her. "Liar."

Margo strode in and wrapped Annelie up in a long, firm embrace.

"I've got you covered, girlie," she said, her Irish accent more noticeable than usual. "I have the best people setting the record straight. Don't you worry." She pulled back and gazed at Annelie. "Have I ever failed you?"

"Not for a second." Annelie swallowed. "It's just…"

"It hurts."

"Badly."

"Come on. Let's sit down and I'll fill you in."

They walked into the living room, Margo greeting Carolyn with a firm handshake. "Thank you for giving me the information so quickly. I'm in your debt."

"When it's about Annelie, I'll do just about anything to keep her safe and happy." Carolyn looked serious. "I was so angry I was ready to…I just knew you were the one to call—and that I needed to come home. I mean, back here." Seemingly not fazed in the least by her slip, Carolyn motioned toward the seat. "Why don't you go ahead and talk? I'll make some coffee."

"Thanks. Coffee's a given at this point." Margo grinned.

Margo's expression softened as Carolyn disappeared toward the kitchen. They sat down, Margo in the armchair and Annelie on the couch.

"She loves you."

It wasn't a question but Annelie replied, "Yes, she does. Fiercely."

"I'd have to be blind not to notice. I like her sense of loyalty. Anyway, let me give you some details. As you realize, Stuart Clint has surfaced in Los Angeles claiming you've neglected him all these years. He's trying to make you out to be a callous daughter who wants a halo for saving the masses instead of caring for an aging, loving father."

Annelie felt the blood drain from her face. "Oh, God."

"Don't worry, girlie. This bullshit isn't going to fly. Sorry for my language. I'm so furious, I'm losing my manners. Stuart hasn't given a damn about you for the last twenty-seven years—not one sign, word, or card from him—and now this. You know the private investigator we sometimes use at the firm? I called him, and this case is now his only priority until we have what we need. I should have all the papers we need from Chicago and California in a day or two."

Carolyn returned with a tray and placed it on the coffee table.

After handing the women on the couch a mug of steaming coffee each, she turned to walk out of the room.

"No, Carolyn, please stay. This concerns you too."

"Yes, stay," Annelie echoed, extending a hand.

"Sure, let me just grab my mug." Carolyn returned with her coffee and sat down next to Annelie. "I overheard the last part. So it's just a matter of keeping our cool for a couple of days, Margo?"

"Yes. I know it's hard on you, Annie, and I can only begin to fathom how you must hate this. He's making an even bigger idiot of himself, since there's no way he can prove anything he's saying."

"I have a theory about that," Carolyn said. "He's hoping Annelie will pay him off to keep him quiet. He's counting on her not having the balls to stand her ground and call his bluff."

Annelie's eyes widened at her lover's choice of words, as Carolyn's vehement tone revealed her fury.

"I couldn't have phrased it any better myself," Margo agreed. "This is a quick, ill-planned scheme for money, and nothing else."

Annelie put the mug down after a quick sip, shuddering as she leaned back against the couch. "I just hate how this affects my charities." Her voice broke and she swallowed twice to try and clear it. "Just the thought of people believing him...thinking such things about me..."

Carolyn moved closer and put an arm around her shoulders. "Now, don't let this get to you. People will find out the truth. The ones you count on would never believe him. In a few days we'll have it all sorted out, and he'll regret he ever tried this."

"He's my father," Annelie whispered. "How can he do this to his child, even if he left me...I just don't get it." Turning to Carolyn, she couldn't hold back the tears.

❖

Annelie cried almost soundlessly against Carolyn's shoulder, making Carolyn and Margo exchange glances of sympathy and concern.

"You're going to be okay, honey," Margo promised. "Just let us do the job. You don't have to make a statement. I'll handle all that."

Annelie looked up, reaching for a box of Kleenex. "I can't ask you to..."

"Sure you can! I thought I'd make a statement to the press as soon as I have all the information I need, challenging this bastard to present any evidence of his accusations."

Carolyn was impressed with Margo's clear-thinking strategy. "For what it's worth, I think you're dead-on," she said. "Annelie should make a personal statement only when we have the proof."

"Exactly." Margo smirked.

"All right," Annelie said, blowing her nose. "Enough of these tears. I'm hungry."

"And I'm running late." Margo jumped up. "Have something to eat, ladies. I'll see myself out. Call you later, girlie." She waved and was out the front door.

"She's an Energizer bunny come alive." Carolyn smiled. "With her taking care of things, you'll be okay, love."

Annelie nodded. "I hope so."

"Why don't you make yourself comfortable? I'll see what's in the freezer."

"You're going to cook?"

Not offended, Carolyn laughed at Annelie's doubtful tone of voice. "I thought so. For heaven's sake, even *I* can defrost a pizza!"

"Okay, okay. Thank you."

Carolyn walked into the kitchen, opened the freezer, and found a family-size mozzarella pizza. After reading the package carefully, she turned the oven on and walked off to use the bathroom. When she returned, the oven was hot so she put the pizza in, feeling confident it would be ready soon. After she set the timer, Carolyn joined Annelie, who stood on the balcony by the railing.

"Twenty minutes from now we'll have a delicious pizza," she promised, hugging Annelie from behind. "In the meantime, can I interest my best girl in some smooching, perhaps?"

Annelie gave a muted laugh. "Some smooching, eh?" She pivoted in Carolyn's arms. "And where is this smooching going to take place, if I may ask?"

"Of course you may. See that corner over there? The only ones able to see us are seagulls and other high-flying birds."

Annelie glanced at the hard wooden bench. "Looks awfully uncomfortable."

"I'll make it worth your while." Carolyn raised her eyebrows suggestively.

"Oh, yeah?" Annelie allowed herself to be dragged toward the bench. "What did you have in mind?"

"Step into my parlor..." Carolyn sat down on the bench, pulling Annelie with her. "Here...just like this..." Looking into her lover's stormy eyes, she hoped the closeness would distract Annelie. She laced her fingers through long strands of hair and closed the distance between them, capturing Annelie's lips with her own. "Open your mouth," Carolyn breathed. "Yes..." Deepening the kiss, she heard Annelie whimper as their tongues met in a tantalizingly slow movement, tasting each other. Carolyn drank her kisses greedily, her passion for the woman in her arms igniting her senses.

Her hands moved down Annelie's back and slid under her sweatshirt, only to find she wasn't wearing a bra. "Oh, God, Annie... this is getting out of control," she murmured. "You feel so wonderful." Letting her lips burn a trail down Annelie's neck, she slid her hands forward, cupping Annelie's full breasts. Carolyn noted with pleasure how hard the nipples were as they prodded her palms. She pushed at the sweatshirt, eager to get it out of the way...

A deafening blare broke the mood. Annelie jerked, looking wide-eyed at Carolyn.

"It's the smoke alarm!"

❖

Dark gray smoke billowed from the kitchen. The smoke alarm's high-pitched tone pierced the women's eardrums as they ran inside.

"What the hell..." Annelie squinted through the smoke, detecting the source. "There's something burning in the oven!"

"I put in a pizza, for heaven's sake! It's only been a few minutes. How can it already be burning?"

"I don't know. Open the door to the balcony and see if we can air out the smoke." Annelie put on a mitt and opened the oven door. More smoke poured out, and she coughed as she yanked out a half-done pizza. She tossed the tray on the stove, then used a spatula to confirm her suspicions.

Carolyn hurried back to her. "I don't get it. What's wrong with the pizza?"

Annelie reached out to a panel on the wall and punched in a series of numbers, silencing the smoke alarm. "Nothing's wrong with the pizza." She tried her best to sound serious. "You just didn't remove the cardboard plate underneath it."

Carolyn's jaw fell as she stared at the oven tray with its smoking contents. "What cardboard plate? It said, 'Bake in oven at 400 F for twenty minutes'—nothing about any cardboard plates."

"It probably was stuck against the bottom of the pizza, and you just didn't notice it. No harm done. The ventilation system will clear the air in half an hour or so."

"Oh, God…I knew I was a bad cook, but this is really ridiculous!" Carolyn groaned, leaning against the cabinet. "What'll we eat now? Not one smoked pizza, I hope?"

"No, this would have a strange flavor. Why don't we send out for something or just have a sandwich?"

"A sandwich sounds great. Nothing to set ablaze."

Annelie laughed at Carolyn's obvious dismay. "True. Why don't we go back to the balcony until the rest of the smoke is gone?"

They walked outside, stood by the railing, and watched the sky become darker as evening approached. "Pretty with all the lights coming on, isn't it? The city noise can be quite a homey feeling," Carolyn said. "Used to, when I came home late after a show, I'd sit out on my much-smaller balcony with a glass of wine. Just relaxing, listening to the city that never sleeps, you know."

"Yes, I know. The difference from the velvety, perfumed nights of Florida is enormous—but I love them both."

"Speaking of sounds, I hope nothing bad's happened. A lot of sirens are screaming out there." Carolyn leaned over the balcony railing. "Oh, look, they're coming down your street."

"Yes, I see the lights. There are two more."

"Wonder what's going on…Oh."

The two women watched as two fire trucks stopped in front of the building and firemen jumped off, looking up.

"Oh, damn, I didn't call the desk downstairs to make sure they knew it was a false alarm," Annelie murmured. "This is embarrassing."

They walked back inside, and Annelie dialed the doorman's desk. "Hello, Fred, this is entirely my fault. I forgot to call. Yes, everything's all right." She paused. "They do? But it wasn't really a fire…just smoke from the oven…Oh, sure. Send them up. I understand." She hung up and turned toward Carolyn. "Since we're on the fifteenth floor, they want to come up and make sure we put it out properly."

Carolyn blushed faintly. "I'll tell them I'm to blame."

"Don't worry. I bet this happens all the time. We might as well open the doors and let our heroes in. Actually, I'm glad they're this conscientious."

A few minutes later, the elevator doors opened and two men in firefighter gear stepped out. "I see we're expected," the first one said with a smile. "Heard your smoke alarm went off, ma'am."

"Yes, but it was only because of a missed cardboard plate in the oven. It's fine now," Annelie explained.

"Let's just have a look, eh?"

"Sure. Come in."

The men gave Annelie appreciative looks before they turned to politely greet Carolyn. "Good evening, ma'am..." After a slight hesitation, the older one continued, "Forgive me, ma'am, but aren't you Carolyn Black?"

"Yes, I am. Good evening. Nice of you to stop by."

Annelie was hard-pressed not to laugh when she noticed Carolyn slipping into a regal tone of voice, as if greeting her subjects.

"I'm a great fan," the fireman said, "and so is my wife. Can't wait to see the Maddox movies."

"Thank you. Please tell your wife I said hello. By the way, this was entirely my fault. I was trying to cook, which I can't, so from now on I'll stick to takeout." Carolyn smiled broadly and raised her hands in a dismissive gesture.

Obviously taken by Carolyn's charm, the firemen quickly checked the oven and the ventilation fan above it. "Glad to see everything's okay, ma'am," the younger fireman offered.

"It was my fault for not calling the front desk. Thanks for double-checking."

"Our pleasure," the other man said, with an admiring glance at Carolyn. "Better safe than sorry."

Annelie had barely closed the door behind them before she started to laugh. "Good Lord, Carolyn, you have admirers everywhere. I thought he was going to kneel before you and ask you to autograph his helmet."

Carolyn walked up to her and wrapped her arms around Annelie's waist. "I would have, if he'd asked me. Right now, I'd like to…write on you…"

"Write on me? How?"

Leaning forward, Carolyn let her tongue trace the indentation at the base of Annelie's neck. A soft purr emanated from Carolyn's throat as she let her mouth travel toward her lover's lips.

Annelie moaned and held Carolyn close. "Trying to continue what you started out on the balcony, are you? Oh, mmm, that feels good…" She felt soft hands under her sweatshirt, stroking along her back.

"You bet. I was onto something good. I could feel it," Carolyn whispered. "I simply can't stop touching you every chance I get."

"I like the sound of that. How about we move into the…Oh!" Carolyn's exploring hands had reached Annelie's breasts and found erect nipples waiting for her touch. "Why don't you go into the bedroom while I close the doors to the balcony?"

"All right. Give me a minute, though. I need to use the bathroom after all this excitement." Carolyn smiled.

"Sure. I'll be there in a jiffy."

Annelie placed a soft kiss on Carolyn's lips before returning to the living room. After closing the door, she heard a faint ringing sound, which she finally realized was coming from Carolyn's purse. She hesitated for a moment and then pulled out her cell phone. The name *Beth* flashed on the display. Knowing Carolyn's sister would reach the answering service within seconds, Annelie quickly pressed the Answer button.

"Carolyn Black's cell phone. Annelie Peterson speaking."

"Oh…hello, Annelie. I'm Carolyn's sister, Beth. Is Carolyn around?"

"Hello, Beth. Yes, she is, but she's in the bathroom right now." Suddenly nervous, Annelie found herself fumbling for a nonexistent phone cord to twist around her fingers.

"Oh, don't interrupt her. How are you doing, Annelie? It's nice to talk to you." Beth's voice was light and cheerful—very unlike Carolyn's.

"I'm doing okay. Thank you for alerting Carolyn today. She told me you called her at work."

"I was stunned at how anyone can be so devious. I don't pretend to know anything about your private life, Annelie, but I know you're a good friend to Carolyn. I had a feeling you'd need the support of your friends once the media started in on this."

"You were absolutely right. Carolyn's support means a lot to me." Annelie stopped there, not knowing what else to say.

"She can be very protective, you know. When she becomes attached to someone, you're her friend for life. If you hurt her, she recoils and has a hard time getting over it. She's more sensitive than most people realize."

Not sure about Beth's motives for sharing this information, if it was a warning or just a heads-up, Annelie replied from her heart. "I understand what you're saying. I don't think Carolyn lets anyone in on her sensitive side very often. She's been wonderful to me."

"She has nothing but good to say about you either," Beth said in a friendly tone of voice. "I can't wait to meet you. I asked Carolyn if I could come and sit in on the set when my pregnancy is more stable, so Joe and I can drive up for a week. Joe's my husband, by the way."

"I know. And your daughter is Pamela. How's she doing? I hear she's her aunt's favorite."

"Oh, she's doing great. Carolyn's her idol, all categories."

"Who are you talking to?" Carolyn came into the living room, dressed only in a towel. "Is that my cell phone?"

"It's your sister. Beth, Carolyn's here. It was nice talking to you."

"Likewise, Annelie. Now you take care and stay strong, okay?"

"Thanks, Beth. I will." Annelie handed the phone to Carolyn. Wanting to give the two siblings their privacy, she had begun to walk out of the room when a strong arm settled around her waist and pulled her down onto the armchair. Carolyn sat down on the armrest, her hand moving through Annelie's hair, caressing her softly. Relaxing, Annelie leaned against her, not listening to her words, merely the husky voice, the warmth of it, as she closed her eyes.

She didn't know how long she had sat there unwinding after the eventful day, and she didn't even look up when Carolyn put the phone down. Carolyn slid down across Annelie's lap, allowing Annelie to cradle her. Their lips met in a kiss that started out gently, only to turn passionate within seconds. Carolyn's towel unwrapped by itself, and Annelie's hands roamed the naked, slightly damp, woman before her.

"I want you," Carolyn whispered. "Oh, God, how I want you."

"I'm yours. You have me." Annelie slid her hand down her lover's stomach, nestling her fingers in the curls below before cupping her mound. "And it seems I have you."

Carolyn readily parted her legs and looked up at Annelie. "Yes, you do…" Her back arched as Annelie carefully parted the slick folds. "Oh…"

Completely enthralled by the sounds Carolyn made when Annelie found the protruding ridge of nerves, eager for her touch, she felt her heart race. Because she had initially not allowed Carolyn to touch her or even see her naked, she realized how vulnerable Carolyn must have felt, being naked while she was fully dressed. The significance of Carolyn's trust overwhelmed her.

"I love you." Annelie's voice almost broke. "Do you have any idea how much I love you?"

"Yes. I feel it, every day…" Carolyn pulled her legs up. "Take me…please…"

Not wanting Carolyn to beg, Annelie complied, pushing two fingers inside and at the same time capturing her waiting lips in a kiss. Ripples of pleasure clasped her fingers together, and rhythmic tremors massaged them as Carolyn tensed. Deepening the kiss, Annelie caught the muted whimpers when her lover came in her arms.

When Carolyn's breath had slowed to normal, Annelie carefully extracted her fingers and pulled a blanket over them. Nuzzling Carolyn's tousled hair, she realized she was still in shock over what her father had done, but her closeness to Carolyn had helped her start to find her bearings again.

"I love you, Annie…" came a husky whisper from inside the blanket. "Am I too heavy for you?"

"No. You're perfect."

❖

Margo rose from her office chair as the fax machine buzzed to life. Several documents emerged, one after another, and she browsed through them with narrowing eyes. When the machine had spit out the last paper, Margo bit her lower lip, but the expression on her face was triumphant.

"Girlie, if I'm right about this…"

Margo reached for the stapler, feeling utterly satisfied at the opportunity to thump something as she fastened the important documents together.

CHAPTER FOURTEEN

Something was choking her. Tossing to the left, Annelie tried to free herself.

"No!"

"Annie, wake up. It's only a dream. I'm here."

Carolyn's voice eventually filtered through, and Annelie opened her eyes to see Carolyn tugging at the sheet cocooning her body.

"I don't know how you managed to get so twisted up," Carolyn said. "You've had a bad night."

"What do you mean?" Annelie was hoarse. All she could remember were fluttering shadows and a sense of frustration.

"You've been tossing and turning since we turned out the lights. I had to hold you to get you to settle down."

"I'm sorry. I didn't mean to keep you awake. You've got a long day ahead." Annelie shuddered and reached for a pillow.

"I don't care. It's nothing some coffee can't fix." Carolyn pried the pillow from Annelie's iron grip and pulled her close. "Why don't we take a hot shower together? Your fingers are like ice."

Annelie clung to her. "I'd like that. Could you just hold me a little longer?"

"As long as you want." Carolyn stroked her back with soft, circular motions. "Better?"

"Yes." Annelie's throat ached and her jaws felt sore, making her wonder if she'd clenched her teeth while she slept. Nuzzling her lover's soft neck, she inhaled the familiar scent of Carolyn's sandalwood soap and felt her frayed nerves settle. "Move in with me?" The words leapt out before Annelie realized what she'd said.

Carolyn shifted next to her, placing two fingers under Annelie's chin, tipping her head back and looking at her steadily. "What did you say?"

"I mean, move in with me during the filming." Annelie swallowed, realizing she was backtracking. "The studio's nearby, so it'll cut your travel time. And I can't imagine you not coming home to me. If you feel crowded…you can always go back to your place." Annelie hated how pleading she sounded. *This is too soon. She's going to turn me down.* Holding her breath, she waited for Carolyn to say something.

"You sure?" Carolyn's voice was noncommittal.

"Very sure." *Am I? Yes, I am. I want this so much.*

Carolyn kissed Annelie firmly, then smiled wryly. "All right. I'll stop by my place and pack some things. I'd love to stay here." Carolyn's eyes began to twinkle. "Of course, I'm only doing it for one reason."

Annelie exhaled, the tension starting to leave her. "Really?" She quirked an eyebrow.

"The pool," Carolyn deadpanned.

Stunned at how quickly Carolyn could distract her, Annelie chuckled. "Naturally. The pool." Then her laughter broke free as she hugged Carolyn. "I'll love having you here. I may not let you leave." Realizing she'd spoken again without thinking, she stopped laughing and put a hand to her mouth.

Carolyn seemed unaware of her lover's discomfort. "You may have to pry me out of here with a screwdriver."

Relaxing, Annelie reveled in Carolyn's embrace and their morning ritual of showering together. *Maybe now I can make it through the day.*

"I'll be back fairly early," Carolyn said. "If you need anything or just want to talk, call my cell."

"I don't want to bother you…"

Carolyn grasped Annelie's shoulders gently and looked at her firmly. "Listen to me, love. You can never bother me."

"I hate feeling this vulnerable. I feel like apologizing."

"Not to me, and not to anyone else." Carolyn leaned forward, brushing her lips over Annelie's. "You're going to work from home today too, aren't you?"

"Yes, I'll be here. Hiding."

"Annie, you don't owe anyone any explanations. You're just waiting to hear what Margo finds out. Then we'll decide what road to take. That's it."

But I feel like such a coward. I'm not used to hiding and letting other people fight my battles. Still, Carolyn's probably right. "All right. I've got a ton of work to do." Annelie smiled wistfully. "Hopefully time will fly."

"I'll hurry home," Carolyn promised. "Gotta run."

Annelie switched on her computer and heard its muted hiss. Sipping some hot Earl Grey tea, she was happy to see Kitty's name in her inbox. Soon she was looking at her friend's smiling face with Sam at a South Beach restaurant.

Raising the mug again to her lips, Annelie blew on the steaming tea and read.

```
From: Kitty McNeil
Subject: What's going on?


Hello babe!
    What's happening in your neck of the
woods? Sam and I watched E! News today,
and your pretty face was plastered all
over the damn thing. Are they insane?
This is even more proof the press is
only out to make a fast buck—not check
their sources! What can a hardworking ex-
journo like me say to redeem my former
profession? Honestly, it's the fat cats
at the top controlling this. If they'd
bothered to check, they'd have known what
a deadbeat your dad is! Damn, this makes
me so mad!
    If there's anything I can do, don't
hesitate to ask—I'll try to call you
tonight if I can figure out the time
difference again. I'll set the alarm if
I have to.
    Oh, by the way, I visited the Diana
Maddox official Web site and saw there's
going to be another convention in L.A.
this weekend. Are you going to be there
```

```
with  the  cast?  In  that  case—pictures,
please!
```
```
    Love  you,  gorgeous.  Don't  let  them
get  to  you.
    Kitty
```

Kitty didn't know about Carolyn and her. Suddenly she longed to talk to her and reached for the phone, but was startled when it rang.

"Hello?"

"It's me." The familiar husky voice surprised Annelie and made her throat ache with unshed tears.

"Carolyn. Did you forget something?"

"Not a thing. I just wanted to hear your voice before I got to the studio. I miss you."

Feeling as if her heart settled in the softest of cotton, Annelie released a wistful sigh. "I miss you too. Are we being silly?"

"Of course not. Will you be all right, love?"

"Yes. I'll be fine." *Now that you've called.*

"Good. Guess I needed to hear that. Oh, we're here. Talk to you later." A kiss sounded through the phone.

"Love you. Have fun, Carolyn."

"I will. Ciao."

Annelie leaned back into her chair. *It's unbelievable how she reaches deep down inside me. All she has to do is speak. The words don't matter. It's how she sounds.* Carolyn's voice resonated within her, warming her. Stretching and finding it easier to breathe, Annelie reached for her mouse and started to work.

❖

Carolyn glanced around the bedroom of her apartment, checking to see if she needed anything else. After putting some clothes and toiletries into two large suitcases, she paused, reaching for her phone and dialing Annelie's number. The soft alto voice replied immediately.

"Peterson."

"Hi, love, it's me. I'm at the apartment and almost done packing."

"Good. I miss you."

"I'll be home soon." Home. Carolyn smiled to herself. "How was your day, Annie?" She pressed the last of her items down into one of the bags, closing it with one hand as she held the phone closer to her ear.

"Long, but okay. By the way, Margo's coming over later with more information."

Carolyn hesitated. "Look, if you need privacy while…"

"No, no. I need you. I want you here when she comes."

Carolyn's heart melted at Annelie's hurried tone. "We're in this together, love. I'll be home soon. Want me to pick you up anything?"

"No, just come home."

"I'll just grab my mail and leave. I'll have it forwarded to your address, if it's okay."

"Certainly. Good idea."

"See you soon." Carolyn placed two fingers to her lips and blew a loud kiss at the phone. Annelie's soft laugh was well worth it.

"Soon."

❖

What will she think of me, meeting her by the door like this? Waiting in the open doorway for the elevator to reach the fifteenth floor, Annelie felt her face grow warm when she thought about how needy she must seem. After a muted ping, Carolyn exited, followed by an enthralled doorman pulling her suitcases behind him. *God, she's beautiful, even when she's worn-out.*

"Thank you so much for your help. I'm fine now." Carolyn tipped him generously, and then she and Annelie pulled the bags over the threshold. "Hello. I'm home."

Closing the door, Annelie wrapped her arms around her lover and hugged her close. "Yes, you are, and it feels so good to hold you." Softly kissing Carolyn's lips, she pulled back a little. "You look tired."

"Long day. We're all set for the promotion picture shoot tomorrow. Regina and I finally settled for a look. Simple but modern." Carolyn continued to tell Annelie how a crowd of fans had been waiting in front of her apartment when she dropped by to pack. "I had no idea they could find out where I live. My number's unlisted."

Annelie frowned. "They have their ways. I've always made sure nobody knows where I live. I'm really glad now."

Carolyn had pulled one of her bags into the bedroom. "Me too. Where do you want me to unpack my things?"

"In that closet and the drawers over there. I'll help you later. Margo should be here in"—she checked her watch—"twenty minutes. I ordered Italian for us, and it's staying warm in the oven."

"Without the cardboard plate, I hope?" Carolyn raised an eyebrow, making Annelie smile.

"No cardboard plates." She walked up to her lover, enfolding her in another embrace. "No fires today…well, at least not in the kitchen." Leaning down, she traced Carolyn's lips with her tongue, coaxing her to open her mouth. "Mmm…oh, yes." Annelie deepened the kiss while stroking Carolyn's back underneath her jacket.

"Oh, Annie…" Carolyn breathed against Annelie's mouth. "I…I better freshen up before dinner…oh…"

Annelie let the passion flare for another minute before she relented. "I know you're right, but it's hard to let go. You feel so good."

Carolyn raised a hand and cupped Annelie's cheek. "So do you, so hold on to that thought. I'll only be a second."

Opening a bottle of Beaujolais Royale, Annelie thought about how Carolyn fit in her arms. *She just feels so right.* The sound of the phone ringing roused her from her daydream.

"Peterson."

"Hi, kiddo, it's Jem. How're you doing?"

Annelie gave a wry smile. "Okay. How are things in Florida?"

"I wanted to call yesterday but didn't want to disturb you. I know all hell's broken loose, and I figured you had Carolyn and Margo there helping you deal with everything."

"That's true, but I appreciate your call. It's been awkward and downright painful, but I'm handling it. Thank goodness, I'm not alone."

"Look, Annelie, I'm calling for a reason. The security guard where you live called, concerned since a media posse's set up camp just outside the gates. I'm not sure how they found out where you live."

Annelie closed her eyes, stifling a groan. "I guess they have their sources. That's all I needed," she murmured. "Thanks for letting me know. Can you get rid of them?"

"They're smart enough not to trespass, so we can't touch them. I know you'll be in New York a long time, so they'll probably give up when they realize you're not here." Jem paused. "Damn that man. I could wring his fucking neck!"

"Calm down. I need you to keep your cool. Have they approached any of the companies at your end?"

"Are you kidding? We've been swamped with calls, but so far we've told them *no comment* until the press conference. You okay with that?"

"Excellent. We'll fax you the statement Margo's going to give the press, probably tomorrow. I want you to give a press conference and use her statement. We have to keep a united front. It's vital to all our projects."

"Got it, kiddo. I'll try to control myself, but you know me. I'm ready to…" Jem was obviously bristling.

Annelie understood. She heard the doorbell ring and looked up.

"I'll get it," Carolyn said, coming out of the bedroom.

"Margo's here. Thanks for calling. Talk to you later, my friend. Take care."

Annelie overheard Carolyn greet Margo. "Hi, come on in. Hope you've got some good news."

"It's looking up!" Margo's Irish accent was more obvious than usual. "Where is she?"

"With our dinner. I just got home."

As the two women entered the kitchen, Margo hugged Annelie firmly. "Hello, girlie. How're you holding up?"

"Fine. Carolyn's agreed to move in with me while she's filming, so that helps."

Margo didn't as much as flinch, though Annelie detected a curious gleam in her eyes. "Sounds like a great arrangement." She winked at Carolyn. "It'll be closer for you, won't it?"

"Yes, but that's not the real reason. I just don't want to be away from her."

Oh, my…Carolyn, do you know what you're saying? Annelie stared at her lover. Carolyn's unexpected candidness took her breath away. Glancing at Margo, Annelie noticed her pleased smile.

"I'm glad you're sticking together. Let's get dinner on the table so I can let you in on what I've found out."

While they ate, Margo pulled out a stack of documents and handed them to Annelie.

"Here's what I've confirmed so far. The media is going nuts, mostly because of the Maddox movies. If things hadn't happened so close together, the press wouldn't have cared."

"Give me the short version," Annelie said, glancing reluctantly at the large stack of documents.

"These affidavits prove your father owed eleven years of child support and didn't pay a single cent. And his rap sheet includes doing time twice for drug trafficking and several DUIs. These complete telephone listings for your house in Florida and the apartment here prove he's lying about trying to call you. And no records exist to show he ever tried to reach you at either the Florida office or the law firm."

"Good job, Margo," Annelie offered, feeling some of the weight fall from her shoulders. "Anything else?"

"Copies of documents when your mother filed for sole custody of you. You were ten, and that's when she quit hoping he'd ever return, if I remember right. She wouldn't say a bad word about him, not even after the court awarded her full custody, Annie. I'd sometimes go off on a rant, but then she'd look at me with those mild blue eyes and remind me that you're his daughter. Without him, she wouldn't have you. Honest to God, girlie, she was a saint."

What would I have done without her silent strength? Annelie suddenly remembered the way her mother's hand had felt against the back of her head, one of her rare caresses. *After she died, I didn't think I could survive without her. More than fifteen years but, to this day, I miss her. Oh, Mother...*

Anna Clint had worked two jobs to support them while Annelie finished high school but had died just before her graduation. "Yes, she was a saint, in a lot of ways," Annelie said. "I don't think she ever raised her voice to me."

"You never gave her a reason, child. Not that you didn't exasperate her, always with your nose in a book or watching your favorite soap on TV—not getting enough sunlight according to your mom." Margo wrinkled her nose at Annelie and winked at Carolyn. "I don't have to tell you which soap it was, do I?"

"No, I can guess." Carolyn smiled. "But I'm not complaining."

"Yes, if she hadn't been completely starstruck with you then— who knows where the two of you would be now?"

"Hey, stop talking about me like I'm not here," Annelie grumbled good-naturedly. "Margo, is this enough to discredit my...father?"

"More than discredit him, girlie. This isn't simple mudslinging. Stuart Clint's trying to damage your reputation. By the way, several organizations you're working with have sent supportive e-mails and telegrams, Annelie."

"I've had several e-mails too. I hope they feel the same way when all this is over."

Margo nodded. "I'm sure they will. The custody papers help prove that Stuart refused to provide for you after you were seven. Even before that, your mother was the one who put food on the table. I know, because I was there and watched her stay up sewing till after midnight every night after she'd worked all day at her real job clerking at the courthouse. And what's more, he's never tried to contact you. This'll blow him right out of the water, sweetie."

"Some facts remain," Annelie objected, her voice almost betraying her. "He lives in poverty. He's on disability. In spite of everything, he's still my father."

Margo frowned. "You don't owe him anything."

"No, maybe not, but it wouldn't cost me much to get him into a program and buy him a decent home."

Carolyn exchanged glances with Margo. "You've got plenty of time to think about that after the press conference. By the way, when is it?"

"Tomorrow at three in the conference room at the office. I'll just stick to these facts. Then the ball's in Stuart's court. I also have our investigator digging for more information. He promised he'd be through by Thursday, at the latest."

Shuffling the food aimlessly around her plate, Annelie looked uneasy. "Sounds like you've got everything covered," she murmured. "I appreciate it, Margo. It's just…"

"Yes, I know." Margo reached for Annelie's hand and patted it. "I know, girlie."

Margo and Carolyn chatted while they finished their meal. Annelie gave up trying to eat any more. Listening to the other women talk, she leaned back in her chair and heard the familiar sound of her mother's voice in the far distance. *After all, he is your father, Annie.*

❖

The women on the couch listened to jazz vocalist Diana Krall and watched two logs burn in the fireplace.

Carolyn sat sideways, her back against the armrest and her legs cradling Annelie's body. Lost in thought, she combed through long, silky hair with slow fingers. To relax like this, holding Annelie in her arms, was almost unfathomable. *Surreal.* Carolyn inhaled the citrus scent of Annelie's shampoo. *She's so quiet tonight. I hate to see her suffer. If I could get my hands on this son of a bitch, I'd...I'd do anything to protect her. Before she left, Margo asked me to look after her and, damn it, I will.*

Annelie raised her head. "Carolyn?"

Pulled out of her dark thoughts regarding Stuart Clint, Carolyn glanced down at her lover, her expression transforming into a soft smile. "Yes, love?"

"Are you sure you're comfortable? Feels like I'm crushing you."

"I'm more than comfortable. Lay your head back down."

As Annelie rested her head on Carolyn's shoulder again, Carolyn kissed her lover's temple, transfixed by the clean smell of lemons. "This feels so good. Can you relax?"

"Uh-huh. I'm finally getting warm."

"Great. You're not shivering anymore. A good sign."

"I liked helping you unpack earlier, but what do you think I enjoyed the most?"

"What?"

"Watching you put the little photos of your sister and her family, and John, on the bedside table." There was a brief silence. "Can I ask you something?"

"Anything."

"Things are moving so fast. Do you have any second thoughts about our relationship? Maybe feel I'm more than you bargained for? I'd understand if you do."

Carolyn gently tipped Annelie's chin back so she could look into her eyes. "Listen to me, love. Of all the places I could be right now, I can't think of anywhere I'd rather be. Holding you, cuddling you by the fire like this is simply marvelous. You're the most amazing person I've ever met, and you're handling this situation so well. I'm honored you've let me in. I love you."

Tears welled up in Annelie's eyes but remained unshed as she clung to Carolyn, turning on her side and burying her face at the base of Carolyn's neck.

"I love you too. I guess I just needed to be reassured. Again."

"As many times as it takes, love. I'm all yours."

Carolyn could feel Annelie swallow hard. "Yes."

Pulling the blanket tighter around them, Carolyn nuzzled her lover's hair. "Close your eyes and relax. I've got you."

A slight tremor reverberated through Annelie before she let go.

❖

"All right, let's see…Helen, wrap your arms around Carolyn from behind. Yes, like that. Carolyn, some more of that gorgeous smile. Good. You love her. Show it."

The camera clicked several times as Hernandez, the young, dark-haired photographer, shot the cast in different groupings.

"We need them closer together. They're a couple, after all," the director, Regina Carmichael, told Hernandez.

"Okay then, let's do it this way," he said. "Carolyn, turn your head a little toward Helen. Yes, that's it. Keep looking at the camera. Helen, look at Carolyn. Good."

"Now we need a picture of them embracing," Regina decided.

"All right. How about the scene at the office?"

"Oh, God, *the* scene," Helen murmured behind Carolyn. "The one the Maddox fans are all dying to know how we'll pull off."

"We can't hide like we did in the audio version," Carolyn whispered back, trying to keep from snickering at Helen's dry tone of voice.

"How about a black background, a wooden desk and chair, perhaps a silhouette of a window behind them, with a pale moon outside?" Hernandez suggested. "I can easily put the window and the moon in digitally."

"Sounds excellent." Regina nodded. "Try it. We need these photos for the convention in L.A. Saturday."

"Got it." Hernandez had his assistants set the scene, then called the actresses back. "Okay, ladies, how about if we try this…" He guided Helen's right arm, arranging it to support her as he made her lean back slightly. "Like this," he continued, taking Helen's other hand and placing it just below Carolyn's right shoulder. "It can either look like you're holding Maddox back or wanting to pull her closer. Tip your head back, Helen. That's it. Carolyn, look at her lips, not her eyes. Great."

The camera clicked as Hernandez took a series of pictures. Carolyn looked at Helen's mouth and suddenly saw Annelie's full lips, knowing so well how they tasted as they parted beneath hers and how they felt against every inch of her body. Feeling her cheeks blush and her eyes narrow, Carolyn held her breath.

"Wow, brilliant, Carolyn. That look's just what I need. Now, Helen, look at Carolyn. Yes. That's it. Good." When he was satisfied, Hernandez unfastened his camera. "Great work. Thanks, ladies."

Regina joined them, waving Helen and Carolyn over. "We'll start tabletop rehearsals tomorrow and take all next week. That's it for today."

Carolyn couldn't wait to see Annelie, since the press conference was probably over. She worried about how it had affected her, knowing how she despised being in the spotlight. Pulling out her cell phone, she walked back to the makeup room with Harvey and Helen.

"How's Annelie doing?" Helen asked in a low voice.

"As well as can be expected. As for the whole sordid thing…I don't know. Margo Dillon was confident about the outcome, but you never can tell."

"Just tell Annelie I said hi, and that all of us know her father's lying."

Carolyn's expression softened. "Thanks, Helen. I'll tell her. Right now, as a matter of fact." She pressed the speed dial on her phone.

When Annelie finally answered, she sounded out of breath. "Hello?"

"Annie, are you okay? What's up?"

"I'm fine. I was swimming."

"I wanted to make sure you're okay. How did the press conference go?"

"Well, first of all, both E! News and CNN covered it. Margo did great, though—she questioned the media's ability and willingness to research the situation. When she gave them copies of her documentation, you could hear a pin drop."

"I bet she gave them hell. She's a champ. Want to stay in tonight?"

"I don't know. A part of me wants to go out and show the world I don't care. The truth is…I do care." Carolyn could hear Annelie take a deep breath. "He's my father."

"I'll be home soon. We can talk about it then. Helen and Harvey send their best. They're rooting for you, love."

"Tell them hi and I'll see them Friday. I'll send them more details about the flight to L.A. tomorrow."

"Okay."

As Carolyn hung up, she hoped Helen hadn't heard the term of endearment. She smiled carefully and relayed the information.

"Great. Gregory told me Annelie's chartered a private jet."

"I think so." Carolyn grinned. "She doesn't want to waste any time. Also, I may be on Jay Leno Friday evening. They've asked the PR people several times. Since we're in town…" She shrugged.

Helen looked at her sympathetically as they walked into makeup. "Rather you than me." She grimaced. "I find those short, gimmicky interviews pretty unnerving."

"I don't mind," Carolyn said. "I rather enjoy sparring with those self-centered comedians."

Carolyn walked behind a screen and in no time was transformed from Maddox into her own slacks-and-denim-shirt self.

"You ready, Helen?"

Walking out toward the busy street to find their waiting chauffeurs, Carolyn turned to Helen. "I appreciate your loyalty to Annelie. She's going through a tough time."

"But she has you." Helen's voice was soft. "You're not your usual competitive self around her. I might even suspect you really like her if I didn't know you better."

Carolyn blushed faintly and was careful not to reveal too much. "Well, what if I do? It wouldn't hurt my image too much, would it? She's an amazing woman."

Helen laughed, put an arm around Carolyn's shoulders, and squeezed. "That she is, honey. That she is."

❖

Annelie looked down at the lithe form gliding through the water like an eel. Carolyn had used the endless swimming pool almost every day. Annelie checked her watch and realized her lover had lost track of time again, since she didn't have to count laps in this pool.

She flipped the off switch, watching the water stop and the body in the black swimsuit reach the wall unexpectedly, then sink below the surface.

Spluttering, Carolyn emerged, glaring at Annelie. "Good Lord, are you trying to drown me? All of a sudden the current was gone and…" She coughed. "Stop laughing, woman."

Annelie tried her best to get rid of the grin on her face. "Sorry."

"No you're not. What's up?"

"Nothing, other than you've been swimming for more than forty-five minutes straight. Look, you're shivering."

Carolyn looked down at her waterproof watch and her trembling arms with genuine surprise. "Oh. All right. I better come out, then."

Annelie watched her move toward the ladder and then noticed that her arms were so weak she couldn't climb it.

"Here, let me help." She extended a hand and Carolyn grabbed it but slipped and fell back into the water. It only took Annelie a second to realize Carolyn's watch clasp was hooked on the end of her sleeve, pulling her down too. Water closed over Annelie's head as she fell in, fully dressed.

"Oh, for heaven's sake, are you okay?" Carolyn gasped in a throaty voice laced with mirth when she surfaced.

Annelie pushed the drenched hair out of her face. "I think so." She coughed. "Was this revenge?"

"Not really." Carolyn tucked Annelie's dripping hair behind her ears. "It was an accident. You look delicious in semitransparent clothes, though."

Annelie, obviously braless, glanced down at her shirt. "God." Looking back up at Carolyn, she immediately felt warmed inside by the mischievous gleam in her lover's eyes. "You like that, eh?"

"Mmm." Carolyn pulled Annelie closer, nuzzling her neck. "Delicious."

"I'd stay here and explore this unexpected use of the pool, but you're still shivering, Carolyn. We better get you into a hot shower."

"Or bath. Together."

"Could be arranged. Hey. Let's not undress in the pool."

"All right, Annie. If you say so."

"What do you mean, all right? Did you think I wouldn't see my shirt floating away from me?"

"Don't worry. You can get it later. It won't get far."

❖

Darkness settled around them, only a small night-light casting a faint glow. Carolyn relaxed against Annelie who, as usual, curled up behind her, warming her back, one hand on Carolyn's hip.

"I just can't figure out what he's thinking about," Annelie whispered.

"Who…oh. Your father."

Annelie sighed. "Why didn't he call or come see me? And why tell such obvious lies?"

"Probably thought you wouldn't risk a scandal—you'd pay him off."

"Or does he resent me?" Annelie's voice was hardly audible as she inched closer, wrapping her arm around Carolyn's chest. "Maybe my mother did or said something…or…maybe I did."

Carolyn turned and looked at Annelie. "Don't even go there. Nothing can justify what that man's done. Nothing."

"For a long time after he left, I blamed myself. I was afraid to ask my mother because she just made excuses for him. I thought he'd come back. When he didn't, I knew it was my fault. You heard Margo yesterday. My mom was a saint."

Carolyn turned over and hugged Annelie. "Listen. I'm sure your mother was wonderful. Just look at you, her daughter. But she couldn't see your hurt or your guilt. And she hurt you by excusing the bastard. I'm sure she didn't mean to. But *nobody's* a saint. She was human, with her own faults and fears. What happened between your parents had nothing to do with you."

"She never said a bad word against him."

"Commendable, but I bet she said a few things in her mind. If she had an ounce of your fire, she did."

"I owe it to him to take care of him now. Without him…"

"You don't owe him anything, love. He threw it all away when he deserted you. Margo agrees with me. But it's your decision. I'll support you no matter what."

"I know, Carolyn. I just can't stop thinking about him. Maybe I somehow…" Annelie's voice trailed off.

"Triggered this? Oh, Annie, of course not. Both of us have reevaluated our lives lately. We've taken a chance on each other against all odds, which gives past demons a great opportunity to dig their claws into us. Your father saw you on TV and decided to take a chance."

"I wish I knew what to do."

"Give it a few days, love." Carolyn put her leg around Annelie's hips, trying to wrap herself around her. "We'll know more tomorrow. Here. Let me hold you."

"Okay." Annelie sighed. "Oh, Carolyn…" Burying her face in Carolyn's hair, she finally began to relax again.

As she cursed the man who was harassing her lover, Carolyn slid her hands under Annelie's T-shirt, feeling nothing but soft skin.

"There you go, just relax. That's my girl." Carolyn kept her voice a low purr, which seemed to work. Not caring how her arms ached, she talked her lover to sleep. After only a few minutes, Annelie slumped closer to her, her breath deepening. *That's right, love. Go to sleep. I've got you. Nobody will be able to hurt you while I'm here, guarding you. I love you so much.* Carolyn inhaled deeply. *I have to harness my anger toward this idiot or I won't be much help to her.* Holding Annelie close, she was determined to protect her.

❖

Carolyn's head ached, a dull foreboding pain, making her reach for her bag.

"Excuse me. I'll be right back." She rushed out of the room where she'd been sitting with Helen, Harvey, and several other actors, reading the first scenes.

In the privacy of the ladies' room, she used her nasal spray, grimacing at how it stung but hoping it would stop the headache. Bile rose in her throat and she swallowed hard. While running cold water on her wrists, she noticed she was pale, but not gray and sweaty as happened during her worst attacks. Checking her watch, she was relieved to see it was almost noon.

When she returned, everyone was breaking for lunch. "Are you okay, Carolyn?" Helen looked concerned.

"I'm fine—just hungry, I guess. I…" Suddenly her phone rang, and Annelie's name flashed on the display.

"Annie, what's up?"

After a pause, her lover spoke. "Am I interrupting? I was hoping you were on your lunch break."

"We're just heading out."

"I'm on my way to the office to talk to Margo. Could I swing by and pick you up?"

Carolyn thought she could detect a slight tremor in Annelie's voice. "I've got an hour. Is that okay?"

"Should be. See you outside the studio in five minutes."

"See you soon, love."

Helen cleared her throat. "Carolyn, I couldn't help but overhear. If you need more time, just call. We can work around you."

Eying Helen suspiciously, Carolyn nodded. "Thanks. But I hate to be the diva on the first day."

"Don't worry about it, Carolyn." Helen winked. "Go take care of your girl."

❖

Annelie sat in the middle of the couch, motioning for Carolyn to sit next to her. Margo sat down on her other side and clasped both of Annelie's hands.

"What are you going to tell me?" Annelie whispered, her voice barely audible. "Please, Margo." She felt Carolyn's arm circle her waist.

"This isn't easy," Margo said, her voice serious. "I've waited until I was certain. I need to hold another press conference, and then our troubles will be over."

"Then why are you looking at me like that? What did you find out?"

Margo's stormy eyes were unreadable.

"Sweetheart, I'm afraid my news is good for everyone…but you." Margo grasped Annelie's arm. "Your father is dead."

CHAPTER 15

What?" Annelie's voice was emotionless.

"The man in California causing all this commotion isn't your father. Stuart died almost five years ago."

Grateful for her lover's supporting arms, Annelie leaned back heavily against her.

"And who's this idiot trying to pose as her father?" Carolyn demanded.

"We don't know yet. We should have more details any minute." Margo still held on to Annelie but let go when she got up and started pacing.

"So this man's motive is money?" she said huskily. "And fame?"

"That's as good a guess as any. Whatever he's after, he's not too smart. Your father had a record, so it'll be easy enough to compare fingerprints."

"How long have you suspected?" Carolyn leaned back against the couch, her eyes narrowing.

"Ever since I saw copies of Stuart's mug shots. Remember, I knew Stuart for several years. Even if the TV footage fooled me, compared to your father's mug shots…" Margo shrugged.

"So my father died and no one notified me," Annelie said from where she stood over by the window. "He probably didn't have anything that suggested he had a child somewhere."

Carolyn rose to embrace Annelie. "We don't know the circumstances yet, do we, Margo."

"No. I hope the investigator lets me know something soon."

Annelie looked down at Carolyn, noting her scowl. Suddenly she realized Carolyn was also pale and trembling. "You're missing your lunch. Margo? Can you get Carolyn something to eat? She has to go back to work soon."

"Sure. I'll be right back."

"Are you okay?" Carolyn rubbed her left temple. "This was quite a shock, for you, for all of us."

"Yes. I don't know what to think...or to feel." Annelie raised her arms, hugging Carolyn closer.

"It's normal to mourn, love."

"Is it? He was gone all those years. Five of them because he was dead and I had no idea—and didn't bother to find out, I guess." Annelie swallowed hard. "And what was this imposter thinking?"

"Who knows? But the puzzling part is he knows enough about you to make his story somewhat credible." Carolyn rubbed Annelie's back with long, soothing strokes, then patted her. "It makes me furious," she growled. "If I ever get a chance to give him a piece of my mind, I would—"

"Have to get in line, Carolyn. You're not the only one. Once the news hits, Annelie's friends are going to have to take a number to get a crack at him," Margo said. "We're in luck. They'd overordered from the coffeehouse down on the corner. Sandwiches and café latte."

Carolyn had paled considerably after her outburst. Her hands shook as she reached for a mug of coffee, and small beads of sweat broke out on her upper lip. Annelie sat down on the couch and patted the spot next to her. "Join me?"

Carolyn nodded, taking another large gulp of coffee. "Oh, this is great. Thanks, Margo." She bit into a turkey sandwich like she was starving.

"You're welcome."

They ate in silence, Annelie noticing how Carolyn's color gradually returned. *She seems to be feeling better now. Thank God.* Annelie frowned slightly as she nibbled her sandwich. *I don't know what to think...or feel. He's dead, but I still have so many unanswered questions. I used to think it didn't matter, that I didn't care. But I do. Why did he leave us? And now...who's this man? What does he want? Everything has gone so fast I can't keep up.* She glanced up at Carolyn. *Then again, I do know what I feel about her. That's the only thing I'm sure of right now, and even that could blow up in my face.* The questions whirled in her mind, leaving her feeling queasy.

"When we're in the air is a great time for the press conference,"

Carolyn said, wiping a daub of mustard from her face. "That way, we're incommunicado when the press goes crazy, because they will. Now they'll focus on this idiot instead of Annelie, but she'll still be in the spotlight."

"Oh, God," Annelie murmured. "They'll want to hear what I think about him, won't they?"

Carolyn nodded. "Probably. They won't give up until you make a statement, but you can still do it through Margo. Think about it for a day or two. You need time to find your bearings, love."

She's right. I feel like running as far away as I can. That old pattern. I'm numb, like icicles are hanging from my heart, my feelings in suspended animation. Well, maybe I won't cut my losses and run, for a change. And then there's you, Carolyn. You're the only one who can reach me now. Everything else seems unimportant.

Annelie shook her head as if waking from a dream. "I'll work on a statement later today. Now I might as well try to get some work done here at the office."

"Good idea." Margo nodded. "I'll see if the investigator has come up with any more information." Leaning forward, Margo kissed Annelie's cheek. "Chin up, girlie. This'll be all right. I promise."

"Thank you. I know it will." Annelie tried to sound convinced.

Carolyn slid closer after Margo left the room. "Need a hug?"

"Desperately." Annelie rolled her eyes at herself but enjoyed feeling Carolyn's strong arms encircle her.

"You're so tense. I despise that jerk for doing this to you."

"I'll be fine. I just need to wrap my mind around it all. I've sometimes wondered if he was still alive, or…" Annelie shrugged, hiding her face against Carolyn's shoulder. "It'll take me a while to deal with this, I suppose."

"Yes. And you know what? I'll be right here to help you. We'll get through it together, Annie. To quote Margo, my new hero, 'I promise.'"

Annelie knew Carolyn didn't make promises easily. "Thank you. I'm going to take you up on that." She hesitated. "I need you so much."

Carolyn paused, then continued to rub Annelie's back softly. "Oh, Annie. I need you too. So very much." She brushed Annelie's hair with a soft kiss. "I don't know how it happened, but you've become the most important thing in my life. I love you."

Annelie felt her heart skip several beats, then instantly speed up and thunder almost painfully in her chest. A sudden heat spread through her chest, melting the ice that had encased it for the last few days. Tears formed in her eyes, and she didn't mind Carolyn kissing them away as they rolled down her cheeks. "I love you too."

Carolyn dug in her pocket for a tissue and handed it to Annelie, smiling tenderly at her. "Here. Blow your nose, love."

As she felt her face grow warm, Annelie settled against the couch, still very close to Carolyn. "How long before you have to go back?"

"Ten minutes. Let's just sit here and relax." Carolyn smoothed Annelie's mussed hair.

Ten minutes won't be enough. I need hours. I need days alone with you, but this'll have to do. Maybe I can make it until you come home from work. "Come closer, then." She pulled Carolyn half on top of her. "Margo will make sure nobody disturbs us."

Carolyn slipped her hands under Annelie's silk blouse, spreading her fingers over her stomach, softly caressing the smooth skin. "I can't stop touching you."

"Good."

"You don't mind?"

"Of course not. I love your hands."

Carolyn soothed a random pattern on Annelie's soft skin.

Nuzzling Carolyn's temples in return, Annelie felt a vein throb against her lips. This symbol of life pulsating in her lover comforted her. She traced the faint blue line with her tongue. "Mine," she whispered in a barely audible tone. *God, how could I ever let you go? Stay with me. Promise me...though I know I can't expect such promises.* Annelie closed her eyes, knowing she had to draw strength from this brief embrace, enough to last the rest of the day. *Nothing else matters right now, this instant. Mine.*

"Yes, love. Yours."

❖

Carolyn pulled the covers over Annelie's naked shoulders, protecting her from the air conditioner's breeze. Annelie had fallen asleep twice on the couch and stumbled to bed only after Carolyn made her.

"I'll be right there," Carolyn promised, as she tucked in her already-sleeping lover.

Walking into the bathroom, Carolyn shed her clothes with relief. The back of her neck ached from tension. She rolled her neck and her shoulders and tried to work it out. Running the water as hot as she could stand it, she slipped into the shower stall and closed her eyes as the massaging water hit her sore muscles.

The readings this afternoon went okay. Made sure nobody noticed I wasn't on top of everything. The medicine and seeing Annelie helped that bitch of a headache. But that bastard who's harassing her! Ow. Feels like a jackhammer in my head. Carolyn quickly opened her mouth and wiggled her jaw to alleviate the pressure.

Got to pull off my appearance with Leno when we get to L.A. And then make it through the Maddox convention Saturday. That's it. No more commitments for me during the filming.

Carolyn had just walked into the bedroom when the phone rang. Snatching it, she moved toward the living room.

"Hello?"

"Annelie? Is that you, babe?"

"Carolyn Black speaking. Annelie can't come to the phone right now. Who's this, please?" Carolyn's voice was somber.

"Carolyn? It's Kitty McNeil. This is a surprise. How are you?"

Carolyn could detect a guarded tone in the woman's voice.

"I'm fine, thanks. Annelie has had a rough day. She's asleep and—"

"Oh, don't wake her up. I can talk to her tomorrow. I'm just calling to see how she's handling this thing with her father."

Realizing how close Kitty and Annelie were, Carolyn uncharacteristically decided to confide in her.

"There's been a surprising development, Kitty." As Carolyn continued to disclose Margo's earlier information, she appreciated Kitty's colorful language about the imposter. "My thoughts exactly."

"So what's going to happen?"

"Margo's holding another press conference tomorrow, while we're flying to L.A. It'll be great to have her straighten everybody out before the new Maddox convention starts."

"I guess she's really been upset. Is she okay?"

Carolyn was too tired to be anything but blunt. "She's had a rough time. I'm staying here with her. In fact, she asked me to move in permanently, and since I don't want to be away from her, the choice was easy."

"Sounds great. Will you tell her I called? I e-mailed her but have been worried about her and wanted to check."

"Of course. Thanks for calling. She'll probably give you a call in the morning before we leave. Or are you asleep then?"

"I'll be awake. I'm keeping very strange hours working on my new novel."

"Excellent." Carolyn smiled. "Any chance of a preview? Remember, I'm an avid fan."

Kitty laughed. "A preview? Well, don't tell Jem…but of course. Just for you."

Carolyn relaxed, finally feeling the connection she'd made with the author when she first met her and during their Disney World adventure. "I won't tell on you, I promise. I look forward to it."

"Cool! Now I know it's bedtime at your end, so sleep well. Give Annelie a hug for me."

"Will do. Take care."

Finally tired and ready for bed, Carolyn padded back to the bedroom. Annelie was still fast asleep, hugging a pillow close to her chest, a faint frown on her forehead. Carolyn dropped her towel and climbed into bed and was immediately wrapped in a close embrace.

"You're here…" Annelie whispered.

"Yes. Go back to sleep, love." Carolyn placed her arms around the warm sleeping form next to her. "Shh, there you go."

Closing her eyes, Carolyn listened to her lover's even breathing and finally slept.

❖

In the jet, Annelie looked at Carolyn next to her on a comfortable couch. She had her eyes closed, and Annelie knew she was focusing on her two upcoming performances. Farther to her left, Helen and the Davidsons were engaged in a muted conversation. Gregory sat toward the back of the plane with a laptop.

Though the *Tonight Show* producers had asked Annelie to appear with Carolyn, she had declined. She did, however, plan to accompany Carolyn to the studio.

Annelie checked her watch and took a deep breath, thinking about the press conference Margo was holding that very minute.

"You okay?" Carolyn asked, placing a hand on her lover's arm. "Thinking about the press conference?"

"Yes. I wonder how it's going. I feel bad for leaving Margo to handle it all."

"Forget it. Didn't you see the look on her face this morning? She was looking forward to socking it to the press for their shoddy research and to this creep for trying a scam in the first place."

Annelie knew Carolyn was right. She reached into her briefcase and pulled out a copy of the document Margo had given them early that morning.

```
Name: Trevor Albert White.
Age: Born in Chicago, January 12, 1945.
Parents: Deceased.
One sister: Geraldine White, location
unknown.
```

Trevor White had lived in the same trailer park as Stuart Clint for many years. The man *was* on disability, mainly because of his drug addictions. As she turned the next couple of pages, Annelie noted that White had left Chicago for California in 1978, just like her father. Apparently, her father and White had been drinking buddies for years, sometimes working on different construction sites together.

Reading further, she discovered their mutual drug addictions had caused them to lose several jobs. White hadn't done time like her father but had been suspected for several misdemeanors.

Leaning back and letting the pile of papers rest on her lap, Annelie wondered if this was how White knew about her. Had her father shared his past in Chicago with him, or had White been part of their lives even before Stuart Clint abandoned his family?

"Annelie?"

The gentle voice made her jump, and she looked up at Harvey standing next to her. "Yes? Sorry. I was daydreaming."

"I just wanted to let you know that Francine and I are completely behind you. It's appalling how a man can treat his child this way."

Annelie motioned for him to sit down. "There's something you don't know, Harvey."

Harvey's eyes narrowed as he listened to Annelie. "First of all, I'm sorry your father's dead. Still, it infuriates me someone would try such a thing. I'm not surprised, though. There are a lot of predatory people out there, ready to do just about anything if they benefit from it." He wavered for a minute, stroking his mustache several times. "How are you feeling?"

Annelie tucked a long strand of hair behind her ear. Harvey's question seemed nothing but kind. Surprising herself, she shook her head. "I'm…a little stumped," she confessed. "Angry, of course, and upset. I'm big on privacy." She gave a wry smile. "Very big."

Harvey patted the back of her hand. "I've gathered that. Remember, you're not alone. Now the press will have another field day—conveniently forgetting they were wrong in the first place—but they'll focus on him. You'll get all the sympathy votes."

Annelie made a face. "I'm not sure how I feel about that, but I understand what you mean. I just don't want the public to contribute less to my charities."

Harvey smiled. "Don't worry. When people learn about this guy's scheme—"

"They'll pull out their wallets, donate money to the charities, and show everyone, including that moron, who they really sympathize with." Carolyn's husky voice surprised them both.

Harvey laughed. "You took the words right out of my mouth, Carolyn."

Annelie glanced at the contented smirk on her lover's lips. She thought back to the precious fifteen minutes she'd spent simply lying in Carolyn's arms early that morning. Carolyn's soft caresses along her back and her whispered terms of endearment had soothed Annelie when she finally realized she would never be able to reconcile with her father—no explanations, no happy ending. Annelie didn't even know she'd harbored such hopes. Perhaps they were remnants from her childhood, when she dreamed her father would return.

Vaguely aware Carolyn and Harvey were talking with each other, Annelie looked over toward the window, the bright sunlight reflecting on the wings of the airplane. It stung her eyes, adding to the tears already forming there. *I can hardly remember him, and I honestly thought I didn't care anymore. We lived our lives well without him, Mother and I. Why am I so lost now? Have I fooled myself all this time?*

Her memories of the tall, lean man were sketchy at best. She remembered dark eyes and how he called her "the child" when he spoke to her mother. *Did he ever use my name?* Her mother had called her Annie and many nicknames based on that. Some were of Swedish origin, and Annelie's favorite had always been "lilla hjärta," meaning "little heart."

Mother was mild-mannered, with a generous heart, soft touch, and pale beauty. He, on the other hand, was cold and selfish. Why did she fall for him? Did she think she could change him? Well, damn it, not even having a child with her made Stuart Clint care much. He lasted for only seven years. I can do this. I can face the media and everybody else. He hasn't played a role in my life, nor did I in his for more than twenty-five years... Annelie leaned back in her seat, the memory of Carolyn's strong embrace vivid in her mind. *As long as I have you, I'll be okay. You empower me when I need it most, and these memories of him make that so important.*

According to Margo, Stuart Clint was a handsome bad boy with a winning smile who had treated Anna well while he courted her. But as soon as they were married, he changed. When Anna gave birth to Annelie, he began to drink heavily and sometimes use drugs. One day he was gone.

A gentle hand took hold of Annelie's, bringing her out of her reverie. "The press conference should be over. Want to call Margo?"

"No. Let's wait till we get to the hotel. We should get there quickly since the security company is meeting us at the gates."

"Security company?" Harvey raised his eyebrows.

"Margo and I talked," Carolyn explained. "Since the convention and the latest about this bozo in California will attract a lot of attention, we agreed to hire bodyguards."

Accustomed to Hollywood and the paparazzi, Harvey nodded. "Good move."

"They'll escort us to the hotel and accompany us everywhere while we're in L.A. Annelie wasn't too keen at first, were you, love? But she relented when I twisted her arm."

Annelie wondered if Carolyn noticed how the tender word automatically slipped from her lips, or saw the twinkle in Harvey's eyes, but she didn't think so and didn't mind.

She scooted closer to Carolyn as Harvey rejoined his wife. "He's such a good man."

Carolyn nodded. "Actually, he reminds me of my father, even if he's not quite old enough. Oh, that's right, you're just a baby. He's old enough to be your father," Carolyn deadpanned.

"Very funny." Annelie rolled her eyes. "All jokes aside, if my father *had* been like Harvey, things would be a lot different."

"You know what? I think Harvey really cares about you. I'm not saying he's about to adopt you, but he definitely acts fatherly around you."

Blushing faintly, Annelie considered this observation. "They're all so nice. I couldn't ask for a better crew."

Carolyn gave a knowing smile. "Oh, Annie, don't you realize Helen, Harvey, and I are the ones who are grateful to be working with you." She caressed Annelie's leg discreetly. "And I'm more grateful than the other two put together."

❖

Carolyn sat next to Annelie in the black SUV and tried not to let her know how badly her temples throbbed. After glancing through the tinted windows and studying the bodyguards who accompanied them, she closed her eyes briefly. She tried to block out the voices of Francine and Helen by concentrating on her inner self. *All I need is a few minutes to relax and I'll be fine. Just a few. Deep breaths. That's it. Maybe that'll help. I can't wait to get to the hotel pool. A quick swim should make me less tense. Wonder how long I've got before I have to be at the* Tonight Show *studio?*

Seeing she had plenty of time unless something unexpected happened, Carolyn glanced over at Annelie. She seemed lost in thought, her hands clasped in her lap. As Carolyn reached over and patted the tight fists, Annelie quickly turned her head, her eyes dark with emotions.

What's going on in her mind? Why the dark thoughts, darling? Wanting to reassure her lover, she locked her gaze onto the pale blue eyes. "We'll be there soon," Carolyn whispered. "Haven't changed your mind, have you? Still going with me to the studio?"

Annelie nodded briefly, not averting her eyes. "Of course I'm going. I'll wait for you in the green room."

As they drove up to the hotel entrance, the doorman approached to open the car door. Forestalling his intention, the man sitting next to the driver held on to the door handle, carefully scanning the surroundings before opening it. He leapt outside, watching over the passengers as they climbed out of the vehicle.

As she walked toward the reception area in the hotel with Annelie, Carolyn heard a man yell. She turned toward the tumult just as one of the bodyguards threw his arm out to shield them, pushing them farther to the side.

"Damn it, she's my daughter! You can't stop me from seeing my own flesh and blood!" A tall man, wearing jeans and a gray jacket, lurched toward them. Reaching out, he grabbed for Annelie.

"No!" Carolyn shouted.

"Hey, look at me, girl!" the man seethed. "Don't you recognize me? Get these idiots off me! I'm your father, damn it!"

Annelie stumbled backward, and only Harvey's grasp prevented her from falling. He simultaneously pulled Annelie toward him and put his arm protectively around his wife. "What the hell..."

Amid the uproar, three bodyguards quickly wrestled the man to the ground. The remaining men hustled Annelie and her party toward the elevators.

"This way," the man in charge instructed. "We've already arranged for your check-in. The penthouse suites are ready."

Once at a safe distance, Annelie stopped to glance over her shoulder, a hesitant look on her face. "Is he the one...?"

Moving closer, Carolyn put her hand in the small of Annelie's back, her touch meant to comfort and protect. "If it is, we'll find out. Hotel security and our guys will take care of the situation. Let's go now."

As they resumed walking toward the elevator, increasingly concerned, Carolyn noticed Annelie was frowning. "Are you all right?"

Annelie merely nodded, apparently too taken aback for conversation. She stood rigidly and stared straight ahead, her eyes vacant. After a silent elevator ride, the group emerged on the penthouse floor where Annelie had reserved three suites for the six of them.

Carolyn watched Annelie anxiously as the bodyguards left them at their door, assuring them they would post a man outside their suites and investigate the incident in the lobby.

After Annelie had mechanically overtipped the bellboy, she closed the door behind him. She leaned against it for a moment and took a deep breath. "God, I wish I knew what that was about."

Carolyn draped her jacket over the back of a chair on her way to Annelie. "I'm sure they'll let us know as soon as they learn anything," she said gently, putting her arms around her lover.

"So you're saying don't assume until we know more?"

"That's exactly what I'm saying, love. They'll get back to you when they've sorted things out."

"I know." Annelie sighed, leaning her forehead against Carolyn's. "I wasn't prepared for such a…"

"Violent display? I don't blame you." Tucking a long tress of hair behind Annelie's left ear, Carolyn smiled faintly. "Good idea about the bodyguards, right?"

"God, yes." Annelie shivered in her arms. "I don't want to think what could have happened if they hadn't been there."

"But they were."

"Yes." Annelie's voice still trembled as she let go of Carolyn and turned toward their bags. "Want me to help you choose between your outfits?"

Realizing Annelie needed something to do to normalize the strange mood after the incident, Carolyn nodded. "Sure, go ahead." As she strolled over to the window and pretended to admire the view, she realized her head was throbbing. Furtively rubbing her temples, she knew she had to have some relief. She couldn't go on Leno looking nauseous.

"Hey," Annelie said, putting down Carolyn's bag. "Do you have a headache? Want me to rub your shoulders?" She walked up behind her lover.

Carolyn shook her head. "You know what I really want? I'd like to go swimming, to try and relax. Come with me?"

"I wish I could," Annelie said. "But I promised Gregory we'd go over some last-minute details about the convention. We put it off all week and now…"

"It's okay." Carolyn smiled. "I'll find the pool and just do a few laps before I leave."

Annelie cupped her lover's cheek. "I'm still going with you to the studio, naturally."

"Thanks, but if you get stuck in meetings, I'll understand…" With no idea why she was almost about to cry, Carolyn shrugged, feeling ridiculous.

"I won't get stuck." Annelie gently brushed her lips over Carolyn's. "Go have your swim, and I'll be here to help you get ready when you come back. Okay?"

Forcing back her stupid tears and clenching her teeth against a sudden stabbing pain behind her eyes, Carolyn nodded. "Fine. I'll just change and grab a quick shower, and then I'm off."

Apparently sensing Carolyn's struggle for control, Annelie glanced toward the alarm clock by the bed. "You know, I've got twenty minutes before Gregory arrives. I'd love to take a shower with you."

Carolyn didn't realize she had a knot in her midsection until it began to unwind. "Yes? You're sure?"

"Of course. I need to make sure you're okay." Annelie began to unbutton her shirt, pale skin appearing as she undressed. "A very definite yes." She reached out, unbuttoning Carolyn's blouse, sliding it back over slightly freckled shoulders. "Surely you know I want to spend every possible minute with you?"

Comforted by the desire mixed with love she saw in Annelie's eyes, Carolyn allowed Annelie to lead her into the bathroom. "I don't feel so good right now," Carolyn confessed. "And…I'm sorry for acting childish."

"You're not acting childish." Annelie started the shower with one hand while caressing Carolyn with the other. "You dropped everything to stand by me last week."

Efficiently, Annelie undressed Carolyn before shedding the rest of her own clothes. "That guy scared all of us, and you have a headache to boot. Come here. Let me rub some of the stress away before you go swim."

Standing under the hot running water with Annelie's hands roaming her body, Carolyn began to think she would find strength to get through the evening after all.

❖

"Ladies and gentlemen, please welcome Carolyn Black!"

Annelie made herself comfortable on the couch in the green room at the *Tonight Show* studio, not taking her eyes off the screen. Carolyn walked toward Jay Leno with her arms stretched out to greet him. After they kissed the air next to each other, Carolyn gracefully sat down in the chair next to the desk. She looked radiant dressed in a sleeveless, emerald green dress that ended just below her knees. Annelie smiled, knowing the diva mode was on.

"You look amazing, Carolyn. Welcome to L.A. You flew in today, right?" Leno echoed Annelie's admiration.

"I did. For the Maddox convention tomorrow."

"Well, we're of course delighted you'd come on the show at such short notice. I hear you flew in on a private jet, with the rest of the Maddox movie cast."

"You heard right, Jay. The production company chartered a jet to save us time, wear and tear. We're getting ready to shoot the movie."

"Sounds like a luxurious way to travel, though I guess the lovely Ms. Peterson can afford it."

Annelie held her breath, seeing Carolyn's eyes narrow. "Ms. Peterson is a very generous boss," Carolyn asserted. "We're all lucky."

"Now, I've just met Annelie Peterson, and she strikes me as a very low-key, unpretentious woman."

Carolyn leaned forward to emphasize the importance of her statement. "You know, she's the kindest person I've ever met—and the most giving. She could be sitting idly on her wealth. Instead she puts it to good use, making life a little easier for the less fortunate. I know you've contributed to her charities over the years, Jay."

Annelie chuckled and thought Leno probably regretted sharing that bit of information in the green room. He looked both flattered and embarrassed. "It's a worthy cause for kids," he said. "There was an interesting development with the man claiming to be Ms. Peterson's father. What do you think about that?"

Annelie pressed her lips together at the intrusive question.

"That's totally up to Annelie Peterson to comment on—or to choose not to, Jay. All I can say is this—I wish the press would do their homework better, instead of going head over heels for a scoop. The damage to people's lives isn't worth it."

Leno's face turned serious, and Annelie wondered if he'd been subjected to his fair share of rumormongering.

"You're right, Carolyn." Leno paused. "It sounds like you and Ms. Peterson have become friends."

The actress didn't hesitate. "Yes, during the time I've known her, she and I have become very close. You know, you just click with some people. She's great."

Leno nodded, and then a broad smile spread across his face. "Now, on a lighter note, you told me a funny story back in the green room, including a near disaster when you visited Ms. Peterson."

Carolyn flashed a broad smile. "Oh, you mean the one about my nonexistent cooking skills and how I ended up signing autographs for some very handsome boys from the FDNY instead of having pizza?"

The studio audience, responding to Carolyn like the crowd at the Orlando convention, roared, stomped their feet, and whistled as she winked at them. Annelie smiled as her lover told the story of the pizza, embellishing it in her special way.

"So, I take it you're a good customer at restaurants?" Leno deduced.

"You bet. That, and catering services. I think I'm solely responsible for my local Italian restaurant's expansion." Carolyn smirked. "I do, however, make excellent coffee."

"Now, the Maddox movies. You've signed contracts to do the first three. How does that feel?"

"It's a true honor to be chosen for this adventure." Carolyn leaned back, touching her lips with an index finger. Her face turned serious. "I'm also well aware of the responsibility. A lot rides on the first one being a success, and since I play Diana Maddox…" She shrugged.

"Yeah, they'll have your head if you screw up," Leno joked. "There's a lot of action in these stories." He wiggled his eyebrows. "Any qualms about kissing the lovely Ms. St. Cyr?"

Annelie closed her eyes and moaned in exasperation.

"Not one bit. Besides, she's a very attractive woman. Wouldn't you want to kiss her?" Carolyn deadpanned.

Leno missed a beat and then shook his head in mock dismay as the audience cheered. "I'm a married man. Are you trying to get me in trouble?" He grinned. "Honestly, Helen St. Cyr is one of my wife's favorite actresses, right up there with you and Alice Kriege."

"All character actresses," Carolyn observed. "Your wife has good taste, Jay."

"Naturally. Goes without saying. She married me, didn't she?"

The audience laughed.

"So, playing Diana Maddox—a tormented, complex, lesbian character—no big deal?"

Carolyn shook her head, giving Leno a somewhat patronizing glance. "I never go into a role thinking it's not a big deal, regardless of who the character is. Playing a lesbian is a first for me, if you don't count doing the Maddox audiobooks, and I intend to do my best to give Maddox credibility and to keep her natural. A certain percentage of all women are lesbians or bisexual—and the concept of love in any way, shape, or form between consenting adults is a good thing, right?"

Looking slightly stunned to be on the receiving end of Carolyn's firm glance, Leno nodded willingly. "Absolutely."

Carolyn was obviously not finished with the subject. "And as for her being tormented and complex, that has more to do with her persona than her sexual preference." Carolyn delivered the correction with an enticing smile, but her voice was forceful.

Leno reached for his tie knot, only to stop halfway. Clearing his voice, he returned the smile. "Now, I only have one final question."

"Shoot."

"Are you going to do all the stunts yourself? I know from the books there's some nudity, for instance."

Carolyn rolled her eyes, making the audience giggle. "Jay, you have a one-track mind. Well, in my contract, I've agreed to partial nudity when it's called for in the story." She leaned toward Leno, putting a hand on his arm. "I suppose by 'stunts' you're also talking about the love scenes?"

"Eh...yeah."

"The only time I'd demand a stand-in or a stunt woman to take my place would be if it concerned...cooking."

The audience roared, and Leno laughed along with them. Annelie knew Carolyn was in control of the show and admired the way she charmed both her host and the spectators.

"I know I said that was my final question, but, if you'll indulge me, what are your plans for tonight? Are you going to paint the town with your colleagues and Ms. Peterson or...?"

Carolyn smiled wistfully. "You know, I'm going straight to bed. Tomorrow will be a long day, and I want to be at my best for the people attending the convention. They're even coming from Europe and Australia."

"Well, we've certainly enjoyed having you here on the show, Carolyn. Thank you so much for coming."

Carolyn rose and took a bow as applause thundered, then left the stage. Normally, Leno's guests remained on his couch, but Carolyn had refused to stay longer than her slot.

Annelie rose and turned to Gregory. "Wasn't she great?"

"Outstanding. She charmed them all. They'll want her back when the movie premieres."

"I'm sure they will."

The door opened and Carolyn entered, with sparkling eyes and a broad smile on her face. "All done," she proclaimed, energy vibrating in her voice. "We can leave right away, can't we?"

"Sure. Are you in a hurry?" Annelie raised her eyebrows.

"I want to get back to the hotel and order something from room service. I'm starving."

"Your wish is my command. We have an early start tomorrow."

Carolyn walked up to Annelie and studied her closely. "I was okay, right?"

Annelie wanted to stroke her lover's cheek, but decided not to since studio personnel were present. "You were awesome. Come on."

Hearing loud music from the house band in the background, Annelie noticed a new bounce in Carolyn's walk as they left the studio, making her realize her lover was on her performance high. When Annelie felt a soft caress of Carolyn's hand on her own, a thumb stealthily rubbing her palm, she shivered and glanced at her.

"Behave."

Carolyn smiled innocently. "All right."

❖

They barely made it over the threshold.

Annelie turned to close the door, and Carolyn leaned past her, shutting it with the palm of her hand and locking the deadbolt. Pushing Annelie against the wall, she slipped her hands eagerly under her white silk shirt and stroked the skin on her stomach.

"Carolyn?" Annelie managed, before the other woman claimed her mouth, parting her lips in a passionate kiss. "You were going to call room service…"

"Shh." Carolyn pushed Annelie's jacket off her shoulders while she kissed her way inside the shirt she was unbuttoning. Tracing the delicate collarbones with open-mouth kisses, she made Annelie moan as she pushed down the shoulder straps of her bra and let it fall to the floor, together with her shirt.

"You're so beautiful," Carolyn murmured. "Exquisite." She closed her lips over a taut nipple, making Annelie arch into the touch. She nibbled Annelie's breast just the way she liked, making her gasp with pleasure and almost moan with pain.

"You're insatiable," Annelie gulped. "What brought this on?"

Carolyn didn't answer. Instead, she unbuttoned her lover's black slacks, pushing them down her hips. Annelie stepped out of them, watching in awe as Carolyn suddenly knelt in front of her, sliding her lace panties down next. Slowly, interrupting her intentions by placing kisses on Annelie's thighs, she undressed her completely. Carolyn's beauty, her dark eyes brimming with desire, made Annelie's heart ache.

Carolyn began to caress her way up. Carefully letting her nails trail up along the smooth thighs, she closed in on the blond tuft of hair, making Annelie tremble.

"Come on, love, spread your legs for me," Carolyn encouraged. "That's it...more...I want to look at you."

Feeling utterly vulnerable and even more aroused, Annelie complied. Carolyn had often taken the initiative in making love, but never like this. The contrast between Carolyn's elegant appearance and Annelie's own nakedness added to the feeling of being exposed. Yet it was such a thrill.

Annelie gasped when gentle fingers parted her folds, carefully exploring. Carolyn rose to her feet, her hand still working between Annelie's legs. "So wet," she whispered. "For me?"

"Yes." Feeling vulnerable about her body's reaction, but unashamed, Annelie closed her eyes at the tender examination. She ached for Carolyn's touch, knowing how her lover could feast on her, drive her toward the abyss with her mouth. "Only for you..."

Watching Carolyn slowly undress, Annelie noticed her lover's hands were shaking. She moved toward her, close enough for Carolyn to feel the heat radiating from her body, then wrapped her arms around her, pulling her tight against her naked frame. Lowering her head, she devoured Carolyn's lips in an endless kiss.

As she pulled back, she gazed into Carolyn's hypnotic eyes— narrow slits shining with desire.

"You drive me insane," Carolyn confessed. "Your voice, your body…your touch. You make me want to do…" Her voice trailed off as she suddenly blushed.

"What?" Annelie whispered, cupping the back of Carolyn's head. "Tell me."

Reaching for Annelie's breasts, Carolyn let her thumbs work the nipples relentlessly. "I have fantasies…" She pushed her thigh between Annelie's. "About us. Doing things."

Oh, God. Annelie swallowed, her head swimming with the sensations raging through her body. The slender thigh between hers made more moisture pool at her center. "And what do we do in your fantasies?" she asked.

Carolyn leaned down and took one of Annelie's aching nipples in her mouth, sucking it for agonizing seconds before replying. "For some reason, I have this image in my head…" Her hand slipped in between their bodies, finding the aching ridge of nerves between Annelie's folds and rubbing it in slow circles. "…of you, on your knees, on a chair, holding on to the backrest …" Her fingers pushed farther ahead, spreading the wetness. "…and me, behind you, exploring all of you."

Two fingers entered Annelie, curling inside her until they found the spot that made her go rigid. "And you ask me to take you, to make you mine…" The fingers began an in-and-out motion while she kissed Annelie's neck, her tongue painting a blazing trail along her jaw. "You whimper my name, and I have access to any part of you I want. Nothing's taboo. You want me to take it all."

"Carolyn…oh, yes…" Annelie was completely caught up in the sound of her lover's voice and what she was saying. The scene she painted was exciting, and she knew it wouldn't be long until it pushed her over the precipice. *Take me.* "And what happens then?"

"I enter you, with my fingers, with my tongue…" Carolyn moved her lips close to Annelie's ear. "I dream of doing this, of taking you completely."

Trembling all over, her breath ragged and her legs becoming increasingly weaker, Annelie was stunned by Carolyn's candor and trust. Not about to disappoint her lover, she gently took a handful of auburn hair, turning Carolyn's face up for another deep kiss.

"It's true, you know," she breathed. "There's nothing you can't do to me, because we love each other. I'll fulfill all your fantasies, one by one, to the best of my ability…I want to, very much." Anything…she wanted to do everything with this woman.

Annelie felt tears well up as Carolyn pressed her drenched sex against her thigh. "Annie, I can't believe how you make me feel… just talking about it, confessing how you invade my thoughts at any given time, makes me feel more than…oh…I've never…I can't believe this…"

Annelie felt her lover push against her, whimpers muted by Carolyn's mouth placing open-mouth kisses along her collarbones. She cupped Carolyn's bottom, helping her ride the thigh lodged between hers. "And how does your fantasy end?"

"Usually, it ends with…uh…me penetrating you with as many fingers as you'll let me…" Carolyn murmured something inaudible.

"What?"

"Nothing…"

"Tell me. You can tell me anything."

Carolyn sighed, her hips jerking, her fingers pressing into Annelie becoming frantic. "You allow me, in my mind, to stimulate you everywhere I want. You let me…Oh, Annie! Oh!"

Carolyn came, and the feeling of her arching against her made Annelie's body convulse along with her. Slowly, her knees gave in as her inner muscles clenched Carolyn's fingers over and over. Lances of pleasure streaked through her body, and she whimpered aloud, clinging to Carolyn. Sliding along the wall toward the floor, she finally sat with her lover straddling her lap, hugging her close while she tried to catch her breath.

"My love…Annie, I love you." Carolyn's voice broke, and muted sobs wracked her. "My precious girl…"

"Shh…I love you too. You're my heart, Carolyn. Only you." Annelie kissed her. "I'd gladly let you do everything in your fantasy. Nothing you want to try could make me uncomfortable, since it's you. I adore you. I have fantasies too. I have so many things I want to do with you…for you."

"Nothing…nobody…has ever affected me this way. It simply has to be you. I can't imagine feeling…this, with anyone else."

Annelie felt her throat constrict at the naked emotions in Carolyn's voice. She refused to cry, but held on even tighter to the woman in her arms. Not doubting Carolyn's truthfulness, Annelie knew she felt the same way.

They sat on the floor until the air-conditioning made them shiver. Annelie helped her exhausted lover to her feet and guided her into the bathroom, where a hot shower warmed them up. After quickly brushing their teeth, they crawled into bed, Annelie cradling Carolyn from behind.

She ravaged me. She pressed me against the wall, insatiable, and turned on beyond anything I've experienced with her...or anyone. Almost asleep, Annelie thought about how Carolyn had made love to her. *She dominated me, but she didn't try to control me. How does she do it? She's had no experience loving women before me. She claimed me tonight. There's no other word for it.*

Carolyn had a habit of calling Annelie hers, but in a way that made Annelie feel loved and protected, not possessed. Perhaps it was because they took turns being the strong one. Cuddling Carolyn, she felt her lover's naked bottom against her sex and suddenly remembered the other woman's fantasy about taking her in every way possible. Not at all shocked by how Carolyn's mind worked, Annelie vowed to turn that fantasy into reality. Soon.

❖

"Can you believe someone will travel great distances for the opportunity to ask one single question—and they want to know if my belly button is an innie or an outie?" Carolyn's incredulous tone made the other passengers double over as the chartered jet leveled out at thirty thousand feet. It was just before midnight.

"I'm even more awed at how you found your bearings and kept from laughing when you replied," Harvey's wife, Francine, offered, wiping tears from her cheeks. "In fact, there were some outrageous questions directed at all of you."

"I still can't get over the question about my boots," Helen added. "Did you hear that girl call them *fuck-me boots*?" She grinned. "I was shocked and appalled. Now I can't wear them without wondering what signals I'm sending."

"Liar," Annelie snorted. "You were flattered!"

Helen playfully swatted Annelie's arm. "Well, can you blame me? The kid was half my age."

"And so infatuated with you, she was ready to climb up on the stage." Annelie laughed.

"Who can blame *her*? She confessed Erica Becker is her favorite character, and there *Erica* was, in the flesh, and—in very special boots." Harvey winked.

"Yeah, very useful boots," Annelie teased.

Helen rolled her eyes at her before sending Harvey a broad smile.

"I'll say." Harvey stroked his mustache, trying to keep a straight face. "But I don't think the girl would've reacted the same way if I'd worn those boots."

"Don't sell yourself short," Carolyn said. "Who knows?"

"Hardly! However, I'm glad we're not doing any more conventions for a while. My hand needs to recover first." Harvey wiggled the fingers on his right hand in the air.

"Your hand? What happened to it?" Carolyn frowned.

"I must have signed more than a thousand autographs. I'm an old man, remember? I can't imagine how many you two beauties signed."

"At least twice that, *old man*," his wife teased. "I think even Annelie signed more autographs than you."

Carolyn smiled as she glanced at her lover, sitting next to her. "You got a lot of attention, didn't you?"

"More than I was comfortable with initially, but, once I got over my first panic, I was fine. People were really kind."

Carolyn hadn't realized until after the performances how people had surrounded Annelie, eager to show their support and wanting autographs. She could well imagine Annelie's first reaction.

"Annelie? I've got faxes coming in for you," Gregory said from behind them. "Want me to bring them to you?"

"No, I'll come back there." Annelie disappeared to the desk area.

"Monday is business as usual, then," Helen mused. "I'm actually excited about continuing the readings. Was it Friday we're starting the first studio rehearsals?"

"Yes, I believe so." Carolyn nodded. "As far as I know, they've completed Erica Becker's apartment. By then, they should've come close to finishing Maddox's place and the interior of the police station."

They continued to talk shop for a moment until Annelie returned with an odd expression on her face.

"What's up?" Carolyn felt her heart flutter.

"The security company faxed a copy of the police report from Friday afternoon. Trevor White is in custody, as we knew, and they expect the ADA to go after him with a list of charges." Annelie sat down next to Carolyn again. "I'm just relieved he didn't turn out to be my father."

Carolyn reached around her, squeezing Annelie's shoulders. "I know, love. So are we."

"Also, Regina left a message. She wants everyone to take tomorrow off and work on your scenes at home. Apparently she has to take care of some problems that have cropped up, but she'll be ready for Tuesday's readings."

"You know, that's not such a bad idea. I get jet-lagged even with the three-hour difference," Harvey said and then suddenly sniffed the air. "Oh, dear God, tell me that's what I think it is."

Annelie, breaking out of her reverie, smiled at the hopeful look on Harvey's face. "If you mean the best hamburgers with all the extras money can buy, it is. The chef's fixing them in the kitchen."

"French fries? Onion rings? Quarter pounders?"

Harvey's eyes widened as Annelie nodded at each suggestion. "And a salad," she added.

"God, are you trying to kill him?" Francine moaned. "He's not a young man anymore. He can't be on a diet like that."

"He won't be after today. This is a special occasion," Annelie said. "We've had so much Italian, seafood, and Japanese food lately. I was in the mood for a regular burger. I can see I'm not the only one."

"All right," Francine muttered. "No onion rings and lots of salad, Harvey."

"Yes, dear." Harvey rubbed his hands. "I'll go see if I can help the chef. Just to carry things out here, dear. Not doing any tasting, I promise." He disappeared toward the back of the plane.

"For an actor, he's such a bad liar," his wife sighed, making the others laugh.

"I'll have to issue a statement tomorrow," Annelie murmured to Carolyn. "Margo said several newspapers and networks won't give up."

"Can't you do it through her?"

Annelie considered. "No, she spoke for me all last week. If this has taught me anything, and you have a big part in this, it's that I have to know when to stop hiding. I'll call a press conference and read a brief statement. If anyone wants any comments after Monday, they'll have to settle for Margo."

"Good girl. I'm proud of you. I know it's not in your nature to do this, but you have a point. You'll do fine." She patted Annelie's knee.

"You're good for me."

Carolyn's heart picked up speed. "And you're even better for me," she whispered.

"Look here, isn't this heaven, I ask you?" Harvey's delighted tone of voice made them turn their heads. He stood next to the coffee table in front of the couch, holding a tray weighed down with hamburgers. "French fries and onion rings coming up!" He shot his wife a sheepish grin. "And salad."

❖

Carolyn pulled her cell phone from her pocket, switching it on as she walked through LaGuardia. Her shoulders ached from sleeping in an uncomfortable position on the plane.

"One missed call," she observed, frowning. "Who on earth's calling me at this hour?"

Annelie reached for the phone. "Here, let me show you how to check it. There, it says *Joe's Cell*. If you press Dial, it'll automatically call his number."

As Carolyn dialed her brother-in-law, an unsettling feeling soured her stomach. No one answered. No one answered at their house either. "Oh, my God, what's wrong?" she murmured. "Why would he call me in the middle of the night, unless—"

Annelie joined Carolyn in the backseat of the waiting limo.

"Do you have any other number you can try? The help they hired?"

"No, I don't have her number. She doesn't work weekends, anyway."

"Did you try your voice mail?"

Wanting to slap her forehead, Carolyn punched in the numbers. She turned the phone sideways so Annelie could listen too.

"Carolyn, it's Joe. Beth's in the hospital. Call me as soon as you can. If I can't answer the phone, call my parents." He gave another

D.C. number, making her scramble through her purse for a pen, cursing violently.

"Easy, Carolyn. Wait till I find a pen, and then let me listen to it again."

Carolyn stared at the passing traffic with unseeing eyes while Annelie wrote down the number.

"There. Now you can dial."

"I...What if she's lost the baby?" Carolyn's voice was barely audible. "It'll destroy her. Oh, God..."

"Don't think the worst. Make the call, and then we'll figure out what to do."

Reaching for Annelie with one hand, Carolyn began to dial with the other. Vaguely she noticed her fingers had gone numb.

CHAPTER SIXTEEN

Annelie glanced at Carolyn, who sat with her hands clenched in her lap. Driving the Volvo down I-95 toward D.C., Annelie was relieved about the lack of traffic at this hour. The car, which handled easily, was more comfortable than her own small sports car.

"I'm glad we decided to take your car. It's only a four-hour drive, probably less at this time of day." Annelie reached out and caressed the fisted hands. "Why don't you take a nap? You'll be exhausted when we get there."

Cold fingers curled around Annelie's hand. "I know. I'm just so worried."

"I'm sure Joe will try your cell phone again as soon as he can. His parents seem nice."

"Yes, they are. When I talked to his mother, she kept trying to comfort me, even though she's worried too. They've really taken Beth to their hearts."

"So no in-law problems for your sister?"

"Perhaps in the beginning, but that was mostly because of me."

"Because of you? Whatever for?" Annelie frowned, surprised at Carolyn's desolate tone of voice.

"I suspect they thought I was this dubious Hollywood person who'd spoiled her young sister rotten. Finally, they came around and started treating Beth like a long-lost daughter. They even warmed up to me eventually."

Annelie heard the exasperation behind the mock sarcasm. *And you suffered through it for Beth's sake, didn't you? You knew how they perceived you and you didn't say a word. Oh, Carolyn, if you only knew how apparent your vulnerability is to me. You may think you're hiding it well, and perhaps you are, from people other than me.* Knowing only too well how prejudice stung made Annelie want to protect Carolyn in any way she could. She realized how impossible that was, but, glancing at the pained expression on her lover's face, she vowed to try. *You'll never have to face such a thing alone again, Carolyn.*

"Close your eyes, Carolyn," Annelie suggested, raising their joined hands to her lips. "I'll put on some music." She turned on the stereo, which was tuned to a station playing classical music. "Excellent."

Carolyn reclined her seat and stretched out. She reached behind her for a blanket from the backseat and spread it over her legs. "She has to be all right," she murmured. "She has to."

"Shh, just relax now."

Annelie set the cruise control to 65 miles per hour and settled back, rolling her shoulders. Traffic was still sparse, and she was confident they would reach D.C. quicker by car than by air. This way, they could drive straight to the hospital where Beth was undergoing treatment for premature labor. According to Joe's mother, who was keeping little Pamela, Beth was hemorrhaging and having contractions.

Carolyn had told her more about Beth's previous miscarriages while they drove from the airport to Carolyn's condo. Not only had she lost the babies, but she'd also gone through some painful complications. *Beth is certainly brave to try again after such ordeals.*

A soft whimper came from the passenger seat. Annelie turned her head and saw Carolyn curling up, a deep frown marring her forehead. Her breaths came in short bursts as she apparently fought some demons in her sleep. Annelie reached out and shook the shoulder closest to her. "Sweetheart, you're dreaming. Wake up."

Carolyn shied away from her hand, moaning. She was trembling under the blanket, and tears outlined her lashes.

Reading the road signs, Annelie saw they were only minutes from a rest area. She pulled off the interstate, parked, and turned to Carolyn. "Sweetheart? Wake up. Come here." She leaned in to hug her.

Carolyn fought her embrace for a short moment, but then seemed to recognize the touch. She looked at Annelie through tears while blinking fiercely. "Annie?"

"You had a bad dream. You're okay now."

Clearing her throat, Carolyn tried to sit up but changed her mind. "Where are we?"

"About halfway, maybe a little more. Are you okay?"

Carolyn's eyes narrowed and a wry smile appeared on her face. "You ask me that a lot, you know."

Annelie smiled, nuzzling her lover's hair. "And so do you. Want some coffee?"

Carolyn raised her seat back and tossed the blanket aside. "Coffee might just do the trick."

"Want me to get it for us?"

"No thanks, love. I need to stretch my legs." Carolyn got out of the car, pulling her coat closer around her as the autumn breeze played havoc with her hair.

Annelie circled the car to stand close to Carolyn. Without hesitation, she pushed the disheveled tresses out of her lover's face, letting her thumb quickly brush against her tightened lips. "Don't worry. We'll be there in no time."

"I know. It's just…"

"…she was once your baby."

Hooking her arm under Annelie's, Carolyn nodded. "I'm so glad you understand. If I didn't already love you, I'd fall in love with you this instant."

❖

"Carolyn!" Joe was pale and needed a shave. "Beth'll be so glad to see you. Hell, *I'm* glad you're here." He pulled her into a firm hug.

"How is she?" Carolyn pulled back, examining Joe's features for any signs of disaster and noticing the dark circles under his eyes.

"She's doing everything they tell her and she's not complaining, but she's scared." Joe glanced over Carolyn's shoulder. "You must be Ms. Peterson?"

"Oh, sorry." Carolyn sighed, wanting to kick herself. "Joey, this is my good friend, Annelie Peterson. Annie, this is Joseph Rossi."

"I guessed as much. Nice to meet you, Joe. Please call me Annelie. I just wish we'd met under happier circumstances."

"Nice to meet you too, Annelie. I'm so glad you could come. Beth can't wait to meet you. Perhaps you can distract her a little." Carolyn noticed her brother-in-law didn't seem convinced. "Come on. She's in room 1412."

Carolyn stopped in the doorway, looking at her sister lying in bed with several IVs connected to her arm. Beth was beyond pale.

Carolyn stepped inside. "Hello, kiddo. How you doing?"

Beth's eyes snapped open. "Lyn!" She stuck out a hand and burst into tears. "Oh, Lyn, it's happening all over again. I'm going to lose my baby."

Carolyn rushed to the bed, pulling her little sister into her arms and rocking her. "You don't know that, honey. Joe just told me how brave you are. He says you're following the doctor's orders to the letter. Have faith in that."

"I can't go through this again. I'm so scared. I was doing everything right at home too. Staying off my feet, letting the help do everything. And Pamela's been good as gold. Why's this happening now? We never should have tried again."

Carolyn's heart ached. Glancing over her shoulder, she saw Annelie and Joe waiting. Annelie raised her hand, indicating she knew Beth was in no shape to meet a stranger. Wiggling her cell phone, she motioned toward the exit. Carolyn nodded.

Focusing on her sister, Carolyn ignored her uncomfortable position, not about to let go of the distraught woman. "I don't know, but I'm here now. So's Joe. We'll see this through, and you and the baby will be all right. I'm not leaving you until you're okay, I promise."

Carefully rocking Beth some more, she hoped her acting skills wouldn't fail her. She wanted to believe her own words, but it was hard.

Carolyn felt the thin form in her arms gradually relax. "That's it, sweetie. Just go to sleep. It's the best thing for you. I'll be right here. Joe too."

Joe came in and helped her lower the now-sleeping Beth onto the pillows. "Amazing," he whispered, stroking his wife's hair. "She's had a hard time relaxing, even when the doctors told her it'd be best for her and the baby. You two have an astonishing connection."

"Yes, we do." Carolyn reached out for Joe's hand. "And so do the two of you."

"Yes, but sometimes you need the person who comforted you when you were little."

"I know I've certainly missed our mother over the years. Beth doesn't remember her, of course, but I do. When Mom died, though I was young, I knew I had to be a mother to Beth. It was odd. Our father was wonderful in many ways, but he couldn't fathom how difficult it all was." She flashed Joe a wistful smile. "Don't get me wrong. Beth was a gorgeous baby and I loved tending to her."

Joe pulled up two more chairs around the bed. "I know you did. You were just a child, and suddenly you had two children of your own."

"True."

Joe stroked his wife's damp forehead. "She was afraid to fall asleep earlier. She was convinced the baby would be gone when she woke up."

"Oh, God, poor Beth. No wonder she was so wound up."

Almost soundless steps approached from behind, making them both turn their heads. Annelie looked hesitant, but Joe rose, pointing to the empty chair next to Carolyn. "Please have a seat. Beth's asleep, but I know she won't mind us sitting here. In fact, I know she'd feel safe if she wakes up to the sound of our voices."

"You sure? Thank you." Annelie sat down. "Carolyn, I called Margo and let her know where we are."

"Good. Everything okay at her end?"

"Yes. I told her to enjoy her Sunday. Everything going on can wait till we go back."

The three of them sat in silence, occasionally engaging in small talk as Beth rested. Joe had been awake all night but refused to leave his wife and go home for a nap. Carolyn admired his stamina.

Looking at Beth's face, almost transparent in its paleness, Carolyn wanted to make a bargain with the devil if only her sister wouldn't lose her child. Suddenly Beth jerked and woke with a start, her body curling up as she gave a muted cry.

"No! Oh, it hurts…"

Joe pressed the alarm and Carolyn rose, taking Beth's hand. "Calm down, Beth. We've called for help. Try to relax, sweetie."

"I can't! It hurts too much." Beth yanked her hand free, pressing both hands onto her stomach as if to protect the endangered fetus. "No, no, no, this can't be happening…" Her voice rose to a loud cry as pain wracked her body.

Annelie disappeared out the door when several of the medical staff entered. Carolyn pressed her back against the wall, watching them administer more drugs and try to calm her sister. Unless they threw her out, she was not about to leave. She'd promised Beth to be there.

Joe looked up at his sister-in-law from where he was leaning over

Beth. "Carolyn? Please try to talk to her again. She's shaking so badly." His dark eyes were brimming with tears.

Circling the medical staff working around Beth, Carolyn stepped close to the bed. She leaned down, hugging Beth. "Please, baby, stop fighting so. Let the drugs do their job and just relax. There you go, try to breathe in and out. Nice and slow. Settle down."

"You don't understand," Beth moaned, tears and drops of sweat mixing at her temples. "You just don't understand. You've never been a mother, and you don't know what it's like to lose a child. It's not like losing a damn role!"

Stiffening at the stinging words, Carolyn swallowed hard, forcing herself to remember her sister was in a lot of pain and under great stress. "Shh, sweetie, calm down. That's it. The medication's working now, right? Can you feel it?"

Slowly the cramps lessened, and after a while Beth fell back into a deep sleep. Carolyn stretched her aching back, looking at Joe and the doctor. "What's happening now?"

"We gave her a new medication," the young doctor said. "All we can do is wait and see. You did a great job of calming Mrs. Rossi down. She's been terrified ever since she was brought in."

"Thank you." Carolyn moved out of the way to let Joe sit on the bed next to his wife. "She needs to see your face when she wakes up."

Joe pressed his lips together in a fine line. "I'm so glad you're here, Carolyn."

"She's my baby," Carolyn said. "I'll go see if I can find some coffee, okay? I'll be right around the corner." She walked out of Beth's room and found Annelie waiting just outside the door.

"You said something about coffee?" Annelie asked, holding up a cup. "Here you go."

Her lips trembling, Carolyn forced a smile, accepting the steaming drink. "Thank you."

"About what Beth said…it was her pain and fear talking. You know that, don't you?" Annelie blew on her hot tea, carefully studying Carolyn's face over the rim of her mug.

"Yes," Carolyn answered quickly. "Of course I do."

Sipping her coffee, Carolyn leaned against the wall, drawing a trembling breath. Beth's pain was her own.

❖

"You look 100 percent better, sweetie."

"I feel better, too." Beth managed a tired smile.

Annelie stood in the doorway, not wanting to disturb the sisters. She recognized the guarded expression in Carolyn's eyes and wondered if Beth noticed it.

"If you're up to it," Carolyn continued, "there's someone I want you to meet. Annelie?"

On cue, Annelie stepped inside the room and walked up to them.

"Beth, this is Annelie Peterson, my friend. Annelie, this is my sister Beth."

"Oh, it's great to finally meet you, Annelie," Beth gushed, color returning to her cheeks. The tormented woman Annelie had seen earlier had disappeared. Now, almost ten hours later, the danger seemed to be over, at least for now.

"I'm glad to see you're feeling better," Annelie smiled. "I've looked forward to meeting you and your family."

"Thanks for helping Carolyn get here so fast." Beth's expression turned serious. "Joe told me you drove all the way."

"I was happy to help."

Beth looked at Carolyn, her cheeks reddening. "Lyn? Won't you sit?" She gestured to the bed. "I…"

Carolyn sat down on the side of the bed, taking Beth's hand in hers. "The only thing that matters is you're feeling better. Both of you."

"No, it's not all that matters. I said horrible things to you. Lynnie, I didn't mean it." Beth clung to her sister's hand. "I was scared, and I didn't mean it the way it came out." Tears dropped from blue-gray eyes so like Carolyn's. "I'm sorry."

Annelie saw the tension lessen in Carolyn's shoulders as she leaned forward to kiss her little sister. "Hush, now. I knew you were in pain. I understand, Beth. Don't give it a second thought."

"You know everything, and more, about being a mom. You're my sister, but you're my mother too."

Feeling tears rise in her own eyes, Annelie had to swallow hard when she heard the love and sincerity obvious in Beth's voice. Carolyn's ready understanding and forgiveness also warmed her heart. Glancing at Joe, she saw him wink at her. Annelie smiled, nodding back.

"Yes, I am," Carolyn agreed. "I know it. You know it." She placed her hand on her sister's rounded stomach. "Pamela's little brother or sister will just have to wait till it's safe to come out and join us."

"I'm sure the baby won't dare argue with *Grandma*." Joe grinned, making Annelie and Beth laugh when Carolyn gave him a lethal glare. "Only kidding, Lyn."

"It's one thing being a mother, but a granny is something entirely different," Carolyn huffed, unable to suppress a smile.

"I'm staying here tonight," Joe said. "Why don't the two of you take my keys and go to the house? You must be exhausted."

"Yes, please do," Beth implored. "We just stocked up the fridge and freezer. I'm sure there's something easy you can fix. Like frozen pizza, or…what?" She looked back and forth between the two women as Carolyn rolled her eyes and Annelie snorted at her words. "What did I say?"

❖

The artificial current in the endless pool slid along her skin like a caress as Carolyn swam forcefully toward no goal. Knowing Beth's condition was stable, she was relieved to be home in New York.

After they had disposed of the car and their luggage, Carolyn had showered and gone directly to the pool, while Annelie headed for the study to take care of business.

Carolyn felt the tension in her joints recede as she kept up an even pace. She was sure swimming would take care of the burning sensation in the muscles in the back of her neck and between her eyes.

When a pair of long legs appeared, Carolyn pressed the Stop button while treading water against the current.

"Finished your e-mails already?"

"Yes." Annelie shrugged. "There weren't that many. I meant to ask you something. Jem e-mailed, and she sounds like she's ready for a vacation after last week's craziness. I think she's pulled all-nighters more than she'll admit."

"Well, why don't we ask her to come stay with us? She'll have the apartment to herself most of the day since we'll be at work. The place is big enough."

Annelie gave a faint smile. "How can you be so perceptive? You always seem to understand."

Carolyn swam to the ladder and climbed out of the water. Reaching for a towel, she returned the smile. "You're so incredibly considerate and always want my opinion about these things. Why wouldn't I do the same? Jem's a good friend of yours, and I like her. If Jem needs a break…Also, she's not stupid. She's figured out the truth about us, hasn't she?" Carolyn walked over to Annelie, wrapping her arms around her lover.

"Yes." Annelie nuzzled Carolyn's damp hair. "Why don't you take another quick shower and dry your hair? I'll just give Jem a call."

"Go ahead. Tell her I said hi." Carolyn let go of her lover, patting her bottom as she left. Annelie raised a sardonic eyebrow at the gesture but had a humorous twinkle in her eyes.

Carolyn followed Annelie's suggestion and then climbed into bed, her body feeling heavy and lethargic. She turned on some soft music, pulled the covers up over her naked body, and settled against the pillows, letting the music surround her.

They had left D.C. after breakfast and one last visit with Beth in the hospital. Carolyn agreed to leave only when she was satisfied her sister was better. Explaining to Beth and Joe she was staying with Annelie during the filming, she'd given them the number to her own line, begging them to keep her posted.

Beth had cried when they said goodbye but lit up when Annelie promised her and Joe a tour of the studio. Carolyn smiled to herself at the look on her sister's face when Annelie had offered to be their personal guide.

"This looks cozy." The cool alto voice made Carolyn's heart jump.

"Come to bed," she suggested, flipping back the covers. "I know it's only late afternoon, but we're exhausted. You did most of the driving."

"Good idea. I'll be right back."

Annelie soon returned smelling of her special grapefruit bath gel, her long hair slightly damp.

"I'm too tired to make love," Carolyn confessed, "but I'd love for you to join me."

"Dressed like this?" Annelie interrupted, letting her short terry-cloth robe fall to the floor.

Standing there as naked as Eve before the fall, Annelie made Carolyn's throat constrict. Gently she cleared her throat. "Oh, my."

Annelie walked over to the bed, crawled under the covers, and pulled Carolyn into her arms. Soft skin against soft skin made Carolyn lose her breath. Too exhausted to think about sex, she let her hands slide slowly along Annelie's body; merely feeling her was enough.

"I know, in a relationship, you don't always have to thank each other," Carolyn murmured. "This isn't one of those times. You've done so much for me, love. And I don't take any of it for granted."

Annelie pressed a soft kiss on her forehead. "I know."

"Is Jem coming?"

"Yes. She's flying in Wednesday morning."

"Good. Will you meet her?"

"I can't. I'm in meetings all day. I'll send a car for her."

Resting on Annelie's shoulder, Carolyn closed her eyes. As she pulled the pillow under her cheek to not weigh her lover down, she sighed contentedly. "This is heaven."

"Mmm."

Annelie's soft curves pressed into Carolyn as she pulled her closer, wrapping a slender leg around her. "Is this okay?"

"More than okay. It's perfect."

❖

Margo looked up from her desk in the heart of the office. "Annelie! Good, you're back. Did all the work you took care of from home yesterday pay off? When I talked to Carolyn earlier, she said you were up past midnight to fine-tune your presentation. How did the meeting go?"

"Excellent." Annelie beamed. "We really made progress, Margo. It looks like we have the go-ahead for those shelters. What did Carolyn want?"

"Just to say hello, I think. She'll call back later."

"Okay. Everything all right here?" Annelie gestured toward the other offices.

"Running smoothly now we can focus on the important things. Oh, speaking of that, there's a package for you. From California."

Annelie had started walking toward her office and now stopped abruptly, her heart speeding up. "California?"

"Yes, from the investigator."

"I thought I'd received all the documents regarding my father and Trevor White. I'd rather not read anything more about that imposter." Annelie scowled.

"I know, but here they are anyway, girlie." Margo handed over a thick parcel. "Seems like an awful lot, just to be documents."

"I'll take a look at this in my office. Hold my calls for now, unless it's personal."

"Will do."

Annelie tossed the package down on her empty desk, then placed her hand on it as if trying to gauge its contents. Suddenly filled with anxiety, she felt her mouth grow stale. She took a deep breath before sliding a letter opener along the edge of the package, opening it carefully, and glancing inside.

She didn't find legal documents or anything resembling what the investigator had previously sent her. Instead, Annelie pulled out two large stacks of small, tattered envelopes.

Breathing hard, she saw her father's name on them and, turning one over, she recognized her mother's name as the sender. They were dated between March 1978 and December 1981.

When she investigated the large package more carefully, she pulled out a single piece of paper, which she skimmed, hoping for a clarification. The package was indeed from the investigator, who explained how the police had discovered the letters among Trevor White's belongings.

With trembling hands, Annelie untied the string and opened the first letter, written only a week after her father left.

Dear Stuart,
    First of all, I hope your trip down south went well and you are feeling better. You were so upset when you left and I am grateful Annie was not home to witness it. She adores you and to see her father in your present frame of mind would have been too much for a child like her.
    Writing you at a post office box is worrying. How will I be able to get a hold of you in case something happens

to either me or Annie? Is there a phone
number I can ring? Please let me know.

Annie asks for you every day when she
comes home from school. It is difficult to
tell her I am not sure when you will be
coming home.

Please write soon, Stuart. We miss
you and I am certain we can make it work
if you would only give me, and Annie,
another chance.

Your loving wife,
Anna

The hopeful tone in Anna's first letter diminished in every letter
Annelie read. She had written her husband for more than three years—
at first, every week, and then every month. Heartbreaking sentences of
how Annelie stopped asking for her father after a while, and how lonely
Anna felt while waiting for her husband to contact her. In the last six
letters, her tone became resigned and resentful. When he had missed
three birthdays and four Christmases, Anna wrote the last letter on New
Year's Eve, 1981.

Stuart,

Annie is ten years old. Her three
last birthdays have gone by unnoticed
from your end. No gifts, and no Christmas
presents…not even a card. If you had seen
her sitting by the phone, all dressed up,
and ignoring the friends I invited to her
party, just waiting, afraid she would miss
your call…which of course never came.

You make me so angry and I have to be
honest—I hate you for what you have done
to her. I don't care what you have done
to me; I'm a grown woman who can take care
of myself. But the child…

Here the letter was unreadable, perhaps from her mother's tears.

...will not write anymore. You have been
an invisible member of this family for
three years now, but no more. We do not
expect to hear from you. If you choose to
return to Chicago, know this; you are not
welcome here.
Anna

Annelie leaned back in her chair, her eyes full of tears and her stomach a tight knot. Anna had hated her father in the end. Who could blame her? *How I wished and hoped he'd return. Every day, for the first year, I expected him to call. When he didn't, when Mom finally stopped reassuring me, I still clung to the hope he would come. If not that day, then next birthday, next Christmas...*

Annelie remembered hoping he'd return and mend their little family. *I don't know why I was so hopeful for so long. He showed me hardly any interest the first seven years of my life. Mom gave me unconditional love, but thinking back, I realize he merely tolerated me at best. And even Mom finally reached her breaking point.* Reading the letters had let her see her mother's more human side, which was a relief.

She jumped when the phone rang, dropping the last letter as she reached for it. "Peterson."

"Hello, love. How's your day going?"

The sound of the familiar husky voice made the tears roll down Annelie's cheeks. "Oh, Carolyn..."

"What's wrong?"

"Nothing...I received a package in the mail. My mother's old letters to my father, and I've just read some of them."

"Oh, Annie. I thought she didn't know where he was."

"She didn't. Apparently he gave her a post-office box as an address. As far as I can tell from her letters, he never replied."

"Damn."

The curse echoed Annelie's feelings. "How're things going today?" she asked, wanting to change the subject.

"Great. We've finished the first scenes, and later this week we'll start rehearsing in the studio."

"What scene are you starting with?"

"The one where Maddox shows up at Erica's place, demanding to know why her partner's acting so strange."

"That's the scene leading up to their rendezvous at the office. Are you nervous about acting it out with Helen?"

"Not really. I think it's good we're doing those scenes first. Strangely, Helen and I are becoming friends. I'm afraid we'd get giggly about it if we become too chummy, no matter how seasoned we are. We need to keep the tension as long as possible."

"Maybe you're right. How does Helen feel?"

"She actually told me of her one, quite innocent, encounter with another woman. It was ages ago and never led to anything, but she thought she'd tap into it when we do the love scenes. I didn't tell her, but I think she guesses I have plenty to tap into."

Annelie had to laugh. "You're bad!"

"No, I'm good at being bad, you mean." There was a smile in Carolyn's voice. "I have to go, love. Are you all right about the letters?"

"I am now. Listen, I'll bring them home tonight. Will you read them over with me? I need to talk about some of the things in them. Or perhaps we should wait, since Jem'll be there."

"We can read them in bed before we go to sleep. No reason to wait and have them weighing on your mind."

Annelie gave a relieved sigh. "Sounds like a great idea. It's a date, then."

As she hung up, Annelie felt the butterflies leave her stomach, at least for the time being.

Her thoughts shifted to Carolyn. *She sounds a little stressed, but that's normal at the beginning of a new job. Thank goodness Carolyn's not too worried about doing the love scenes. What if I'd become jealous because she's going to be almost naked with another woman in a couple of scenes? Now I know how Carolyn and Helen plan to approach the scenes, I certainly don't have anything to worry about there.*

Shaking her head, Annelie checked her watch and realized Jem must have arrived at the apartment. She dialed her home number.

"Peterson residence."

"Peterson herself here. How was your flight?"

"Short and turbulent. I tried to work on the flight, but it got so bad,

I think I made permanent indentations in my laptop. It was all I had to hold on to."

"You were working on the plane, Jem? Isn't this supposed to be a vacation?"

"A something-in-between, I'm afraid. I just received two new manuscripts, and they need my opinion before the week's over. One's really promising and the other one…well, let's just say I can't get a grip on it."

"Intriguing either way. If you need another opinion, just let me know."

"Sure. By the way, when will you be home? I'm cooking."

Annelie grinned. Jem's cooking skills were one of her best-kept secrets. "Sounds wonderful. I'll be home around six—Carolyn, soon after."

"Good, then I'll know what to aim for. I'll run down to a grocery store I passed about a block away. It looked promising."

"Marco's? They have everything you could possibly need. Especially their seafood section."

"Is that a request?"

"Well, you know I love any kind of seafood."

"How about gratineed lobster with a salad?"

"Excellent! See you around six, then?"

"I'll be the one wearing the apron."

Hanging up, Annelie tried to envision her chief editor in an apron. Jem intimidated a lot of people, since she didn't tolerate fools and made no bones about it. Perhaps if they saw her wearing an apron and a chef's hat, they'd think differently.

Her mood suddenly brighter after her two phone calls, Annelie put her mother's letters back into the package. She'd get through things, one at a time.

❖

Nothing remained of the meal. Carolyn looked down at her rounded stomach, wondering if she'd be able to fit into her clothes at work. They were going to shoot the first scene a day earlier than expected.

"Jem, you're going to cause me all kinds of trouble. Yesterday lobsters, and today this incredible casserole. I'll pop the buttons in all of my clothes," she groaned.

"What can I say? I love to cook. I don't have time when I'm home because I work so much and, frankly, cooking for one isn't very inspiring." Jem shrugged. "I'm glad you liked it."

"Liked it?" Annelie moaned, unbuttoning her jeans. "I don't think that's the right word."

Looking at the empty plates, Jem grinned. "I take that as a compliment."

"We've got to have the Davidsons and Helen over one night," Annelie said. "We can't keep Jem's skills a secret like this. They'll never forgive us."

"I like Helen St. Cyr," Jem said. "She seemed really down-to-earth and nice when we talked briefly at the Orlando convention."

"She is," Carolyn agreed. "We get along better all the time, and I think she and Annelie really hit it off flying back from L.A."

"She has a great sense of humor." Annelie shared the story about Helen's *fuck-me* boots.

Jem laughed out loud, leaning back into her chair. "Oh, God, the things people want to know. I'm still laughing at the smooth-or-crunchy-peanut-butter question someone asked you, Carolyn."

"In L.A., it was about my belly button," Carolyn said. "It's pretty innocent, though."

"We ought to invite some people from the set." Annelie ran a finger over her lips. "Perhaps Regina and Gregory."

"And Margo."

"Yes, that'd be a lot of fun," Annelie said. "We can make it a casual get-together, nothing fancy. Except the food, of course. I promise to be your kitchen slave, Jem."

"Good. I hate to wash dishes."

"I'll just call for maid service."

As they cleared the table and filled the dishwasher, Carolyn moved with care, since flashes of light sparkled behind her eyelids. The food hadn't stopped her escalating headache. Not wanting to worry the others, she turned to Annelie with a casual smile. "Think it's time for my swim, love. I'll join you in the living room later."

Annelie frowned. "You look pale. Do you have a headache?"

"A little one. It was a long day. A swim will take care of that." Carolyn forced herself to smile.

Annelie didn't look convinced, but she relented. "All right. I'll make you some café latte."

Carolyn smiled again, this time more genuinely. "Oh, you're such a treasure. Royal Copenhagen?"

"Of course." Annelie kissed her on the nose. "Go on."

Carolyn shot Jem a glance and was relieved to see her grin. "You two are too cute for words," she said.

Rolling her eyes in mock exasperation, and immediately regretting it since it sent a jolt of pain through her temples, Carolyn went to get ready. Examining her face in the bathroom mirror, she realized Annelie was right. She *was* pale, with dark shadows under her eyes.

As Carolyn pushed through the cool water, her arms seemed heavier than normal. Changing from the breaststroke to a crawl, she tried to ignore the pain in her shoulders. The current seemed stronger than usual, making her wonder if she'd accidentally changed the settings. After another ten minutes of the searing ache, she decided to stop and was stunned at how difficult it was to climb out of the pool.

Stumbling into the shower, she let hot water flow down her body, relieved at how it relaxed her. Carolyn closed her eyes, willing her breathing to calm down. *I can't let Jem and Annelie see me this way. I've got to keep these silly headaches under control.*

After her shower, Carolyn avoided the noisy hairdryer and instead swallowed two Relpax, knowing they'd knock her out.

Jem and Annelie were in the living room talking, low music playing in the background.

"Ladies, I'm heading for bed."

Annelie's head snapped up. "Already? It's only eight thirty." She walked over to Carolyn and pressed the back of her hand against Carolyn's forehead. "Don't you want your coffee?"

"No. I'm sorry, love. Not tonight. I must be anxious about the first day of filming. I'm exhausted."

"Let me tuck you in. Be right back, Jem."

"Don't worry about me," Jem smiled, waving a DVD cover in their direction. "I found a movie I haven't seen. Mind if I pop this in?"

"Of course not."

After Annelie folded the covers back, Carolyn climbed in, dressed in one of Annelie's long T-shirts. "Thanks, love."

"Shh, just relax. Want me to rub your temples?"

"Could you kiss them instead? It helps when you press your lips right where it hurts."

Annelie leaned over Carolyn and kissed her forehead. Slowly the pain dissipated, fading to a faint throb. "Oh, yes."

Not saying anything, Annelie kept kissing her forehead. The motion was hypnotizing, and Carolyn felt herself drift off into the half-conscious state just before sleep. "…so much…" she murmured.

"Better?"

"…love you…"

"I know. Go to sleep. I love you too," Annelie whispered against her skin. "You'll be fine. That's it. Sleep."

Carolyn wanted to say how much she appreciated Annelie's care, but the words forming in her head never reached her lips.

❖

Regina Carmichael waved the script in the air, a sure sign she had something important to say.

"Listen up, ladies. You've got to make the audience realize how much the denial and evasions of their mutual attraction torment Erica. This scene will ratchet up the tension for the all-important one where Erica kisses Maddox. Carolyn, play Maddox as bewildered, yet furious. Helen, Erica is defensive and equally angry. You did a great job at the tabletop exercise. Now show me you can take it over the top. Everything clear?"

Carolyn nodded briskly. "Yes."

They moved into position, Carolyn standing below a concrete staircase that led up to Erica's apartment and Helen upstairs, behind a green door. The crew rustled around them.

"All right, people. Look sharp. Camera!"

"Camera running."

"Silence! Scene twenty-two. Take one. Action!"

Carolyn hurried up the stairs and knocked on the door.

"Cut! Sorry, Carolyn, the mike was in the picture. Again, please."

Walking back down, inhaling deeply, she braced herself for the next attempt.

After a few adjustments, Regina gave her command again. "Take two. Action."

Carolyn repeated her maneuver and reached the top of the stairs. "Good. Let's move on to the next scene while you're still up there, Carolyn. You ready, Helen?" Regina said after the third take.

"Yup."

Swallowing against her nausea, Carolyn prepared for Helen to initiate the quarrel scene.

At the director's command, Helen yanked the door open and glared at her. "Diana, what a surprise," she said resentfully. "Working around the clock as usual. What's up?"

Carolyn leaned against the door frame, staring at Helen with narrowing eyes. "You left in the middle of our conversation."

"Conversation?" Helen huffed. "You were lecturing. I swear, if you ever talk to me in that condescending tone of voice again, I'll—" Her voice broke off, completely falling out of character. "Carolyn?"

Sweat was pouring down Carolyn's back under her shirt and black leather jacket. Everything blurred, and the stairs to her left swayed. She tried to move away from them, but her legs wouldn't cooperate. Nausea made her swallow hard, and she began to fall.

"Oh, God. Carolyn!"

As her pain became unbearable, taking away her vision, she felt hands clutch at her jacket. She fell, expecting to slam into the concrete steps, yet unable to stop herself. In the distance she heard loud voices shout her name.

❖

Helen watched Carolyn go beyond pale. In fact, she quickly turned gray. When she began to fall toward the long stairs, Helen acted on impulse. Reaching out, she managed to grab the lapels of Carolyn's leather jacket and pull the other woman toward her.

Carolyn's body slammed into hers as they both fell into the hallway of Erica Becker's apartment. Landing painfully on the floor, Carolyn on top of her, Helen lost her breath for a minute.

When Carolyn didn't try to move, Helen managed to make her voice work. "Carolyn? You okay?" Then she freed a hand and touched Carolyn's cheek, which was cold and damp. "Carolyn!"

CHAPTER SEVENTEEN

K eep the change." Annelie pressed some bills into the cabdriver's hand and jumped out of the car. She wanted to scream with impatience when a family of at least six cut her off at the hospital entrance.

Inside, she frantically looked for the emergency room, her heart pounding. Half running toward the ER entrance, she clung to what Regina had said. Carolyn was awake when the ambulance drove away from the studio. She had to be all right.

The nurses' station in the ER was as crowded as the front door. Trying to draw even breaths, Annelie waited in line. She fought an overwhelming urge to push the people ahead of her out of the way, knowing they had equally pressing concerns.

"Annelie? Over here!" A familiar male voice made her whirl around, and Gregory walked toward her. "They're over here."

She forced herself not to run. "How is she? And what do you mean by *they*? What's happened?"

"Helen's here too. She needed a couple of stitches in the back of her head after the fall."

"What fall?" Annelie felt confused and unable to focus. "What're you talking about? I thought Carolyn fainted. What happened to Helen?"

Gregory gently took her by the elbow and led her farther down the corridor. "Carolyn did faint. From what they told me, she already looked pale this morning. After running up and down some stairs several times during rehearsal and later, during the takes, she passed out."

"Oh, God," Annelie murmured, stopping outside the curtains. "And who fell?"

The door behind them opened, and Helen stepped outside, dressed in pants and a hospital robe. "We both did. Carolyn landed on me when she collapsed." She walked up to Annelie and hugged her. "She's okay, Annelie. She just came down from X-ray and the doctor's with her now." She gestured toward a door across the corridor.

"Helen saved her," Gregory added, drawing a stern look from the actress. "Well, you did. Regina said if you hadn't pulled Carolyn toward you, she could've fallen down the stairs."

Annelie felt her knees buckle and, for a second, only Helen's strong arms held her up. "What?"

"Gregory! You've got the tact of a bulldozer." Helen turned back to Annelie. "She scared us all for a minute. At first I couldn't tell if she was breathing or not."

"And then?"

"People came running from all directions. The staff nurse made everyone leave Carolyn alone and not move her while she examined her. When they finally moved her, Carolyn woke up, dizzy and with a headache, but able to stand on her feet."

"Can I see her?" Annelie's eyes brimmed with tears.

"The doctor should be out soon." Helen kept her arm around Annelie, who welcomed the comforting touch.

When a doctor finally appeared, Annelie approached him, eager to see her lover. "Doctor, I'm Annelie Peterson. Is my—is Carolyn all right?"

The doctor peered at her over his reading glasses. "Are you next of kin?"

"No, but…yes, in a way."

"I can only answer questions from immediate family members. Sorry." He started to walk away.

"We…she's my…We're like family, doctor." Annelie felt a jab of pain in her stomach while she tried to explain.

"Sorry. Unless you're her sister, I can't share any details." As he began to walk away again, Helen grasped his arm.

"Can we see her?"

"She really needs to rest. Until her family gets here, there's nothing I can—"

"Doctor, these are my friends, and Annelie's right. She *is* my family," a husky voice interrupted. "I realize you're only protecting my privacy, but, in this case, it's unnecessary."

Annelie pivoted and saw Carolyn standing in the doorway, looking pale and smaller than usual, but with a familiar firm expression in her eyes. The doctor frowned.

"Ms. Black, you really should rest and not—"

"I'll rest, and my friends will keep me company. It's up to me to decide who can stay or not, don't you agree? I feel a lot better, thanks to the medication you prescribed. Start the procedure of having me released, please." Annelie recognized Carolyn's commanding tone of voice.

Not caring if anyone saw them, Annelie walked over to Carolyn and put her arms around her, holding her tight. "You scared me."

"I'm sorry." Carolyn's voice was a mere whisper. "I didn't mean to. God, another hospital, another scare. We can't keep doing this." She tried a smile.

"I know."

"Gregory and I'll find some coffee. See you ladies later." Helen pulled Gregory with her toward the waiting area, tucking the hospital robe tighter around her.

Returning to her room, Carolyn sat down on the gurney, still holding Annelie's hand. "I'm so glad you're here."

Annelie examined Carolyn's face, raising her free hand to touch her lover's lips. "I'm devastated you're here. You scared me. Regina called and all she could say was that you fainted, were unconscious for a while, and they called the paramedics. I…Apart from going with you to see Beth, I haven't really been in a hospital since my mother died."

"Oh, love, come here." Carolyn pulled Annelie closer. "This doctor, in spite of his harsh manners, is very conscientious. He's going to refer me to a different neurologist."

"A neurologist? What does he think is wrong?"

Settling against Annelie's shoulder, Carolyn closed her eyes. "Same as before, but with a twist." She sighed. "He started asking me how my latest weeks have been, and at first I thought, no more stressful than usual, considering how I live my life. Then I began to list everything that's happened. It's been crazy, Annie. Falling in love, the contracts, the imposter, the movie, Beth…The CAT scan was negative, so no reason to think it was anything else than my usual migraines gone awry."

Annelie brushed Carolyn's disheveled hair from her forehead.

"I'm glad they did a thorough check. And you're right. It *has* been one thing after another. So what did Dr. Standoffish think?"

"That I need to start taking much better care of myself. My blood pressure was elevated—not dangerously high, but still up there. My level of stress, well, the list says it all. I'm not on the most effective medication for my type of migraines, so he's going to take care of that. I'm going to see a dietician—or perhaps it was a nutritionist—I don't remember, to learn more about my condition. The only thing I was doing right was the exercise. He told me to keep swimming."

"Whatever it takes, darling," Annelie sighed, kissing the top of Carolyn's head. Feeling her stiffen, she pulled back. "What?"

Carolyn looked at her with wide eyes. "You called me darling."

Annelie opened her mouth to speak, but closed it again. Blushing faintly, she cleared her throat. "So I did. Do you mind?"

"No, no. It was just such a surprise. You never use terms of endearment." Leaning against Annelie, she closed her eyes again. "Why now? Because you were worried?"

"I don't know. Perhaps. I never use words like that because they're so common and meaningless. I guess it happened because that's what you are."

"I'm what? Common? Now I'm confused."

Placing soft kisses along her lover's hairline, Annelie finally realized Carolyn wasn't in any danger. "Silly. You *are* my darling. I love you."

Carolyn held on closer. "I love you too."

"What happens now?" Annelie didn't think she could let go of Carolyn.

"They wanted to keep me here overnight, but I refused. I'll be very careful and not do anything but rest this weekend, I promise. I just want you to take me home."

"All right. Home it is."

❖

Jem stirred one pot while lowering the temperature on another. "Was that the doorbell?"

"Yes, I'll get it. Helen's on her way up."

Carolyn stayed in a chair by the kitchen table. She felt better but was still shaken from her ordeal earlier in the day. "It smells wonderful, Jem. Casseroles are the perfect autumn food."

"Couldn't agree more. Easy to make, and if there's enough left for the next day, it usually tastes even better. Ah, here's Helen now." Jem wiped her hands on a towel and greeted their guest.

"Nice to see you again, Jem." Helen smiled. "I better warn you, I'm starving."

"Good. I've made enough to feed a small country."

"I'm glad you could join us," Carolyn said. "You don't need to be alone when you just banged your head. Or should I say, *I* banged your head."

"Didn't they want to keep you in the hospital?" Jem asked while they all sat down around the table. "I thought a twenty-four-hour observation was routine."

"The doctor was pretty exasperated with me, and Carolyn, for going against his recommendations. I pointed out I never lost consciousness so he agreed I could take care of myself. He sent me home with pretty strong pills to take if the headache gets worse."

"Well, I'm glad you're staying with us," Annelie offered, reaching for a bottle of mineral water.

"To be honest, I agree." Helen sighed. "I feel okay, but I do feel headachy."

"Some food and rest will fix that," Jem assured her, rising to check the stove again. "We're lucky Annelie has plenty of space for all of us."

"How long are you staying, Jem?" asked Helen.

"I have to leave Tuesday. I hate to go, because I've really enjoyed evaluating manuscripts in a different environment."

After devouring Jem's chicken casserole, Annelie and Jem took care of the dishes, having pushed Carolyn and Helen into the living room. The actresses sat down on the couch, Carolyn looking at Helen appraisingly. "I never got to thank you earlier. Gregory said you saved me from a nasty fall."

"It was nothing."

"And that *nothing* made you have several stitches in the back of your head."

"Better that than a broken neck." Helen gazed back. "Really, apart from this silly headache, I'm fine."

Carolyn looked down at her hands, not sure how to phrase what she wanted to say. "Listen, Helen, I'd like to talk to you about something." She paused, looking squarely at the other woman. "I know you're aware of my reputation for being ambitious and competitive. Rumor has it I'm prepared to walk over corpses to get the role I'm after."

Helen propped her arm on the back of the couch, waiting for Carolyn to continue.

"For a long time that was true. First, because I needed the work and the money, and then…because of habit and ambition, I guess. Since we're becoming friends, it matters to me what you think. I used to not give a damn about other people's opinions, and I've never really been friends with another actress, but lately that's changed. I'm tired of competing with everyone."

Carolyn fiddled with the hem of her shirt, twisting it between trembling fingers. "And it's not just about me anymore. I've got someone in my life I care very much about. I want this someone to be proud of me, not only as a professional, but as a person. One way to do that is to be friends with a few special people like you, and to be true to them." Carolyn tried to disentangle her fingers from the shirt, while giving a faint smile. "Am I making any sense at all?"

Helen returned the smile, reaching out for Carolyn's restless hands. "Carolyn, don't worry about it. Yes, I've heard through the grapevine about your ambition. I'm a fairly uncomplicated person with a simple outlook on life. You, Annelie, and now Jem have never treated me with anything but kindness and respect. That's so much more than I bargained for when I agreed to do the audiobooks and the movies. To be accepted into this inner circle of wonderful, caring individuals—that's pretty awesome. As for our budding friendship, I'd say it's more than budding. You're a good person underneath your facade, Carolyn. You just have to realize that for yourself."

Tears rose in Carolyn's eyes at her unexpected feelings of vulnerability.

"Hey, no tears," Helen exclaimed. "Annelie will fire me on the spot." Her face turned serious. "Maybe you've bought into the rumors a little too much? If people say things about you enough, you start believing them. When you go into your professional mode, you're very much Carolyn Black, diva extraordinaire. Maybe it's easy to lose sight of who you really are."

"The last few months have helped me see things from another perspective," Carolyn said. "Being in a relationship and seeing my sister several times, not to mention my niece, have helped keep me grounded."

"Are you happy?" Helen's voice was soft.

"I've never been this happy and content...or dizzy and infatuated either, for that matter." A tender smile played on Carolyn's lips. "You guessed pretty quickly, didn't you?"

"It took me a while, but when you rushed home to Annelie when her so-called father entered the scene, I was sure. You've got a bad case, my friend." Helen gave a cheeky grin, making Carolyn roll her eyes.

"Yes, I do."

"You're keeping it a secret?"

"We haven't discussed that yet. I guess we'll have to agree on a course of action before the whole hoopla around the movie begins."

"What hoopla would that be?" Annelie entered the room with a tray of steaming mugs. "I know you're supposed to cut back on caffeine, Carolyn, but I didn't think a very mild café latte would hurt."

"Thanks, love." Carolyn lit up, grabbing a mug before answering. "Maddox movie hoopla. We were just talking about all the hype about *Dying for Fame*. It's going to be brutal." She winked at Helen.

"We're going to be interviewed to death. Leno was just a small taste of what's to come." Helen moaned. "Can you imagine? Letterman, Conan..."

"Actually, the producers of *The Oprah Winfrey Show* have approached us." Annelie sat down next to Carolyn. "We'll do two whole shows based on the books first, and then the movies. This isn't until the premiere, of course."

"Oprah's another matter." Carolyn smiled. "I've never been on her show, but I look forward to it."

Jem slumped back into one of the armchairs. "Who knew, when Annelie signed Delia Carlton—completely unknown at the time—she'd write such an international hit?"

"Oh, that's right. I checked my mail earlier," Annelie added before sitting down next to Carolyn. "I didn't have a chance to tell you all the news."

"What news?"

"You've got to promise me this stays among the four of us." Annelie looked serious.

"Now we're all dying of curiosity." Carolyn turned her head, trying to determine what was up from Annelie's expression.

"Delia Carlton just submitted another manuscript. There's going to be a fourth Diana Maddox book."

"What?" Jem exclaimed, her jaw dropping. "When did you learn about this?"

"Just before Helen arrived. I meant to share it over dinner, but we started talking about other things."

"Does this mean another audiobook and another movie?" Carolyn raised her eyebrows.

"Possibly. I'll read it and then pass it on to my editor." Annelie winked at Jem. "If it's up to her usual standards, which it probably is, I foresee at least an audiobook."

"The fans will go crazy," Helen said. "The secret's safe with me."

"I'm so glad Delia Carlton wrote these books." Carolyn smiled. "So much has come from it."

"Clever lady, in all she does." Annelie raised her mug. "Here's to Delia, without whom none of us would be exactly where we are."

They all raised their coffee mugs.

"To Delia!"

❖

Annelie pulled Carolyn onto her shoulder, nuzzling her hair. The familiar scent of her lover's shampoo made her relax into the embrace.

"You all right, love?"

"Shouldn't I be asking you that?" Annelie murmured.

"You have. Several times."

Not sure if Carolyn was being facetious, Annelie moved, looking down at her. "I was worried."

"I know, Annie, but I'm fine now. No headache, no dizziness. The new medication works like a charm."

Frowning, Annelie sank down on the pillows. "Please don't downplay it. You scared me today."

Apparently realizing how serious she was, Carolyn rolled over on her side, landing almost nose to nose with Annelie. "I know I did. I think you were paler than I was, at the hospital. I'm sorry."

"No, no, it wasn't your fault. You couldn't help being sick, but I need you to acknowledge my feelings. I sat in the cab forever, in the traffic gridlock from hell, and had no way of knowing how serious your condition was. I was rushing toward a hospital for the second time in a week, and—" Annelie stopped the gush of words when memories of another hospital, another time, overwhelmed her.

"And?" Carolyn prodded gently, wrapping her arms around Annelie, rubbing her back.

"And I was afraid I wouldn't make it in time."

"I'm guessing you didn't make it to the hospital in time when your mother died?" Carolyn's voice was soft.

"I tried to get to her." Annelie gave a muted sob. "I had a test in school, an important one, and I'd studied so hard for it. I took the test, and when I came out, the principal was waiting for me. She drove me to the hospital. Margo met me at the door and told me. Mom was gone."

Carolyn tucked Annelie's ice-cold hands into her armpits, and her freezing feet tangled between her own. "I'm so sorry to hear this, Annie. It must have been so hard for you."

"You went through something similar and you were only twelve, with siblings to raise."

"True."

"And at twenty-one, when you were left completely in charge. We've both been there in different, but still similar, ways." Annelie clung to her lover. "You feel so warm."

"You'll be warm soon too. What time is it?"

Annelie turned her head toward the alarm clock. "Two thirty. Wonder why I can't settle down. I'm keeping you awake too."

"Don't worry about it. It's Saturday. We can sleep in."

Annelie frowned. "Yes, but you still need your sleep. I'll go have some warm milk. Want some?" The disgusted look on Carolyn's face made her smile. "Guess not. I'll be right back."

Annelie grabbed her robe, tiptoeing through the hall toward the kitchen. When she passed the two guest rooms she spotted Jem coming from the bathroom. "You okay?" Annelie whispered.

"Yeah, just too much coffee. What's up? Can't sleep?"

"No, and I'm keeping Carolyn awake."

As Jem began to walk back to her room, something caught her attention. "What's she up to?"

Helen stood motionless farther down the hall, almost ghostlike in her long, white nightgown. Her hair was tousled around her shoulders, and she didn't appear to notice them.

"Helen?" Annelie said in a low voice as they walked up to her. "What're you doing out here?"

There was no reply. The actress's eyes were open, but unfocused.

"She must've taken the pills the doc gave her," Jem said. "She's asleep."

"You mean she's sleepwalking? Should we wake her?"

"No, I don't think so. I'll help her." Jem carefully circled Helen's shoulders with her arm, nudging her toward the guest room. "Come on, honey. Let's get you back to bed." Walking behind them into Helen's room, Annelie watched Jem help the sleeping woman sit down on the bed. Then Jem lifted Helen's legs and coaxed her to move up onto the pillows. "That's right. Up we go." Jem grabbed the sheet and blankets lying on the floor, spreading them over Helen's motionless body and tucking her in. She stood watching the sleeping form for a moment before walking back to the hallway with Annelie.

"Is she all right?" Annelie resumed walking toward the kitchen.

"She's pretty out of it, but she responded when I was talking to her. Still, she took quite a fall today. Speaking of that, is Carolyn okay?"

"Yes, she claims she's fine." Annelie took a carton of milk from the refrigerator, poured some into a mug, and placed it in the microwave. "Want some milk?" Unaware of it, Jem mimicked the face Carolyn had made only minutes before.

"No, I'll head back to bed. I hope that'll do the trick for you, though."

"Me too."

Carrying the mug back to the bedroom, Annelie found Carolyn still awake and waiting for her. She carefully climbed back into bed, sipping from her mug.

"You look like a kid, all tousled and drinking milk," Carolyn whispered. "You're always beautiful, but this is the first time I've ever seen you look cute."

"Cute?" Annelie wrinkled her nose. "Thanks. I think."

Carolyn placed a soft kiss on her cheek. "You're welcome."

Finishing the milk and finally feeling warm again, Annelie curled up close to Carolyn, holding her in her arms. "I want to ask you something." She held her breath for a moment while pushing back stray strands of hair from her lover's face. "You tried to hide the fact your headaches were getting worse, and I guess you meant to keep me from worrying. Like you protect Beth, for instance. I don't want to be protected, nor do I need to be. If I'd known you were feeling worse than usual, I might not have gotten the shock I did today."

"Annie…" Carolyn's voice was a mere whisper.

"I'm not trying to tell you what to do. I'm trying to tell you how I feel and what I need from you. You don't have to tell me every little detail, but don't try to shield me from what's important. If it concerns you, it concerns me. Let me take care of you when you need it, and I'll come to you when I need you to care for me—to put your arms around me and love me." She rose on one elbow, looking down at Carolyn. "This is important, darling."

Carolyn cupped Annelie's cheek gently and brushed her lower lip with her thumb. "Well said, Annie. I promise to do my best. It's my nature to be protective, but I can try and change the way I do it. I'll try not to shy away from asking for help, your help. You've been there for me so many times."

"And you for me." Feeling it was easier to breathe the air in the bedroom, Annelie settled onto the pillows, closing her eyes. "I love you."

Carolyn's fingers combed lovingly through Annelie's hair, smoothing it before traveling farther down her back. Annelie buried her face into her lover's neck, again inhaling her intoxicating citrus scent. Carolyn tugged at the covers, pulling them up and arranging them in a warm, cozy cocoon.

As sleep finally overtook her, Annelie saw jumbled images of Carolyn playing behind her eyelids. A panther, an eel, a pool, concrete stairs. She half jerked. Then she saw her lover stretched out on the deck of a boat, relaxing in the sun, with the ocean all around, and she smiled.

❖

Entering the kitchen, Annelie encircled Carolyn from behind, sliding her hands up under the half-open silk robe to cup her breasts.

"Mmm," Carolyn murmured as Annelie's lips found naked skin where the robe slipped off her shoulder. "Did you sleep well?"

"Yes, eventually. I missed you when I woke up, though. I should've realized the thought of coffee had enticed you to the kitchen."

"I promised the doctor to cut down, especially late in the evening, but my morning cup…" Carolyn shuddered. "Can't do without it. I'd be impossible to live with." She tilted her head back onto Annelie's shoulder, turning to kiss her lover. "I don't want you to kick me out because of caffeine withdrawal."

Trapping Carolyn against the kitchen counter, Annelie claimed her lips again, deepening the kiss. "There's no way I'd let you go, darling," she whispered, only a breath away from Carolyn's mouth. "With or without caffeine."

"Good morning," a sleepy voice said from the doorway. "Oh, sorry, ladies…" Helen stood holding onto the door frame. "Didn't mean to interrupt."

"You didn't." Carolyn smiled, her arms still around Annelie. "As a matter of fact, you're just in time for coffee."

"Did someone say coffee?" a second voice asked. Jem walked up behind Helen, her short, dark hair standing up in all directions. Patting Helen on her shoulder, she gave her a sleepy smile. "How are you doing this morning?"

"I'm feeling much better. My scalp is sore, but no headache. I took some painkillers last night, and they knocked me right out. I had the weirdest dreams."

Jem shot Annelie a grin. Putting her arm around Helen's shoulder, she guided her toward the kitchen table. "Oh, really? Do tell."

"I can hardly remember, but everything was swaying, and I believe you guys were there."

"Well, that makes sense, because we *were* there. Annelie and I found you standing in the hallway." Jem shrugged. "We couldn't very well leave you there, so I helped you into bed and tucked you in."

Helen blushed, covering her eyes with a hand. "Oh, no. I *have* been known to sleepwalk, but it was a long time ago. I'm sorry."

"Whatever for?" Jem asked merrily. "You were downright beautiful, if a little spooky, dressed in white silk in the middle of the night. So, anyone want pancakes or waffles?"

Helen looked dazed at the quick change of subject.

"Waffles!" Annelie exclaimed, rubbing her chin against Carolyn's hair. "You're such a whiz in the kitchen, Jem. I think I'm going to hire you."

"You already did." Jem grinned. "So, bring out the waffle iron."

Restricted to the dining room, Carolyn sat down next to Helen as the aroma of Jem's cooking filtered from the kitchen. Handing her a mug of coffee, she sighed in contentment and leaned back in her chair. "This is my idea of a perfect Saturday morning."

"Feeling less stressed?" Helen sipped her hot drink.

"Yes, a lot. Annelie and I talked for hours while we were trying to relax last night, and something she said stuck in my mind." Carolyn tucked her disheveled hair behind her ears. "I possess a certain arrogance."

"She said that?" Helen raised an eyebrow.

"No, no. But she made me realize that I don't share my weaknesses. I have to be strong and able, all the time. Or at least I think I do. Annelie wants me to share everything, warts and all."

Helen nodded thoughtfully, turning her head to look at the two women busily making breakfast. "First of all, I think you struck gold, Carolyn, and I don't mean in the monetary sense. She adores you just the way you are. You'd be a fool to let her go."

"Don't worry. I don't have any intention of letting her slip through my fingers. She's stuck with me. You said *first of all*—what else?"

"I don't see you as arrogant at all. You may interpret your actions and motivations like that, but I see it as being considerate of others. I don't want to sound presumptuous, but I think you're too hard on yourself sometimes."

Carolyn saw the warmth in Helen's eyes and smiled. "Could be."

Jem approached them with hot plates and utensils. "Won't be long now. What are your plans for the weekend, ladies?"

"You know we had plans for a little get-together, but since I'm under orders to rest, I'll just relax, study the script, and swim every day, of course." Carolyn helped her set the table. "What about you, Helen?"

"I'm going to my temporary home later and kick back, watch TV, and like you, reread the script. It's a nice day outside, so I think I'll walk home. It's only six blocks or so."

Jem exchanged glances with Annelie. "Helen, if you like, I can walk you part of the way, since I'm going grocery shopping for tonight. Marco's is on the way, I believe."

"That's very nice of you, Jem." Helen looked pleasantly surprised. "I'd like some company."

"And remember, in New York six blocks is farther than you think," Annelie cautioned. "Take a cab part of the way if you don't feel well."

"Goodness, you're all like mother hens." Helen gave a mock groan. "I sleep funny once, and all of a sudden you're going all protective on me."

Carolyn patted Helen's hair, exaggerating a worried expression. "It's because we *luv ya*, babe," she drawled.

Helen broke out into a fit of laughter, taking the others with her. Once they calmed down, the waffles were ready and Jem filled their plates. "Enjoy."

Carolyn let maple syrup run over her waffles. "You sure you need to go home Tuesday, Jem?"

Helen looked up, swallowing her first bite with a dreamy expression on her face. "Oh, Jem, we sure will miss you."

Jem rolled her eyes at the comments. "You only want me for these carnal pleasures," she muttered good-naturedly. Despite the broad grin on Jem's face, Carolyn noticed a vulnerable expression in her eyes.

❖

"I want to show you something." Annelie walked into the living room where Carolyn sat on the floor by the fireplace, leaning against an armchair.

"Yes? Come sit by me, then." Carolyn scooted to the side, making room for Annelie.

"I went through some of the letters my mother wrote my father, and when I looked into the package they came in, I found these." Annelie handed over some yellowing clippings.

Carolyn browsed through them with careful fingers. Annelie leaned her cheek against her lover's hair, watching.

"These clippings are of you as an adult." Carolyn turned one of them over. "Look, here's a date on the back of this one. March 12, 1994. Here's another one. April 28, 1999. Did they belong to your father?"

"I think so. This explains how Trevor White knew who I was. The thing is, they also raise a whole new set of questions. Why did White delay until now to try and get money from me? Why did my father keep clippings of me? If he took such an interest—I mean there are at least fifteen clippings—why didn't he try to contact me?" Annelie swallowed. "I'm getting upset again, and I promised myself I wouldn't." Tears ran down her cheeks.

Carolyn placed the clippings on the chair behind them and took Annelie in her arms. "Listen to me, love. You can cry on my shoulder any time you want. As for your father, I don't think we'll ever know his motives for saving these clippings. But I think it's safe to say this is how White made the connection. Perhaps your press coverage sparked his interest and made him think he could pull it off. It wasn't the smartest of plans."

Annelie had to laugh through her tears. "No, it wasn't. I believe they're holding him on several charges." Wiping her cheeks, she moved closer to Carolyn. "I'll just have to accept it—some parents simply don't want to be parents."

"I know. He didn't deserve you. He blew his chances with you a long time ago."

"Somehow I must have known a reconciliation was out of the question, ever since I was little and gave up hope he'd come back. I never tried to find him."

Carolyn didn't say anything but stroked Annelie's back in long, languid movements.

"I had my mother and, later, Margo. I told myself I didn't need a deadbeat dad." Annelie moved, placing her head in Carolyn's lap, pressing her face into the soft fabric of her T-shirt. Carolyn kept up the soothing motion of her hand. "The truth is, if he'd come back…I'd have listened and told him how much I'd missed him. I wouldn't have turned my back on him, even if it *had* been all about money."

"That's because you've got the biggest of hearts, love," Carolyn whispered. "You're that kind of person."

"He lived in misery. Why didn't he ask me for money when he discovered who I was?"

"Pride, regrets, some shred of honor…who knows, Annie. At least you know that the man who tried this scam wasn't your father. That's always something."

Annelie put her arm around Carolyn's waist, feeling safe and cared for. "Yes," she breathed. "It's something."

❖

Carolyn looked up from her script as Helen walked through the door. "How was lunch?"

"Oh, God, you did the right thing, staying here with a sandwich." Helen sat down on the couch with a thud. "Monday. Lunchtime. New York." She made a face. "Ew. It got ugly at the cash register."

"Did you get anything to eat? Want a sandwich? They're actually not bad."

"No, thanks. I managed to get a salad. Next time the kids try to drag me away for lunch, remind me of this."

Laughing, Carolyn promised she would. "I've got a few issues with the big scene between Erica and Maddox that everyone's making such a fuss about."

Helen nodded, reaching into a bag by her feet for her script. "What's your problem?"

"Well, I've done my share of love scenes, and they're not my favorite part of the shooting. I don't like to have the crew there. I'm sure Regina will be sensitive enough to shoot these scenes with a skeleton crew. Still…"

Carolyn regarded Helen carefully, wanting to be sure she understood. "Normally, with a man, we have rehearsal, very schematic, and usually very cut and dried."

"I know," Helen said, "and I really want to get it right. I'm not worried about feeling awkward, since both of our characters are supposed to be reluctant and nervous."

"That's exactly it. When Erica confronts Maddox in her office in the middle of the night, they're both tired and frustrated. Erica's angry, feeling Maddox is running instead of dealing with the obvious attraction. Maddox is angry with herself for being afraid of her own feelings."

"So they kiss, and neither of them can say for certain who started it." Helen dragged a hand through her hair. "As I've already told you, I've kissed a woman once in my life, but it was a very chaste kiss. We didn't deepen it, and I was rather young."

Carolyn was grateful for her candor. "You know I'm with Annelie, but that's where my expertise on the subject ends."

"And? What's your verdict, kissing men versus women?" Helen made a funny face. "Any major difference?"

"Stubble."

Helen's jaw dropped. "What?"

"No stubble, beard, or mustache."

"And that's it? The only difference?"

Carolyn couldn't keep a straight face at the sight of Helen's perplexed look. Laughing, she had to pull a tissue out of her purse and wipe the corners of her eyes. "No, of course not. With Annie, it's softer, gentler, and, because it's her and I love her, it's more passionate and soul-claiming."

"Oh." Helen rubbed the back of her neck. "So is that what we aim for? To make the audience believe in softness, passion...and soul-claiming?"

"Yup, that's it. Think you can handle it, St. Cyr?"

Helen grinned. "I'll damn well try, Black."

"Speaking of Annelie, I believe she and Jem'll be here for a tour soon." Carolyn looked at her watch. "In a few hours, in fact. You must be looking forward to tonight."

"Yes, I am. Wasn't it great how Jem and I discovered our mutual passion for musicals? I've wanted to see *Mama Mia* for a long time. I was really impressed with how quickly Annelie managed to scare up two tickets on the Internet."

"Yes, I'm starting to think I'll have to buy one of those laptops and learn the basics." Carolyn laughed. "I know, I know, I'm still getting the hang of using the cell phone."

The door opened and a young man poked his head inside. "Regina wants you in the conference room, please. Five minutes."

"We're coming." Helen rose from the couch, taking her bag with her. "I need to do something important before rehearsal." She pulled out a toothbrush and gave Carolyn a smug grin. "I come prepared!"

❖

Annelie watched Carolyn exchange some final words with Regina and then say goodbye. The studio was quiet.

Carolyn walked up to her, her eyes shining with excitement. "They looked at the dailies, and Regina is thrilled with what we did today. That's pretty rare with her. She's usually hard to please. Seems Helen and I nailed it."

"I'm happy for you, but not surprised."

"You're biased." Carolyn looked around the empty set and then kissed her gently on the cheek. "I'll just go change into my own clothes. I can remove the makeup later. The girls have all gone home." Checking her watch, she frowned. "It can't be that late."

"Your watch is on Maddox time. It's almost midnight."

"Late enough. I'm not very tired yet—I must still be on a high. You ready to get out of here?"

"Don't change yet. I want to see you in your office as Maddox. I haven't seen much of the shooting."

Carolyn cocked her head. "We've only shot a few scenes," she explained. "I think you want to see me as Maddox in the office because Helen and I shot *the* scene today." She winked, making Annelie blush. "See? I was right."

Annelie took her by the hand, pulling her toward Maddox's office at the far end of the studio. It was furnished with an old, scratched desk, a leather chair with a tall backrest, and several filing cabinets.

"That's some ambiance," Annelie said, looking around the set. "The prop guys have done a great job."

"Yes, it looks wonderful." Carolyn sat down on the corner of the desk. "I'm going to spend a lot of time here."

Annelie sat down next her and leaned back. "Erica Becker was sitting on Maddox's desk like this, wasn't she? I saw the promo pictures today."

"Oh. Well, she sat like that, but with her legs slightly parted, like this." Carolyn's eyes glittered when she stood up, gently nudging Annelie's legs apart. "And Maddox was standing very close, like this, pushing her away and pulling her close at the same time."

Annelie's breath caught in her throat at the sight of Carolyn, still looking like Diana Maddox. Dressed in a black pantsuit and white shirt, with the prop gun still bulging under her left arm, Carolyn looked every bit the famous character.

"You look so beautiful, like Maddox, but still yourself. Perhaps you *are* her…or vice versa?"

Carolyn backed off a little and something in her face altered. Eyes suddenly fiery, she said, "I don't know what you're talking about. You barge in here in the middle of the night, when I'm trying to get some work done. You know how backed up we are. What the hell's going on?" She glared at Annelie, half-playful, half-serious, coaxing her to tread the line between fantasy and reality.

Annelie leaned back on her arms, sitting on the desk the way she'd always imagined Erica would in this scene. "You know very well what's going on," she said, eyes narrowed. "For days you've acted like we're no more than casual acquaintances."

"We're working on a case involving a dead kid, Erica. There's no time for anything personal."

"Don't even go there. If you had your way, you'd skid around this issue, case or not. Why do you think I'm here now, in the middle of the night?" Annelie imagined Erica hurt, distraught, yearning for more than Diana was willing to give. Her tone conveyed her emotions. "Because you're here... alone. And there's nowhere to run."

"You want to talk, so talk." Carolyn stood, arrogant and outrageously desirable, her thighs almost between Annelie's legs. "What the hell's going on? Can you explain that to me? We've worked together for more than two years. We've been to hell and back, witnessed the things monsters do to innocent people, and we've supported each other through all of it. I thought we were friends!"

Annelie raised her hands and took Carolyn by the shoulders, barely able to resist shaking her. "We *are* friends! We're friends and so much more." She pulled her closer, lips trembling. "I'd give my life for you, Diana."

Carolyn tried to pry Annelie's hands off her shoulders but ended up stroking the soft skin instead. Her hands slid up Annelie's arms to the softness of her neck.

"Oh, God, Erica. If you let me touch you..."

"What are you afraid of? This?" Annelie lowered her hands to Carolyn's waist and drew her so close she could feel the damp of their merging breaths.

❖

Carolyn stopped resisting as soon as Annelie's tongue entered her half-open mouth and found hers. Moaning out loud, she kissed Annelie deeply in return, lowering her onto the desk. "All right," she whispered feverishly. "If this is what you want."

"It's all I've ever wanted," Annelie gasped. "You're all I want, Diana. Only you. I've waited so long…for this…"

Carolyn's weight descended on her, sliding between her legs. She pushed Annelie's skirt up and traced the naked skin above her stockings with hands that shook slightly. Devouring her with long kisses, she caressed her way up to the lace and satin of her panties. "So you want me to make you mine here and now?" She rubbed the damp fabric between Annelie's thighs. "No romance, no declaration of love, nothing?"

Annelie went rigid, turning her head away from the insistent words. But she was unable to prevent herself from undulating against the probing fingers. "You don't understand. It doesn't matter…"

Carolyn stopped moving, her hand slowing down. "What do you mean?"

Annelie faced her squarely. "It's impossible to make me yours."

"So it's just sex."

Annelie pushed herself up, sitting on the edge of the desk, Carolyn's hands still between her legs, waiting. "No. Never just sex." Tears ran down her face, and she threw her arms around Carolyn's neck, holding on tight. Her hips started moving against Carolyn's motionless fingers. "Don't you see? It's a done deal. You can't make me yours—I already belong to you."

Carolyn's eyes suddenly brimmed with tears, and she shuddered slightly as she gave in to Annelie, accepting what she offered. Kissing her deeply, she pushed the panties aside and entered her with two fingers, evoking a low moan.

Annelie arched and whimpered as Carolyn took her thoroughly on her desk. Clinging to her, she gasped as yet another finger entered, stretching her. "Diana, please…" She reached inside Carolyn's jacket, her fingers sliding over the gun harness as she unbuttoned the white shirt. Pushing the bra up, she eagerly sought the soft skin so long denied her.

Carolyn whimpered as fingertips found her nipples, the sweet torment increasing her efforts to bring Annelie pleasure. "Oh, yes."

She held Annelie close with one arm, her fingers on the other hand caressing the shivering woman. Feeling her own sex convulsing while Annelie tweaked her nipples, Carolyn didn't take her eyes off her lover for a second. "I love you, Annie…I love you so much."

"And I love you. Don't let go of me."

"I won't. Ever."

The leather couch in the office was useful when the two women needed a more comfortable way to catch their breath while adjusting their clothes.

"I can't believe we did that." Carolyn nuzzled Annelie's cheek. "You bring out the strangest behavior in me sometimes."

"Strange as in *good*, or strange as in *bad*?"

"I'd say this was pretty good. Any better and I'd be unconscious."

Annelie smiled and raised her eyebrows. "You play well, darling."

"And you make an excellent Erica, completely irresistible." Carolyn winked at Annelie. "I always knew playing Maddox would be rewarding. I just didn't know how right I was."

Annelie leaned down for a kiss. "How clever of you. Why don't we go home before the guards begin their rounds, and I'll show you just how many rewards you deserve?"

Returning the kiss with fervor, Carolyn hugged the woman she loved close. "You gorgeous woman, you. You're full of excellent ideas this evening. Yes, let's go home."

EPILOGUE

Carolyn stood motionless by the balcony railing, her hair the only thing moving in the wind.

Annelie stopped on the threshold, enjoying the view for a moment before walking up to her. "A penny for them?"

Impressed with how Carolyn didn't even flinch, Annelie encircled her lover's waist.

"Just listening to the city. So many lives, crammed into one tiny island."

"Why this philosophical mood?"

Turning, Carolyn cupped Annelie's cheek. "I came out here to get some air after a long day at the studio, and it hit me." She gestured toward the busy city below them. "Can these people possibly be as happy as I am right now?"

A warm glow started in the pit of Annelie's stomach, spreading toward her heart. "Some of them, surely."

"I don't know. I'm here with you. I love you more than anything or anyone. I've never felt like this in my life. Playing Maddox is the role of a lifetime, which will make me financially secure for the rest of my days. I called Beth earlier, and she's doing fine. She'll be home tomorrow. We're blessed with such good, loyal friends..." Tears rose in Carolyn's eyes. "The only cloud is...what if I lost you?"

Annelie took her by the hand. "You won't. Unless I fall under a bus, which I have no plans to do, you're stuck with me." She guided Carolyn into the living room, where a fire crackled in the fireplace. Looking expectantly at Carolyn, Annelie held her breath.

"Oh, my, when did you do this?"

On the floor in front of the fireplace, on a red wool blanket, lay an assortment of cheese and crackers, a bottle of chardonnay, and several large pillows. An Eva Cassidy CD played in the background, her clear voice filling the room.

"While you were deep in your reverie on the balcony. But I admit I planned it in advance. I thought we'd have a romantic evening together, now that we're alone again."

"You're a genius." Carolyn expressed her appreciation with a firm hug, which soon turned into a heated kiss. "Why don't we sit down, and you can pour me some of that wine."

They lounged in front of the fire, arranging the pillows so they could rest comfortably. After filling the rounded crystal glasses, Annelie raised hers. "To us."

"To us."

Sipping her wine, Annelie looked at the contented expression on Carolyn's face. She'd never seen her look this relaxed. Carolyn had changed her routine and now swam for half an hour every morning before heading to the studio. It seemed to lessen the unavoidable stress and pressure of playing Maddox.

"Carolyn, have I told you today how beautiful you are, inside and out?" Annelie smiled at her surprised look.

"Well, no, not today."

"Then let me tell you. I have a secret. When I wake up in the morning, I spend a few minutes just looking at your face and any part of you that's visible, absorbing how beautiful you are. Sometimes I have to pinch myself to realize this is true—you're here with me."

Carolyn's face softened, and she dropped her actor's mask completely as she put her glass on the floor. "You do?"

"Yes. If you're afraid of somehow losing me, then I'm just as afraid, if not more, of finding you gone one day. I know, it's an irrational fear—but it's there. I've gone from worshipping you for the work you do to loving you for the woman you are. You know I was nervous about us in the beginning. I was afraid you'd realize you weren't ready to be with a woman, with me, after all. I don't think like that any more, but in my darkest hours, the fear can reemerge."

Carolyn took a chocolate-covered strawberry and offered one to Annelie. "You're all I could ever want. If you watch me in the morning, I watch you during the day when you're not paying attention. I look at how you move, how your ponytail snuggles against your neck, and how you hold on to your left wrist with your right hand behind your back when you're nervous. I love how you eat with a knife and fork the

European way, and it excites me how your breasts move underneath your shirt when you're not wearing a bra. Most of all…" Carolyn leaned in and placed a soft kiss on Annelie's lips. "I love how I'm allowed to touch you, hug you, and make love to you."

"You do?" Annelie whispered. "I had no idea. I find you so extraordinary, so fascinating, and so divinely beautiful."

"No, you are." Carolyn smiled and sipped her wine. "You're exquisite. There's no better word to describe you."

Annelie felt a blush creep up her neck and color her cheeks. "I've been meaning to ask you something."

Carolyn waited, but when the words caught in Annelie's throat she leaned forward and kissed her. "Yes?"

"We decided you'd stay here with me during the filming, and I'd like to know how you think it's working out." It wasn't at all what she meant to say, but she couldn't think straight.

"I've loved every second of it. And you?" Carolyn gazed at her over the rim of her wineglass.

"I don't want to think about how it would feel when…" Annelie's voice faded and she cleared her throat. "I don't want to think about waking up and you not being here, darling. Do you think you could…I mean, can you see yourself…" Furious with herself for sounding completely lost, Annelie jumped when Carolyn took the glass from her fiddling fingers and placed it on the floor with her own.

"Are you asking me to stay on after the filming? To move in permanently?"

"You don't have to answer right away. Just think about it and—"

"Yes."

"What?"

"Annelie, I don't want to be away from you. I don't want to go back to my lonely apartment when you and I can be together, sharing our days, waking up and falling asleep in each other's arms. I never want to leave."

Suddenly Annelie lunged forward, threw her arms around Carolyn's neck, and buried her face in Carolyn's hair. As she inhaled the familiar scent of musk and sandalwood, she closed her eyes and felt her heart rate slow down.

"Do you know how amazing you are?" Carolyn murmured, her hands moving in soothing circles over Annelie's back. "You can drive me crazy with one look, one touch, and at the same time you evoke all these protective feelings in me. I love holding you, just like this, and yet I adore it when you take control and let me surrender to you." She softly kissed Annelie's cheek. "I love you."

Tipping her head back, Annelie looked up into Carolyn's eyes, surprised to see the usual streaks of gray drowned out by the clear blue. "Kiss me."

Lowering her head, Carolyn obliged, deepening the kiss as they clung to each other.

"I love you too," Annelie whispered. "I adore you."

As they shed their clothes into a growing pile, the fire warmed their naked flesh. Looking at Carolyn's body, watching the flames cast flickering shadows on her lover's pale skin, Annelie knew she would never grow tired of this sight.

"Mine to touch," she whispered, never averting her eyes.

"Yours to do with as you please."

"Then let me love you."

"Always."

About the Author

Gun Brooke combines her lifelong love for science fiction and romance novels by writing both genres—always with romance at center stage. She resides in the Swedish countryside with her very patient family in a village displaying remnants from the Stone Age and Viking era.

Having first written fan fiction, Gun caught Bold Strokes Books' attention when she entered an online writer's challenge, and the international second edition of *Course of Action* is the happy result. Creating character-driven stories about relationships, whether set in the future or contemporary times, now keeps this Swede occupied full-time.

Putting her fascination with the latest technology to good use, she keeps in touch with friends around the world through the Internet and maintains her own Web site, http://www.gbrooke-fiction.com. She has also been known to create Web sites for other people on occasion.

When not working on her next book, Gun loves movies, reading, cooking/eating/talking, and creating computer graphics. She also enjoys traveling and meeting new people, whom she stores in her ever-growing gallery of characters for future stories.

Look for her next release from Bold Strokes Books, *Supreme Constellations: The Protector of the Realm*, in December 2005.

Other Books Available From Bold Strokes Books

Course of Action by Gun Brooke. Actress Carolyn Black desperately wants the starring role in an upcoming film produced by Annelie Peterson, a wealthy publisher with a mysterious past. How far is Carolyn prepared to go for the dream part of a lifetime? And just how far will Annelie bend her principles in the name of desire? (1-933110-22-8)

Justice Served by Radclyffe. The hunt for an informant in the ranks draws Lieutenant Rebecca Frye, her lover Dr. Catherine Rawlings, and Officer Dellon Mitchell into a deadly game of hide-and-seek with an underworld kingpin who traffics in human souls. (1-933110-15-5)

Rangers at Roadsend by Jane Fletcher. After nine years in the Rangers, dealing with thugs and wild predators, Sergeant Chip Coppelli has learned to spot trouble coming, and that is exactly what she sees in her new recruit, Katryn Nagata. But even so, Chip was not expecting murder. The Celaeno series. (1-933110-28-7)

Distant Shores, Silent Thunder by Radclyffe. Ex-lovers, would-be lovers, and old rivals find their paths unwillingly entwined when Drs. KT O'Bannon and Tory King—and the women who love them—are forced to examine the boundaries of love, friendship, and the ties that transcend time. (1-933110-08-2)

Hunter's Pursuit by Kim Baldwin. A raging blizzard, a remote mountain hideaway, and more than one killer for hire set a scene for disaster—or desire—when reluctant assassin Katarzyna Demetrious rescues a stranger and unwittingly exposes her heart. (1-933110-09-0)

The Walls of Westernfort by Jane Fletcher. All Temple Guard Natasha Ionadis wants is to serve the Goddess, and she volunteers eagerly for a dangerous mission to infiltrate a band of rebels. But once she is away from the temple, the issues are no longer so simple, especially in light of her attraction to one of the rebels. Is it too late to work out what she really wants from life? (1-933110-24-4)

Change Of Pace: *Erotic Interludes* by Radclyffe. Twenty-five hot-wired encounters guaranteed to spark more than just your imagination. Erotica as you've always dreamed of it.
(1-933110-07-4)

Fated Love by Radclyffe. Amidst the chaos and drama of a busy emergency room, two women must contend not only with the fragile nature of life, but also with the mysteries of the heart and the irresistible forces of fate. (1-933110-05-8)

Justice in the Shadows by Radclyffe. In a shadow world of secrets, lies, and hidden agendas, Detective Sergeant Rebecca Frye and her lover, Dr. Catherine Rawlings, join forces once again in the elusive search for justice. (1-933110-03-1)

shadowland by Radclyffe. In a world on the far edge of desire, two women are drawn together by power, passion, and dark pleasures. An erotic romance. (1-933110-11-2)

Love's Masquerade by Radclyffe. Plunged into the often indistinguishable realms of fiction, fantasy, and hidden desires, Auden Frost discovers a shifting landscape that will force her to question everything she has believed to be true about herself and the nature of love. (1-933110-14-7)

Beyond the Breakwater by Radclyffe. One Provincetown summer three women learn the true meaning of love, friendship, and family. Second in the Provincetown Tales. (1-933110-06-6)

Tomorrow's Promise by Radclyffe. One timeless summer, two very different women discover the power of passion to heal and the promise of hope that only love can bestow. (1-933110-12-0)

Love's Tender Warriors by Radclyffe. Two women who have accepted loneliness as a way of life learn that love is worth fighting for and a battle they cannot afford to lose. (1-933110-02-3)

Love's Melody Lost by Radclyffe. A secretive artist with a haunted past and a young woman escaping a life that proved to be a lie find their destinies entwined. (1-933110-00-7)

Safe Harbor by Radclyffe. A mysterious newcomer, a reclusive doctor, and a troubled gay teenager learn about love, friendship, and trust during one tumultuous summer in Provincetown. First in the Provincetown Tales. (1-933110-13-9)

Above All, Honor by Radclyffe. The first in the Honor series introduces single-minded Secret Service Agent Cameron Roberts and the woman she is sworn to protect—Blair Powell, the daughter of the president of the United States. First in the Honor series.
(1-933110-04-X)

Love & Honor by Radclyffe. The president's daughter and her security chief are faced with difficult choices as they battle a tangled web of Washington intrigue for...love and honor. Third in the Honor series.
(1-933110-10-4)

Honor Guards by Radclyffe. In a journey that begins on the streets of Paris's Left Bank and culminates in a wild flight for their lives, the president's daughter and those who are sworn to protect her wage a desperate struggle for survival. Fourth in the Honor series.
(1-933110-01-5)